FIFTEEN BILLION YEARS II

SECRET OF THE LEGENDS

"Then I saw a new heaven and a new earth; for the first heaven and the first earth had passed away..."

Revelation 21: 1 (RSV)
Holy Bible

By Rand McLester

InfusedMedia Co. LLC
www.infusedmedia.co
1-888-251-6088

DEDICATION

For family and friends…

The glue that binds when the going gets tough,

…Those who sustain us.

ACKNOWLEDGEMENTS

I would like to thank Rozi and Amy for their assistance with editing and proofreading; and also express my appreciation for Rozi's excellent work with the book's cover design. And, of course, I'd like to thank the Infused Media team who put it all together.

Thanks to all of you.

PART III

CHAPTER ONE

A faraway place, a distant future…

…"Hey Doc, I'm *baaack*." Reed rounded the curve on the path, his easy smile in the forefront, the scar across his forehead faded to a white line, his mark of distinction. It had been some time since they were reunited at the crater, time they needed to rest and heal. So few had survived.

All traces of the battle with the Trogs were gone. Dead were buried, defense ramparts dismantled, the jungle renewed reclaiming the scars of war. Probing through the trees, dappled sunlight warmed the village as early morning dew slipped away in shimmering wisps of grey[1]. It was good to be alive in this beautiful place; there was peace in the land of the Renoloi.[2]

Ames and Tian[3] laughed when Seana[4] leaped from the roof of a hut taking Reed to the ground. Reed and Seana were young and in love, and they played like that. Watching them wrestle, Tian leaned into Ames, amused as Seana quickly got him in a full nelson and leg lock. She was an adept student. He was secured.

"Bust me with a hickory switch, Seana, let me up."

"Not unless you squeal like a pig." It was an expression she had learned from him.

Almost choking, "Not in a million years," grimacing, "you don't even know what a pig is."

"Oh, short-timer," she bantered biting him on the ear and growling lovingly as they began attracting a crowd, she mustering moral support. Reed knew he'd better think of something quick, one of those macho moves that impressed the girls. Face down on his stomach with Seana clamped on his back, he pushed himself up, ducked his head and somersaulted —over— carrying her with him, surprising her when she found herself beneath him, flat on her back.

"Now will you let go?" he gasped; her arms still cinched around his throat.

"Reed, you are squishing my boobs."

Tian looked at Ames. "Where do you suppose she learned something like that?" And the grin.

Innocently, "Beats me."

"Sea—na," Reed sputtered, "you're choking me."

Ames, still straight-faced, "Why're you looking at me?" Tian just sighed. "Oh sure, I get blamed because he's a heathen."

Lovingly she backhanded him on the chest with a twinkling of deviltry in her eye.

Seana grunted, "Reed, you are squishing the air out of me."

"Okay, okay, I'm getting up." He'd squished the air out of her once before. Both winded, they got up brushing one another off, and when he spent a bit too long dusting her breasts, she slapped his hand. "They are not dirty, and I do not want them bruised either."

"Just little bruises perhaps?" She smacked him again.

Tian interrupted, "Meal time."

"What are we having?" Reed asked prefatorily.

Seana swatted him playfully. "The same as yesterday, Chiqua. You know that."

Not quite sarcastically, but almost, "My favorite." Reed thought the small animals resembled a cross between hybrid kangaroo rats and reptilian spring hares, but was never able to explain that to the women, and bowing with a sweeping arm gesture offered royalty, "After you, m'lady," indicating Seana.

Following them, warm and secure within Ames' embrace Tian smiled as they headed for the meeting circle located at the edge of the village on the lower end of the path. Affectionate words: "He never changes, does he, John?"

"Nope."

Continuing to pester Seana, Reed overheard. "Tian, are you implying that I sorta grow on you?"

Ames answered. "Yeah—well so do warts."

"Cheap shot."

Tian smiled. Good friends. She had no way of knowing how soon they all would need one another again... to survive in the land of the Renoloi.

* * *

At the meeting circle...

...Preparations were already underway. Too few had survived the battle with the Trogs to live separately, so Tondra, Denen, Lita[5] and Tian had combined their villages and now led as a council, an evolution of government.

Talking quietly, women sat in small groups while children tended to roasting Chiqua and extracting juice from leafy stalks. It was essential for the young to learn to care for themselves as early as possible—survival skills.

This was still a primitive world.

Approaching the circle, seeing Denen and Lita, Tian excused herself without speaking. Ames nodded then ambled off with Reed and Seana.

Entering the crowd, a swarm of smaller children promptly began gravitating toward Reed. He was their storyteller and they loved him like an uncle, and even though his tales were oftentimes modified, even unorthodox, the stories were delicious and not one child among them had any doubt they were absolutely true. Kneeling, he scooped an armful of his tyke-admirers hugging and grizzling them; he loved the attention —and he loved the children more.

Seana stood quietly watching the little ones converge upon the man. She didn't understand exactly what it was she felt inside, but it was good, warm. It wasn't the same as watching children with their mothers, the hermaphrodite connection; this feeling was different. Without Seana being aware, as it had occurred, Reed, a stranger, had not replaced the Renoloi, but now fulfilled what had not been there before. It was as though inside her something had been somnolent, something incomplete of which she had never been aware; and this man was the missing part. She still belonged to the Renoloi; but now, she belonged more to this stranger and she didn't know why —but it was good. Seana and the Renoloi did not yet comprehend the father concept; she sensed though that the men knew, something part of a world far away, a long time ago.

The meals served two purposes, sustenance, and perhaps more importantly, keeping the people a family. It was a time to talk and share; ties that outside distractions could not dismantle allowing them to drift apart. Since their genesis and earliest known records linked to their beginnings, their leaders had insisted the meal ritual be maintained. It had always been and always should be a leisure affair; young and old gathering and interacting, maintaining the constant bond of communication and trust. The meals were unhurried, the experience enriching. Their leaders were wise.

Discussing survival tactics, Tondra and Nitana[6] sat with Kalo,[7] a young Renoloi who absorbed their every word. Kalo was reluctant to interrupt, and Tondra, sensing her confusion at times, would intentionally pause and explain in detail things the young girl seemed unsure of. Tondra was patient, an excellent teacher.

Ames rejoined Tian and Lita; then several others gathered discussing cloud formations. The Renoloi instinctively knew that cumulonimbus were storm clouds, and cirrus, the feathery high-altitude wisps were fair weather; but the women had never given them names. Ames told them of stratus, nimbus, cumulus, cirrus, barometric pressure, deciliters of mercury, and other meteorologic terminology; and in exchange they offered their perspective, they explaining as much to him as he to them. The Renoloi were easygoing, and their lack of inhibition and candor would at times surprise him; but that aspect he accepted simply as part of their charm.

She was watching Reed as he, Denen, Seana and a few others were collectively speaking across the circle from Tian and Ames. Her bright blue eyes blinked with wonder and admiration for this stranger who was not an enemy; and her perception of the man was known only to her. Jade, one of the youngest children, had adopted Reed as her own; and she was so taken with him that it was her attraction that Seana had first observed.

Seana then noticed his connection with other children as well. In some it was very subtle and with others more obvious; but almost without exception the young ones identified with him, thrived on him, loving his time and attention. They cherished it and couldn't get enough, and whenever possible he made a point of spending time with them. Reed knew the children were the future —and besides, they called him 'Uncle Reed'. Were it necessary for him to pick his favorite, he would likely choose Jade.

* * *

The meal finished…

…Reed looked around furtively, being sure they had completed their chores, free for every detail of his next story. He grinned. The children had instituted a tradition of their own, and they were waiting. They had never heard of bedtime stories. They had aftermeal stories.

"Okay," he said at last, "today it's 'Jack and the Beanstalk'." The children, who had been edging closer in anticipation, swarmed him in earnest, congregating in a compressed group of snugly packed little bodies. And as part of the new tradition, he would arrange them just so.

They loved his stories, naturally, because his stories were good.

"Now, once upon a time there was this guy named Jack, and he had these magic bean seeds that he bought at one of the big-box chains for fifty-percent-off from the discontinued items basket, or blue-light special, or some such promotional discount." He paused, had their undivided attention, and went on, "Now Jack planted the magic seeds outside his condo window and watered them copiously with mineral-spring water —'bout a five-gallon jug, if I remember correctly."

"The next morning Jack awoke all bright eyed —he could do that 'cause he's fictitious you know. The rest of us wake up like Oscar the Grouch; but that's a different story, so forget that for now. Anyway, Jack looked out the window, and lo and behold there was a humongous beanstalk that grew all the way up into the clouds." His stories were appropriately accented with voice inflections and hand gestures, creating just the right effect.

"So being the adventurous soul he was, Jack popped on his iPod with his tunes and headed out climbing the giant beanstalk, all the way to the sky. About the time Jack got almost to the top of the beanstalk, on the ground far, far below, along comes this gnarly logger jock named Paul Bunyan and his kick-ass blue ox, Babe. So, ole' Pablo says to Babe 'Look at that tree boy. Lots of board feet there,' and Paul Bunyan chopped through the beanstalk with one stupendous swipe of his mighty ax." The children—all ears.

"Of course Jack is unknowingly and raucously dislodged from the beanstalk, plummeting toward certain death below." Quick glance. "For all you non-raconteurs that means he was screamin' like a sissy on the way down. When from out of nowhere, this turbaned dude named Aladdin swoops by on this magic carpet —and Jack plops right onto the rug beside Towelhead. But it's kinda crowded on the carpet now 'cause Aladdin's already got another passenger named Ahab and his trusty camel Clyde who he just snatched from Patina's tent. So the four of 'em go careening through the sky, having fun doin' high left and right banks and such. Howeversobeit unbeknownst to them they're losing altitude." Reed paused, leaving them hanging, suspense builder, wondering what was going to happen next.

"Next thing you know, cruising along they go into a low-level tail spin," he abruptly continued, "but by now they're miles out to sea and ole' Jack is buffeted and tossed overboard and bites a big wave when he goes into the drink. And even more bad luck, Aladdin can't stabilize the rocket rug 'cause by this time Clyde the camel is freaked out and airsick and in such a dither he's sitting on Aladdin's head puking on Ahab, so Carpet Jockey couldn't see where Jack went into the soup. So with heartfelt regret, after several unsuccessful reconnaissance passes they sadly give up on him and the magic carpet zips on out of sight with poor Jack left adrift in the ocean."

"Now for purposes of self-preservation Jack treads water for a couple of hours, but he's getting mighty tired—rhumatiz' and whatnot—when finally he sees a boat coming. So he starts waving his arms and yelling, and the boat changes course to rescue him." He paused again. "Good story, huh?" He needn't have asked because by now his audience was spellbound. "Turns out it wasn't a boat at all, but a giant whale named Moby Dick; and that sucker opens his big-ole' toothy-trimmed mouth and swallows Jack right down whole." From somewhere a muted gasp. Reed grinned.

"Next thing Jack knows he's inside Moby with this little wooden dude named Pinocchio. So, he says, 'Sorry, Pinocch' but I need your legs and arms', and he pops them right off Puppetboy. Then he proceeds to rub the arms together vigorously, just like he learned in his 'Boy Scouts of America' handbook —and, *poof*—" gesturing, "Jack's got a campfire going. A'course Pinocchio will never be the same again —but that's another story too."

He took a breath and continued. "Now as rightly would be expected by some not-to-be-named, pain-in-the-ass environmentalists, the campfire smoke eventually made old Moby Dick sneeze —*ker-choo*— and he shoots Jack airborne like a 007-supersecret James Bond torpedoman. Goes for miles and miles. Then Jack hits the water and skips along the surface till miraculously he glides gently onto a beautiful beach somewhere in the tropics —most likely Borneo or some such tourist locale."

One of the children raised her hand. "I have to pee."

"Okay." He and the others waited as the little girl ran into the bushes and rustled about. Scanning his audience, "Suspense will do that sometimes," he whispered, "—make you have to pee." Several nodded. They already knew that. A moment later she reappeared at a trot still pulling up her black leather skirt. "Ready?"

"Yes. All done," quickly reclaiming her spot.

"Okay, so now Jack's wandering around on the beach when who do you 'spose comes strolling out of the jungle but this little girl with sparkly red shoes, a cowardly lion, a tin man without a heart, and this ditzy strawberry blonde scarecrow. The five of them engage in casual discourse until unexpectedly, out of the ocean a herd of turtles come plodding along, shells polished to their Sunday best, shiny as herringbone. And then from the jungle, comes a mob of hares, or maybe it was rabbits —well nevermind that. Anyway, without being aware, Jack and Dorothy, along with her friends, have all arrived just in time for the annual race festivities. Of course, upon closer examination they do finally notice the lane-marker flags strategically placed along the beach leading off into the jungle."

"It's almost high noon and race time so the turtles and bunnies all line up and—*they're off*—the race begins. But little do the fuzzy Leporidae lepus realize, these are world famous flipper turtles, and each time a hare tries to pass one, the bugger shoots into the sky and plops down on top of it squishing the unsuspecting rodent — *splat!*" slapping his hands together. Concentrating, eyes blinking, everybody flinching simultaneously, he startled them. "There's little bunny carcasses smunched into the sand everywhere before they even make the beach-stretch of the first lap. It was certainly a hare-racing experience." Time for a breath.

"What happened next, Uncle Reed?" Jade asked.

Grinning and eyeing his tense little audience he continued, "The race is gonna be perilously close for sure. They're neck-'n-neck coming down the back stretch when all of a sudden the sky is blackened by hundreds of ugly little flying monkey suckers with bat wings —and the Wicked Witch of the West is leading them. So these bad guys start dive-bombing Jack and his friends, trying to rip 'em to pieces and turn 'em into shredded wheat. I mean to tell ya there's fuzzy furballs flyin' and they're getting in Dorothy's hair and pooping on the tin man —it was just awful! And all seems hopeless until at the very last minute, from out of the sky comes the Millennium Falcon with lasers blasting —and Luke Skywalker and Han Solo rescue Jack and his pals. And they all kick ass on the wicked witch and her flying monkeys then blast off to the Dagobah

System to learn the ways of the Jedi Knight and become one with the Force, and live happily ever after… the end."

The children applauded and cheered for the heroes as Tian shook her head wondering, "Where did Reed ever learn such stories, John?"

Droll, he answered, "That stuff really happened."

Playfully bumping him with her hip, "Sure, like Br'er Rabbit." Tian enjoyed Br'er Rabbit most, the characters were more colorful; but she still had no idea what zip-a-de-do-da meant. She smiled when he finally couldn't help leaking a grin. "We will go for a walk," she said.

* * *

On a winding trail…

…They ambled quietly, unhurried; time together, special time, synchronous connection, physical contact. Holding hands they followed the path through the jungle, along the cliffs of the escarpment, and eventually arrived on the rimrock. Before them lay the ruins of the Sacred Temple and the collapsed mountain range beyond. The day was clean and beautiful, the jungle rich with saturating deep-green chlorophyll life, the air sweet and pure.

They sat together on the rimrock at the same place Tian had waited for Ames when he went Beyond. It was the place where he had risen like the Phoenix and returned to her. It was their place. The Prophecy was true. It was in the Legends.

Words not really necessary anymore, for a while they sat quietly holding each other as Ames scanned the collapsed mountain range and temple ruins, where the geodesic time sphere had been before the Renoloi moved it into the jungle and hid it— cold storage. His mind was focused, calculating, always working to solve the riddle that continued to haunt him.

"They are there somewhere," her words whisking him from his thoughts; he didn't say anything, just returned a thin smile. "We will find a way," she assured snuggling next to him, his body comforting; she leaned against him. Since his return they'd had time to grow closer and she had begun to understand the man-woman concept as her awareness increased and she had developed, grown, become more complete. She knew it was the same for him. That was how life was meant to be. And she knew other things; she was a hermaphrodite, a Renoloi, and the Renoloi possessed a gift.

He nodded, "They're down there somewhere," still considering the timeline to the present—all that had happened, all he was able to recall.

He remembered himself, Alex, and Kristina on the sixth sub-level of the Complex, and the deuterium reactor auditorium. Then he and Kristina and General Smith… in a dark room somewhere— had to be the sub-levels of the Complex, but that was where things became incongruous, disjointed. He could recall bits and pieces of a confrontation with someone, or something, but couldn't sort it out— and it hadn't been so long ago that he would forget; but from that point what happened seemed vague, almost obscured.

Then the Light; he would always remember that light. It was like nothing he'd ever felt before, still clear in his mind's eye, so pure and intense; and paradoxically, other things so clouded. It had been so dark and dreary, and smelled so awful —then the light— everywhere.

People and what, what else? Horses… but they didn't smell like horses. In his mind he thought he could see them now, those huge white horses, steaming and lathered. *But they didn't smell like horses,* and that didn't make sense. *Massive unshod hooves thundering overhead, but why overhead?* He was lying on the ground —*no, a concrete floor*— or inside the Sacred Temple. *No, that wasn't right.* He remembered the temple. It had to be in the sub-level, in that room. *But how could white horses be there?*

The light reappeared in his mind—*pure, clear, warm… and Someone smiled.* He remembered the smile.

"John—John," Tian nudged bringing him back; he blinked, beside her once more. "You were far away again, were you not?"

"I suppose I was. Pieces are missing."

And that bothers you, she knew without saying it. The missing pieces pulled him away more often now than before. When he first returned it had been only occasionally, but now his subconscious was searching for answers. She knew him, sensed it nagging him, what he yearned to find. He called them missing pieces… the answers.

They were together. It was meant to be. That unity was their bond, and with the bond she accepted him as part of herself and she as part of him. They must find the missing pieces together, what he called a puzzle that would complete the image, a reflection on the still surface of a pool of water. That was how he had explained that word to her. She understood reflections, but not the word puzzle.

Perhaps the 'Prophecy of the Strangers' was also part of the puzzle. Even now Tian sensed that the last line must have meant more; she could feel it somehow. *And they would change our world.* But its intimation was still unclear, something she could not yet understand. John was absorbed with his own puzzle so she kept her thoughts and feelings to herself; and she would consider the prophecy. She believed when it was time she would know, she would understand what it really meant *—and they would change our world.*

Looking at him, "Do you wish to talk?"

"No." He squeezed her affectionately and smiled. "Let's walk."

She knew without asking. He wanted to go into the crater again, to walk the mountains again. Somewhere within the collapsed mountain range was a passage, a fissure, crevice, cave, or tunnel. It must be there, only they hadn't discovered it yet. Out there, somewhere, was an access to the Legends.

They got up, and unhurried, began walking, past the crumbled ruins of the temple. They had searched there before, scrutinized every stone, now concluding it was entirely destroyed with no possible way to what might be beneath it.

The Sacred Temple was once a peak of the mountains that held the Legends. According to Tian and the Renoloi, long ago a violent storm had mysteriously caused the entire mountain range to collapse into this planet leaving only one peak still jutting forth. That solitary peak was called the Sacred Temple, honeycombed with passages and caverns that were chiseled with writings from a time long ago, presumably from Earth.

The Inscriptions mystified Ames. How could they be here, on this world; and who carved them inside that mountain? He didn't believe those questions might ever be answered the day he followed the Trogs into the temple to end the bloodshed and preserve the Renoloi race. That day the reign of the Trogs came to an end when the magnesium oxide core of the mountain destroyed them, also sealing the mystery within. Magnificent, unexplained, timeless. The Inscriptions.

Even now, Ames knew he should not be here—but he was—and not understanding was something he couldn't, wouldn't accept. In spite of every possibility he considered, it was an enigma that continued to haunt him, not an obsession, but a manifestation in an incomplete dream. Still, it was more than he could ignore. It was his nature to study, decipher, and understand. For everything that happens, there is a reason; there must be a reason.

Why was he here, still alive? How had that happened? Pieces were missing. How had he gone back, been catapulted through time; and how had he returned? He was here with Tian and Reed; that alone was more than he could comprehend.

The temple and Inscriptions were incredible; but there was more Tian had said, much more. Perhaps the ceremony of the 'White Warrior and Serpent' was an unknown holographic technology from the Legends, singular technology beyond his comprehension, and they were here, beneath the ground he walked on, somewhere within the mountain range, secreted just beyond reach. Tian had seen them, studied them, but could not explain them —and the dust was real.

Somehow, John Ames knew he must find them. He needed to know. He must learn the Secret of the Legends.

* * *

Climbing craggy formations…

…Of plagioclastic granite, they explored for hours. Always deeper, toward the center of the mountain range, constantly searching —every slide, coulee, crevice, fracture and rise that might allow passage to the depths below. Ames was certain there was a cave or tunnel somewhere descending into the mysterious darkness of the mountains that once towered high above this land.

Without talking, making their way around jutting precipices, crawling over unstable slides or between tumbled boulders, they covered the barren, rugged topography that was once above the treeline and lacked vegetation. Jungle had not yet enveloped this part of the mountain, but with the passing of time was now encroaching upon the rock faces. Nature was reclaiming the craggy landscape with her nourishing chlorophyll medicine: grasses, plants, shrubbery and saplings, eventually to be replaced by larger trees and mature jungle. The cycle would transform the austere into life of endless variety.

They continued tirelessly until late afternoon.

Tian's stamina born of living in an untamed world surpassed even Ames, who had always kept physically fit. Flabby, untoned muscles in this land were as fatal an affliction as cancer. Here, Stairmaster, Soloflex, Image, Nordic Track, Tunturi, Pro Form, Weslo, Orbi Trek, and exercise videos were unnecessary superfluous gadgetry. Darwin had arrived at sound conclusions, 'On the Origin of Species'. Herbert Spencer summarized the concept then coined the phrase, 'Survival of the Fittest'.

The pair finally stopped just below an outcropping and sat down to rest at the top of a draw before beginning their return to the village. They had covered eight miles distance by line of sight, and actually several times that considering the meandering search pattern they used. Another day and a thousand nooks-and-crannies without success; but Ames was determined and Tian steadfast. They would search again, as long as necessary; but this day was winding down. Time to go home.

The sun would be setting soon and they would arrive at the village after dark.

"You tired?" a concerned whisper.

"No." Tian smiled. "Are you discouraged?"

"No. We'll find it."

Just then —above them, from the other side of the outcrop— stone clatter and a cascade of dirt sending rocks tumbling down the opposite side of the rim. Disrupting the prolonged solitude of their day, the commotion startled them and their first reaction was to duck; then realizing the slide was on the other side, they exchanged glances knowing something had caused it. Ames in the lead, both were on their feet and scrambling to the top.

Crashing noise. More loose rock sloughing and rumbling, cascading down the other side.

As Ames arrived at the top and stood up, the massive rising head, yellow-green eyes and potent jaws full of six-inch teeth confronted him. Tyrannosaurus Rex —mere feet from him— close enough to reach out and touch. Stumbling, its footing unstable, the dinosaur was just gaining the summit and sliding on the loose rock and dirt; but determined, it was still climbing.

Face to face, blinking surprise, the man halted and the dinosaur expelled hot, rank breath in his face. His heart stopped —or at least skipped a beat— as the T-Rex swung its huge head, opening its awesome mouth, and Ames saw saliva-sheen teeth and a deep scarlet throat. He froze. Jaws opening, it reared its ungainly head and roared; then the yellow-green eyes blinked him into focus and its jaws clamped shut with a crunching, *pop.*

"Holy shit!"— startled and terrified, jumping back then beginning to fall.

Something grabbed him as a fist-sized rock sailed passed his head striking the dinosaur solidly just beneath its eye. Tian threw with one arm and snatched him with the other, seizing him with such precision and speed Ames swung in an arc away from the dinosaur —around her— both of them sliding on loose rock —*going down*— and tumbling, temporarily beyond reach of the hulking reptile.

Instantly on their feet and propelled by fear, they ran. Two cats springing, running and weaving among rocks, they were bent on escape, descending the draw —in flight— mere flashes of motion. Moving synchronously Ames followed her. As her foot rose from a boulder or stone bound for the next, his foot landed there then rose again —tracking— his steps a single footfall behind her. Tian was fluid with agility and speed, honed to perfection from being a part of the jungle; and Ames had watched her and practiced learning her skills that now might save his life.

Stepping forward its clawed toes dug into the dirt and loose rock with a gritty crushing sound, and when the other leg followed attaining the summit, the Tyrannosaur rose up. Looming over the peak of the outcrop and throwing back its head, it screamed a long, drawn, boisterous roar, then leaned forward —reptilian eyes following the prey. It hunted by sight.

Ripping up debris the Tyrannosaur was awesome, lunging thirty feet at a stride, dirt and rock erupting from beneath its treacherous feet. Its eyes were locked on, tracking the woman and man as they appeared and disappeared with their flight, its size and stride enabling it to cover distances requiring several leaps for Tian and Ames.

They were incapable of the dinosaur's speed, knowing it would quickly overtake them, so outrunning it would not be an option. Without weapons, killing it was impossible. Their only hope lay at the bottom of the draw down which they were running, its irregular granite spires rising above them might possibly impede the dinosaur's attack, their best cover as they fled. Ames saw the high rock wall beyond the draw —*that crevice*— two feet wide, allowing room enough for them but not the predator, and he knew Tian was already intent on escape through the passageway. She had long ago learned to be aware of her surroundings; that awareness could mean life or death.

Splintering spires—rattling ground. The Tyrannosaur was closing, its enormous bulk thundering upon them with astounding speed and agility for such a huge animal. Flying stone—splatter-debris. Rocks kicked and hurled by its menacing feet clattered as they ricocheted and spun past Ames when the dinosaur stumbled crashing into a spire. Almost exploding, the jutting formation shattered shooting fragments. Something hard smacked the back of his head as shards whizzed past and clouds of dust swirled from behind up around him. Larger chunks thumped splattering the ground. Pieces hit him in the back *—don't look, go faster—* he didn't slow down *—where was her foot, land there.* Terror and speed, just one step behind, *keep running.*

The dinosaur fell headfirst, skidding —then rolling, went over sideways— a rumbling collision of heaved dirt, dust-scatter and spattering rock. Legs straight out, tail flailing and finally sliding, it slammed into Ames' back hurling him across the open area and to the rock wall just behind Tian. With unbelievable speed the Tyrannosaur completed the roll and was on its feet again; but the fall gave the pair just enough time to reach the hundred-foot escarpment and disappear within the crevice, the dinosaur's massive head ramming the vertical wall inches behind Ames' back —a gristly-thick, *crunch—whump.*

Not stopping, they kept running through the narrow passageway as the Tyrannosaur bellowed rage and frustration behind them —the vertical walls were close, felt cool, were solid, felt safe. After several hundred feet within the confines of the crevice, the two emerged on the other side of the rock wall, in the open again. Only then did they stop to rest.

Out of breath he bent over clasping his knees until the adrenaline-rush started to die and he could finally suck his lungs full. Shaking his head, he chuckled a little, then sort of laughed.

Breasts heaving, fingers almost pumping, Tian leaned back against the rock face catching her breath. Aside from the stabbing pain in her side stinging with aggravating regularity, she was aware her feet hurt. Lifting them lightly one at a time she looked around then checked the top of the rock wall, just to be sure. No dinosaur.

Running to avoid certain death can distract one's attention for a while, but eventually realization will return; and even though accustomed to being barefoot, running on such rugged terrain tended to bruise even the most callous soles. Aside from that, she was also puzzled. "What is so funny?"

"Nothing really; nervous laughter," he explained. "Seems a lot funnier now than it did a minute ago. That sucker almost got us."

"That is not funny."

"Bet your butt; don't I know it."

"If the dinosaur had not stumbled it would have caught you and eaten you."

"That's the whole point; I didn't know it fell. I thought it had me for sure —and I was so scared and puckered up, the thought that flashed through my mind was, 'eat shit and die'."

Tian frowned. "You worry me."

"Why's that?"

"You are beginning to sound like Reed."

He thought about that; then at the edge of concern, "You really think so?"

More frown.

He considered, "That is kinda scary, isn't it?" Then dismissing the idea and grinning again, "So much for a hair-raising episode at T-Rex hill —*whew.*"

"T-Rex hill?" she inquired, curious. He nodded and she allowed, "Appropriate enough." From that time on, this place would be known as the rock wall below T-Rex hill. Both lingered catching their breath, until she mildly complained, "My feet hurt."

"Mine too." Ames lifted his right foot to examine it, found a rock-cut across the arch with coagulated blood and dirt packed in the wound, "That granite is some nasty stuff to run on," picking at the wound.

Tian noticed him trying to wipe the cut clean. "Leave it alone. The mud will draw the wound and it will heal faster."

He grimaced, "But there's so much gunk caked in there it'll make me walk lopsided."

She smiled. "It will wear down as we walk." He began to protest again, but she interrupted him. "You know I love you—and you know I am right... so leave—it—alone." She was already getting good at this man-woman thing, getting really good. It wouldn't do any good to argue.

A tepid, "Okay," and without further discussion they began walking. Then, perhaps exaggerating just a bit as he limped alongside her, he feigned a whine; just had to try one more time. "But if I tip over sideways from walking lopsided, you realize of course, it'll be your fault."

"I will catch you and tip you up again," she responded almost automatically. Sure enough, she was a natural.

"You take such good care of me," shaking his head as he slipped his arm around her waist.

"I know, John." And they headed home.

Their return to the village took several hours of steady, careful travel. Negotiating the unforgiving crevices and drop-offs in the dark was hazardous, and in a primitive world such as this, a misstep could mean death. A broken ankle or leg would mend; but without mobility an injured individual was easy prey for the elements and predators.

* * *

It was late…

…When the pair arrived at the village and they entered the hut quietly; but Tian was restless, bothered by something she had not yet told him. He sensed her uneasiness and knowing she wouldn't sleep suggested they go to the pool to swim. There were times when his perception touched her, even surprised her, though perhaps it shouldn't; being there when she needed him was one of his innate aspects, reassuring. They were not really a pair any longer, but two halves of the same one. The love they shared was only a part of much more: trust, understanding, closeness, and a unity. Alone each was incomplete; now the other made them whole. That was their love.

* * *

Quiet…

…The pool was soft and serene in its solitude, a picture postcard of a tropical paradise. Unseen, beyond the water's edge crickets and myriad insects regaled creating a soothing background cacophony from countless sequestered niches. From untold secret places they composed a rhythmical, natural symphony of the darkness; but there were no birds, this was the era of dinosaurs, birds not yet having arrived. Still, nature's music was beautiful, highlighted with the luminescence of swarming lightning bugs, candleflies Tian called them. Blinking yellow embers glowing in the night, nature's mating ritual unfolding before them. Cicada and frogs riveted a musical chorus from the trees and water lily fronds rooted near the opposite end of the pond, the air warm and enchanting, incited them to warbling and croaking every now and then.

This was the night music of the jungle... in the land of the Renoloi.

Silently Tian and Ames stood facing one another on the large flat rock overhanging the pristine water. She pulled the sleeveless black leather shirt over his head and let it drop. When he had returned at the crater his other shirt was so badly torn and soaked with blood it had to be replaced. Running her hands softly down the contour of his chest Tian recalled the old shirt, with the blood on it.

John had never been able to explain what happened... just another of the missing pieces.

She slowly unbuttoned his Levis, now torn and laced with holes. He had refused to part with them though, not willing to accept black leather shorts she had offered. He told her the jeans were like old friends, an expression she did not understand; and Reed must have felt the same, because he still wore his as well. Although Tian could not understand the men's sentimental attachment to the cloth pants, neither did she mind; it excited her, made her tingle inside when she would entice John and make the bulge within the jeans.

That bulge would make her wet. John could do that.

As he stepped out of his jeans, Ames ran his hands over her body and cupped her breasts drawing her nipples rigid beneath the leather. Their gaze connected, he removed her top and let it fall to the ground, hands softly squeezing and massaging, capturing her nipples between his fingers then gently closing and manipulating them creating twinges of excitement that shivered from her chest to her groin. She loved the way he touched her. The pleasure flowed through her and she closed her eyes as his hands traced down her sides to her waist, night air wafting between her legs when her skirt slipped away.

Embracing, they drew together quivering with excitement and anticipation, neither ever tiring of the sensations of the other. Each time they made love it was better than before, and each time their bond grew stronger than before. As they kissed slowly and passionately, they went down together, lightly upon the rock, he turning onto his back and drawing her to him. She lay on top of him and spread her legs, feeling him enter, sending tingling pulses and burning excitement throughout her body, her long golden hair flowing gently over them, veiling them from the world.

They were all alone, together in their own panorama.

She slid gracefully, effeminately and lovingly upon him, their bodies liquid with the perspiration sheen between them. With each movement her breasts caressed him and compressed with his pectorals, their nipples brushing together in lubricated rhythm. Moving slowly at first, she could feel him inside, the sensation sending cravings to her abdomen; the more she pressed upon him the more intense her hunger, electric pulses creating an acute overwhelming desire. Sealing him more securely she drew him deeper inside escalating her sensual yearning, her desire in harmony with her body.

Rhythmically they moved, sharing themselves, two becoming one... the ultimate intimacy.

Drenched with perspiration, waves of pleasure flushing through them time and again, increasing with intensity, every sense mounting to its zenith, she kissed him with feral aggression sealing her mouth upon his to muffle her scream, her orgasm creating an incredible rush as his body arched and tensed. They climaxed together.

After that they lay quietly for a time holding one another, she nestled to his chest. An hour passed, then two, and they slept soundly until she stirred waking him.

"Do you want to swim?" he whispered.

She snuggled, kissed his chest. "In a moment, but now, please hold me." Pressing against him they lay together on the rock on their cushion of clothes. At last Tian sighed. "You are very patient with me."

"When you're ready," his eyes moving down to her.

She looked up from his chest and told him, "Something is wrong, John… very wrong."

"What do you mean?"

"Never before have the beasts, the dinosaurs, crossed the river from the Forsaken Land, yet today the dinosaur was in Legend Mountains. That should not be."

He tried to reassure her. "The Tyrannosaur was—or is—territorial by nature. More than likely that one was only expanding its range in search of food. Just because one crossed the river into the mountain range doesn't necessarily mean anything."

Genuinely concerned, "I wish that were so; but it is not."

"Why do you think that?"

"I do not know; but something is not as it should be."

"Things change. The one constant, since the beginning of time, has always been, that things change."

"Perhaps. However, what will happen may be more than we know, much more than we expect." She trembled as he pulled her a bit closer brushing hair from her face with a gentle hand, her hazel eyes sparkling in the moonlight as she looked at him. She tried to force a smile, but the effort was obvious and she conceded pressing her cheek against his chest. With a worried sigh she whispered, "Something is wrong, John. I can feel it."

"We're together," he assured softly kissing her head, "we'll be all right."

Drifting, he looked up from the woman he loved, past the highest reaches of the treetops, to the countless diamond stars flung across the heavens, and for a moment he lay quietly pondering her premonition and the new world he was in, still unable to comprehend it all. How it had all come to be.

Taking a deep breath and caressing her back with a tender hand, he finally spoke again. "Let's go for a swim." She looked at him. "We're together," he said, "whatever happens, we will face it together. Remember, for everything that happens, always… there is a reason."

"Yes, I know." This time her smile came more easily. He rose offering his hand and they stepped to the edge of the flat rock overhanging the pool. "How is it John, that you can always make me feel better?"

"Because, with all that I am, I love you," he whispered. "And because… there are always possibilities."

CHAPTER TWO

Daybreak burned off the ground fog...

...And the morning meal was finished; but the Renoloi remained at the circle, word having spread like a virus of the dinosaur in Legend Range. A serious matter, this had never been before, requiring the presence of the entire village. Tian, Ames, Reed and Seana sat together.

Unobtrusively, Kalo crouched on a high flat rock just behind them, tentatively waxing the string of her new bow. She was still very young but her desire and persistence had been rewarded; she would be an archer. The girl had been practicing ardently, obsessively, alone in the jungle, honing her skill and aim; and as always, today she had chosen a place near her leaders whom she emulated. Kalo was quiet, intent, wanting to learn.

From atop a large boulder opposite them, Lita raised an open hand, and, *hush,* moved through the crowd. She motioned to Tian on the other side of the gathering.

A tip of her head acknowledging Lita, Tian rose, stepped forward and addressed her people. "Yesterday in the mountains beyond the temple ruins, John—Mr. Ames, and I encountered a beast," then corrected, "a dinosaur. Never before has a Tyrannosaur crossed from the Forsaken Land into ours, and although we escaped, it remains a threat." The crowd murmured agreement until Tian raised a hand, and the people quieted, listening as she continued. "We must assemble a party to hunt the dinosaur, to kill it.

"But we kill only for food," a voice from the crowd. Neme stood.

"True, that is the way of our people," Tian allowed, "however, as it was with the Trogs, we must also kill to survive." The woman understood, nodded, and sat down. Tian concluded, "It will be done."

Lita motioned several Renoloi to her and they began organizing the hunt as Tian sat down with Ames. Reed, seated on her other side with Seana, leaned over and nudged Tian.

"Short, sweet—to the point. Cool." Tian smiled and mussed his hair playfully. As he began smoothing his hair down Reed chuckled then asked, "Was that a gesture of affection?"

"Yes, it was, and perhaps I will do it again," she warned.

"Good thing," he threw back, "else I'd have to mess you up. Don't be frizzing my hair anymore."

Tian leaned over bumping him with her shoulder. "I let Seana do my light work. She whips you on a regular basis."

Automatically Reed looked around Tian, to Ames. "She learned that from you, didn't she, Doc?"

Straight-faced, "Don't be involving me in this. I only told her you're self-conscious about going bald."

"Aw shit, that's lower than a gully snake. Why would you go and tell her something like that?"

"Because it is true," Tian taunted, "and you *are* losing your hair."

Almost panicked he turned to Seana. "That's just bullshit, right? Am I losing my hair?"

Seana, composed, softly, with deadpan innocence, "Some, but not a lot." Then she elaborated as she pointed touching the top of his head near the back, carefully selecting a spot he could never see without two mirrors, "Well... except for right here. Most of your hair is gone from there."

"Aw shit," he gasped, "that's male pattern baldness, sure as shootin'. Runs in my family." He turned to Ames again. "Doc, I told you the magnetic fields in the time sphere..."

"—Shoulda worn a baseball cap with a button on it," the other interrupted.

"It ain't funny."

Affecting empathy, "Damned shame actually."

"Doc…"

"I know it's serious," he agreed, "but for the life of me I can't figure out why it hasn't had any affect on me —only you."

"Well hell, that's easy," Reed offered, "you're old, and things like that don't affect old guys, just young ones."

Ames chucked. "Think so?"

"Well sure. That's a proven scientific fact. Shoot, next my gonads will probably start shriveling up."

Tian observed, "We should be wearing boots."

Reed regarded her disapprovingly; then back to Ames and asked, "Why do you teach her stuff like that?"

Seana jumped in. "Well, what about Bloody Bones, Reed? You tell me stories about Bloody Bones all the time."

A snap-reaction, both men in unison, *"Bloody Bones is real!"*

"Oh yeah, well real *this!*" Seana gestured, grabbing her crotch with a cupped hand. Abruptly turning, eyes stabbing Reed, Ames stared with disbelief.

"I only did that once, Doc," he spontaneously defended. "Christ, she absorbs shit like a sponge —and she never forgets anything."

Shaking his head, "Reed, I can't believe you would teach her something like that."

"And he showed me the bird," Seana volunteered, flipping them the finger. Then she went on elaborating, "It was originally a Greek gesture." Reed grabbed her hand, folding her extended middle finger back with the others.

"Aw jeez, Seana," he pleaded, "don't help me, okay?"

"He showed me many other things too, Mr. Ames, but I will have to take my clothes off first…"

"Seana—" he begged.

"Jesus, Reed!" Ames began to say.

Disrupting their banter —shattering branches, a splintering *craa-ack*— two massive trees split apart and were still falling as the Tyrannosaur lunged from the jungle snatching Lita from the high rock. Unsuspecting, the woman was dead before realization set in. The dinosaur was lightning with monstrous jaws that sliced through her in a heartbeat then flipped her body into the air and caught it. Renoloi popcorn.

Drooling viscous gruel as it bit her in two, the reptile gulped the top half letting her legs and abdomen fall to the ground with a blood-splattering, *thud,* hips twitching, feet kicking dirt. Cloudburst of panic and terror flashed everywhere at once, women scooping up children nearest the dinosaur and fleeing toward the other side of the clearing as the Tyrannosaur swelled its chest, reared its head, and roared.

Tian seized her spear, Ames another, Reed grabbing the last as he pushed Seana back toward the rush of fleeing people, other Renoloi lances also rushing forward from throughout the commotion of bodies. Pushing their way to the front Tian, Ames and Reed filled a gap in the line. Time to fight —win or die.

Kalo was onto her feet, a virgin warrior, stone cold and steady.

The dinosaur spun, its tail slamming into a tree —tipping over— dirt clods scattering with the earthen ball boiling up shredding and snapping roots. Lances flew, some punching holes, others glancing off, arrows piercing the hide of the dinosaur's neck and chest with non-lethal effect.

Kalo calculated, carefully choosing her target.

The tree crashed to the ground. T-Rex lunged —a ground-trembling stomp— and Tian and the others attacked.

Reed's spear punched through the abdomen, tearing it, drenching him with a heave of eviscerated intestines and deluge of blood along the shaft. In the rush of rancid stench and steam he slipped and fell then slid under the animal in a twisted pile and slop. Almost blinded by blood and fluid-flush he scrambled frantically between the huge clawed killing feet.

Thinking, *do something—now,* Ames screamed —distraction— the dinosaur reeled.

Blurs of motion. Hands and knees, erupting blood and mud, fingers digging and pulling, feet pushing and kicking, Reed scrambled with uncanny speed, frantically —under the tail— a roll as he dove. The dinosaur blinked and he was gone.

Eyes narrowing, Kalo drew her bowstring.

Looking for him, the Tyrannosaur sidestepped and spun whipping its tail sweeping three warriors from a ledge, their broken bodies catapulting into the surrounding trees. Then quickly turning back and lowering its thickset head the dinosaur spewed saliva and hot breath in Ames' face. Defiantly the man stood his ground ramming his spear down the monstrous throat, blood squirting from the wound as bone-crushing jaws slammed shut snapping the spear in two and splattering him in crimson.

Kalo aimed, following her target.

As Ames fell backward Tian rushed forward throwing her weight with her spear, sinking half the length of the shaft in the dinosaur's neck. In her hands and her head she could feel it: the popping sound as the spear pierced leathery hide, the ripping sensation as the point sliced through muscle, the crunching-gristly grinding as the tip severed tendons and cartilage, and finally the thick sensation of, *thuck*, when the spear burrowed into soft tissue of the throat three feet inside.

Raising its awesome head, the dinosaur roared then vented, shrill like a scream, lifting Tian from the ground. Heart racing, adrenaline pumped and splattered with blood, she dangled, a rag doll clinging obstinately to her weapon, recalling an encounter in the past —a Trog— when her spear was broken. That would not happen again.

Echoing rage, the Tyrannosaur's scream drowned everything else out; and it blinked its hungry, yellow-green eyes. The target.

Absorbed, focused, Kalo released the bowstring, a powerful —*snap*— the feathered missile slicing through air —*ssst-thwack*— and struck with consummate accuracy, splattering lens, severing the optic nerve, scrambling brains, then stopped in the back of its skull.

Standing dead, the Tyrannosaur teetered with Tian still dangling clutching her spear, then collapsed sideways crashing to the ground with a heavy, dead weight collision and dark splattering mud. Jumping clear at the last instant she landed and rolled out of harm's way as Ames rushed forward to help her up and others moved in.

Still not certain what had happened, it was then Tian saw the fletching and shaft of an arrow barely protruding from the punctured right eye of the monstrous reptile. Wondering, her gaze traveled from the dead dinosaur, over the Renoloi, to Kalo, still standing on the boulder, stone cold... a Renoloi warrior.

Tian smiled.

Still wiping blood from his face, thoroughly impressed, Reed complimented, "Robin-a-Hood."

* * *

Dead weight…

…Tyrannosaurus Rex. It took several hours for the Renoloi to drag the huge dinosaur from the circle into the jungle, where it was gutted and cleaned. Claws, teeth and bone would be sharpened for weapons, ribs used for bows, hide, too heavy for leather, stretched on wooden frames for shields, entrails cleaned and tied for waterskins, and the meat salted or smoked and preserved. They wasted nothing.

By late afternoon bonfires were roasting corpulent slabs of meat for the evening celebration, with women and children scurrying about orchestrating a medley of commotion. Tian and Ames stood together observing, Tian keeping vigil over her people, her eyes repeatedly traveling back to the high flat boulder where Kalo sat unpretentiously, almost blending into the background. Ames noticed.

"The meal will take some time to prepare, would you like to walk, John?"

"Sure."

"Do you mind if others join us?"

"Not at all."

"Reed, Seana—" she signaled over the activity. They waved, starting toward her. "Nitana." She also responded. And last Tian called, "Kalo."

The young girl was overwhelmed. She hesitated, such an honor to be summoned by her leader. Dropping smoothly to the ground she darted through the crowd, as others, who also heard Tian, observed.

Delighted, Kalo beamed with pride. "Yes, Tian?" stopping abruptly before her. They were all together now.

"We are going for a walk. Would you care to join us?"

"Would I—oh, yes!" She almost bounced.

Until now, concealing something in her hand behind her back, Tian opened it offering Kalo a dinosaur tooth strung on a leather thong. Kalo, rising on the balls of her feet and admiring the six-inch tooth could hardly stand still as Tian slipped the trophy necklace over her head. "For you," Tian said.

As they began down the path Kalo bubbled, "Do you see it, Reed?"

"Well heck yes I see it," overtly praising her. "Sure can't miss that baby. It's bigger than your boobs."

"*Ree-ed*," Seana admonished slapping his shoulder.

"Well, it is," he defended. Tian, Nitana and Ames, in the lead, exchanged glances just shaking their heads.

"It is *so—beautiful*," Kalo regarded.

"It sure is," he encouraged. "It's an incisor."

"Yes," the girl agreed, having no idea what that meant. "My own beast tooth."

"A Tyrannosaur tooth," he counseled, "that's what the dinosaur is called."

"Tyrannosaur," her eyes bright.

"Yes. Well actually, Tyrannosaurus Rex," he explained. "They were huge carnivores that lived during the Jurassic in the Mesozoic Era, back even before my time —and of course here too, now."

"Why are they called by such a strange name?"

Reed grinned mischievously. "Oh, well, that's because this little paleontologist guy named Tyrannosaurus Rex first discovered their fossilized bones and classified them: phylum, class, order, family, genus, species, and so on. It was a custom back then that the species be named after the person who discovered it." Then stoic, interjecting a footnote, "But people became quite exasperated trying to pronounce Tyrannosaurus —well actually they pitched a royal bitch— so the paleontologist relented and let them call his dinosaur T-Rex. Pretty cool, huh?"

"Yes, it is," she agreed enthusiastically.

Teasing, Ames chaffed, "This is beginning to sound like a character reversal of Lucy and Linus in a Peanuts cartoon." The Renoloi didn't understand, but Reed did. Unruffled, he ignored his friend and continued the dissertation, which grew more outlandish as it progressed, and didn't end until they had arrived at the lowland bordering the river.

* * *

Gnarled, ancient trees…

…A primitive world; the battleground had healed. Lush grass carpeted the dark loam that months earlier was torn ragged and saturated with blood shed by warriors from both sides. Broken trees and liana were now absorbed within the jungle's camouflage, another of nature's cycles. And once again the river sang its burbling, wind-flutter song, the never-ending musical rhythm of water flowing to somewhere unknown.

The jungle had healed, but Tian had not. Only rarely did she come to the lowland with the memories it kept. Why she must be here today she did not understand herself; but she could feel it, something intangible, something within drawing her to the river. Today would be important.

They walked quietly together along the bank, no one saying much. The mood of the lowland had overtaken and captured them. Perhaps one day they would build a memorial in honor of those who fought so bravely, and died here. They were still here, like stepping into a church, that feeling—*their spirits nearby.* Finally, the six stopped on the beach.

Tian breathed deeply and slow, sighed; then said to no one in particular, "We must expand the sentry perimeter. More dinosaurs will cross the river."

"It will be done," Nitana replied quietly. Tian acknowledged Nitana's response but said nothing more. She gazed over the flowing water.

"Why do you think more dinosaurs will cross the river?" Ames asked.

"They will come." Tian looked from the river to Kalo, standing silently close by, then back to the river.

"Tian…" Ames almost whispered; she turned, "why are we here at the river?"

"Today is important. I can feel it."

Reed broke in. "What is that?" pointing over the water. His attention redirected, Ames turned, scanning the river.

"Something yet unfinished," Tian murmured; but neither man clearly heard, nor understood what she said.

"Where?" Ames asked Reed.

"Out there, floating in the —well nevermind— I'll get it." The others waited onshore while Reed waded into the chest-deep water, to the middle of the river, where he retrieved an object, examined it briefly, then headed back toward them. Beaming with excitement and nearing the shore, he called out, "Hey Doc, you're never gonna believe this." Slipping his hand under his shirt he concealed the object as he sloshed onto the beach and teased, wheedling, "You won't believe it, not in a million years."

"What is it?" Seana queried.

Avoiding her probing hands Reed turned. "No fair peeking."

"What?" Ames asked.

From beneath his dripping leather shirt Reed produced a green glass bottle sealed at the neck with a short length of stick and containing a small piece of paper rolled up like a scroll. He handed it to Ames. The man took it, looked it over, then handed it back.

"What?" Reed was puzzled.

"Aren't you going to open it?"

"Oh—yeah." Reed fumbled prying the stick loose, then pulled it free. Gently thumping the bottleneck on his hand, the scroll emerged slightly and Seana carefully eased it out. Focusing on the scroll as he and Seana tenderly unrolled it, Reed handed the bottle to Ames.

The note read:
We must leave our mountains
Hunters have returned
Safety lies across the water toward the rising sun
We go to the Island

— Lent

They listened intently, no one quite sure what to make of the message. For a moment each considered silently until finally, Reed said the obvious. "Curious."

"Yes," Seana agreed.

"Not the note, Seana," he explained. "This isn't some exotic parchment, or even cambium. It's plain old cellulose pulp."

"What is cellulose pulp?"

Reed looked at her. "It's common paper, from a spiral notebook."

"A note in a bottle," Tian said, "something important," reigniting Reed's smile. "There is another Renoloi village, and we must help them."

"Absolutely," he agreed.

"Across the water, to the Island," she recited.

Reed made the analogy, "Robert Louis Stevenson's, *Treasure Island*, a real pirate adventure." Turning from Tian to Seana, "Isn't that cool?"

"Yes, it is." Then she asked, "What is a pirate?"

"Buccaneers, corsairs, the scourge of the high seas, pillaging and plundering Spanish galleons." He thought about it wringing his hands, "Oh, this'll be great, a pirate adventure," anticipating, ready to go.

"Reed, take a look at this." Ames handed him the bottle. He took it, gave a cursory examination, but didn't notice. "The bottom," Ames instructed. "Read it."

Turning it to make out the molded wording, he read aloud, "Coca-Cola Bottling Company, Newton, Miss, 1952." Scratching his cheek, "I didn't know Coke ever came in glass bottles, only plastic and aluminum cans."

"How did a Coke bottle get here?" Ames proposed.

Reed grinned. "Curiouser and curiouser."

Turning from Reed to Tian with a sideways glance, "We go upriver?"

"We go upriver," she said. "They are in trouble and we must help them."

Reed thought, *the adventure begins.*

"How many shall go?" Nitana asked.

Her gaze again drifting over the river, Tian considered. "Myself, John, you, Reed, Seana, Denen, and ten each lances and archers."

"May I go?" Kalo asked, speaking for the first time. Tian turned, looked at the girl, then away without answering. "Please, Tian," she pleaded.

"It will be dangerous. You are too young." Ames listened, but said nothing... watching Tian's eyes.

Reed, puzzled by Tian's reluctance, stepped forward on Kalo's behalf. "Tian, she has proven herself. She's earned the right. I have only known one person better than her with a bow and..." cutting his words short. Tian's eyes burned into his; and even as he had spoken, Reed saw the pain in her face, a ragged blade cutting through to her heart. He hesitated, then whispered, "I—I'm sorry. I didn't mean to remind you."

Tian squeezed his arm with her hand. "I know, Reed." She had to be strong. "I know. She is gone."

Ames listened, and said nothing... watching her eyes.

"*Please*, Tian," Kalo begged. Tian looked at the young Renoloi but didn't respond. "*Please*, Tian; I would *die* for you."

"I know you would." The woman blinked, her eyes welling with tears, emotional strength ebbing, and she abruptly turned and walked away from them. Tongue-tied and ill at ease Reed vacillated standing with the others, feeling awkward, unsure what he should do.

Ames' hand touched his shoulder. Hushed, somber words: "Go back to the village. I'll stay with her."

The younger man looked at his friend. "I'm so sorry, Doc. I didn't mean to upset her."

"I know." Ames sighed. "Ghosts. She needs some time alone." Without speaking Reed and the women began to leave turning back toward the village when Ames subsequently added, "Better get the pulse laser from the sphere."

Reed nodded, answering quietly over his shoulder, "Will do." He, Seana and Nitana continued walking as Kalo lingered attracting Ames' attention without speaking.

"I'll try," he said. "I'll talk to her."

"Thank you, Mr. Ames." She left, hurrying to catch the others.

Tian had walked along the beach for some distance, now standing silent, absorbed in thought. Ames followed part-way then stopped, leaving her alone. The mood of the lowland murmured sadness in the air, haunting recollections of loss transported on zephyr wings. He sat down on the sand. He would wait.

Looking out over the river Tian stood for some time, motionless, statuesque with the exception of her hair rustled by the breeze, waist length, exquisite strands, flowing golden, the dance of the wind. But the wind could never carry away the pain inside. Her loss. For an hour she stood there; and for an hour Ames waited. From time to time her body would tremble as she cried, her soul trying to heal from within.

Finally, she turned and walked toward him, head down, eyes red with pain, face lined with tears. He rose to his feet, waiting. She did not say a word and did not look up, just walked to him, to the security of his arms as they wrapped around her; then she cried, sobbing intensely, trembling so violently he held her to prevent her from falling. Ames hurt so badly for her, but despite his fervent love for the Renoloi leader, this time, even he couldn't take away her pain.

For a long time, she cried, and he held her, caressing her softly, *cry... let it go.*

At last, she was quiet. Wiping tears from her face, she looked up to him, "Am I wrong?"

"I believe so," he answered. "Strange as it may seem, this time I have to agree with Reed. Kalo has earned the right to go."

The admission: "I miss Kimo."[8]

"She isn't Kimo." Ames already knew. He had seen it... in her eyes.

Her lips quivered. "I do not want her to die too. She reminds me so much of Kimo. She moves like her, sounds like her; she even looks like Kimo." Tian pressed her cheek against his chest then continued, remembering, "Even as she died Kimo was not concerned for herself. She said to me, 'You are safe. Perhaps we will meet again... in a world somewhere beyond. Please, remember me'. When Kalo said, 'I would die for you', it was more than I could bear. She is young, too young to die."

Tian was still, and the silence dredged recollections in Ames of a little old man with bright green eyes, a scraggy beard and a rag-a-muffin's body; the spirit who had been dead for twenty years. Old Sam.

"I'm here," Ames said to her.

For a long time, Tian talked, and cried, and finally... began to heal.

* * *

Cirrus clouds, and just rising...

...A waning moon. It was late by the time Tian and Ames returned to the village, the celebration well underway. Shadows danced beyond the roaring bonfires and spits laden with charbroiled dinosaur meat seasoned to perfection and basted in a sauce of savory wild herbs. The people were felicitous, relaxed and relishing the camaraderie and an air of contentment that permeated the gathering.

Kalo saw the couple approaching on the path and moved quickly, intercepting them before the festivities of the banquet would interfere. As Tian and Ames neared the perimeter of the circle, pushing ferns aside she stepped out in front of Tian. Momentarily the leader considered, glanced at Ames, then back to the young Renoloi; and at length she placed her hand on the girl's shoulder. "We leave at dawn; will you be ready?"

"Oh yes, I will! Thank you, Tian." Thrilled, Kalo looked at Ames. He winked, and grinned.

"I am hungry," Tian commented, a matter-of-fact pretext.

"Come then," Kalo encouraged. "Tyrannosaurus Rex is very delicious. Reed says it tastes like chicken." She led them into the crowd and as they were absorbed within the confusion Tian finally smiled, and as she did, she slipped her arm around Ames' waist.

"You were right, John," she conceded.

Tian was ready for tomorrow.

* * *

Reed hailed…

…Motioning them over, from across the crowd. They joined him. Tonight would be a time of cordial relaxation spiced with Reed's somewhat-twisted and uniquely demented folklore. It would be an evening of pleasant memories. And for some, it would be their last time together. This was still a primitive world.

"You gotta try the T-Rex," Reed recommended as they were given large portions and others made room so they could sit down. Reed's beaming smile encouraged them as he, Seana, Nitana, Denen, Tondra, Kalo, and an entire entourage waited expectantly.

"Very delicious," after swallowing her first bite.

"It is," Ames agreed a bit surprised.

Reed: "Tastes like chicken, doesn't it?" Ames nodded and continued chewing. "Bet your ass on a biscuit."

"It is different from Chiqua," Seana remarked.

Rather droll, Reed turned to her. "After having Chiqua seven frickin' days-a-week for months on end, anything would taste different. Hell, T-Rex is a whole new food group."

"Well," she defended, "Chiqua has not hurt you. It has put a little pot belly on you." She patted him affectionately indicating the precise location of excess accumulation.

"Oh my achin' ass, that's relaxed muscle."

"That muscle is not relaxed," she needled, "it is comatose."

Surprised, "Where did you learn a word like that?" Then accusingly, to Ames, "Why do you teach her stuff like that, Doc?"

Innocently, "Who, me?"

"You know bitch 'possum well where she learned that." Ames smirked while Reed carped, "She went straight from being terminologically challenged to termagant."

"It does not matter," Seana decided. "I will tighten your stomach up because I am horny and you are going to do me tonight."

Ames coughed—laughed—almost spit out his food. Tian's jaw dropped. Not knowing what to say Reed sputtered until Ames finally managed to swallow and chastised wryly, "Well we certainly know where she learned *that*, don't we." Statement, not a question.

"It is true," Seana explained innocently. "I thoroughly enjoy when Reed sexes me; his stomach muscles become *sooo* tight."

Ames burst into laughter and would have tipped over if Tian hadn't caught him; however, she was laughing too, so hard she couldn't keep from shaking.

"Aw, runnin'-mouth-squealer..." Reed protested, "Seana will you *plee-ease* quit talking."

Seana snapped, good-natured but defiantly, "I will not —and you are going to sex me tonight." She sat up straight puffing out her chest. "See these; want some?" Then she turned to Ames proudly. "He taught me that too." He couldn't take anymore; both he and Tian went over backward from laughing, sprawled on the ground, tears coming to their eyes.

"Seana, for crying out loud—" then, almost pleading, "for God's sake, *plee-ease, shut up!*"

"That is not what you said when you had that string with the beads, is it?"

"Aw—jeez, why not just put it on the bulletin board. What ever happened to the concept of a private sex life?" his face pitifully into his lap, completely embarrassed.

Ames was roaring. His side hurt, and he couldn't get up. Tian lay wedged, her arm beneath him, jubilant, thoroughly wrapped up in the moment. She needed the laughter; medicine for the heart, therapy for the soul.

Later—

The children swarmed Reed, insisting he tell them a story. The fare for the evening was the harrowing tale of Peter Pan and Tinkerbell, and their narrow escape from Captain Hook and the crocodile in 'Never Never-Land'. Luckily, they were saved just in the nick of time when a rhinoceros with a Ouija board impaled on its horn stampeded and obliterated Captain Hook's ship. After that part, the yarn experienced a rather bizarre turn of events and became really strange; but it ended well, with Peter and Tinkerbell riding scout for General Custer —at the Little Bighorn.

The whole time Jade sat in Reed's lap, never taking her eyes from him. Reed was a gifted storyteller.

The evening passed too quickly, entirely delightful; Reed steadfastly refusing to elaborate about the string and the beads though, and Ames, knowing his friend was creative, didn't press for details. At any rate, Seana was grinning like a Cheshire cat when she led him home, and as they entered their hut and the door closed Tian and Ames both heard her say, "Now Reed, take—your—clothes—off."

Not a word, but both grinning, they continued up the path, and arriving at their hut Tian stopped and without prelude passionately kissed him. "Nice custom," she remarked coyly. "I enjoy it." The door rose. They stepped inside, and draping her arms around his neck, Tian said sweetly, "Are you going to *do* me?"

Smiling, "I certainly hope so," and the door closed.

As they lay on the stone couch together, dim reflections of the burning sepulcher playing mysteriously over the walls of the room, holding one another, they talked softly. For both, these were the times that meant the most, knowing they could discuss anything, everything, without fear of reprisal, ridicule, anger or misunderstanding. And perhaps these were the ingredients, blended with patience, that created the matrix of their love as each grew into the person they were, their trust enabling them to believe in the other, and in themselves. That faith allowed them freedom to overcome insecurity that might otherwise arise to strangle them with suspicions and jealousy, the green-eyed monster.

But this time there were no green-eyed demons. Reed, Old Sam, and one other; green eyes, windows to kindred souls, links of a chain and a spiral of circumstances and...

...Something yet Unfinished.

For Tian and Ames their trust, their love, their bond was absolute. And later they made love... softly, tenderly, slowly. They held each other, intimately exploring, sharing one another. It was a precious time. Time together, sealing themselves away from the rest of the world, the two of them in harmony so close and intense nothing could sever the bond between them. Their unity and commitment would last forever... more so than they knew.

Ames had no way of knowing, this night would be the last time he would ever make love with the Renoloi.

CHAPTER THREE

Greylight, not quite dawn...

...Kalo sat quietly waiting at the meeting circle, no one else having yet arrived. Admiring it almost reverently she stroked the Tyrannosaur tooth, her most precious possession, second only to her bow. She was an archer, a Renoloi warrior; and although still very young, she had been accepted as a member of this expedition. Anticipation made her restless. The girl could not imagine what the adventure would bring, and perhaps that, the unknown, was the greatest adventure of all. Kalo, the girl, would embark... but the girl would not return.

Footsteps padded along the path. Arriving at the circle Nitana and Denen walked together, next Seana and Reed, then Tian and Ames followed by nineteen lances and archers. Kalo rose, all of them assembling near the fire circle containing remnant embers of the previous evening's bonfire.

"Everyone here?" Reed asked, the pulse laser slung over his shoulder. With groggy unspoken, *good mornings,* the team began preparations as Tondra and several others arrived to see them off.

Denen, to Tian: "I believe we are ready."

"Looks like it's going to be a nice day," Ames said, a glance to the sky then back.

"Perhaps," Denen considered, "but a long day."

"A very long day," Tian agreed, then ordered, "Nitana, Kalo —point." Without question both moved nimbly assuming the lead positions.

"De'ja vu, Doc?"

"Seems like."

Reed quipped, "We're off to see the wizard."

"Uncle Reed, please do not leave me," a child's voice whimpered from the obscurity of bracken. As he turned Jade scampered headlong across the clearing and seized his leg despairingly. Not having realized the depth of the child's attachment Reed carefully lifted her from the ground offering his easy, comforting smile of reassurance.

"Hey, Kiddo, what are you doing up?" he asked, tapping her lightly on the nose with a fingertip. "Don't worry. I'll be back 'fore you know it."

"My mother told me that too," Jade appealed, "but she did not come back." She flung her arms around his neck and began to sob causing Reed's eyes to tear so quickly he almost choked. With her plea, he was acutely reminded of the day Jade's mother bravely went to war against the Trogs, and never returned. Like many others, Jade was an orphan. He tried gently to pry her loose, but the tiny girl clung to him with desperate tenacity; and sensing his awkwardness Tondra stepped forward to intervene.

"Jade," Tondra quietly said, taking the girl in her hands, "Reed and the others will come back. You must be brave." She, coaxing the small child gently, "You are a Renoloi."

"I am not brave," Jade pleaded, "I am little."

"But you still must be brave," Tondra whispered.

Tears streaming down her cheeks, the child sobbed brokenly as her grip began to loosen. "Uncle Reed, I love you."

The pain in her voice stung in his heart, and hugging her for a moment longer Reed whispered into her ear, "I love you too." A single tear tracking down his cheek, "If it's the last thing in this world I ever do, Sweetie... I absolutely promise, I will come back."

More confident, "Absolutely promise?" she sniffled.

"Absolutely," he assured. She wiped the tears from her face with a dainty hand, then abruptly kissed him on the cheek.

"I love you, Uncle Reed. You absolutely promised," she reminded.

"I love you too," he told her carefully turning her over to Tondra's waiting arms. Without saying anything more he turned and the team moved out knowing it would be easier for the child if they were quickly out of sight; and Seana knew, it would also be easier for the man.

Within a moment the jungle absorbed them and Reed and Seana were walking together on the path leading to the cliffs along the river, "It isn't right," he finally muttered. "It ain't natural."

"What?" Seana asked.

Reed looked at her. "To love a little kid so much… when she isn't even your own little girl. It just isn't natural."

Taking his hand, squeezing it lovingly, Seana wiped the tear from his cheek. "Yes, it is, Reed."

* * *

The first two days...

...Were long and hard, following the cliffs shadowing the meandering ribbon of river far below. This was not a leisurely journey, rather deliberate and swift. The pace set by Nitana and Kalo was fleet and constant as they maintained their distance on point pushing the others to keep up. Expeditiously miles of familiar jungle lay behind the band of travelers, the terrain now new and unexplored; virgin territory, unknown wilderness, none having ever been this far upstream before.

The next day was the same, travelling upriver by greylight, not stopping until the jungle absorbed the very last of the sunset.

* * *

Late, the third day…

…Darkness now creeping in from above and around them, they were bone tired. A makeshift camp was in place, sentries posted for early watch, the team gathered around a small fire. Tonight would be the dark of the moon, not a good night for the diurnal Renoloi, but an opportune time for nocturnal creatures.

They were camped in the foothills of mountains that rose almost vertically, their peaks towering within an inky abyss of limitless dark sky. The river's wandering oxbow course had dramatically altered today, now transformed to a cascade of waterfalls from above; the origin of the river sequestered there, waiting somewhere beyond those peaks.

They were close now, and were tired but anticipating, a sense of expectation that kept them nervous, alert. It would be a difficult ascent. They would climb at first light.

"Tomorrow we should find the source of the river," Denen said calmly. Nitana nodded, brushing hair from her face.

"Perhaps," Tian reflected, "but what will we know? Whoever wrote the note will likely be gone; and we will follow." Denen agreed.

"You tired, Doc?"

"A little. You?"

Reed grinned. "Yeah. I will admit, any one of these women could have kicked ass in the Boston Marathon. Twenty-six miles ain't shit to a Renoloi," he mused wiggling his toes, "and without Nikes too."

Tian looked across the fire to Kalo. "You have done well," she commended.

Tired but determined Kalo smiled, proud of Tian's recognition. Gently stroking the dinosaur tooth, "Thank you," was all she said.

Tian leaned against Reed. "Why not tell a story?"

Flattered to have been asked, he quickly offered, "Okay, what kind of story would you like?"

"A Bloody Bones story," Seana suggested.

Reed hesitated. "Well, how about something else for tonight?"

"No, Bloody Bones would be good," Tian agreed, inveigling. She and Seana both smiled mischievously and Ames quickly realized what they were up to.

"Come on, Reed," he joined in, "Bloody Bones would be good."

Being cornered, Reed opted for a graceful exit. "No, Bloody Bones is for the kids —you know— back home. It's no good for a road trip story." He scratched his chin. "Just give me a minute to come up with something else." He noticed Seana's grin, then saw Tian and Ames smiling too. "Oh, that's really low, Doc."

Innocently, "What?"

"Oh, that is *ree-eally* low," he emphasized. "I can't *ee-even* believe you told her."

"Told her what?" he asked, deadpan.

"About that little pop-out-of-the-dark Compsognathus in the Forsaken Land bouncing off my lap and startling me, just a little."

"Just a little?" Seana teased. "Ronto told me you almost peed your pants."

"That's not…" then realizing the joke was on him, "you guys are all in this together, aren't you?"

"Not at all," Tian assured straight-faced, and turning to Ames, who sat solemnly beside her, "we just thought a Bloody Bones story would be good."

Ames: "Yeah, that's all."

"Yes you are," he insisted, "and I'm not in the story mood tonight. I'm tired and I'm going to sleep." He lay down, and before Seana snuggled in his arms she gave the others a quick, approving wink.

To him, "I love you," she whispered.

"I love you too," he whispered back, then continued mumbling to himself. "Little sucker almost gives me a heart attack and you guys all think it's a big sick-o-joke. Just beats me how we're all such good friends sometimes." Seana tried to suppress her snicker but was shaking so much he noticed, and she, Tian, and Ames finally all laughed. "Cute, you guys," he grumbled. "My friends; real frickin' cute." A little more teasing… then not long after, everyone in camp was sleeping soundly.

Several hours later, during the night, from one of the sentry posts there came an abrupt cry of pain —and *snap*— but everyone in camp was asleep; too tired to hear the noise.

* * *

"Tian, wake up!" her voice hushed, urgent…

...Groggily, still drowsy, "What is it, Kalo?"

"Rawlin is gone. She was on second sentry. I awoke and walked the perimeter just now and she was not there. The others have not seen her."

Tian was instantly awake, completely coherent. "Wake Denen and Nitana. Take six with you and search."

A nod and Kalo was gone in the darkness. Ames, awakened by their voices, reached over shaking Reed.

"What?"

"A sentry's missing. They're going to search."

"I'm awake." Reed was on his feet and moving almost as he spoke. "Kalo, where are you?"

"Here, Reed."

"Okay, kid," swinging the pulse laser to the ready, "you and the others stay alongside. Don't get in front of me. Wouldn't want to blow a hole in a good guy by mistake." The pulse laser was in the time sphere when Ames returned at the crater.

Although Kalo had never seen what Reed's weapon could do, Ronto and Tian had, in the Forsaken Land, and word spreads quickly in a small village. Seana, awakened when Reed moved, began stoking the campfire, added some twigs and rekindled it. They needed the light; it was still a while until sunrise and very dark.

Barely a whisper, "Who's missing?" Reed asked.

"Rawlin."

"How long?" as they headed from camp into the understory.

"I do not know. I only discovered it minutes ago," their voices fading with them in the darkness.

After the first reconnaissance of the area and no luck locating the missing Renoloi, those remaining in camp waited anxiously, but not hopeful. The second, wider sweep also produced nothing; no woman, injured or dead, no blood or sign of a struggle. No trace. She had vanished. It was daylight when the search team returned to camp and the others already expected the news would be bad.

"Nothing?" Tian asked.

Perplexed, Reed shook his head. "Even her spear is gone, nothing indicating a struggle."

"That's peculiar," Ames allowed.

"Peculiar isn't the word for it, Doc. On the second sweep we easily found our own sign, tracks and whatnot; but the sentry had to be snatched out of the tree and never even touched the ground, not a drop of blood." He shook his head sourly. "It's just not possible to vanish like that… 'cept maybe for voodoo juju and spooky-weird shit. But this, I just don't know."

"Voodoo isn't real," Ames said.

"I know that," Reed agreed, "but this is."

Ames, to Tian: "It's up to you." She considered, remain and continue searching for someone most likely dead, or protect the welfare of the others. Something inside made her uneasy.

"Rawlin is gone; we must not remain here." They broke camp and within minutes moved out.

* * *

The ascent was difficult…

…In many places almost vertical, scaling cliffs and rock faces, crawling between jutting formations, constantly following the backtrail to the water's source. Three hours into the climb Nitana and Kalo, still working point, found Rawlin's body, or what was left of her, near the mouth of a cave. Nitana signaled to those below; a raised open hand, then fist, pulled to her chest, the sign one of many used by the Renoloi, meaning trouble. Voices carried great distances and could attract attention. Seeing the signal, Tian understood immediately to hurry, and within minutes the team caught up with the scouts.

They were on a steep incline honeycombed with caves, their openings and the immediate area littered with scattered leavings of humanoid skeletons. The victims had not all died at the same time as evidenced by varying conditions of the skeletal remains. Some were bleached white by the sun, while others appeared to be more recently deposited with pieces of skin and torn, dry tissue still stuck to the bones. Only one body appeared to be newly acquired, Rawlin's, the others all beyond any manner of identification.

Wary, Nitana pointed to Kalo standing near Rawlin's remains, then made a sweeping arm motion with an extended index finger and the team understood; the, *on guard—search,* command. Without a sound the women formed a defense perimeter, scanning the area for an unknown enemy. Tian, Ames, Reed and Denen walked to the body.

"Jesus, dead as a frog in the hot sun," Reed whispered.

"Re-ed—"

"Well shit, she looks like a raisin."

Within the protective ring of warriors he and Ames knelt to examine the corpse: completely dry, parched, and in fact wizened. Without touching it they carefully scrutinized the body.

Tian turned to Denen, and under her breath, "I have never seen anything like this before, have you?" Nervously, Denen shook a, *no.*

Ames examined the head and neck; her face dry and brittle as stretched parchment, lips and eye sockets drawn tightly back, eyeballs collapsed dingy black and white marbles, tongue a protruding shriveled remnant of what it once had been. The woman's entire body was drained, breasts flat pancakes of skin compressed upon her ribs, abdomen completely collapsed to her backbone, hips protruding in absolute anorexia nervosa, thighs and calves withered to bone twigs. Every drop of fluid was gone from the corpse.

"The neck..." Reed whispered.

"I see them," Ames said studying the gruesome puncture marks where large holes entered the proximity of the carotid artery on either side of the neck.

Reed reflected morbidly, "Gives an entirely new meaning to the expression, 'I'll suck you dry', doesn't it?"

Ames shot him a disapproving glance, then reexamining the body observed, "You're a demented individual, you know it."

"Guess it was just one of those perverted thoughts that go 'blink' in your brain, and you can't really control them." He looked. "Know what I mean? We all have 'em, Doc."

Ames, wryly, "No we don't; not all of us."

Back to the corpse, Reed considered, then almost inaudibly, "Well some of us anyway. Happens to me all the time."

Tian knelt beside him. "John, what could do such a thing?"

"I don't know. But I do know, it wasn't a dinosaur." Ames carefully took the cranium in both hands and tried to lift and turn it, gingerly, to better study the penetration wounds. When he did there was a crackling sound like a spoon into cornflakes —and the head broke loose and the body went, *plop*. Startled, he hesitated, unsure what to do with the decapitated skull in his hands. He looked nervously to Reed.

"Snap, crackle, pop—Rice Krispies," Reed recited in a monotone lyric. He looked from the skull to Ames. "Sorry; just one of those blinks." Ames glared incredulously, and not a sound.

"John, what does he mean?" Tian asked, referring to Reed's almost musical comment. Eyes still fixed on Reed, Ames carefully put the head on the ground, in place at the shoulders, then rose to his feet, as did Reed and Tian. "What does he mean?" she persisted.

"You really don't want to know."

"Couldn't help it," Reed offered in defense.

Slowly shaking his head Ames said, "You are one—sick—puppy."

Reed turned to Kalo, still standing silently nearby. "It's an involuntary, subconscious thought process response, to disrupt suppressed anxiety," he explained. She had no idea what that meant and no intention of becoming involved.

Nitana returned.

"You should take a look," she advised in a soft but urgent voice. Moving quietly and quickly the four followed her to the nearest cave, and all but Kalo instantly understood her concern.

Tian: "We must leave this place—now." Both men agreed and Nitana signaled the team to clear the area immediately. As they hurried up the mountain Reed held back covering the rear. He was deadly serious now. Kalo stayed with him until the others were safely away.

"Let's go," he ordered as they quietly but hastily followed.

Alert, prepared for danger but not yet understanding their concern, Kalo asked, "Reed, what is wrong?"

The man, moving quickly, pulse laser ready and still watching their backtrail, cast her a glance as he answered, "Those weren't caves. The mounds of dirt pushed out at the openings... they were burrows." Then he explained, "Whatever killed Rawlin... we were right in the middle of an entire colony of them. Not a good place to be."

* * *

Tension, and empty silence...

...Within an hour the team arrived at the top of the ridge. Before them lay a great sprawling plateau sculpted with mammoth bluffs, ragged ravines and rolling forested hills where the river dispersed into fingers that diminished to rivulets and small streams feeding in from throughout the reaches of the landscape.

The plateau was still and silent. No wind rustled through the foliage. Too still. If there were animals inhabiting this region, they made no sounds. Too silent. This place was heavy with premonition. Something was not right here. It was too quiet.

With subliminal intuitive dictum, the travelers sensed something was wrong. The presence of an unknown malice drifted ominously in the air causing the fine hair on their arms and the back of their necks to tingle. That feeling. Without speaking Tian looked at Ames. It was his turn to choose which way they would go. He pointed and they moved on. He had no idea why he'd chosen that particular stream and neither did Tian; but to her it seemed he had chosen correctly. She sensed it. It felt right.

For two hours the team moved swiftly and silently following the stream, always within sight of it. No one uttered a sound: alert, watchful, focusing and refocusing, observing every miniscule detail for any movement however slight and seemingly insignificant.

That nagging sensation hung there, wafting around them, almost beckoning it silently warned, *this land is not safe; there is danger. Beware.*

Late that afternoon the group arrived at the source of the waterflow, a pristine, artesian spring surrounded by a narrow strip of sand. It was a tranquil place, the pool seemingly untouched, encompassed by trees. For a moment no one spoke, all carefully surveying the area; and as they did, Kalo saw it, pointing to the bushes on the opposite side where, partially concealed by vegetation, lay a green glass bottle. Upon closer examination the words, Coca-Cola would be clearly legible, molded within. The girl circled the spring, and kneeling to pick it up, through the trees she saw the huts.

Eyes wide with excitement she turned to Tian and whispered, "Renoloi village."

* * *

Quietly, alert...

...The travelers entered the village, its dwellings identical to their own. Constructed of the familiar gray-tan stone with no windows and bronze doors, even the smooth foot-worn path bisecting the village, only the arrangement of the huts was altered. This village was the same as their own, with one glaring exception; it was deserted.

Upon closer examination there were other differences, less noticeable with first impressions: a Stanley hammer was splattered with paint, and some nails lying near a doorway, a rusted Mercury Monterey hubcap was lying flat and half full of rainwater, a tricycle with a bent wheel some child might have played with. The X-Z hardbound volume of a 1978 *Encyclopedia Britannica* formed a tent in the grass, an Ekco spatula with the black plastic handle broken off, a highway speed limit sign shot through with bullet holes covering a fire pit, less noticeable perhaps —still— trifles that should not be here.

Looking over the deserted village, "This is strange," Tian said nervously.

Reed looked at Ames. "She does have a penchant for understatements, doesn't she?" He was referring to the random collections of artifacts littering the village, which meant little to Tian.

"More than strange," Ames agreed.

Tian signaled, *on guard—search*, and the Renoloi instantly spread out exploring the huts and the area. As the warriors investigated Tian, Ames, Reed and Denen waited, observed, and considered.

The Renoloi searched in teams of three, finding nothing of the missing villagers. Had there been a battle there should be casualties; there were no bodies. Possibly there might be new graves; none were located. The village appeared intact, as though abandoned casually; considering the note, that didn't seem likely. The surrounding countryside appeared undisturbed, very peaceful and quiet; too quiet. But most puzzling to the men was the presence of random, neglected, miscellaneous articles from a time long since past, from an insignificant blue planet in a Milky Way galaxy of a time long ago... how could they be here?

"It will be dark soon," Denen observed, "we must make camp."

Troubled, "There is danger here," Tian said softly.

Chewing his lip Ames considered, "Then we'd better be prepared..." and offering her an encouraging smile, "just in case." Then serious again, "Denen's right; we really don't have much choice."

"Feels like Sherwood Forest," Reed voiced under his breath. Tian felt it too and looked at him without speaking. "*Re-eal* spooky," he whispered.

"Death," Tian intimated.

Surveying the area Reed nodded, "Yeah, that's it."

The bland, tasteless sensation of death lingered thick in the air, hovering unseen, moving through the trees without motion. It was all around them, colorless, transparent, nagging in the back of their minds. It was intangible, but very real, always just a footstep away. And tonight, with the dark of the moon... *it* would return.

Watching. The scouting parties were returning from their reconnaissance, none indicating they had discovered anything of the missing villagers.

"Post six sentries, teams of two, no one alone," Tian ordered.

"I will see to it now," a Renoloi responded.

Denen added, "Three perimeter fires." A glance; Tian agreed.

The Renoloi had been in dangerous situations before, past experience having taught them to form a perimeter closer than usual using the outer fires and a larger fire in its center to illuminate the entire encampment. The sentries in the trees above the outer fires would be able to more easily see movement below, offering more protection for those sleeping within the enclosure. Since Rawlin's disappearance and death, two sentries would now stand watch together.

They all knew that something was out there, and it was nocturnal, stalking the land after sunset, coming in the darkness... a Night Hunter.

* * *

Everything quiet…

…Too quiet. The fires had burned down. It was very late and very dark, the travelers in camp asleep except one, the sentries alert, watching. Then a quick rushing of claws ripping bark; two brief muffled cries —*snap, snap*. It was over.

"Reed, wake up." Kalo's urgent whisper and her small hand on his chest instantly roused him. "Do not move," she told him. "I heard them. They are in the trees."

Without a sound Reed rolled onto his stomach palming the pulse laser, scanning the thick limbs and low-hanging branches circling their camp. His movement woke Seana who gently kicked Ames' leg. Silently they alerted one another, all lying still, waiting in the dark.

Branches rustled at a sentry post. Again, the rushing and ripping sounds of claws tearing tree bark and two quick screams of terror cut short —*snap, snap*.

"They're in the trees!" Reed yelled rising to his knees, turning, triggering fearsome laserlight of pulsing energy, launching a nearly continuous stream of powerful, blinding fury and incredible white explosions that shredded the canopy. Screaming loudly Denen ordered the sentries out of the trees, and in the continuity of luminous flashglare and detonations only two of the six dropped to the ground scrambling for the protection of camp.

Branches and treetops swirled as slivers and ribbons —ragged explosions swallowing them— brilliant flashes of white light and radiant flame shattering wood and leaves, laser blasts splintering and shredding them. All of it pieces! Astounded, shrinking and cowering, the Renoloi beneath him, Reed on his feet, still turning, swept a circular arc of nearly continuous linear white fire destroying everything in the canopy around them. They had never seen anything so incredible —so astonishing— cringing on the ground, terrorized and awestruck as —light pulses screamed!

The drone of shrill whines climaxed with deafening noise and rattling, magnificent, explosive bright light. All eyes were locked on Reed, a flickering dark silhouette with gritted white teeth and green twinkling eyes reflecting each muzzle flash.

A chain reaction of violent explosions ripped the treetops and foliage to pieces —monstrous limbs, entire trees torn to shreds— branches twirling, trunks splitting apart, catapulting and crashing in domino fashion. Again and again laser pulses blazed a blizzard of destruction. Airborne chunks of timber were blown into slivers until nothing remained but debris and loose twirling leaves that rained from the darkness flitting down upon the travelers, every single tree disintegrated for fifty yards in all directions around them.

Blinding streaking light and fiery explosions —then sudden darkness— silence.

Poised, watching as he turned, surveying the ragged perimeter and destruction around them: tree trunks severed completely, branches shredded to pieces no larger than wood chips, and mounds of twigs and leaves in a clearing large enough to play football.

In the dark, on this night, four Renoloi sentries were missing. Whatever had taken them was remarkably agile, exceptionally quick, and extremely dangerous. As were the sentries, the Night Hunters were gone.

Cowering at Reed's feet Seana was spellbound and overwhelmed by the man with the weapon standing over her; to her he had always been a very gentle and playful companion. The powerful, serious, determined man towering above her now was a different person. During the battle with the Trogs they were separated by distance. Seana was on the ridges when the Tyrannosaur killed Tarin and she had not seen Reed then, never seen him fight. As Seana looked up she realized he was completely masculine. She respected this stranger who was not an enemy, this man.

He made one final, visual sweep of the area; then protectively extending an open hand taking Seana's in his, looked down at her lovingly. "It's all right," he said gently as she rose to her feet, "they're gone now."

Fascinated by his weapon Kalo reached out and touched it, carefully, almost reverently caressing the black-steel laser rod housing near the muzzle. Reed felt the pressure of her hand on the barrel and looked at the girl. She stroked the weapon delicately, admiring it, then smiled and said, "Cool," imitating him.

He began to respond then stopped and looked at Tian and Ames, both of them waiting. "No, Kalo," he finally said, "not really." Kneeling, "This weapon has only one purpose—to kill," face to face, "if it's necessary to survive... but it isn't cool." She seemed puzzled and he gently fingered the tooth on her necklace. "We kill only if we must. Do you understand?"

Kalo looked from the necklace, to Tian, then back to Reed and somberly said, "Yes, I understand."

He kissed her on the cheek, wrinkled his nose and smiled. "Then that's cool." As he rose he glanced at Tian, who nodded approval; and for some unfathomable reason, it made him feel good inside. He, Seana and Kalo walked away, to help the others search the area.

Tian leaned against Ames, and in spite of the tension and terror of the past few moments she couldn't help but smile. Softly, "Sometimes he surprises me."

Ames, eyes following Reed: "Yeah, me too."

Watching the others, then to the sky, Tian observed, "It will be daylight soon. We must leave this village."

"Which way do we go?"

Echoes of, *Something yet Unfinished,* lingering in her mind, she looked at him earnestly. "We came to help. We go toward the rising sun."

The search that night, for their people and whatever had taken them, would prove to be fruitless. Four sentries, and the Night Hunters... gone, without a trace.

* * *

Morning...

...Of the twenty-six, twenty-one remained. They broke camp and were moving with the first rays of a rising sun touching the plateau, none knowing what lay before them, only aware they must see their undertaking to its conclusion. Silent, in this world of verdant camouflage they moved carefully until midday when they stopped in a deep-forest grove to rest. The area was quiet, shaded by large deciduous trees with exposed tentacle root systems like those of the Banyan. The ground was spongy, soft dark loam thickly overgrown with bracken, moss, lichen and mushrooms: chanterelle, shaggy mane, king boletus, puffballs, morels, death cups and truffles. Flourishing, they crept from under fern thickets, venturing out into the open in the scattering of protective shade.

No one spoke as a waterskin was passed around, then a leather pouch of Chiqua jerky. They were all alert to the slightest sound; anything that moved could be danger. Resting against the tangled root system of a gnarled tree, as Seana sat beside Reed she leaned over and quietly asked, "Was your journey to the Forsaken Land like this?"

Fiddling with a stick he looked at her, grinned absently, then looking around answered, "No, not really; it was different. We knew what we were up against then."

"What do you mean?"

Looking down, drawing a circle in the dirt with the stick he explained, "The enemy here is intangible; can't fight what you can't even see." Thinking, he went on, "Granted the Trogs were physically powerful; but they had weaknesses so we could deal with them. This is different," looking at her, "we don't know whom or what the enemy is here, only that it uses the darkness to its advantage. That makes it more difficult."

"But we will be all right?" she asked. Realizing the direction of her inquiry he flipped the stick away slipping an arm behind her back, drawing her close.

"We'll be just fine," he assured smiling with that easy confidence he could project. Seana reciprocated, returning his smile, perhaps less certain than he was, or pretended to be. Reed looked overhead at Kalo as she crouched silently, vigilantly watching from a thick sprawling branch. "Right?" he asked winking at her. Soberly she looked down and nodded, then resumed watching again.

"Excuse us please," a muffled, gruff little voice chimed from behind them as something poked Reed and Seana in the butts.

"What the—" Reed blurted, spinning onto his knees and leveling the laser at the gnarled roots and a small hole in the ground he hadn't noticed before. All of them coiled, prepared.

A walking stick popped out of the burrow; next, the head and body of a dwarf three feet tall, then a second dwarf, identical in every aspect to the first. Both wore dark blue watch caps, red and blue plaid flannel shirts with the sleeves rolled up to their elbows, and bib overalls with cuffs primly rolled up over black, laced work boots —children's, size twelve. Sling-shots sticking out of their back pockets, both individuals were gray-skinned, the color of dry mud, and walking purposefully and businesslike they marched directly to the center of the group taking a moment to brush loose dirt from the palms of their hands and the knees of their pants.

"Please, kind sir," the first gray dwarf began, raising a short-fingered hand to Reed, "your weapon is unnecessary. We are not hostiles."

Reed looked from the newcomers to the pulse laser trained on them, and unable to perceive any threat from such small people, "Oh, sorry," he apologized lowering his weapon. The others followed his lead. Kalo crouched silently overhead, unnoticed.

"Allow me to introduce myself," the first twin began. "I am Phineas Taylor Barnum," he announced proudly.

"U.S. showman and circus enterpriser, eighteen ten to eighteen ninety-one," Reed recalled almost inaudibly.

"I'm 'Just Plain' Wilson," the second dwarf said with a contrite manner. "He got the good name."

"P.T. Barnum," Ames mused with a novel grin, "and Wilson?"

"Yes indeed, Sir," Barnum confirmed.

Reed couldn't believe what he was hearing. "Where did you guys come from?"

"From down there, quite obviously," Wilson answered, pointing to the burrow secreted within the tree roots.

"I think he means, what are you doing here?" the other man clarified.

"Oh— we're workers," Wilson explained. He walked to the satchel of jerky, looked at a grinning Tian and respectfully inquired, "May I?"

She nodded, "Certainly," with her smile.

Wilson retrieved two pieces of jerky, returned to his twin giving him one, both munching contentedly as the conversation continued.

"You're workers?" Reed repeated. Both dwarfs, chewing industriously, shook their heads.

"What do you work on?"

"Anything and everything," Barnum answered. "Anything that isn't finished..."

"—And everything that has to be done," Wilson wound the disclosure up.

"Well, I guess that makes sense," Reed conceded, even though it made none to him. Of the entire group, Tian was the only one who might actually grasp what P.T. Barnum and Wilson had just told them. Prodding further, "What *specifically* do you work on?" Reed asked.

Ripping the piece of jerky he clenched with his teeth, Wilson commented, "This is excellent. It certainly is."

"Why are you gray?" Seana asked.

Ostentatiously Wilson examined his hands and forearms, then P.T.'s, and finally, quizzically Seana and the others. "Well, what do you know," he said at last, "we are different colors, aren't we?"

"Yes. Why are you gray?" she said again.

Barnum quickly answered for Wilson, who seemed at a loss for an explanation. "We really don't get out much."

"What?" Reed joined in.

"Faded— just a bit faded," Wilson explained.

"—And dirty," Barnum added. "Yes-siree-bob, just faded and dirty." Then he changed the subject. "And thirsty." He pointed to the waterskin, inquiring of Denen, "May I, please?"

"Of course you may," Denen obliged. Both little men took a moment to quench their thirst and ambled around the group meeting some of the others; while inside Ames' head, words clicked, words he had heard before —*yes-siree-bob.*

Reed stepped alongside Ames and Tian, nibbling his lip and considering; then commented under his breath, "Phineas Taylor Barnum and 'Just Plain' Wilson, midgets. Ain't this some curious shit?"

Ames couldn't help but grin even though he corrected his friend. "Dwarfs, little people, Reed. Not midgets." Then he conceded, "Yeah, curiouser and curiouser."

Reed smiled. "Touché."

Meanwhile, overhead Kalo remained silent, observing.

As the two dwarfs mingled engaging in friendly conversation, which seemed to be as naturally a part of them as their outgoing personalities, Reed noticed that each carried a slingshot in his back pocket. They lived here in this forbidding place armed only with walking sticks and slingshots. For several moments the engaging dwarfs visited with the strangers, being always courteous and polite in everything they said and did, some of their gestures and mannerisms so quaint they were even a bit amusing, and the Renoloi befriended them without reservation, as though it were meant to be.

Finally, Reed's curiosity prodded him to inquire, "Mr. Barnum," he said, attracting the little man's attention.

"No need for such formalities, Reed. Please, feel free to call me P.T. Everyone does."

"P.T. then," Reed agreed congenially, then asked, "your slingshots... where did you acquire them?"

Barnum responded with the rather odd preface of, "I am so pleased you noticed," however he didn't elaborate. Instead, he drew the slingshot from his pocket and offered it to Reed; one-piece formed stainless steel frame, surgical rubber tubing, and cowhide leather projectile cup. Both men instantly realized that it didn't belong here. "Beauty, isn't she?" Barnum quizzed, then added, "—and powerful too."

"I'll bet she is, P.T. And where did you say you came by it?" Reed feigned innocently.

Barnum grinned knowingly and wrinkled his nose. "Actually Reed, I didn't say..." pausing, then continuing, "but, because you asked me a direct question, I can tell you that I found it in the cove. It's not too far, in *that* direction." Barnum made an overt gesture, carefully pointing out the exact way the travelers might want to go. "There are many interesting things in the cove," he explained, making direct eye contact with the man.

"Thank you so very much, P.T.," Reed said almost involuntarily. He didn't know why he suddenly felt so giddy; and he certainly didn't talk like that. He was beginning to sound like Barnum —and he didn't know why.

"Would you care to try my slingshot?"

"That would be great," Reed replied. Barnum poked into his pants pocket and withdrew an assortment of jacks that children might play with, except he didn't have the little red rubber ball; and cat's-eye marbles, clear glass with the colored cat eye streaked inside them.

"I have lots of ammo," Barnum said, offering Reed his choice.

Edgy, Wilson tugged on Barnum's shirtsleeve and whispered, "Perhaps we should be going."

"Oh nonsense, we're fine," the twin replied as Reed selected a jack and targeted one of the trees, its trunk likely five feet in diameter. He aimed, carefully stretching the surgical rubber band's full length, then let fly. The jack sailed —dead on— and stuck solidly in the tree's trunk. "Excellent, excellent," P.T. delighted.

"Now you do one," Reed coaxed.

Wilson whispered so only Barnum could hear him. "Don't be a showoff; you'll get us in trouble."

"Just one," Barnum quickly whispered back. "No harm in just one is there?" Wilson offered a stern look, but didn't say anything more.

"Come on, P.T.," Reed cajoled.

Although more than willing, the dwarf first pretended to be reluctant; then quickly agreed. "All right, just one; but then we must be going. We've still much to do." Reed smiled as Barnum selected a marble. "I like the cat's-eyes," Barnum admitted. "The glass is so clear, pure if you will, and the eyes are really beautiful."

"Let's see what you can do," Reed flattered, wheedling. "Let 'er rip."

Barnum grinned knowingly, drew the slingshot and let go. The marble's speed created a small sonic boom as it bullet-burned cleanly punching a perfectly circular hole all the way through the tree trunk with a sharp, *whap-zing* —then again, *whap-zing*— as it spit through a second tree deeper within the forest. Then, more faint —again and again— until the reports finally faded in the distant woods.

Stunned, Reed peered with utter disbelief through the hole in the massive tree trunk. Not a single word.

"P.T., you'll get us in trouble one of these days," Wilson chided. "You always have to be such a showoff," hustling his dwarf twin to the burrow entry. Giggling, Barnum scampered out of sight.

Just before going in himself, Wilson stopped and looked up, directly at Kalo. She didn't move a muscle. As she watched the dwarf, Wilson made direct eye contact —and blinked twice.

Inside Kalo's mind she heard, *ask me.* She thought, *the Night Hunters?* Wilson blinked twice. Inside her head she heard the word, *fire.* Then Wilson vanished, into the burrow, underground, out of sight.

Without knowing why, Kalo began picking lichen from the tree limb and wrapping it around the tip of her arrow. Wadding.

CHAPTER FOUR

Traveling the way…

…P.T. Barnum had sent them, they discussed their peculiar callers; a random occurrence in an out-of-the-way forest inhabited by an unknown, nocturnal killer? Their meeting was too unusual. But 'why and how', they had no idea.

"Curiouser and curiouser don't make it, Doc. Those two midgets didn't just pop out of a hole in the ground by accident."

"Little people," Ames corrected quietly.

"Yeah fuckit—whatever. And P.T. was too puny to shoot that marble all the way through a big-honking tree like that." Reed was perplexed, and aggravated.

"Through several trees," Seana volunteered.

Looking at her as they walked, "Oh for pity's sake, I know that."

"Does it bother you that you were not able to do it?" she asked plainly.

"No, it doesn't," he puffed, "the point being, it would be impossible —period— unless that marble was launched by a missile."

"What is a missile?"

Now even more exasperated, "For cryin' out loud; Doc, would you please help me out here? I have this overwhelming urge to choke the living shit out'a something."

"You seem to be doing fine."

"Yeah right; thanks."

To Reed, "Why do you suppose they were so gray?" Denen wondered joining the discussion; she'd been thinking about that.

"*Ex-cuuse me*, Denen; I'm still trying to figure out how he shot the frickin' marble through the tree."

"—Trees," Seana corrected.

"Okay, what—*ever*—the *treees.*"

"A missile," Seana decided.

Reed looked at her. "No, it wasn't. I looked at those marbles..." cutting himself short, then, "this is stupid." Ames and Tian both grinned.

"Why do you suppose they were so gray?" Denen wondered again.

Reed looked at her. "Just a bit faded —and dirty."

She nodded agreeing, "That makes sense to me." Biting his lip and glaring he studied Denen as they walked.

Next, Seana asked, "Where do you suppose they found such strange names?" musing, "Phineas Taylor Barnum, and 'Just Plain' Wilson."

Blandly, "That's easy, the Bureau of Vital Statistics, Bethel, Connecticut. Just surprises me it wasn't Phineas Taylor Barnum and James Anthony Bailey." He shrugged, considering, "Where did they come up with a name like Wilson?"

Affecting sincerity Ames surmised, "Probably someone's idea of a joke."

Seana agreed. "You are likely correct."

"Seana, you don't even know who Barnum and Bailey..." Reed stared at one then the other, then decided, "This just really sucks. You're all screwin' with me now."

"Curiouser and curiouser." Tian grinned.

Just then, both moving swiftly and breathing hard, Nitana and Kalo emerged from the woods ahead of them, joining the party as the others gathered to hear what they had to report.

Nitana whispered, "We found the cove. Come quickly." Her eyes darting from one to the next, "This is very strange." Without further conversation, the scouts assumed the lead with the others close behind.

Reed shrugged, "Strange... imagine that," and he followed them.

* * *

Out of the trees…

…Onto a rise of breaker sandbar, the cove was a backwater inlet filling in from an ocean. As far as the eye could see the great body of water spanned the distant horizon in a gentle arc defining the convergence of sky and sea. Like a living, breathing entity, slowly rising and falling with perpetual motion, the surface shimmered silver and blue beneath the afternoon sun. Breaking waves born in the constant rhythm of rolling tidal swells gently etched the shoreline with rustling turbidity undercurrents that pushed onto the sand, then receded, over and over again. Farther out the seascape blended to a fluxionary surface of water touching sky and seemingly going on forever.

The magnitude of the ocean was impressive, and it belonged here, a natural part of this world. What drew their attention did not belong here; not the cove, rather the flotsam accumulated upon its net of sand.

Beyond the water's reach was an accumulation of driftwood riprap left at the peak of high tide and rough weather. It was matted with thick tangled strands of kelp and sargasso[9] seaweed, now all crisp and dry.

And there were other articles collected by the cove. Large wooden crates were scattered about, and fifty-five-gallon drums once painted blue, red or green, now mostly rusted through. In the mishmash of sargasso was a styrofoam ice chest nibbled to pieces by small creatures, as well as two Folgers coffee cans with the plastic lids still tightly sealed.

All around was a random menagerie of commonplace items… and the most singular artifact the cove had dredged from the sea.

It was a sailboat, sixty feet in length; its once-burnished triple hulls now faded dull white. Fitted with outriggers, it lay stark. The fore and aft rigged sailing cruiser boast a mainmast fifty feet in length and foremast of thirty, both laden with sails reefed securely to the spars at all reef points. The boat had been deposited near the tangle of driftwood beyond reach of the tide, rudder buried in the sand and the daggerboard, or centerboard, setting it askew on the beach.

Never before having seen such a thing, the Renoloi stared and wondered.

"What is it?" Denen asked.

Ames: "A catamaran."

"No, Doc, a trimaran," Reed corrected, "three hulls—and even the outriggers." To Seana: "Can you believe it?" She had no idea what it was, and a quizzical expression was all she offered in reply.

Tian asked, "What does it do?"

"Hopefully," Ames began; then looking at Reed as they both began to smile, and answered together, "it floats."

"Kick me with a peg leg Long John Silver," Reed marveled, "a real pirate adventure." They stood surveying the beach a moment longer, until Reed said it out loud. "Where did all this stuff come from?"

Within minutes—

Warm sand between their toes, they were on the beach rummaging through boxes, barrels and the clutter abandoned there. Carefully studying the craft, the men circled the sailboat twice, and finding no fractures or holes, both considered it promising, seaworthy.

Speculating, "Fiberglass hull," Ames guessed, "wonder how it held up. Seems like it would have decomposed."

"No, I don't think so. Looks like carbon fiber laminate, stronger and lighter," Reed said circling to the bow again, his third time around, and finally noticing. "Oh, this is interesting."

"What?"

"It's moored, dry dock —well, sort of anyway." Reed traced the bowline to the beach, pulled, and the anchor rope ripped out of the sand —snaking— a burning fuse crossing fifty yards of beach then stretching taut and flinging sand as it snapped tight tied to a tree at the edge of the woods. "A storm or the tide may have brought it ashore; but someone tied it down. I guess technically it's lagan, tagged for ownership." Both considered that.

"You know, Doc, she's a pretty big boat; but if we dig the rudder out of the sand and pull the daggerboard, then tip it onto one outer hull and outrigger we should be able to drag it into the water." A glance to the women beachcombing, "There are enough of us." Ames nodded. "And it's not like we'd be stealing it —you know, just borrowing it."

"I doubt they'll mind. Let's do it."

* * *

Two hours later...

...The trimaran was floating stately in the cove, moored fifty yards offshore, its twin masts swaying gently in cadence with the undulating water. The carbon fiber had survived the ravages of time, remaining intact and watertight. The center hull contained a cabin equipped with sleeping quarters and galley, and the outer hulls provided room for additional bunks and storage, or could be converted to a hold for ballast in the event of rough water.

Sun going down, aboardship—

Seana, Kalo and Reed had just finished cleaning up accumulated hard-packed sand and dry seaweed inside the cabin and on deck, anticipating a more thorough going over the next morning. Reed had reset the daggerboard in its watertight slot and the trio had run up the sails for inspection discovering recent repairs by an unidentified but proficient seamstress, who had apparently used a leather awl and commercial grade, polyester carpet thread. The blue thread didn't match, but the repairs were stalworth, more than sufficient.

Others had portaged water from an artesian spring just within the treeline and filled the craft's potable water tank, although they discovered when launching that the entire ocean was not salt, but fresh-water. Another team, led by Denen, was foraging for Chiqua to supplement the jerky; that also, now stowed on board within the cargo hold.

A fourth group had scoured the beach collecting miscellaneous articles, all having one common denominator; in one form or another, every object was broken, nonfunctional, junk. There was a Ludwig drum set with the skins torn off the bass and one missing Zielgen cymbal, and lamps with no shades or broken pedestals. There were red-clay flowerpots, all cracked or broken, pink Corning fiberglass insulation melted into blobs on craft paper; a red, white and blue striped barber pole with the drive gears missing and a cracked globe. There were aluminum lawn chairs with crushed frames and frazzled nylon webbing, and a Victrola phonograph without the crank handle and needle.

The fifty-five-gallon drums were all empty, and all but two of the large wooden crates were opened, having already been rifled. The two remaining crates, bearing faded stenciled markings, 'M2A1', in block letters four inches high, were hasped, bolted and secured with heavy steel strapping tape and appeared to possess their contents still intact. The travelers hadn't had time to open and inspect the sealed crates, intending to do so the next morning prior to departure.

Three dove from the boat and swam ashore joining the others.

Arriving at the campfire he reported, "Good to go. We can make sail first thing in the morning." Tian nudged Ames and they scooted down the driftwood log making room for him and Seana, both dripping water, making wet spots on the sand.

Remaining near the fire to warm her, Kalo unobtrusively picked up her bow slipping the quiver across her back; then sensing something she studied the timberline, and a moment more, she closed her eyes.

Their makeshift camp was on the beach between the high-water mark and the water's edge where they were waiting for Denen and her team of eight to return from the forest. They'd gone a third time and now the sun had set with twilight fading, darkness already obscuring movement within the trees.

"They should have been back by now," Nitana worried. "It is getting dark."

"Denen knows to be out of the forest," Tian assured.

Scanning the treeline Seana saw them moving just inside the woods. "There—" pointing as Denen stopped, raising a hand signaling, *all clear.*

Eyes closed, inside the silent Kalo felt it, and she whispered, "No, in the trees." Then blinking open, eyes wide with terror, she screamed, *"No!—They are in the trees!"*

Glancing up Denen didn't have time to move, even to lower her arm. From above a quick rushing of claws tearing bark —it was upon her— the creature's curved twenty-inch fangs slicing savagely into her neck, locking in position —*snap.*

It was enormous; six feet tall and jet-black with a twenty-foot leg-span —a Spider!

Its cephalothorax-head had four pair of glowing, white night-vision eyes and its pedipalps, front leg-like appendages, seized her with its incredible crushing grip. Like a gigantic wolf spider clinging to overhead limbs with its ragged-barb legs fixed with bale-hook claws, the pedicel connecting the head and body let its posterior abdomen drop down like a counterweight as the huge arachnid snatched Denen from the ground by her head stretching her neck. The chelicerae, its mandible jaws, drove its fangs with lethal precision; and sleek and blue-black as a raven, its rear section covered with coarse-bristle hair bobbed then contracted as the Hunter injected its prey.

Denen's body inflated —liquid bloat— venom and digestive fluid stretching her skin water balloon-tight as her insides and organs almost instantly dissolved. Liquid diet. Unhesitating, the monster drained her with its hollow fangs, Denen's body contracting and shriveling —all within seconds— her withered husk hanging in its chelicerae —a skeletal raisin, crisp and dehydrated— and that quickly, Denen was dead.

Tian screamed, *"No!"*

In the first sudden attack six others died the same gruesome way, only two being able to avoid them, escaping onto the beach, terrified, running for their lives. Dropping from the canopy, moving with unbelievable speed, the horde materialized from the greenery.

And within those few twilight seconds Reed reacted, bringing the laser to bear on the descending dark shapes as they sprang from the trees. Realization clicked —*they're already dead*— so he focused on the two fleeing women screaming for help —dozens of shadows behind them, blurs of commotion and glistening black speed. Pack hunters.

Target—to—target, laserflames splattered Hunters to slivers of chitin and vapor-wind muck. He had to stop them, prevent them from catching the terror-stricken women sprinting for their campsite, crossing the beach. Streaking spears of lightning ripped through the sleek predators swiftly overtaking them from behind —terror, running feet— twirling shrapnel pieces and sticky gray juice showering the Renoloi time and again.

—But now the darkness of treeline was filled with cackling white noise of savagery and trilling, chattering animalistic screams!

Too many of them, they were everywhere, gigantic dark killers leaping from the trees onto the beach. Pouncing eighty feet, claws ripping into her, an arachnid jerked one of the fleeing Renoloi from her feet —a whorl of kicked-up sand— shrieking a terrorized scream as fangs stabbed into her neck. Envenomed, she swelled in midair before a laserflash splashed the Night Hunter's eyes and front half away —just a heartbeat too late. Bloated, the hapless warrior beachballed onto the sand then bounced as she rolled squirting fluid from the broken fangs still stuck in her neck, four more sinking their claws in her grotesque, lifeless body.

Stumbling, the second woman fell then tried to get to her feet —but they had her— two monsters on top of her tearing her apart from crotch to neck —bloody spray and a splash of red on the sand!

With near-disbelief Reed spit, "Awww—*fuck!*" as laserflames strafed punching ghouls as they came.

Hunters were splattering bits and sticky dark rain; but there were hundreds now, everywhere, covering the beach —the sky wild with white noise of savagery and shrill with animalistic screams as they poured over the driftwood riprap, laser blasts shredding them, flinging them back. He couldn't stop them, couldn't kill them all.

Tian and the others stood fast, spears and bows against the onrushing tsunami of jet-black. No longer able to hold them off alone, Reed was backing up as he killed —arrows flying, taking some down— but the Hunters kept coming.

Inside her head Kalo heard the word, *fire,* sweeping a wadded arrow through the flames of the campfire, then drew her bow, choosing her target, clustered night-vision eyes. *Snap—whoosh,* trailing alizarin flame the arrow sailing dead center into malevolent white eyes.

—Splattering fire, a swirl of hot liquid wind,

Its head disappeared in torrid roiling flames —a billow of rush— across its pedicel and abdomen, down its legs enveloping and spiraling around it. Suddenly engulfed in inferno the demonic creature careened frantically screeching horror that cut through to bone —then collisions of fire, blinding and wild— maddened monsters, swirling smoke, and yellow-orange blaze!

Skipping spider to spider, the roar of infernal explosions smothered the guttural animal screams knifing the darkness as viscid incineration blew through their maniacal push —savage flashburn of ocher and bright flare— evaporating twilight in brilliant flamespray!

They were ravaged fiery legs with wicked splintering claws and scorched, crinkling eyes popping from flaming black heads —and charbroiled abdomens purging hot bubbles of foam. They were helter-skelter flame-eaten autoclaves running wild, a frenzy of skip-speed infernos skimming with blinding celerity until they pressure-cooked and ruptured as clouds of plasma-soup fumes and crisp smoldering chunks.

—Fire and speed, vomited bubbling froth—and explosions, hot rain!

Pumped with intensity and adrenaline, chunks and leaking hulls piling up around them, Reed kept taking them out. Next to him Kalo sent another flaming arrow into the driftwood and ravel of kelp, the seaweed and wood going up with a flashover that ran both directions. Night Hunters climbing over the debris were instantly taken in flames, as others jumping the snarled barrier caught fire and bolted across the beach being chased by their own smoking trails. But undeterred, still more of them came.

—Sickening, burning dervishes of speed trailing white noise of savagery and ribbons of twisted alizarin flame!

Side by side Ames, Tian and Seana fought the jet-black rush lunging at them; leaping and attacking they were everywhere now, ragged legs sheathed with lethal claws slashing around them, compressing the warriors into a half-circle, being forced back toward the cove.

Over the piles of dead one leaped forty feet high, legs wide, intent on Tian, twenty-inch fangs already dripping venom. Landing — claws coming at her— she ducked —intercepting— her spear slicing between its jaws with a gush of vomited froth —and *crunch*— out through its head and those glowing-pixel white eyes. As her lance sank inside it, she sensed the grizzly then gooey-thick punch; and as the spider collapsed she dropped and rolled clear wrenching her spear free —then nasty dark blood all over the ground.

One grabbed another warrior, bale-hook claws raking her flesh, its fangs sinking in her neck. Liquefying, she expanded and stretched spraying from her wounds, then deflated as the horrific suction compressed her to a voodoo-like withered-dry doll.

Far outnumbered and now backed to the water's edge, they kept killing the demons; but there were just too many to withstand the unending onslaught. Taken by a leg, another warrior went down; then two more had her ripping her apart as she vanished in flailing black and scissoring jaws. Pungent, the beach reeked the stench of death —no matter where they looked— frantic commotion screeching trill of deadly animalistic screams!

Firing furiously, bits and pieces flying as he withdrew, Reed tried to keep them away, then tripped and fell flat on his back. Glimmering white eyes were instantly there, closing down upon him —laserflashes— streaking white blasts. An unending rain of chunks and blood —bursts of white light and splattering gray— but all he could see were the slimy black jaws and those eyes in the rush. There were fangs in his face, but he refused to give up, to die in the crush —and he screamed— a maniacal long wail of defiance. Three more —exploding wind-missile shards and splatters of shockwave muck, the laser disintegrating two— but the third was on top of him, jaws coming, aciculate fangs closing. There was nowhere to go; he couldn't get out of the way, couldn't move, couldn't fire, death no more than an instant away…

…He didn't feel it or hear it; but he could see it, the sensation of stop-motion confusion splashing images in his eyes. Dead silence.

One frame at a time—

Kalo's arrow streaking just above him and slamming home, halting the spider's forward momentum with a noiseless —*thwack*— the arrow's shaft punching through then disappearing in its eyes —into the head and pedicel, down the pipe of its neck. Stopped —rigid— the spider was stuck with its fangs in mid-strike barely inches above him; but it couldn't go lower, couldn't get to him, slicing together as they locked —an awful, silent, *snap!*— narrow miss.

Stunned, he watched venom shoot from the fangs but not into him, the yellow stream of poison spraying just above his neck.

Reality clicked—

Sudden noise. He could hear himself screaming, and something had him by the collar and nape of the neck; something was dragging him from the sand into the water. Foam of cold wet commotion was swallowing him, pouring over him —still pulling the trigger. There were deafening shrill whines and unending flickers. There were flashes of light.

Sound and realization snapped back into focus. He was still alive, still killing them. Night Hunters were still exploding in whirling clouds of sticky dark wind, but they weren't still coming and crawling all over him. They were swarming the shoreline but not entering the water —too many to count. And finally realizing what was pulling him back, what had dragged him into the water —the powerful fisted hand of his friend. Together, Kalo and Ames had just saved his life.

Relief spit cold in his face and flushed through his chest like a gut-wrenching wash that ached with the knot of adrenaline rush —and he sniggered. Shaking, trembling with cold, his eyes suddenly went wide —and he laughed— still pulling him. And he kept laughing until finally he screamed at the Night Hunters.

"You dumb sons-a-bitches..." still being hauled away, waves pounding the back of his head, *"you can't even swim!"*

Ames jerked him to his feet, his voice hoarse, snatching him back to his senses, "Reed, let's get out of here!"

Still going backward, farther into the cove, they struggled with all they had left until suddenly snatched by the undertow. Boiling cold and froth lifted them from the bottom buoyantly dragging them out; then kicking themselves into deeper water and finally to safety beyond the hideous barbed claws of the dancing killers on the sand.

Highlighted by the blazing driftwood wall and burning spiders behind them, pumping up and down on the shoreline the sleek black giants scrambled back and forth stabbing sand on the beach. Rearing on hind legs they were apocalyptic demons of darkness; clawing maniacally, slashing empty night sky at the water's edge, trilling and screaming an unholy animalistic chatter of emptiness and soulless insanity. Driven by environmental stimuli they were predators of unparalleled savagery piercing the darkness with white-glowing, night-vision eyes...

They were relentless,

    They were monsters,

        ...They were Night Hunters!

Tiptoe on the bottom Reed stopped as Ames urged, "Let's go!" from behind.

But Reed glared at them, *no chance;* and without looking back vowed, "This ain't over yet," raising the laser, sighting down the bore —and fired!

Searing white bolts screamed at the speed of light; skimming fireflashes clipping and slicing rolling breakers, illuminating the dark water and reflecting off waves. The shrill continuity of whines climaxed in blistering rupture-explosions splattering through the capering black hoard on the beach, their hulls splashing to sliver-whorls of slurry sludge and viscous gray mist. Shredded burning cephalothoraxes and abdomens were hurled from the sand as twirling severed legs and specks of white eyes spun away.

Running the waterline and clamoring at the water's edge, in the midst of hellish flames they kept screaming and dying. And adamant, vengefully he kept killing them —until the muddy bottom suddenly vaulted heaving then sloshing himself and Ames with a violent surge of upward-roil…

—Uh-oh, that's not 'sposed to happen,

…Water froth swirling with the undercurrent rise as it rolled rushing toward the beach. Then he could see the shoreline as it started vibrating and pounding toppling gigantic spiders when it shifted like a sidewinder breaker —and the first wave hit engulfing it, tossing it all up— then just explosions of water and sand!

The entire beach erupted splashing upward with water and burning debris in belching storms of muddy sand; the seismic shearwave hurling arachnids, barrels, crates and junk into the air — *everything up*— then falling back down. Confusion and chaos —the surge flashing inland beyond the beach— ripping into the forest, tearing, uprooting and razing trees, violently bringing them down.

Almost immediately a second tremor followed, more powerful than the first, the entire landscape vaulting as it wrenched again —timber, spiders and sand thrown in the air— roiling ground crumbling and coming apart, the whipsaw motion opening sinkholes and crevasses dragging some arachnids under —then again, *up!*

It was a subterranean sidewinder cresting twelve feet high. Beyond the beach hundreds of mammoth trees were falling, being toppled like dominoes shredding the swaying understory on their way crashing down. More shockwaves followed —crackling, cracking and jolting— causing outward-expanding devastation of consuming darkness, destruction and fire.

Unsure what was happening as they struggled for the boat, the remaining Renoloi fought the sudden whitecaps and turbulent water washing over them, shoving and dragging them under. Reed knew that something was wrong, but he didn't know what; so he quit firing, shooting a look to his friend, both of them baffled, bobbing corks being tossed recklessly about. "Dump me in a milkshake, what—?"

A sudden-rising swell swept over them burying them —vacant waterswirl waves— they popped back up. Sloshing around with wet hair stuck to his face, being pitched by the mud-boiling roller coaster bottom Ames spit out a mouthful of water and yelled, "Earthquake!"

Roiling, the cove was now treacherous swirling undercurrents and sporadic leaping whitecaps making it almost impossible to stay afloat. Tumbling again, they were dragged to deeper water by the undertow, while farther out the constantly bounding trimaran strained on its moor line. With a glimpse over his shoulder Ames saw the last Renoloi being pulled aboard the heaving deck through the combined efforts of the others.

Onshore fires were burning, the beachhead was quavering; even the water seemed to tremble. The shoreline was covered with dark glistening spiders; tremors continuing inland, timber swaying and snapping branches as they tottered back and forth, others splitting and forcibly cracking.

Terrain was rattling. Ancients were wavering.

Deep underground tectonic plates were shifting, reverberating with guttural rumbles; while from inland came hundreds of sharp resonant snaps of trembling, splintering trees. Shredding substratum, successively intense upthrust pressure-waves swelled fracturing the surface's crust with tension billows that began ripping the plateau— the night sky thick with echoes of heavy crashes as unseen gnarled ancients uprooted, listed and collapsed.

—And fighting water, going under in, *the rush!*

Each time they submerged their heads filled with the noise of swirling watersplash and the distortion of rustling bubbles. These were sounds they would remember. However, more than that, the most definitive sound was the one they didn't hear, but could feel.

First the silence, as seconds passed; then it was something more. Quivering vibrations swarmed around them rising from somewhere deep below. Then gradually the pulses began increasing in intensity with the portent of constant, mounting pressure that seemed ever so slightly to lift the entire plateau.

Next a low, deep rumbling followed, gathering strength of incredible squeezing compression focused toward a single fault lying directly below the abandoned village three miles inland.

Finally, the incredible climactic surge as pent-up pressure and liquid fire burrowed searing into the vent, then blasted through the granite crust obliterating the village, unleashing clouds of superheated steam, smoke and ash that catapulted miles into the night sky.

—Billowing, boiling, roaring and climbing!

Hurling ejecta and fractured landscape, molten magma rocketed and fantailed expanding with gagging opaque clouds of sulfuric mustard gas. It was two thousand degrees of frothing, raging, fiery broth bathing a nocturnal landscape in amber light and liquid flame. Spewing viscous inferno-spray a thousand feet across, splashing viscid molten fire five miles high —the volcano erupted!

Solemn, both men watched, overwhelmed by the natural fury born in their presence. Amazed, Reed almost whispered, *naaah... this shit ain't real.*

Ground-rattling violent, the volcano disgorged steam, smoke and brimstone in a remarkable fountain-fire display of rushing liquid flame as heaving, pounding tremors vibrated the beach to a sifter of sand. Night Hunters scattered and ran —chaotic— their instincts scrambled, everything jolted, all of it tossed, the plateau on the brink of destruction.

Incredible seething pressure rocketed ejecta upward then out in graceful defining arcs —lava bombs— trailing searing smoke and flame. Streaking into the dark, out of sight —then from the sky— the starburst molten globs of liquid rock returned as plummeting meteoric firewings flashing down from the churning plume. Impacting like artillery shells, hundreds of them smashed into the forest quickly setting trees aflame. Again and again lava clods jettisoned from the volcanic cloud, bombed the jungle and cratered the beach turning trees into firestorm and sand to melted-hollow depression puddles of glass. In less than a minute the entire plateau was afire.

Now a skyfire of searing inferno blocking their flight, the Night Hunters' treetop canopy was aflame. For them there was nowhere to

hide, skirmishing mindlessly back and forth at the water's edge —
and two-thousand-degree death coming down.

Along the shoreline flames were eating the clamoring piles of
gigantic spiders while mad as a hatter they ran —all directions—
eight legs of jet-black fireball torches trilling animalistic screams
until they collapsed crackling and popping and burning to crisp
cinders.

A lava bomb hit the cove shattering the cold water —near them,
too close— exploding as a thousand-pound fragmental grenade of
splattering liquid shrapnel skipping sizzle-streaks through steam
and waves. Treading water and watching the carnage on the beach
Reed slung the laser over his head. Then to Ames, "Fuckit—fight's
over—let's get out of here."

Steam-mist was quickly gathering.

Rough breakwater waves crashing over them, both swam for the
trimaran; and between gulps of yellow-brown sulfur-tainted water
Reed shouted to the boat, "Hoist the mainsail!" Dodging pelting lava
bomb scatter-clutter sizzling and dancing on deck, Seana and two
others ran to the foremast to untie the reefs. "No, the other one..."
he splashed fighting waves, "the big one!"

To the mainmast— the women working feverishly, freeing the
canvas from the boom.

Steam-fog was forming.

Sloshing whitewater, hair plastered to their heads with waves
slapping them in the face, the turbid water was slowing them down;
swimming to the surging boat seemed to take forever. Now hurling
farther out, lava bombs were reaching greater distances and landing
closer as magma accumulated around the volcanic fissure forming
the characteristic cone called a composite landform.

Streaking down from the dark as fireball trails issuing glowing
ribbons of smoke, the globs of flaming rock were hitting the cove all
around them now. *Ska-woosh,* explosions.

Forty yards away a molten blob smashed into the inlet with a blast
of shattering vaporized water and intense detonation-explosion. The
lava bomb splintered in fiery pebbles that shot into waves spinning

sizzling shrapnel-scatter that skipped on the surface like bounding pebbles of dancing fire until they finally cooled enough to sink, *skizzzing* into the murk.

Crashing behind them, a second molten glob detonated in a rush of steam and fragment-clutter, a whistling barrage of red bullets hot enough to sear completely through them. Then the sudden trailing stench of vaporized sulfuric water flashed passed in a driven-mist of sultry hot air.

Three miles inland, more pounding explosions, the landform was breathing and growing. Power and molten flame.

Determined, they swam through the brown roil, and almost to the trimaran, pulling with a crawl stroke Reed saw it coming; from the dark, a fiery ball of pulsing plasma-flame and glowing froth. He stopped, treading water, watching to be certain.

"Incoming—five hundred yards!" he screamed. Ames looked up—saw it. "Dive, dive!" Reed roared. A breaststroke and both surged gulping lungs full of air then went under the scramble of waves in opposite directions.

—Shattering fire, horrific steam-flash!

Alongside the boat the massive lava bomb crashed on the surface where only seconds before they had been. Exploding, the opaque water detonated in a bursting orange depth charge of rupturing blast and instant rush of expanding bubbles spun with twirling, glowing molten slivers that sizzled careening underwater.

The primary force of impact was absorbed in the surface explosion when the lava bomb blew apart in a rupture-pulse of superheated steam, quaking waves, and shattering discharge flinging marble-sized fragments. Splattered globular chips skipped sizzling across the surface and skittering onto the deck of the craft pelting everything with bits of hot ore. Already thoroughly soaked the trimaran was suddenly shrouded within spiraling rises of steam from the fizzling lava pieces that spotted and discolored the carbon-fiber deck. But acting quickly and splashing it down, Nitana and others scooped buckets of water washing the hundreds of blistering pebbles overboard. No serious damage.

Resurfacing, Ames yelled, "Weigh anchor..." then coughed out explaining as he swam, "pull it up." Tian and Kalo sprang into action towing in the line; and as both men bellied onto the deck the mainsail was unfurling and climbing the mast. Bare feet splashing across the deck, Ames ran to help secure the sail's rigging as Reed took the helm bringing them about.

The anchor was up, the boom coming in, sweeping the deck, "Heads up, coming about," Reed sounded; but they didn't look. "Tian, Kalo—get down!" Standing amidship they ducked just in time avoiding the spar as it swooped over their heads. Ballooning with air the mainsail filled launching the trimaran with a powerful uplifting surge, then steady, and the sailing cruiser effortlessly glided over pounding crested waves and ragged breakers.

Bound for open sea.

* * *

Moments later...

...And beyond the fire, they plied over a watery world beneath a sky of ash plume illuminated by heat lightning's intermittent shimmers. Yellow-thick the taste of sulfur still hung heavy in the air; but the cove, and the Hunters, were behind them.

"Dive, dive," Ames mocked with a nervous grin as he returned aft and sat down beside his friend. "We're about to be char-broiled out there and you're doing, 'Run Silent, Run Deep'." Finally having a moment to rest, he took a deep breath, exhaled, then cordially, "You're an idiot, you know it."

Reed smiled. "Well, it eases the tension; you know —blink!" He blinked his eyes for emphasis. And still shaking his head, Ames smiled too.

Looking back, the survivors could see the volcano's composite landform building around the vent, inexorably rising with belching fountains of lava as it grew from the corpse of a burning plateau. With an aurora of flame the night sky glowed amber and bright illuminated by a volcanic beacon that was visible for miles. And although fading now, the roar of pressurized gas and steam was still audible spewing imbued gray-brown saturated clouds that climbed the sky. Alive with lightning, the opaque expanding pool of churning deadly atmosphere was crawling across a horizon lighted by fire, blotting out stars as it spread.

Farther out, attracted by moisture and blitzkrieg flakes of particulate ash, heat lightning flickered as crooked flippant scratches leaving trails of fading embers. And last, thick snowflakes of volcanic ash began falling, a dark blizzard of fluffy, charcoal manna.

From the deck of their sailing cruiser beneath sails bellied with the wind, for a while they all solemnly watched the lightshow of firestorm. Finally, Reed turned. Then, one-by-one so did the others. Now, before them only night sky, the wind, and the waves.

In awe and anticipation… ten sailed out to sea.

CHAPTER FIVE

The horizon...

...A sky of greylight, the sun soon coming up. Behind them, a sky of expanding dark particulate cloud now carried aloft on currents of jetstream wind. They could no longer hear the volcano's molten eruption; but in the distance the plume and orange glow of the corona was still faintly visible, miles away now. Sailing strong and confidently the trimaran skimmed gracefully over the water, both masts pulling her steadily with sails filled by the wind.

Its three parallel hulls intercepted the onrushing waves; keels slicing then tossing spray and foam to the wake, creating the sensation of slow-motion horse and rider. The wind quivered as it swept across the sailcloth with a fluted, whipping sound, arrhythmic and pulsating but enchanting nonetheless; part of the mariner's lore, perhaps a fragment of that inexplicable attraction which had drawn so many to the water so long ago.

Today, there were ten. They had survived.

It had been a long night—

Ames, Tian and Seana slept soundly near the helm. Nitana and four others lay amidship, some curled fetal, others sprawled on deck. Exhausted, Reed leaned heavily upon the wheel keeping himself on his feet, his eyelids closing then blinking open as his flaccid body reflexively jerked, trying to stay awake. And last, Kalo, the youngest, sat somber and silent on the deck at the bow.

She hadn't moved all night, except when once in awhile she'd trembled a little. Reed had been watching from the helm and at first thought the damp night air was causing her periodic shivers. But the longer he'd watched, the more evident it became, she wasn't cold; she was crying. He thought about calling her to the helm, then reconsidered, deciding she might better spend some time alone, contemplating, sorting through what troubled her.

Gradually the night had blended to predawn, and she still hadn't moved. Now, the man was becoming concerned for Kalo. And he was exhausted.

Hazel eyes opening blinking slumber away, Tian saw him hanging limply upon the wheel. Slowly his knees bent then folded and gave way, and Reed slipped wrenching suddenly awake. He pulled himself upright again. Spent, he forced his eyes wide one more time.

Not wanting to wake him, Tian eased free from Ames' arm then rose and stepped over to Reed wrapping her arms around him, helping him stand. He offered a tired, appreciative smile and she kissed him on the cheek.

"Teach me," she said quietly. "Show me what to do."

"I'm okay," he told her, "but I think she needs someone to talk to," nodding forward and indicating Kalo sitting alone at the bow. "She hasn't slept all night."

Tian was puzzled. "You have not slept either."

"I know; but I really think she needs someone to talk to." He was serious.

Tian looked at the girl again; then knelt and squeezed Seana's arm waking her, whispering, "Then teach Seana, and I will speak to Kalo." Seana, pert with the prospect of being chosen for such a marked responsibility—to operate the boat; Reed nodded and Tian left for the bow.

"You will teach me?" Seana was both honored and nervous, but more than willing.

Quietly, "Yes, but first things first..." hesitating, "well, don't I get a kiss?"

"You teach me, then you get a kiss," and she smiled as she said it. Reed couldn't fathom that as acceptable and frowned. "Then after you sleep," she went on furtively indicating the cabin below deck, "we will sneak down there and I will do you."

A whisper: "What, like they're not gonna miss us? This boat *is not* that big, Seana." But he was interested. The grin: "Fuckit—deal." She quickly snuggled within his arms, against the wheel, and as he began to speak she abruptly turned and kissed him.

After the kiss, "What was that for?"

She smiled and quietly said, "You are *sooo* easy."

"Yeah, easy my ass; now pay attention." But he couldn't help smiling as he began explaining, "Right now we're sailing on the wind, because the wind is blowing from just about where the sun is rising. We can't sail directly into the wind so we're tacking, zigzagging in an upwind direction." He paused. "With me so far?" She nodded eagerly. "Okay then, right is starboard, left is port," indicating as he spoke, "and the wind is blowing from the left side, portside, so we're on the port tack." Moving aside to give her more room, "Now you take the wheel." She did, blushing with enthusiasm as they held their course together for a moment.

"Now we'll change tack. This is called jibing," he explained. "Rule number one—don't ever change course without letting everyone know beforehand, so when the boom, or spar as it's sometimes called, sweeps the deck, you don't hurt someone—you know, knock 'em overboard."

"The boom?" she asked.

"You'll see." Then, although the others were asleep and Tian and Kalo were both at the bow, Reed called out moderately, demonstrating, "Prepare to jibe… jibe *ho—oo*." He and Seana spun the wheel together altering the trimaran's course, and simultaneously the booms of both masts, being controlled by the stay lines, swept majestically across the deck, the two sails ballooning with full bellies on the opposite tack.

Darting him a glance she beamed, "Reed, that is—so—cool."

Hugging her, "Yeah; it is kind of incredible isn't it."

At the bow—

Holding it in her cupped hands, the young Renoloi had taken off her necklace, studying it, leather thong wrapped around her palm; she tenderly caressing the dinosaur tooth with both thumbs, absorbed in thought when Tian sat down. Keeping her face close to her hands the girl examined her most prized possession, until Tian finally spoke.

"Kalo, what troubles you?" No response. A patient moment, she asked again, gently, "What is wrong?"

"Nothing."

"Look at me when we speak. You are a Renoloi warrior and you must act like one."

Kalo peered up from her hands through suffused, reddened eyes, murmuring, "But I am not..." and she stopped, not finishing what she was about to say, quickly returning to the security of her palms.

"You are not what?" Tian prodded; but the girl wouldn't face her. Finally, Tian ordered, "Kalo, look at me."

"Please, Tian, do not make me," she simpered.

The leader considered, remembering John's patience in the lowland; then calmly responded, "When you are ready; we will talk then." That said, Tian began to rise and Kalo reached out grabbing her wrist and turning her hand, then reverently placed the necklace in the woman's palm. Tian was stunned, silent, her expression asking, *why?*

At last Kalo looked up to her leader and began to explain. "I am not..." but tears flooded her eyes and she buried her face in her hands crying and trembling piteously.

"Why?" she asked softly, empathetically; but the girl would not answer, could not face her. She wanted so desperately for Tian to be proud of her. Tenderly wrapping her fingers, closing her hand and sealing the precious necklace within, Tian rose and quietly walked astern.

Confident at the wheel, Seana was glowing, her gaze fixed upon the horizon and just-rising sun, the wind tossing her hair as surely as it filled the sails. Reed stood at her side, his smile of approval evaporating as Tian approached; he could tell something was wrong.

"What is it?" he asked. Without speaking Tian opened her hand, the necklace in her palm. Reed was taken aback, not being able to imagine Kalo relinquishing her most precious possession. Serious, he looked at it, and at length almost inaudibly exhaled, "No way. Why? This doesn't make sense."

"I do not know. She will not tell me."

Extending a hand, "Give it to me." He took the necklace, turning the tooth in his palm with his thumb and index finger. Then to Seana, "Can you handle her?"

"Yes, I can."

"Starboard tack, port tack, into the sun," and he grinned as she bobbed confidently. Then serious again, he glanced at the necklace and started toward the bow mumbling, "Nope —no way."

Kalo sat with her arms wrapped tightly around her legs, gathered to her chest, her chin resting upon her knees. She stared listlessly and exhausted at the ocean sweeping toward her in gliding, rolling swells. Reed, without prelude or invitation sat down Indian fashion next to her, the holes in his ragged Levis stretched so tightly his knees popped through. Elbows propped on his thighs, without speaking he manipulated the necklace in front of him for a minute or two; then looking across the open sea let it drop and dangle from his finger by the leather string until he was sure she was watching. Without looking away from the sea Reed calmly extended his arm holding the necklace inches from her face.

"Sure is a beauty. This belong to you?" he asked plainly. She looked from the tooth to him, silent, still staring out over the ocean.

"It is beautiful," she admitted. He said nothing more, looking straight ahead, scanning the waterworld before them while holding the necklace in front of her face, suspended precariously by a single finger. He was leading her—Psychology 101. Her eyes traveled back and forth from the tooth to him, the necklace meaning so much to her, him seemingly unaffected, detached from it. Kalo did not know that once upon a time King Solomon employed a similar technique, only he used a baby. Reed bent his finger ever so slightly, and the leather thong slid, almost to his fingertip. Still not making eye contact, continuing to look straight ahead, he said nothing, until nervously, eyes transfixed on the tooth, she whispered, "Be careful... please." Now he had her.

"Be a damn shame to drop such a beautiful necklace. Surely would." And as he said it, Reed let the string slip from his finger. Kalo, compelled without realizing, caught it, not able to let it hit the deck. She cradled the tooth within her hands, studied it, then looked at him.

"But I am not..." she began to say, then stopped. He still wouldn't look at her, only waited taking in the rise and fall of a vast ocean — and he would not ask. At length she said, "I am not worthy."

Now he turned and looked her in the eye. Direct, serious. "That's bullshit, kid; you are." The door opened; post traumatic stress. Now she could talk, get it out.

"But I was so frightened. They were so many and we were so few, and I could not stop them as I did Tyrannosaurus Rex. I have never seen anything so horrible as Denen hanging there..." and she broke down and cried, sobbing and heaving with violent jerks. Reed put his arm around her, pulling her to him, not saying a word. He let her cry into his chest.

Five long minutes passed.

Finally, she was ready to talk some more. "I am so ashamed," she professed weakly.

"Why?"

Kalo looked up from the security of his shirt, to him. "Because I must be brave, and I was frightened. I was not brave and eleven died."

"No," he corrected, "you *were* brave... and ten lived." Her expression betrayed confusion. "Kalo, being afraid is not cowardice; don't ever confuse the two." She said nothing, listening, so he continued. "Killing is terrible, but we will when we have to, to survive —and not all of us will survive. That's a warrior's destiny. We fight when we must and tremble later. Under those circumstances being afraid is natural. You'd have to be nuttier than ole' Crazy Guggenheim not to have been frightened." He paused, then added,

"I thought I was spider juice for sure. Hell, I was scared shitless. You and Doc saved my ass. I expect it of him Kalo; but I owe you one."

The girl inquired softly, "Are we friends?"

Earnestly, "Till death do us part."

Seriously, "Friends do not keep track."

Reed smiled. "You're learning, kid." Then, as he took the necklace to slip it back over her head, "Here, put this back on."

"Would you really have dropped my necklace?" she asked suspiciously.

Reed grinned —dropped it— and as she gasped, quick as a wink he caught it with his other hand. "Naw, I wouldn't have let it hit the deck. That might chip it and it's too important to you." And slipping the thong over her neck, "Would you mind if I just sit here with you for a while?"

"That would be nice." Now more at ease she snuggled inside his arm and they stretched out together.

"Cool."

A quiet moment, then, "Reed, who is ole' Crazy Guggenheim?"

The smile. "You've never heard of Guggenheim?"

"No."

"Oh, well… now there's a *real—good* story; but I'll have to tell you later 'cause right now I sorta need to unwind. How 'bout you?"

Curious, she asked, "What is unwind?"

Reed grinned. "Just close your eyes."

From the helm Tian and Seana had been watching and Tian commented, "Seana, he still surprises me."

Seana smiled, love in her eyes. "What can I say... he is *just* Reed."

Right about then, two thoroughly exhausted people at the bow fell soundly asleep.

* * *

"Prepare to jibe, jibe *ho—oo*..."

...Seana's voice awakened him shortly after midday. The girl still cuddled against him; they had gotten some much-needed rest.

Washing drowsiness away Reed yawned. Placid, he lay still and watched the rise and fall of the sea, his mind passively absorbed with the exhilarating sensation of freedom and being alive on the ocean. Then, feeling the powerful rush of the twin booms sweeping the deck with the bow slicing smoothly as they veered changing tack, he was satisfied and pleased. Seana had done well.

Kalo stirred and sat up rubbing her eyes in the glare of vivid sunshine. "Good morning," her smile imparting the warmth of affection.

Teasing, "Ready to get up, kid?"

"Yes I am, old man," playfully smacking his chest with an open hand.

He sprang to his butt, sitting up. "Old man, what's this old man shit?" But four steps ahead of him, she was already on her way astern. Onto his feet, he followed as Tian, Ames and Seana stood waiting, Seana still at the wheel. Arriving aft, "Did you hear that?" Kalo still grinning like a Cheshire cat.

"Hear what?" Ames asked.

Pointing at her, "The kid called me an old man." Ames smirked.

Tian taunted, "Imagine that."

"Well age is relative," Ames considered, then added wryly, "Shades of de'ja vu—whispered echoes of haunting reckoning," gesturing 'ghostly' with crooked fingers. Not believing their insensitivity Reed turned to Seana.

Poker-faced she said, "Life is a bitch."

Throwing his arms in the air, "Great, my friends. This just beats me all to pieces. You guys are screwin' with me again."

"But Reed," Kalo insisted, "compared to me, you are old... well, older anyway."

"Sound familiar?" Ames needled, and they all smiled—except Reed.

He squared playfully with Kalo. "Hey kid, I'm not *that* old." Pointing at Ames, "He's old; I'm just..." at a loss for the word.

"Older," Kalo ended his sentence.

Staring her down, Reed glowered playfully, thought about it, then sniffed and shook his head. "This sucks —and you realize of course, I'm gonna get you for that."

Kalo beamed. "If you last that long."

He grabbed her by the waist playfully lifting her and twirling around, holding her in the air. "Kids— should just sell 'em all on the Black Market to South African slavers while they're still precious, cuddly little munchkins —and be done with it." As he finished speaking, he set her lightly upon the deck.

Giggling subsiding, she looked at him, then serious, told him, "I have no idea what that means."

He turned to Ames. "This is hopeless; she's gonna drive me crazy."

"You won't have to pack a picnic lunch," Ames considered dryly.

"You guys," Reed began, then decided, "ah nevermind," turning again, this time to Seana. "How we doin'?"

"Starboard tack," she answered, "on the wind." He winked, obviously proud.

"You want to spell her, Doc?"

"She's doing fine."

Reed nodded. "She is at that. Okay then; let's teach these landlubbers a thing or two about sailing. Nitana, you and the others gather 'round," motioning to them.

As they approached, he began. "What we have here is a Star Craft, twin mast, sixty-foot, trimaran sailing cruiser; and you're about to get a crash course as oceanic navigational personnel, otherwise known as sailors before the mast." He took a breath. "That expression, by the way, originated in olden days because the crew's-quarters was located forward, in the front of the boat —thus— before the mast." He gave the crew the once-over. "Okay, let's get started."

He began with nautical terminology, then various aspects of the boat and how each component interfaced, combining the parts to construct the whole, interlacing everything to present a comprehensive picture in their minds. Finally, he answered questions demonstrating as he did, absorbing the better part of an hour. The women were eager to learn and keenly astute, remembering everything to the most innocuous detail.

"I guess that should do it then," he said at last.

Tere,[10] one of the younger Renoloi, raised a hand and he acknowledged with a tip of the head. "What are the spikes in the mainmast for, Reed?" He looked at the stainless-steel spikes ascending the fifty-foot mast, all the way to a short cross spar or yard above the sail peak.

"To access the stays and canvas should it get tangled."

"And a sentry's post," she inquired, "a lookout?"

"You mean a crow's nest?" Studying the horizontal cross spar he considered, then answered, "Sure, I suppose so. But we're doing six or seven knots, up there the wind is likely thirty or more, it could be sorta dangerous."

She raised her hand again saying, "I volunteer for first watch." With that, she was on the mainmast and with easy agility climbing for the top.

"Well okay," and reluctantly, "but be careful and hold on up there. Little as you are a strong gust of wind might blow your puny carcass right out to sea."

Glancing down she called back, "Aye, aye, mate." A moment later she was sitting atop the yard, her legs and arm securely wrapped around the mast.

Reed nervously walked aft, and as he approached Tian and Ames, he turned again looking up toward the masthead. "She still up there?" He squinted blocking the sun with a hand.

Ames, nonchalant, "Yes."

He called out, "Tere, you all right up there?"

"It is *sooo* beautiful. You should see the view from here," her voice trailed back, but the sun was in his eyes making it impossible for him to see her.

"No thanks," he mumbled as he started to walk away, then stopped for another quick peek at the masthead. "You know, Doc," he said seriously, "these guys are so gung-ho… sometimes they just make me nervous."

"She is fine," Tian assured. "She has climbed trees since she was big enough to walk."

"Sure, I know that; it's cool." He sat down mumbling again. "No kidding boy, these women are some crazy bitches for sure. Just Doc and me and all these crazies, curious all right. Beats the shit out'a me... enough to make a guy wonder."

Overhearing, Ames asked, "What did you say Reed?"

He looked up. "Nothing; just talking to myself."

"That's a sign you'll go crazy."

"Don't even start on me again, okay?"

Nitana broke in, "May I take the wheel?" Ames looked at Reed, who looked at Seana. No one spoke.

"Your call, Seana," Reed told her. "You have the helm." She agreed and Nitana enthusiastically assumed command. Trading places, Seana nudged her and whispered more loudly than necessary.

"Now I want to do Reed."

"Oh, for cryin' out loud," he wailed, "just put it on the six o'clock news." Then he pleaded, "And —*plee-ease*— don't start talking about sex again."

Seana squared with him emphasizing each word. "Reed, you are *sooo*—easy," and she laughed playfully thumping him on top of the head as she sat down snuggling next to him.

Rubbing his head where she smacked him, he countered, "Don't mess up my hair either."

"I did not mess up your hair. There is no hair in that spot."

Ames looked down at the top of his head. "Shoulda worn a baseball cap —with a button on it," he said dryly. "She's right though…" the pretext of a sigh, "too late now." Tian joined in, stroking his head tenderly.

Knowing she was up to something Reed glared at her. "Okay, what?"

"The wrinkle…" she answered, "just smoothing it out." He slapped at her hand, but she was too quick.

"Get away from me you guys."

Kalo approached Tian. "May we talk?" Playful vanished as Tian nodded indicating the cabin. They went below.

In the cabin—

Tian sat on one of the bunks while Kalo remained standing, uncertain but determined, maudlin adolescence aside, time to be mature.

"Sit here," Tian said laying a hand on the bunk. The girl complied and they quartered to face one another.

Kalo pushed her shoulders back, took a slow breath and sat up straight. "When you said I could come on this journey I was so honored, and I wanted very much for you to be proud of me; but I am not worthy and I am ashamed."

Softly Tian asked, "Why?"

"I let Denen and the others die."

"You did not let them die," Tian ensured benevolently, perplexed, "no one could save them. Why would you believe it was your fault?"

"Because, Tian," the girl said urgently, "I knew the Night Hunters' weakness —only not until too late."

"Fire?" Tian asked. Kalo nodded. "How did you know?"

"'Just Plain' Wilson told me."

"'Just Plain' Wilson told you? But you did not speak to Wilson; you were in the tree."

"Yes; but before going into the burrow, when Wilson looked at me he talked to me. I heard him speak inside my head; but I did not understand."

"You heard him speak... but he did not talk?"

"Yes," Kalo answered, then explained, "he knew their weakness and he and P.T. Barnum came to warn us, to help us so we would know." She considered, then continued. "He told me; but I said nothing and eleven died. If I had told you, Denen and the others would still be alive; but I was not certain and said nothing." This time staunchly refusing to cry, "They died because of me."

For a moment Tian thought quietly, searching her memory for something her mother had shown her once a long time ago, inside a mountain. The passageway was separate from the others, an oubliette, a dead end, unto itself, where there were words chiseled in stone and inlaid with gold. Now, however she tried, she could not recover the words, and it would haunt her. "What was it?" she murmured.

"What was what?" Kalo asked. Her voice brought Tian back.

Blinking, "I was trying to remember from my youth, something important, a prophecy." A pause. "Kalo," Tian began again, "just before Denen was killed you cried out." The girl nodded. "Why did you cry out?"

Kalo hesitated. "I want you to be proud of me. You will think I am foolish."

"No," Tian assured gently, "I will not."

Reluctantly the girl confessed, "I knew the Night Hunters were in the trees, not because I could hear them, or see them… but somewhere within, I could feel them." Tian was silent. Waiting for a response Kalo looked at her intently, until finally she nervously inquired, almost a whisper, "Tian, do you believe me?"

"Kalo, we will speak of this again, another time," and she began to rise.

"—But Tian, do you believe me?" she asked, almost pleading.

Calm, Tian sat down beside the girl again placing a gentle hand upon her cheek. "Yes, I believe you." Then she told her, "Kalo, the voice you hear and the premonitions you feel are truth. Trust them. Believe them. They will guide you and never lead you astray."

"I am sorry Tian. Will you forgive me?"

Tian closed her eyes, touched the girl's forehead with three fingers, then opened her eyes. "You need not be sorry; there is nothing to forgive," she assured. "You are young and perhaps you have begun a journey, one you cannot envision, a journey that others will follow. There are many things we do not know today and we must each face our destiny one day at a time, one step at a time. What you sense inside you must treasure; nurture the voice and the feeling. I am proud of you; but even more than that, you must believe in yourself for you are worthy, more so than you know. Today you are a Renoloi warrior... perhaps beyond that lies your destiny."

"What do you mean?" the girl asked.

"More than that I do not know; perhaps your answer will come with time." Tian rose, smiled affectionately, then left the cabin. And as she did, she thought, *something important. The Legends.*

On deck—

Bantering congenially the others lounged easily in the sunshine enjoying the day. The ubiquitous foreboding lingering on the plateau had evaporated with the nautical miles now separating them from the mainland. This was a new chapter in their adventure, the ocean invigorating and reviving their spirits with each rolling swell met by the bow. Beneath them the triplex keels sliced with rhythmic liquid melody of waves tossing foam in the spray, while above them wind-whipped canvas carried the trimaran on with its strength. A siren's song in the sails.

Relaxed, sprawled on deck near the companionway Ames complimented, "Reed, I didn't know you were such an accomplished sailor."

Flattered, "Well thanks, but remember, I'm originally from the Midwest." He grinned. "You native Montanans thought the Fort Peck Reservoir was a major body of water; but Minnesota alone had ten thousand lakes, and Wisconsin, almost that many." The pause. "And then there were the *real lakes*."

"The real lakes?"

Reed laced his fingers behind his head, kicked back for bragging rights. "Sure: Ontario, Superior, Michigan, Huron, and Erie; the Great Lakes."

Ames granted, "True enough, but you've made a topographical error that was pretty common back then; and you lived in Montana long enough to know better."

Brow wrinkled, thinking, "Really, what?"

"The Fort Peck Reservoir was located between Glasgow and Miles City," the native reminded, "technically, we didn't consider that to be Montana. It was West Dakota."

"Oh, yeah —forgot."

Ames concluded wryly, "That's where the sheep jokes originated."

The other chuckled, "Natives."

A few minutes later Reed began humming a catchy chantey and eventually worked up to the lyrics. Ames vaguely remembered and accompanied, and their off-key duet instilled the others to hum along. Even Kalo, who also had returned to the deck, joined in. She sang a beautiful soprano, if only she weren't so quiet all the time.

When they finished, Ames asked, "What's the name of that tune?"

"Don't recall, but it's really old; no pun intended either." And they sang it through a couple more times, finally winding down. "And now for my next number," Reed quipped, "a true pirate ballad, a genuine buccaneer ditty." Then he began, "Fifteen men on a dead man's chest, yo-ho-ho and a bottle of rum. Come on," he encouraged, "sing along." And they did.

When the song ended, "You know, Doc," he commented seriously, "I just realized that every now and then I miss the radio." He thought about it. "Guess I just always took it for granted before. But there are times… yeah, I do miss it sometimes."

"Just goes to show, it's not a perfect world," Ames remarked.

"But we've got the next best thing."

"I'll bite; what?"

Reed smiled. "Me."

Ignoring that Ames asked, "You know any other sailing songs?"

"Only one…" Reed was interrupted as a gray shape torpedoed up —out of the ocean— and a voluminous splash alongside the trimaran, the column of spray bursting to droplets and swept by the wind, raining across the deck. All were instantly onto their feet. Ready.

Again, the porpoise-like creature surged from the depths, leaped then crashed into the next rising swell, and disappeared.

Worried, "What was that?" Seana asked.

Reed: "Can't be a Cetacean; mammals haven't evolved yet."

"The vertical tail," Ames observed, "an Ichthyosaur, early marine reptile similar to the dolphin. It must be thirty feet or more."

Two more breached —propelled airborne, sailing— then splashed with explosions of watery spray. Soon others appeared, an entire school bursting from the depths then skimming the waves alongside the travelers, some leading, others trailing, all circling and joining the craft as if it were one of their own.

Ichthyosauri surface running, skimming shallow and fast; then disappearing, going deep and rising in an explosion of water and foam; the breach. The reptiles were swift and adept in their habitat, a mysterious, watery world; and adopting the fleet trimaran as a playmate, they crisscrossed before the bow, sparring with it and jockeying, outmaneuvering the boat. They leaped time and again. Rolls, somersaults and airborne spirals—beautiful, sleek, graceful bodies with the speed and agility of aquatic torpedoes. Water games at sea.

"Aw' right!" Reed whooped, and he began singing, 'Calypso', a song originally dedicated to Jacques Cousteau, a pioneer in oceanographic exploration, and recorded by John Denver, but auspiciously persevering to become what Reed considered one of the greatest sailing songs ever written. By the second chorus they were all singing at the top of their lungs, wrapped up in the moment, the music, the trimaran and the Ichthyosauri accompanying them on the fresh-water ocean.

An incredible day.

CHAPTER SIX

Reflecting sunlight on seaswells...

...Water sparkled silver-crystal beneath blue. For two hours the Ichthyosauri accompanied the boat entertaining the travelers with their aquatic acrobatics and nautical antics. But the afternoon sun was now slowly passing behind them, the horizon before them gathering storm clouds faintly outlined as building cumulonimbus rims. A final watersplash and the Ichthyosauri suddenly vanished, wind shifting, portending danger with its scent.

Sails relaxing, just a flutter. Calm moving in.

The trimaran glided a bit longer, slowing as the canvas quieted; a moment more, the sea still flowing easily with gentle, rolling swells. But the wind was passively diminishing and strangely becoming still; like a vagabond leaving, it softly evaporated and the sailcloth lethargically went flat. Undulating in irons.

It became very quiet. Too quiet.

Peering over the edge between the outer hull and outrigger, perhaps Maya thought the Ichthyosaur would return. They did not. Hoping they might, the Renoloi leaned from the deck looking into the water —a flash of gray from below, two black eyes rolling white, deadly jaws opening.

Not having even an instant to move Maya would die; the great white's massive body exploding through the surface, slamming between the outer hull and outrigger, heaving the boat sideways and her from the deck. Before she could scream she was gone, jaws slamming shut, crushing and slicing through her with rows of angled teeth designed only to kill. The power and savagery of the bite ripped her nearly in two spewing a crimson cloud in the air.

One second, the Renoloi and shark disappeared vanishing into the sea.

Two seconds, the cloud of blood splashed onto the deck soaking it red.

Three seconds, the liquid slosh of the shark's wake swept over the boat washing it clean.

Both disappeared that quickly. The only evidence that either was there three seconds before, was the diluted remnant trail of wine-tinge water trickling from the deck back to the sea.

Then everything was quiet again. Too quiet.

Bated breath and jangled nerves, no one spoke. It happened so quickly it seemed illusory, some demented mind trickery; but what happened was real, not their imaginations. Reed moved carefully nearer to the edge of the deck, where vermilion water still gathered to puddles then slid away dribbling into a watery oblivion. Weapon ready, he stood there waiting; a long minute ticked passed. From below there was a glimmer of movement, the water's refraction displacing the object and surface reflection obscuring its image, as coming slowly it rose to the surface. He thought he could see it; but couldn't quite make it out… yet. Then, hair flowing liquid, dead lifeless eyes and mouth open in a scream, neck trailing trachea and arteries, Maya's decapitated head serenely surfaced and swayed with the flow.

Numbed, he watched, then raised a hand trying to push her away as Tian stepped forward. "No don't!" —too late.

Tian gasped transfixed by the horror of the spectral head, the gruesome image instantaneously imprinting in her brain. Ames grabbed her and held her, and unnerved, together they saw the decapitated woman's lips move; then her mouth closed and her head slowly descended again... all the while her dead staring eyes were watching them as she slipped away, sinking out of sight.

Now, there were nine.

Backing away from the edge of the boat, not speaking, the three slowly moved to the helm, now knowing the shark had been very real.

"What was it?" Nitana asked. Each in turn looked at her, but no one would answer. And as they stood there a cold wind swept overdeck filling the sails, the bow dipping in a trough then easily rising on a moderate swell… and in the distance, it was there.

"Off the port bow—" Tere called down from her lofty perch at the crow's nest.

One after another the voyagers spotted it; to their left, more than a mile away, silhouetted by the amassing thunderheads beyond. Tian moved closer taking hold of Ames' arm while he studied the creature, his friend carefully slinging the laser over his shoulder and diagonally across his back, muzzle pointed down. Seana pressed against Reed.

Ames, to Reed: "Plesiosaur." The other agreed.

Nervous, Seana whispered, "What is it?"

Still watching the marine reptile, the younger man replied, "The Loch Ness frickin' monster." And anticipating her next question, "No," he said gravely, "that one ain't friendly."

More visible now, the Plesiosaur was moving closer, its hump-backed body a capsized boat with broad horizontal, pectoral and anal flippers, and an abrupt powerful tail. Eyes constantly searching, its neck was long and slender with serpentine movement and a viper's head. Submerging, stretching its neck and propelling forward with the fluid strength and symmetry of a dolphin, it swam like a seal, first pushing easily with paddling limbs, then gliding and rearing its head with its uplifted neck forming an 'S'. It surveyed analytically to seek out its prey.

"Think we can outrun it?" Ames asked.

Reed considered, "With the rising wind and full sail we might make fifteen or twenty knots, but I doubt that'll be enough." Then looking at his friend, "Given a choice, I'd prefer prehistoric dolphins."

"So much water and nowhere to hide," Ames mused.

Scanning, Reed speculated, "Not necessarily."

Ames glanced at the crow's nest. "Tere, all hands on deck." Without question she quickly descended the mainmast joining them aft near the helm.

Reed spun the wheel to quarter the wind as he yelled, "Prepare to jibe —everyone down— watch the boom." Both he and Ames knew there wouldn't be time for protocol; this race could mean life or death. "Jibe ho—" sounded as the twin booms swept the deck with pronounced, *swoosh—pfoomfs*. The canvas filled, and tacking, they altered course to avoid the marine dinosaur.

"What do you have in mind?" Ames asked, the trimaran gaining speed.

Eyes shifting between the Plesiosaur and the storm boundary, "Probably something foolish," indicating the mushrooming towers of opaque thunderheads amassing in the distance, "we're going into the storm under full sail."

Nervous: "Reed, we could broach."

"I know; but if we can get to that weather it'll give us some cover, and with a little luck we'll have a couple of minutes to reef the main and try the storm on the foresail before the wind tears us apart." Both of them drenched with misgiving, he added, "Hell, if Nessie takes us on, we'll never make it; we're too light. She'll capsize us for sure."

Ames knew he was right, musing, "How long can you tread water?"

A glance, then shaking his head, "That was a blink, right?" and a tangle of nerves wreaking havoc in his gut, resigned to their decision —and their fate.

"Do it," Ames agreed.

The low-pressure mass forward boundary with its intruding influence on the preceding high-pressure ridge, combined creating the storm. Cold stable air undercut and displaced warm moist thermals causing violent atmospheric turbulence, gradually rousing the ocean.

Entering the front, the wind began to rise.

Green and powerful the sea awakened with rolling fluid strength, her steadily increasing swells building in size. Troughs that had been evenly spaced predictably succeeding the one before, began pulling apart and separating, running obliquely between the rolling volumes of fresh-water sea.

Stretched taut, the sails pulled strong, ballooned, bellies full with the wind. Tracking the dinosaur Reed held the wheel fast, boltropes and stays angling the canvas bent to the mast for maximum aerodynamics and speed.

Ten knots increased to twelve.

The Renoloi holding on to the rail along the cabin wall found small refuge from the building sea, the trimaran's triplex hulls surging into oncoming swells that pounded then poured with mighty washes breaking overdeck. Slicing, the boat dipped in the troughs then knifed through the swells as water cut by the keels cascaded over the carbon-fiber craft, flinging light green foam with the spray.

Twelve knots, now sixteen… a sky growing darker.

Sitting lighter and higher with its speed as wind whistling underdeck created a hydroplane effect, the trimaran swept forward bursting through thirty-foot seas tossing streaks of wet cotton blown away in their wake. Pushing powerfully, bow angled up they breached another swell, the weight of the craft then bringing them down; but with the trough already passed the trimaran heaved into the next rising waterwall and again climbed to its crest. All around them tumbled a choleric waterworld with lashing wind that was increasing in strength.

Sixteen knots mounted to twenty… churning clouds turning black.

Now they plied through waves so quickly the bow seemed to leap from the rolling water, skimming the troughs then plashing into the succeeding water-rise of the next onrushing swell. Knifing from the forty-foot waves the ten-foot daggerboard was now clearly visible above the troughs as it launched from each roll of ocean bound for the next.

Dark as a shadow… Nessie, still coming.

The storm boundary rushed closer, its cumulonimbus formations wringing hail and drenching rain from a wall of gray cloud stretched sideways with the bleak downpour dumped from the sky. Guiding the bounding trimaran, Reed's objective was the cover of zero-visibility within the protective cloudbank.

Nessie—

Momentarily it watched them. Then stretching out the Plesiosaur laid low, extended its slender neck and dove into the ocean, its powerful horizontal flippers propelling the seal-shaped body with a serpentine head. The dinosaur closed in.

Looking to port, "It's coming," Ames yelled over the wind.

Stance wide, maintaining their course Reed barely glanced; his concentration focused on the ocean pouring toward them. Bearing the intense strain of a ragged storm in her sails rattling sheets of soaked canvas dumped wash blown away in the wind; the twin masts held fast, boltropes whistling, stays quivering binding the sailcloth together. Beneath them the triple keels sliced defiantly onward as the stabilizing outriggers' *sweeze,* plowed liquid furrows through an unending field. Cutting wave to wave through wind and cold, an uncompromising ocean pounded them.

Waterspray in their faces. Now the trimaran rushed forward at thirty knots, the speed and strain testing its structural design. But defying the fifty-foot seas the sturdy craft persevered plying over green, wind-driven hills capped with mysterious drool and blisters of froth. Rises of ocean poured toward them in an unending seascape, the small craft swiping wedges from her breast, crashing into onrushing walls of water rimmed with green-gray foam and bluster of spray. Riding the mantle the canvas was straining the rigging, bellied and drawn and stretched to its limit; but solid and steady the trimaran cut water bounding from one massive rise to the next within a wild and dark realm flashing lightning's scatter-white wires through the sky.

Hold together, Reed prayed.

Battered and sloshed by water and boat the women huddled on deck clinging desperately to the cabin rail. Surging from swells the trimaran repeatedly dropped from beneath them, abandoning them like gonfalons dangling in midair; then with the untamed rush of oncoming ocean it would crash into the succeeding wall of uplifting, petulant sea. Over and over, rising then falling, surging then slicing the small craft determinedly plunged with the troughs and rode up with the swells; pounding slams of the rise, the ocean's unharnessed ride, while above a dark sky fired slashes of lightning and spit wind through their hair.

Now absorbed in a world of pouring... and Green.

Both men stood at the helm fighting the wind's tremendous strength; losing control of the craft would mean almost certain disaster. Either the trimaran would turn sharply to lessen the wind in the sails, or the booms would swing wildly out of control with enough force to take down the masts and splinter the hull. Without forward momentum the next roll of cresting whitewater would capsize them flipping the craft like a pop-bottle cap.

The sea was reckless and wanton, its magnitude dwarfing their presence —and they still had not reached the boundary, the frontal edge of the storm.

The trimaran met the next sixty-foot swell, and as the great wave crashed onto the bow with three feet of water cascading overdeck, Tere's legs were washed from beneath her. Torn from the cabin rail and flushed aft with the rush, she screamed desperately for Seana; Seana reaching out, grabbing her wrist —locked together— both fighting the wave, before being swept overboard.

As the craft cleared the wave bounding above the next trough Tere flopped in midair like a dangling wet rag. Determined, Seana hung on; but her other hand was slipping along the rail, and realizing their plight Tian swept her legs around Seana's waist locking her ankles, trying to save them both. Unnerved, Reed and Ames couldn't help; they could only watch from the helm.

Kalo immediately grabbed Tian, and Nitana Kalo, forming a chain ardently clinging to one another, each life dependent upon the others. The boat cleared the trough and pared into a swell —vaulting up. In a huge splash of gray-green the wet rag slammed back onto the deck locking her arms around the rail as her terrified wide eyes blinked; for the moment, safe.

—And the ocean erupted!

Loch Ness dinosaur-seal exploded from beneath them shattering the port outrigger with its rise and heaving the left side of the trimaran from the sea. Pieces flying, the craft vaulted —tipping up— forcing the starboard outrigger underwater creating a roostertail-spray thirty feet high. Abandoning its customary hunting grounds within the deep scattering layer[11] and green darkness below, the Plesiosaurus rose in quest of easier prey above.

As the portside rose the incredible drag on the starboard outrigger, tilted masts, and full sails caused the boat to veer violently to starboard on two hulls with the port keel sweeping from the ocean then raking the length of the Plesiosaur's humped back. The dinosaur reeled swinging its long slender neck —vicious pit-viper speed— lashing out at the two women crowded against the cabin on the high side of the boat.

Starboardside. Nearly submerged and fighting the wash of crashing waves pounding over them, Tian and those on the cabin's trailing side were being battered by the ocean —hanging on for their lives.

Portside. Wind whistled and howled as it came again… snake's strike—empty air …the Plesiosaur missed.

Waterspray and wind…a world soaked in green.

Surging as it cleared the swell, the trimaran righted itself, the port hull slamming back down on the storm-swept sea. Washed back by the monstrous wave, the dinosaur dove into the wall of rolling water like a reptilian seal with powerful appendant flippers, chasing to recapture the boat.

Knowing in such wild water the wind-driven spray would scatter the pulse laser's beam of white light rendering it useless, and unable to come up with a plan, Ames and Reed exchanged worried looks. Both also knew if they couldn't get rid of the marine dinosaur, now closing from behind, their only hope would be the cover of downpour and hail below the thunderheads within the storm's boundary. Very close now.

Ames gave a fleeting glance at the laser slung across Reed's back, next, the Plesiosaurus closing on their wake and maneuvering to attack on their starboard; then forward, to the deluge of rain and hail blowing so hard it came sideways.

"Go!—" he yelled through the gale, booms sweeping the deck, the wind's sudden-slam surging them forward as they turned on a swell jettisoning back on course.

The sea heaved upward on the starboard as the Plesiosaur emerged alongside them colliding with the boat as it was veering to port. Slamming down the dinosaur's brutal flipper shattered the starboard outrigger shearing the support braces at the outer hull, all of it disappearing within the next tumble of wash; dinosaur-seal then circling as the boat listed to port with ocean rolling overdeck engulfing the two women along the left cabin rail. Howling wind and momentum vaulted the craft upright again flinging both from their feet like helpless banners tossed with the wind, and Dira[12] lost her grip and was thrown into the air where narrow-slit eyes and rattlesnake's strike snatched her in midair from hurricane winds that smothered her scream. She was gone.

The marine dinosaur's hinged jaws crunched its solid swill, then flicked Dira in the air taking her headfirst, devouring her whole. Reminiscent of a cottontail bunny being eaten by a snake, it stretched its neck and began gulping the oblong bulge. Peristalsis pushed her; and with each succeeding swallow, Dira's body traveled the tunnel of the neck, sliding inexorably down to the stomach below, later to slowly liquefy and digest. Predator and prey: the gambit of life and death transpiring before their eyes.

Soaking wet, she searched for what she needed; then Kalo spied it. A coil of rope was lashed to a cleat on the cabin wall. Hooking her thin arm through the rail as another enormous wave slammed over the boat, she washed along the banister to the bundled rope. While the Plesiosaur bounded alongside the trimaran swallowing its meal, the young girl, fingers stiff with cold, feverishly began untying the knots binding the coil.

It was a violent world of windroar and waterstorm on a raging green sea incensed with fury and power; above electric fire flashing fried, crooked fingers trailed by thunderclap percussions that rattled the deck. At the wheel, both men knew whatever it might be; they must do it now. Before the trimaran could reach the camouflage of blinding sheet-rain and pummeling hail, the marine reptile would attack again.

Reed yelled, "Take the wheel!"

Putting his shoulder and strength into it, "What are you going to do?" Ames yelled at the top of his lungs.

Over the wind, "Buy us some time," stepping through the spokes of the captain's wheel so he could stand without holding on, Reed leveled the pulse laser on the marine dinosaur alongside them.

Emerald sea, slate sky and gale force —then a flash from the dark— eclipsing wild wind and green water, was a whine and the blast.

The laser flamed, and almost instantly deflected by wind-swept spray the light pulses split into spiraling rainbow-torpedoes of color. Firelight red, sunburst orange, bright yellow, medium green, cobalt blue and umber violet, burst in tight parallel spirals of sparkling bright light —slamming into the dinosaur— then ricocheted disintegrating. He fired repeatedly; but even at close range the weapon could only stun the creature, not seriously wound it.

The laserlight effect was dazzling: pure, brilliant colors of helical flame flashing an absolute contrast to the gray-green darkness around them; explosive detonations of rainbow clouds. Startled —blinded— the marine reptile reared and swept away from the craft and acute splattering colors stinging its wet leathery hide. Momentarily it withdrew.

Trembling and still working the lashings with numb fingers, Kalo finally managed to untie the heavy rope bundle. Wasting no time she wrapped the free end around the cabin rail, tied a knot and jerked it tight, then swung the coil of rope around herself and behind her back looping it twice around the rail, binding herself against it.

"Nitana!" she cried out throwing the coil to the Renoloi archer. Nitana snatched the rope from midair, yanked it tight, wrapping twice, behind her back, then twice again, and tied herself in. Both warriors, now securely lashed to the cabin, were finally able to fight.

Wind blowing ragged, the sea growing wild; the archers were ready.

Still building and climbing, the sea rolled churlishly as it rose with an eighty-foot swell. Pushing upward on the wall of water the trimaran climbed almost vertically; but the pair remained standing, bound firmly to the rail, arrows nocked to their bows, riding the wave toward its crest. The dinosaur was coming; its neck a majestic 'S', rearing its head, arched to attack.

The storm's boundary darkness was almost upon them, impenetrable billowing black clouds. Water pelting them, thunder pealing then bursting overhead, electric skyfire of lightning, the clamor, the sound. Tremors vibrated through the boat, shattering inside their heads. Wizard-fingers of lightning ripping fiery holes through the sky, brilliant scattering flashes of intense ragged flame.

Stone cold and steady, Kalo drew her bow... following her target.

Dripping water, Nitana stood ready, steadfast, waiting a heartbeat more. She inhaled slowly; held it. From the corner of her eye, she could see them at the helm. Reed had quit firing; holding their breath, waiting and praying. He had bought them the time they so desperately needed... and now, two Renoloi archers would decide the final outcome.

The Plesiosaur came, jaws opening, teeth bared, its neck a blur of speed, a snake of snapping whip. Rain and wind howling through gray —straight and true two arrows spit forth— intercepting the snakehead in flight. Razor-sharp and lethal Nitana's arrow sliced through the throat then up into the head. Kalo's arrow spit through an eye, into the brain.

—*Tick,*

The sound that no one heard out there in a watery world when two arrows instantaneously crossed paths in its brain and ripped through the back of its skull. Tightly wedged inside the Plesiosaur's head the arrows lodged touching one another, forming an "X", and with eyes frozen wide the dinosaur's head and neck slammed a dead weight of thunder onto the deck then slid overboard dragged back to the sea.

In the tumult of storm—

Green Sea brought to a rage, thunder's roiling collisions, wind screaming wild wailing howls, lightning's flashdance of fire; they looked at the girl standing there, soaking wet and small, holding an empty bow.

Stone cold... Kalo, the warrior had returned.

* * *

Wind moaned…

…The sea seeming to breathe as it rose in an uprising swell, drawing their eyes to the bow. Then from above and behind lightning's crackle —*sudden static*— the megavolt's fiery blast splashing the peak of the mainmast and cross spar with a ball of luminous blue-white flame. A thunderclap shattered —*too close*— then slammed overhead —*duck*— avoiding the intense percussion pulse spray.

Split in half and torn from the mast the crow's nest spun wildly ripping the burning mainsail as the canvas flared in wind-stretched yellow flames. Twirling around the mainmast rigged with sheets and halyards, the cross spar got tangled in the ropes that held the burning sail —and reflecting the flames the storm boundary was there.

Before them the incredible wall of water continued to build, rising, climbing and piling above the mastheads, more than a hundred feet high. Towering awesome and deadly, tearing apart at the crest with billows of lather and webs of wind-driven spray. It was coming.

Thick sheets slit with streaks of gray, mountainous opaque thunderheads were pouring sideways rain, the wind turbulent and blinding, the howl of a hurricane gale. Lightning crackled within a rabid fireflash sky igniting swirling, angry charcoal-dark clouds. Extraordinary, rising before them.

The voyagers were helpless, at the mercy of nature's fury, desperately hanging on as the trimaran ascended with the monstrous cliff of nearly vertical ocean rise. Quickly extinguished by overspray the burning canvas was tearing from the rigging and disappearing in the wind. Seconds were agonizing. Tension wound tight as heartbeats of fear squeezed abdominal knots; all eyes transfixed on the overwhelming, unbelievable wave that would surely overpower and drown them. Towering over them, coming in —a peeling skyscraper of water— they all held their breath.

As—

Rolling and reaching it crested above them, then arcing and pouring it came crashing down in an incredible collapsing surge — *then the slam*— of pounding, rushing ocean colliding onto the craft, swallowing and submerging them within the gigantic monster wave. Sound swept to distortion as the craft went under a rushing freight train of crushing, gurgling bubbles and strangely twisted noises. Confusion and darkness. Everything cold. Everything wet.

Can't breathe...

Millions of tons of coursing, swirling water buried the trimaran pushing it under with the force of horrendous rushing waves. Compressing and pounding, all of it moving in streams of chilling slow-motion and liquid-filled shadows, an inexorable, unending underwater gale.

...Then, Air!

The water was gone, erupting from the backswell from under thirty feet of ocean —a kayak in wild water— the bow rose, both masts holding, gushing foresail and torn mainsail pouring overdeck. The boat boiled from the deluge like a submarine exploding onto the surface; and cold and trembling, again they could breathe. Made it through.

And again—

Another unbelievable wall of water came at them, but the steadfast trimaran refused to succumb to the sea's treachery as it climbed with the rise of the storm. Angled up, keels furrowing, riding the second phenomenal ascending green cliff churning white at its peak, they held on. Tenaciously the travelers clung to their craft, a toy boat being violently beaten, torn and tossed in a waterworld seemingly intent on killing them. Crawling, waves breaking overhead, the trimaran seemed to momentarily stand still —all eyes fixed— until all at once the craft surged for the crest, a deluge flooding her deck and washing astern —and in a torrent the wave was gone.

As the bow fell the ocean suddenly leveled to a scrambled, choppy surface pelted with hailstone-splatter dumped by a murky sky of flowing dark-fluid mist, pursuing the leading edge of the weather. The huge storm front was rapidly sweeping beyond them with floating hailstones now accumulating so quickly that the undulating water resembled an unstable ice flow, a facade of dissolving landscape inches deep with a racket of hail still coming from above. Lightning continued burning voids through the clouds, after-shadowed by explosive collisions of thunder.

Then abruptly the hail let up, floating away, atmosphere and ocean settling. With the storm front now behind them, the lightning and thunder diminished moving beyond in their wake, and the trimaran, carried steady by the wind, swept forward beneath a hazy gray sky... with fog moving in.

Eight were alive.

Vindicated seaworthy, the defiant craft had persevered. Although now two less in number and sustaining structural damage, the boat had brought them through the storm boundary's battering fury. With broken, jutting supports at the outer port and starboard hulls, both outriggers were lost to the sea. Rigging twisted askew on the mast, the disabled mainsail hung tangled and burnt, a sheet of canvas now partially draped from the boom, able to carry only a half-belly of wind. But their greater loss was two valiant Renoloi fallen victim to the savagery of a primitive world.

The sea, with its dark, mysterious green secrets lay before them, an undulating mantle of perpetually shifting unknown. Unsuspecting, the voyagers had not sailed through the storm, rather into the storm, the eye of the hurricane, an enigma of mystery.

Part of... *the Puzzle*.

Spanning twenty miles across, the storm now completely encircled them as the trimaran moved through drafts of chameleonic fog flowing over a seascape encompassed by the storm's boundary wall. In all directions an opaque veil churned with obscuring gray rain born in the towering thunderheads. They were inside a bleak ever-changing amorphous barrier rising miles into the sky. Remnant

Christians thrown to the tigers in a Roman amphitheater, an arena of ocean…

…And in this arena, the Tiger was one they could not have imagined.

With the intense immediacy of the storm past, for the moment the voyagers breathed a bit more easily. Ames and Reed stood aft at the helm, surveying the damage. Kalo and Nitana were still lashed to the starboard cabin rail with Tian, Seana and Tere huddled near them. And clinging to the portside rail was Quell, the eighth survivor. Without speaking Tian looked at each woman in turn, then to the men.

Reed finally muttered, "Shoot, when it rains… *it rains.*" Then looking at Tian he asked, "You guys okay?" Hair a tangle of wet strands, clothes still dripping water, she nodded. "Seana?"

"Yes," she said weakly glancing at Kalo and Nitana, next across the cabin to Quell, then back to him. With measured steps she and Tian moved aft while the men continued assessing the craft's damage.

Voice moderate, almost subdued, "We can sail, but we'll have to let off the main and reef it," Reed decided. "With only the foresail we'll lose speed and maneuverability; but the main's trashed, it's gotta' come down." Combing hair stuck to his forehead with his fingers, he let out a deep breath.

"All right," Ames agreed, "but first, let's take a minute." As he spoke, he reached, then wrapped his arm around Tian as she crowded against him. Reed turned, Seana waiting a couple steps away, frightened to the verge of tears. Opening his arms, she willingly accepted, and as he held her, she trembled.

Whispering into her ear, "We're okay," he assured.

Looking up at him, "I was frightened."

"Yeah, fuckin-a', me too." Then he squeezed her again.

"Reed," Ames interrupted gently, "take the helm." The younger man complied and Ames and Tian went forward to the others.

As Nitana and Kalo untied themselves from the cabin rail, Quell moved from port to starboard joining them. All together now, they hugged and milled speaking quietly, unraveling frayed nerves and pent emotions for friends taken by the perils of their journey. What had begun a mission to rescue a previously unknown Renoloi village had now become an odyssey of survival, the rescue team itself struggling for self-preservation. None had anticipated so many would die, and with only eight remaining, survival itself now loomed a daunting challenge.

Reed and Seana stood together at the helm, him guiding the trimaran to an as yet, unrealized destiny; Seana holding him close, her face pressed to his chest, Reed, ever watchful, scanning the seascape.

Out there—

In the distance a dark object gradually appeared between them and the far storm boundary wall. Wafting flows of fog and the perpetual rise and fall of ocean frequently obscured the dark mass; but he could tell it was enormous. Concentrating he tried to make out the shape and detail of it as it grew larger, coming closer. Standing silently, one hand on the wheel the other holding Seana, he watched... even larger, and closer.

Tian looked at Nitana. Words weren't necessary, her eyes conveying gratitude for the woman's decisive action and bravery; all knowing the pair had likely saved them. Their proficiency with the most primitive of weapons had again spared the lives of their companions warranting respect and appreciation. But in this world, it was just another day of surviving.

Tian turned to Kalo tenderly fingering the tooth dangling from the leather thong, then placing her open palm on the girl's cheek. Ames stood silently, proud, as Tian pushed Kalo's hair back over her ear with a gentle hand and asked, "Were you afraid?" Kalo nodded. Tian commended, "Renoloi warrior."

The girl understood. And touching her treasured necklace... she almost smiled.

* * *

A voyage of mystery...

...On a Green Sea, and More.

"Doc," Reed called out, interrupting, "you might want to see this."

"In a minute."

"No, you *really—should* take a look."

Half-irritated Ames returned to the helm as Reed tilted his head indicating the direction; and through the fog he saw it. "What— the...?" his voice trailing off.

Reed, hand on the wheel, bringing them ten degrees to port, said, "Yeah." Then, they could hear it; unheralded, the constant mechanical pumping of pistons becoming audible as it got closer.

The rusted steel-hull freighter bore down upon the trimaran as Reed altered course allowing the behemoth passage. The colossal vessel was thick with mud, encrusted barnacles and accumulated marine growth that evidenced the centuries since its demise. Adorn in tangled seaweed clinging to the deck and tentacle fingers of kelp that hung from the rails then draped to the sea, she wore a green bridal train that followed in her wake. Lost for eons, she lay still and silent on the bottom immersed in mud and mystery below, now rising again to transport cargo in an inexplicable, eerie afterlife. A ghost ship.

Unhurried, the dead ship sailed toward the voyagers. The mechanical noise of churning propellers and her submerged screws' methodic melancholy became louder, moving the ship on with awesome turbulence-whorls and trails of confused bubbles that rose from the sea's murky depths. Steady, the pounding drone of hammering pistons echoed from within the dark hollow giant, gaunt and empty as a downcast, soulless apparition... bound for nowhere.

She was a leper with gaping dark holes infecting her skin. Rotted and torn with the ravages of time, her hull's partially exposed superstructure of I-beams and steel was pitted, oxidized, and eaten away. Water entering near the bow washed heavily through the ship spilling out at the stern, then back to the sea. No law of physics could explain the empty vessel's ability to remain on the surface; less than supernatural or surreal, it should not be there.

Plying through green water and fog, coming upon the voyagers the freighter navigated an undeviating course, a ponderous gray and rust hulk bound with metal-dead skin. Then slowly, like strangers in the night, the vessels began passing one another, the huge freighter's bowels echoing a cadence of metallic-clang pounding, the symphony of her engine room's noise. When finally the gigantic ship came alongside the trimaran, its waves buoyed the smaller craft with undulating sideswells; and as the voyagers gazed upon the specter, mystified and uncertain, not one of them uttered a sound.

There was no one aboard the entire vessel. Even from below, looking up to the deck they all knew the ship carried no crew or passengers; the feeling of it, empty, dead, completely alone... a journey to nowhere.

—A foghorn blare,

Startling them, the sudden plaintive blast cut through the encompassing grayness as a solitary, painful wail —long, drawn and hollow as the ship itself.

—Then silence.

It ceased creating the impression it may have been their imagination; and with spooky-quiet still ringing in their ears they exchanged glances, not wanting to ask, wondering if it had been real. Each believed they had heard it, but couldn't be sure.

Reed focused on the bow trying to make out her name while Tian and the women studied the thing, never having imagined something so huge could even exist. To the Renoloi the trimaran was one of a kind; but this, whatever it was, was beyond comprehension.

Almost disbelieving, Ames watched it, and wondered. In places the rusted holes in her hull appeared dark and blackened concealing the interior within; but with others dim light was visible ferreting through from the opposite side. There was no logical way, no possible way it could remain afloat; yet there it was, rusted and hollow, dripping water and mystery, gray as death itself, wearing a bridal train of seaweed and mire dredged from the depths of an unexplored sea.

It was an eerie scene of shadow and mystery and creeping gray fog. She was vacant and despondent, from the deck high above them laden with tangled seaweed and layered blue mud, to the barnacle-encrusted hull that groaned with the contagion of leprosy, to her bones of exposed I-beams creaking moans of despair. The sullen mood of darkness lingered inside her hollow, lifeless carcass, almost whispering… ushering recollections of prose and poetry that stirred reviving dark and layered images of Edgar Allan Poe.

Undulating with the sideswells they all just watched, while around them crept an unsettling presentment. Pushing onward it moved passed the small craft with the churning propulsion of engines secreted within the darkness of her bowels, until again the foghorn blared, an empty bawl of lament —long, distant and removed from reality… the painful sound of a soup-fog night.

But more than that, it was the vessel's warning call to seafarers within a mystical realm, the dregs of eternity, and a cycle long gone. Almost as though a hushed voice was carried on the wind, they felt the sensation, the intimation… as though beckoning, *beware*.

Still the travelers watched, unnerved and baffled, until the rhythmic, dispirited mechanical pumping of pistons eventually diminished, absorbed by distance. A bridal train of seaweed following her into the fog, the ghost ship moved on pushing slowly through green water with secrets untold. Then silence again.

And as they watched the behemoth vessel, gray and dark as it was… faded. It was as though the curtain of fog had taken it away, or swallowed it up. Hollow, empty and dead, the ship disappeared leaving upon the surface a floating legacy of seaweed and kelp, green and tangled as the mysteries of the deep… on a voyage to nowhere.

Shaken, Reed slowly shook his head, then whispered, "Can't be."

Ames lay a hand on his shoulder, asking under his breath, "What's it called when several people imagine the same thing?"

"A clusterfuck."

"Be serious will you."

Turning, "You want serious?" Reed asked. "Could you make out her name?"

"No."

"'Marine Sulphur Queen'."

"So?"

Hesitant, "Nothing," he said, "forget it."

Seana: "Tell us."

"Yes, please," Quell entreated.

"No," he replied, reluctant.

But Seana persisted, "Please."

Serious, deliberate, Reed turned as he told them, "There was a place, a long time ago, in our world, a part of the ocean located between Florida, Puerto Rico and the Bermuda Islands. It spanned almost a half million square miles and spawned a like number of mariner fables, sailor's folklore for lack of a more appropriate term; others even claimed the region was haunted. There were pilots who avoided flying over it and some sailors feared navigating the waters within its boundaries."

Moderately, continuing, "On the seabottom lay a range of limestone mountains honeycombed with caves formed by unusual entwined waterflows created within overriding, swift, prevailing currents, and a floor of quicksand. The water depths averaged five thousand feet along the Florida Straits and varied from six to twelve thousand in the Northeast Providence Channel." All were listening now. "That channel abutted an expansive basin that lay below most of the area and was about eighteen thousand feet deep." He paused, thinking, they waiting until he continued again. "But therein also lay the Puerto Rico Trench, the deepest known formation and the greatest known depth of the Atlantic Ocean, estimated at thirty thousand-one hundred feet. Almost five miles deep."

Seana asked, "What does that have to do with us?"

"Deep water, very deep... perhaps nothing," he considered, "but then again... I don't know."

"What do you mean?" she prodded while the others quietly listened. Reed elaborated, offering additional circumstance.

"There were many tales, sailor's stories of bizarre magnetic fields that skewed compass readings, or unusual chemical components present in the region's seawater, alien abductions, the lost city of Atlantis, sea birds and seaweed where no land was within hundreds of miles, weird unexplainable lights in the night sky." Another slow breath, then he went on. "Conjecture even went so far as to speculate a time warp or wormhole or, if you will, a hole in the sky." Listening intently, Seana absorbed every word, almost involuntarily darting a glance overhead.

"Reed," Ames cautioned, "you're scaring them."

The man looked at his friend. "That's not my intention." Then chewing his lip, "But something's not right here. Something's going on."

"Reed," Ames whispered, almost a warning.

"Doc, supposedly—allegedly—over the years it was reputed to have amassed a score of at least one hundred-forty ships and planes, and a thousand lives lost within its waters. Whether it be called the Sargasso Sea, graveyard of the Atlantic, Davy Jones' locker, Devil's Triangle, or the Hoodoo Sea. Be it random occurrence, geologic anomaly, or supernatural phenomenon, something out of the ordinary was possessed of the Bermuda Triangle."

Ames insisted, "If you're leading up to something, or in some way making a point, what is it?"

"I am, and the point is this; you likely will recall the famous, albeit infamous Flight 19, in 1945. Five Navy Avenger torpedo bombers vanished in the Triangle without a trace. Never located, recovered, or explained."

"Yes," Ames conceded, "with the frenzy of notoriety and sensationalism, every newspaper and tabloid printing ink to a rag, connected with the occult, psychic or supernatural, at one time or another, made a point of exploiting the incident."

"1950, the American freighter, SS Sandra, gone without a trace; do you recall?"

Trying to remember, "No."

Reed nodded expectantly. "I'm not surprised. Wasn't nearly so famous; logged and documented as just another ship lost at sea."

Almost irritated, "Reed, what is your point?"

"In 1963 another ship went down with thirty-nine crewmembers —American freighter, four hundred twenty-five feet long. No distress signal, no wreckage ever found —no trace— lost at sea within the Bermuda Triangle." A careful breath, "Her name was the 'Marine Sulphur Queen'."

Ames blinked. "That's impossible."

"I know it's impossible." Reed's gaze then drifting to the fog where the freighter had been, "I have no idea where she came from, nor do I understand how we managed to do it... but somehow we've sailed right smack-dab into the middle of the Bermuda Triangle." Then back to his friend, "And only we could do something as foolish as that." Seana said nothing, unaware of the implication.

Ames lay a finger along his lower lip, mused, reminding, "But that was then... so long ago."

Crooking an eyebrow, "Yeah, I know. So maybe we've got the revised edition," Reed allowed.

Surprisingly, Ames grinned. "Aberrant fodder. 'Things that go bump in the night'."

Reed turned to Seana. "And you guys think I'm weird."

Seana didn't respond, and Ames only smiled. For a few moments no one spoke, catching his or her breath, hoping the worst was over.

That was not to be, their fate vacillating with mood swings of a fitful seascape. The wind was rising.

* * *

And minutes passed...

...The fog lifting, on a Green Sea, and More.

"Oh—no," Reed muttered studying the sky, "it's going green." Seana had no idea what his statement implied; but Ames understood. "Doc, take the wheel; I gotta get the mainsail down."

"It'll go faster together."

"Better not; if it hits you need to be here. I'll get the canvas — and besides," Reed reminded glancing over a shoulder, "you're too old to be climbing the mast. Shit, last time you fell out of a big-ass tree." Ames cracked a smile with his reference to the Pterosaur as

Reed stopped at the mainmast, looked up at the tangled rigging and fluttering canvas at the masthead, then back to him.

"What?"

"It is true that lightning never strikes the same place twice, isn't it?"

"'Fraid not; that's just an old wives' tale," matter-of-fact.

Grimacing Reed began climbing the mainmast, and as he did, Ames was sure he heard him mumbling something to the effect of, "Wouldn't you know, it's only a wives' tale. Just my luck."

Watching Reed climb Seana asked, "What does he mean, 'going green'?"

"A phenomenon that precedes tornadoes, when weather conditions are just right." She didn't seem to understand and he explained, "A whirling windstorm." That she understood. "The air becomes calm and the sky sometimes turns a peculiar, inky gray-green color when a tornado is imminent. You might even feel a tingling sensation on the back of your neck." He inhaled, let it out slowly surveying the sky. "Out here, it'll be a waterspout." Uneasy, looking at her, "Turning out to be quite a day, isn't it?"

Seana frowned. "I have had better."

The grin. "You're starting to sound like Reed."

From amidship Tian volunteered, "Reed, what can I do?"

Hanging on at the masthead he called down, "Secure those strips of torn canvas on the boom. Either cut them free or tie them down —rope, wire, anything— so they don't catch the wind."

Already at the main spar, "Aye, aye," she yelled back as the others quickly joined her on the cabin and the width of the deck. Seana started that way, but Ames, with a hand on her shoulder, stopped her.

"Better stay here." She seemed perplexed. "They can reef the damaged sail, but if the wind comes up too quickly I may need your help." That said, alongside him, she lay a hand on the wheel.

Some of the mainsail was burned from leech to foot, with parts of the sheet draped from the boom, lying overdeck like heavy fluttering canvas semaphores. The large strips were saturated making the task more difficult for the Renoloi to secure them. Standing on the cabin and deck and working as quickly as possible with a moderate but persistent wind, they gathered armloads of the brittle sailcloth heaving it over the boom and wrapping it around the spar. The chill and spray may have made them feel anxious and cold; then again, perhaps it was something else.

The rigging—

Fifty feet above Reed hung by his legs from the masthead, knife in hand, slicing and sorting the maze of twisted ropes. Separating, untangling and arranging the rigging, he quickly realized it would be necessary to free the broken cross spar that had been their crow's nest prior to the lightning strike. It was split in half and wound tightly within the boltrope near the sail peak.

The bounding momentum of the trimaran amplified by the height of the mast hampered his progress requiring he move carefully—a twenty-something nightclub's mechanical bull ride; although bucked from this ride there would be no foam mat to break his fall, only the deck or a churlish ocean below. As he dangled upside-down and glanced toward the sea a ludicrous thought sprouted in his head — *how long can you tread water?* Stupid —but it made him grin and work a little bit faster.

The boundary—

Skittering the storm boundary encompassing the voyagers, heat lightning shimmered as it ran the cloudbanks in a race of obscured white electrical flames. Like a mystical dance of fox and hound, vanishing pulses of static charge flickered then halted and backtracked, skipping the opposite direction. Quiet as a thought, overhead the display glimmered enigmatically presenting a special-effects lightshow within the churning amalgam of cumulonimbus sky, continuing to pale as mounting electrical shimmers silently skimmed. And the more the lightning flickered, the more defined the eye grew... and the more it went green.

On deck—

Securing the torn sheets of sail Quell, Nitana and Tere worked as a team on the cabin middeck from the mainmast, gathering and wrapping the largest strips of the stiff canvas around the spar. The trimaran, on port tack with the boom extended beyond the starboard side, pulled smoothly with the wind as Kalo, beyond them, was making fast remnant smaller pieces. And last, Tian was at the outer edge of the starboard deck standing on the severed outrigger, reaching as far as she could, trying to tie down strips toward the clew. Holding on with one arm draped around the boom, her progress was slow.

With the, *whoosh,* the trimaran rose on a swell pushing to the trough, then leveled with the ocean, gliding steady. Unexpectedly, again the sails relaxed, gently fluttering then went slack as abruptly the calm moved in. The wind hushed. The sea settled, and stilled.

An unnatural sensation swept over the water; an invisible flow companioned with skittering heat lightning flares, silently pulsating within the sky and boundary cloudbank. Overhead, Reed instantly sensed it, that uncanny feeling of, *uh-oh.* On deck, Seana now understood what Ames tried to explain, that sixth sense of awareness creeping in with spooky invisibility; that peculiar feeling, the tingling rustling of the fine hairs on the back of her neck, sensations singularly preempting tornado.

Ames studied the sky, gray-green and imminent. Still —absolute calm, air gone dead— soon-coming fury taking a breath.

"Starboard bow!" Reed yelled down, all heads turning, eyes focusing front and right; where wound with twisted intensity the funnel tendril emerged as it snaked free, a roarwind serpent spawned within the overcast of revolving, darkening sky.

A claw of gray rimmed with black, the whirlwind finger descended in a furrowing arch, its wall cloud inevitably reaching the ocean then tearing into the seascape with a blizzard of spinning liquid spirals that were drawn up and absorbed within the ceiling of cloud. Now moving more quickly, the tendril rose flinging spray, then stretched and reached again strafing the surface ripping explosive lather and green. Mysterious as Mother Nature, graceful as a twirling ballerina, destructive as a force-five three hundred mile-per-hour phenomenon wind; the first twister.

Pointing to their wake Seana squeezed Ames' arm as a second funnel descended behind them. With a broad spiral updraft cloud, it was much larger and nearer than the first, a charcoal helix of violent wind possessing a burgeoning roar. Plummeting into the ocean then erupting and dragging swirling water to the sky, the second waterspout was born.

Still clinging to the boom and fighting the sudden rising gale, "Port bow—" Nitana yelled. A third funnel appeared.

"There!" Tere screamed, pointing toward a fourth.

Caterwauling wind was rousing the sea, climbing, rolling swells capped with rabid lime-colored froth; seastorm was mounting around them. Bow rising and heaving, the trimaran plowed onward, her boltropes taut and whining with strain, the remaining canvas strips snapping loudly, resembled horizontal gray sheets of stretched flame. Increasing with intensity and power, searise was building to massive walls of pouring green incensed by winds that whistled an eerie lament of wailing ghosts from a long distant past.

Wind in their faces, dark ocean beneath them, it was waves and waterspray, wave after wave. The voyagers watched with abraded nerves as the churning canopy formed more tightening knots of twisted-cloud that constricted as they spun and momentarily hung in the sky, then weaseled and descended spawning three more spinning funnels. Now, there were seven.

Touching down then skipping wave to wave, the whirlwinds shifted and leaped in animated bounds, or slid the troughs like sidewinder snakes. Almost surrounding the voyagers, unpredictably the funnels tore water from the heaving seascape like spiraling belly dancers, leaving them little chance for escape. They were sea-green water serpents wound from ocean to cloud, skating erratically within the storm's boundary, tenaciously sucking volumes from the awakened sea then whirling it to a congealing dark sky.

The weather was becoming unmanageable, the storm's fury intensifying and expanding beyond their ability to cope; but the damaged sail was causing too much drag for the craft to maneuver, so Tian and the others fought to tie down the remaining canvas scraps. It must be stowed if they hoped to survive.

Rising then falling, rolling whitecaps vaulted the boat with intense liquid power as skreeking turbulence buffeted the deck with yowls akin to imaginary gale-goblins roused from the depths of those unseen dark waters below. While above, twisted gray-green and spectral, the canopy wound and tightened with superstition's lore… as the hurricane's eye manifest a hole in the sky.

Knowing they were running out of time Ames yelled over the roar of the wind, "Reed, how much longer?"

From the tangle of rigging, vaulting and sea-flung, he shouted back, "Almost clear." Waiting, Ames held his breath. "Ahoy below— spar coming down. Toss her away."

All hands anxiously watched as Reed lowered the broken cross spar from the masthead with a rope; but buffeted by the wind it swung wildly, rotating propeller-like as it swept to and fro. A trapeze artist's finale performing the spinneret's twirl, it was spinning too fast.

Nitana, Tere and Quell knew trying to catch it was too dangerous; so together they quickly gathered the last strip of torn sailcloth flinging it over the spar as it swept overhead, cinching and pulling the beam to the deck. Fighting the elements, the trio hurriedly untangled the snarl of canvas, untied the spar and heaved it overboard just as a mounting swell vaulted the craft almost vertically—then nearly airborne. The trimaran surged then collapsed; dropping from beneath them as it crashed back onto the sea.

Above, the whipsaw motion amplified by the height of the mast threw Reed off-balance —almost falling— grabbing the stayrope run from the peak to the clew supporting the outer end of the boom, where below, Tian was still working alone. The sudden pitch of the craft caused his foot to slip from the peg pinning his ankle between the mast and halyard, the rope ascending the mast used to raise and lower the sail.

Knowing he was in trouble, "Oh—great," trying to free his leg, now wedged between the halyard and mast. The wind was causing so much tension on the remaining halfsail that it seemed the only way to free his foot would be to cut the sail entirely free. That would leave him only the foot peg and stayrope run the span of the leech, from the top of the mast to the outer end of the boom. Akimbo above, "Well now this is gettin' just a little bit serious," —and another wet blast in his face.

"Reed—" Ames yelled from below. He didn't answer. "Forget the sail; it's too rough." Still no response.

"Reed, please!" Seana cried out.

She sounded worried —couldn't ignore that— grumbling, "Stuck and jumbled," so he yelled down, "I can't come down right now."

From below, "Why not?" her voice piercing the bawling wind.

From above, "I'm sorta stuck."

On deck they all looked uneasily at Seana, then Ames; then overhead as Seana admitted sourly, "Only *he* could manage something like that."

Equally anxious, but trying to cheer her up Ames reminded, "Well, he is *just* Reed," the only thing he could think of.

From Reed's vantagepoint the wind and sea were a mixture of smeared turbulence and ever-shifting green drenched by a sky pouring sideways rain. Then from the strata, at first barely visible, six more appeared as spirals of wound cloud emerging from the gray — rotating inverted spires of dark tendril and atmospheric distortion— and with their descent, the seven were thirteen.

Gathering strength and size the cyclone winds touched down savaging swells and tearing flesh from her breast, whorling and winding ripping ocean away. Seemingly surrounded, the craft cut skimming the mountainous flows, avoiding the evil pillars with dark liquid shafts of explosive wild water and wind-twisted spray. They were everywhere now.

The stage was set.

A storm boundary perimeter flashing fire and light —the coliseum. Thirteen roaring funnel spouts maneuvering and looming in revolving columns of destruction from seascape to sky —Roman pillars. A small boat and voyagers on a tumultuous sea —remnant Christians in an arena of ocean.

On deck—

Tacking, the trimaran sailed onward with steadfast determination slicing from one pouring searise to the next. Cutting at thirty knots, the able craft clipped swells and negotiated troughs as the man and woman thread a trail among the twisters closing around them in a field of watery confusion, a wet blizzard of stinging gray. At the wheel Ames and Seana were narrowly avoiding the shifting waterspouts as they descended then withdrew like leaping destructive sentinels; ever-twisting, tearing and whirling, lacerating the oceanic theater of voracious dark rolling water.

Through biting wind and slashing rain, the cyclone waterspouts seemed to pursue them   cheered on— enhanced by the howl of dark tempest and lightning's excited blue-electric fire. Companioned, the elements were deafening, unmanageable, intimidating. It was a devil's storm.

"Tian—" Ames screamed, "get amidship!" Clinging to the boom, soaking wet, she began inching along the spar; but a quartering swell rising on their starboard slammed onto the boat swamping the deck, washing her feet from beneath her. As she vanished in the wave, she flung a leg around the boom lost in white-green colliding water; then as the wash swept astern and the deck cleared, she reemerged, hanging on, facing the mainmast. "Crawl to the cabin!"

Fingers blanched, she began creeping along the spar toward the boat.

"Look out!" Seana cried. Ames saw it. A monstrous waterspout coming from starboard —unexpected— dark, cold-twisted ferocity directly in front of them. Then suddenly it stopped and backtracked blocking their path —looming— revolving and churning, resembling an erect charcoal cobra —waiting for them— preparing to strike.

Hoarse, Ames sounded, "Tian—hang on—jibe hooo!" heaving the wheel...

—*Crashing Spray!*

...Responding obediently and sure, the small craft veering to port, with the turn's momentum the starboard bow rising from the ocean as the masts tilted to port...

—*Swoosh!*

…Both booms and Tian rushing over the deck as the others watched helpless and dreading. Locked on, Ames watched her. Eyes closed, arms and legs clinging desperately, wet hair swept in a wave of the wind —she flashed past!

Reed, still tangled in the halyard, swooped down with the masts as the trimaran careened to the left almost onto its side, the outer port deck being overrun by rushing water —lower, and lower— until he was suspended virtually alongside the listing boat.

The boom bearing the remaining halfsail —and Tian— splashed into the sea on their port carving a torpedo furrow and thirty-foot roostertail of green and white spray. The halfsail, being beaten with spray and instantly gathering wind on the left side of the boat — bellied, filled, ballooned— *poomph!*

For just an instant Ames could see Reed beyond Tian, still caught in the rigging and clinging to the masthead, his eyes wide, an expression of complete disbelief clearly scrawled on his face. Then as the foresail filled the wind surged the trimaran forward again, and emerging from the ocean —booms rising, the craft righting itself— both masts climbing in a majestic arc as the starboard deck descended splashing back onto the ocean. The trimaran turning acutely, avoiding the waterspout…

—And above everything else, Reed's voice, being carried back overhead, resounding, *"…Peter Pan I'm—flyyinnng!"*

With the rising boom the roostertail vanished and Ames' chest collapsed in relief. Leeched to the outer end of the spar near the clew, Tian was still there. But respite was short-lived, no more than a breath. As the trimaran rose on the next mounting swell, passing on the left side of the dark-monster waterspout, another funnel attacked. It came for their bow blocking their flight, Seana gasping with horror, both heaving the wheel to avoid the roaring spire of whirling green water…

"Jibe *hooo!*"

—*Swoosh!*

…The booms gliding powerfully over the deck again, sending the craft veering to starboard, lancing around the first waterspout.

—Poomph!

The sails filled —then strained— surging them forward —no time to spare— correcting the wheel, shredding whorls of water and wild spray in the air. The trimaran sliced between them, both funnels so close that fish were visible whirling around within their spiraling, turbulent-liquid flames. Thunderous, the windroar was deafening, drowning out sound, the reverberating, twisting streaks of violent water revolving so fast they looked like grainy blurred rings resembling slowly backwinding, smeared, crawling veins.

Barely avoiding them, the tip of the boom clipped the waterspout on their right shearing a blast of white-blizzard confusion. Ames watched —a heartbeat of unknown— attention completely focused. The trimaran cleared, and Tian was still there.

The valiant craft launched from the swell, lancing above the trough and plowed underwater as the succeeding searise swept over her bow. Behind them the funnels crashed together, twisting into one another, shredding flung water to roiling opaque broth of wild flying ocean. Separating like warring gladiators, then colliding again: titans entwining and parting, repeatedly clashing like two giant water snakes in furious twisted combat rivaling for the prey.

Above—

Still pinned between the rope and mast, Reed mumbled, "Don't tell me the Devil's Triangle isn't real." Then pulling and straining again for all he was worth; he stretched the halyard from the mast *—just a little more—* and with a resolute effort jerked his leg free *—finally—* the sigh of relief. Looking over the panorama of choleric green water and wind, hanging on with vice-grip fingers, his eyes scrolled the ocean counting, "Thirteen tornadoes. Now all we need is a Halloween black cat."

Refusing to submit, the intrepid craft rushed onward defying a hostile, constantly moving, volatile world. Pouring in untold volumes the seascape rose and rolled turning dark green water and tattered wind-driven froth, conveying thirteen deadly twisters that seemed to pursue them. Spiraling down upon them then ascending again, their debris clouds tore the ocean to wet shreds, relentlessly closing in. Like phantoms of superstition and legend they were contortions of green-dark demons… from a world a cycle away.

Above them thunderheads within the shroud of black-angry canopy shattered and pealed forming a circular arena of impossible weather. Around them wind shrieked yowling like ghosts from a charnel somewhere, lightning leaping and streaking, highlighting the seascape with ragged fingers of vacillant flame. They were captured within a perfidious realm of churning darkness and treachery, a waterworld of turbulent mystery and green.

Eight gladiators in an arena of ocean…

…Only in this arena, the Tiger was one they could not have imagined.

Remnant Christians: Tian, arms and legs wrapped tightly around the outer end of the boom at the clew, Ames and Seana standing side by side at the wheel threading their course; Nitana, Tere and Quell hanging onto the cabin rail, Reed, up there in the wind, one arm around the masthead, one foot on a peg, a hand clinging to the stay rope. And a young girl standing alone.

Inside, Kalo felt it…

Powerful, mysterious, awesome, and deadly,

> …It was coming for them.

"Tian!" she screamed leaping onto the boom then crawling, trying desperately to reach her, slipping but refusing to stop. Tian watched, amazed, her eyes asking the question. "Climb in—now!" the girl screamed. "You must get away from the water!"

"Stay there, Kalo! The boom is too slippery." Tian was still unaware.

"No— get away from the water!" the terrified girl insisted. *"The voice inside!"*

The woman was stunned…

The wind howled,

> …And the Tiger *roared!*

Rising on a swell Reed was first to see it. "What—the…?"

Ames, below: "Oh—my—God…"

"What—*is*—that?" Seana stammered.

Before them the ocean wound green-and-dark to a tsunami mounted three hundred feet high. Incredibly, the seascape revolved pushing the surface to a circular rise five miles wide. Huge, unbelievable waves were rolling over one another cascading and crashing with nonpareil crushing strength, as though intent on swallowing the world.

Whitewater churning, colliding and pouring…

As it formed,

  …And the Whirlpool opened.

Unworldly, monstrous waves rolled inward crashing upon themselves, pouring and collapsing within the expanding vortex creating whitewater explosions that were absorbed and lost in spiraling volumes of green rushing sea. It churned thunderously and deafening, like looking down into the core of a tunnel, a slow-motion watery maelstrom of inexplicable origin. Revolving water spawned in the depths of this mysterious ocean was rising to the surface in an unimaginable rotating waterstorm with liquid gaping jaws...

  …The Tiger.

Overhead lightning flashed ragged fingers of fire —sizzling and crackling through swirling clouds of gray-green— spectral blasting firebolts of electrical light that illuminated…

  …A 'Hole in the Sky'.

Atmosphere rushed back setting free crushing thunder that exploded in the clouds, pounding the voyagers and rattling the world with climactic shock pulse detonations. Filled with pain and soaked wet with spray, wind moaned the song of mystery from a distant, past time; a drawn, incessant lament capable of infecting the mind, resurrecting ghosts and demons kept for too long, and hidden therein.

The ocean roared with supreme fluid power as the awesome whirlpool wound with green colliding water and unbelievable monstrous waves thundering through its vortex, drawing the waterworld in. And deadly, miles across, it churned everything within the roiling white-green destruction, spiraling down to…

  …The Graveyard of the Sea.

One small boat. Eight determined voyagers. A revolving world of supernatural dark water. They were helpless, being drawn by its might. Unable to escape the unparalleled fury of the anomalous whirlpool formed within the core of the circular storm, the trimaran was swept recklessly onward following the rush. Spellbinding and unexplainable it lay winding before them, awaiting their arrival, the trimaran and eight unsuspecting sojourners embarked on an odyssey of survival, and Mystery…

…And Green.

Agonizing, uncertain, Ames studied the phenomenon. "Sweet Jesus…"

While fifty feet overhead, not quite able to believe his eyes, Reed contemplated, "No black cat, but we got the next best thing…" swiping spray from his face, "a giant-ass whirlpool in the middle of the ocean —*shi-iit,* we're gonna die." Seeing —and still disbelieving— "This ain't happening."

Looking to the helm he saw Ames looking back at him with an identical expression: dread, confounded. Reed's eyes locked on the whirlpool again, calculating: *counterclockwise rotation.* Port would send them against the incredibly powerful, winding rush; their only possible hope was to try to sail around on the right side using the current to propel them along. His eyes clicked back to Ames; waiting. *"—Starboard!"*

Unquestioning Ames and Seana spun the wheel, the craft surging as it met a building seaswell, then veering to the right and plowing a determined course within the intense flow of ocean. Into a world of wind and rabid water, and tumultuous whitewater-green.

Swiftly the trimaran was helplessly captured within the pouring torrent catapulting the voyagers at sixty knots through whitewater rapids of incomprehensible, unparalleled magnitude. Monstrous waves were breaking apart above them, swells rising more than eighty feet around them, the sea's unmeasured power exploding and heaving up from below and crushing in from all sides. Pounded by water that was unbridled and furious beyond their wildest imagination, incredible waterflow and white commotion was so intense and unpredictable that the trimaran was being swallowed by waves and battered and drenched from all sides at once. Windstorm and liquid flame!

Tsunami swells launched the boat forward into a trough that compressed within the fore and aft swells, and rose then collapsed as the opposing walls of water crashed together swamping the trimaran under forty feet of thunderous crushing ocean. The entire seascape heaved up and the boat erupted as it breached from below, sails sloshing rushing water as waves poured overdeck. Defiantly the boat held its own, withstanding the worst weather possible to imagine.

They were terrified—three Renoloi hanging onto the cabin rail, Reed at the masthead, Kalo midway, Tian desperately clinging to the boom, Ames and Seana trying to avoid the waterstorm and guide them around the whirlpool's monstrous, turbulent rim. Wild water, and green.

Despite their uncompromising effort the overwhelming power of the whirlpool was unbounded beyond reckless, the valiant craft and courageous crew being drawn inexorably along with the spiraling torrent. Washes of whitewater blasting from everywhere jetted them violently through sheets of waves that poured from the sails in explosive backwash and runoff. The rushing vortex was the deafening roar of Niagara Falls pounding around them—intense, resounding, relentlessly mounting, all the while it was dragging them in.

As the trimaran battled to sail around the crest of the whirlpool, the voyagers perceived the mythical Tiger's manifest roar. They could hear it. They could sense it. But they could not see it. Originating somewhere deep below within the maelstrom's blackness of tightening whirlpool-sea, emanated an unimaginable, resonant, wind-tunnel-effect. Twisted and compressed, it came from the unseen depths, a howl that was so eerie it seemed to flow from its core. It was a roar of the wind spawned in a waterworld's storm, now violently escaping releasing long-imprisoned fury.

Circumnavigating the whirlpool's rim with the rush, the powerful updrafts began lifting the port bow from the descending wall of the vortex plunging the end of the boom, and Tian, into the streaking turbulence of water flashing passed. Submerged in green-liquid fury the spar pared a roostertail with Tian a knife blade slicing the sea, carving a whitewater furrow that immediately closed—relentlessly dragging her, slipping along the boom.

Extraordinary and unceasing the ocean's turbulent force pulled the desperate woman with unrelenting power, drawing her toward the clew at the end of the boom. Battered with waterspray she couldn't hang on, the wooden spar too slippery for even her determined grip. One hand reaching for Kalo with terror defined in her eyes as the whitewater rush swallowed her to the waist; she was slowly slipping away.

Still being drawn into the rushing wall of frenetic water, in a final act of desperation Tian let go of the boom seizing the stayrope spanning the leech from the clew to the peak at the masthead. Now submerged almost to her breasts she was inexorably being dragged into a waterwall of flashing seastorm. Stricken, she clung to the rope; but this was a struggle she could not win, the ocean was overwhelming and would quickly exhaust her. She was already tiring; now, seconds were precious.

Horrified, Ames couldn't help; too many lives were at risk. Should he or Seana let go of the wheel they would all be dead in an instant. Desperate to save her leader, Kalo knotted her legs around the wrapped canvas reaching as far as she could; but with seaspray and tears in her eyes, she knew Tian was also beyond her small ability to help. More than deafening the roar of the vortex drowned out all sound, a trillion tons of green water pounding and crashing, blotting everything else out.

In a glimmer of reasoning and grit, above Reed analyzed, calculated, and said, "No—way—not today," then acted.

Unhesitating, he cut a canvas strip left over from the sail, flipped it over the stayrope grabbing it with his left hand, sucked a deep breath, then leaped slashing through the halyard collapsing the remnant-shredded main. It plunged down toward the deck clearing the leech of obstruction as it went, and like Errol Flynn in a high-seas swashbuckler, legs spread wide Reed rappelled the run of the stayrope, to Tian clinging desperately below.

He landed, hard, straddling the boom with an awful pain that shot through his groin. But there wasn't time for pain. Reaching out he seized Tian's wrist and said, "You are not alone," conviction defined in his eyes, "we are in this together."

Terrified, Tian's eyes blinked profound amazement and gratitude, letting go of the rope and grabbing his wrist with both hands — memory flashback— they had been here before —the Forsaken Land— the impassable swamp of 'Black Water' where his sheer strength and will to prevail had saved her. She trusted him. He would not fail, would not let her die. She believed in him. He was her friend.

Holding the stayline of the leech in his left and Tian with his right, Reed flexed and pulled, his powerful arms and chest pumped solid with strength, adrenaline and blood. The test: his muscle and will against a violent green sea flashing passed as a smear of savage, untamed water intent on taking her. Gritting his teeth, face grimaced with strain, the man fought for her life; chest quivering, arms straining, gradually gaining by inches... slowly prying her from its clutches.

Thunderous wound-water roared as shrieking wind howled from deep within the core bemoaning netherworld groans spawned somewhere below. Together they wailed a spectral lament manifest as a drawn, hollow, discursive foreboding moan; a world of wind and rabid water, and tumultuous whitewater-green.

Seastorm raging around them, an incredible sea wall risen against them, everywhere they looked was dark water and tumult—the roar of wind, the whirlpool drowning out sound. It was overwhelming and deafening—ragged white flames of lightning searing wires through a furious gray-green of sky.

Life and death and desperation, clinging together, Tian and Reed heard it. From the howling depths of the vortex abyss it came as an unnatural, ominous, guttural whisper...

...Something yet Unfinished.

Their frightened eyes locked together with unmitigated disbelief. And drawn with the tremendous strain, the stayrope failed —*Snap!*...

Swallowed, both disappeared—just gone.

The boom was empty.

Transfixed with terror, Kalo watched.

Horrified, Seana screamed!

...Nothing there but whitewater and green.

Suddenly the whirlpool and cataclysm wound more quickly and tighter, constricting as it began collapsing and crashing together deep below with explosions of unbelievably monstrous waves colliding onto one another. Then the sudden incredible sinking rush of collapsing ocean, and a tremendous uplifting heave —sealing itself closed— then exploding with a furious roar like a depthcharge blasting upward from the core.

Ames saw it coming, and at the same time with inhuman strength cranked the wheel violently to starboard —into the whirlpool's waterwall of liquid flame! The trimaran veered into the rabid, rushing sea of the whirlpool wall, plunging into the maelstrom —submerged, engulfed— disappearing within the furious confusion of water.

Time suspended...

...Seconds ticked past.

Then explosions of water and noise, bow pointed up targeting the sky, vaulting from below the craft breached and went airborne. Blistered wind howling underdeck thrust it from vertical —and backward— it broached and capsized crashing upside down onto the ocean in a slow-motion collision of carbon-fiber, whitewater and canvas.

The gigantic whirlpool closing in an immense rising mound of sea, then heaving, collapsing the entire core —and exploding— beyond the surface, two miles high! An incredible climb of waterspout blasting into the atmosphere then shattering in a windswept canopy that rained torrential deluge for miles. Backlash of spray was flung into the sky, scattering with the wild wind and raining down as a cascading pour veiling the clouds and a mysterious waterworld, until finally descending...

The searise settling but still churning, everything gray,

...And after the roar of the impact, mist filtered away.

All that remained were garbled, gurgling sounds of water filling their ears in an abstract world blurred with the confusion and disguise of underwater sensations—echoes, rushing bubbles and distorted boils of liquid commotion and froth. Everything tangled —all of it. Confusion and chaos —everywhere. While down there, somewhere, Ames tumbled end over end, the cold ocean burning his searching, horrified wide eyes as inside his chest swept a twisted knot of terror...

...And his silent scream, *"No-ooo!"*

Falling, tumbling, rolling over and over, absorbed in the rush of a deep swirling mystery and impenetrable abyss of a black emerald world of...

...*Dark Water and Green.*

CHAPTER SEVEN

He had sand in his face…

…Warm with the sun's radiated heat; but it made his eyes burn, irritating and painful. He didn't want to move, to open his eyes, get up, too much confusion still scrambled in his brain. Reality waited, impatient and nagging, persistent. It was there alongside awareness, both calling his name. Inside his head he answered, *leave me alone*.

"Mr. Ames, please... do not be dead. Please, wake up," uncertain and anxious Kalo's poignant, hushed words pleaded into his ear.

"Leave me alone."

"Mr. Ames, you are alive!" her voice wavering with urgency and relief. Shaking him again, her delicate trembling fingers full of wet black-leather shirt, "Mr. Ames, it is me, Kalo."

Awareness had him; he was conscious. "Where are we?" his eyes slowly opening, squinting; they fluttered irritated by both sand and sunlight.

"I do not know."

"The others?" At least he and Kalo were still alive.

"I do not know; so far, I have only found you." As she spoke, her eyes scanned the beach and treeline searching for the others. Ames tried to get up but was held fast almost completely buried in the sand, then smoothed over with a receding tide and left submerged to dry.

"I can't move."

"It will take only a minute." On her knees, feverishly she scooped flinging sand between her thighs, a beautiful flaxen-hair puppy digging him out. A moment more and he could sit up; then quickly pulled his legs free.

Brushing himself off they sat together on the beach for a moment, surveyed their surroundings: an azure sky laced with cirrus clouds, a blue ocean, her breast rising and falling in the tranquil undulation of liquid breathing, and tracing the beach margin, a lush jungle of chlorophyll-green. This was a quiet place with simple, placid sounds, the wispish rustle of wind through verdant trees and the repetitious wash of waves burbling onto the beach, followed by the swish of retreat. The wind would be there, then vanish; but the waves were regular, constant.

Kalo was nervous, aloof; and sensing her apprehension Ames drew a breath assuring, "They didn't all drown." She looked at him, tried to force a smile; but it was more than she could manage. Once more she longingly gazed down the beach, then turned back to him with vacancy in her eyes. Withdrawn, she didn't respond. "Kalo, they aren't all dead."

The girl blinked, "I know," then told him, "I only sense death a little. What I feel more is—space. Something cast away, abandoned."

"What do you mean?"

"In here..." placing her hand to her breast, "I feel something lost, empty." Frustrated, she shook her head. "I cannot explain."

"It's okay," he said, "let's go find the others." Rising, they finished brushing themselves off as best they could; then looking around Ames considered, "Which way?"

She, almost involuntarily, "This way," offering her hand, he accepting, gently wrapping his fingers around her delicate palm. Together they started down the beach, hand in hand.

* * *

A short time later, walking...

...The sand beneath their feet lay a smooth, unblemished table of light brown. Storm tide had washed away all traces of trespass upon its ever-shifting mantle leaving it undisturbed all the way to the treeline. Not a telltale footprint except theirs; one set large, one small. They walked together, not talking, constantly watchful, searching. Within a few miles the young girl detected inconsistent movement at the water's edge, perhaps a fish flopping with the waves as they pushed ashore. She didn't speak, instead squeezed Ames' hand and pointed.

Both immediately ran to the fish and dropped to their knees in the water, hoping against hope, but both well aware they were too late. It wasn't a fish, rather a woman's left arm, the rest submerged beneath the seawater and sand. They scooped purposely quickly uncovering her left leg, then the right, her torso, and finally the head. Her eye sockets, nostrils and mouth were all tightly packed with gritty sand that obscured her identity. Still digging her out and at last touching the body, Kalo immediately let go and covered her mouth with her hands, the reality of death so close and wretched almost making her gag. Sometimes death could be impersonal, uncaring, and gruesome. And at times, emulating death, life could be the same.

As Kalo writhed and trembled trying not to vomit Ames carefully pulled the corpse from the sand. Once free, he lowered the body and the next incoming wave washed the skin clean. Death glared; the anguished expression, eyes wide with terror, skin drawn tight, stretched and waxen, mouth agape in horror.

Inside, Kalo felt it… heard it. Quell's final scream.

Realization seized her and she vomited into her hands clasped over her mouth. Projectile vomitus squirted from both sides of her face and into her nose. Coughing, gagging, vomiting and choking she sprang to her feet and ran a short distance then dropped to her knees into the sea plunging her face into the cold water, crying and spitting, trying to wash away the horror, the sadness, and her shame. She wanted so desperately to be strong just as the others always seemed to be; and with each new test of her tensile, she believed she failed. But the girl was still young, with lessons to learn.

As she coughed her frustration and tears away a muscular supportive arm wrapped around her, holding her by the waist. Ames was there.

The girl looked up to him, reluctantly, uncertain. "I am sorry." For a moment he said nothing, eyes fixed on hers, thinking. Finally, he cupped a handful of water and gently washed a bit of foreign matter from her cheek.

At length, "Are you all right now?" he asked.

"Yes," a soft reply; then she continued, "I am sorry I am so weak. It makes me feel ashamed."

Considering, Ames chewed his lip, then replied, "Kalo, when something like that does *not* bother you... only then, should you be ashamed."

On their knees in the surf with water lapping around them, the girl looked to the man for strength and reassurance, his strong hand still holding her by the waist. Physical contact —and their eyes connected. Inside, Kalo felt it; an intense, incredible pain within her. The anguish was so acutely focused it burned, so vehement and severe it sent an overpowering chill through her.

The vision: *Tian and Reed and the whirlpool wall.* The flash: *both vanishing, being swept away in a rush of green water.* The pain: *more than she could bear.* Startled, the image caused her to jerk and his hand slipped from her waist, and instantly the picture, emotions and sensations were gone. The hurt and pain were lost.

"You okay?"

"Yes," she murmured, "please, just let me wash my face." Cupping her shaky hands, she did.

"You're sure?" he asked again. Kalo trembled, shivering while the chill flushed away, acknowledging with an abrupt nod. Sadly the man told her, "We have to bury Quell."

He rose; helped her to her feet, then turned walking to the drowned Renoloi. Kalo momentarily watched Ames, his back to her as he lifted Quell's lifeless body and carried her toward the trees. It was then that Kalo realized what she had felt; that incredible, burning pain was not lost... it was his pain. It was somewhere deep inside him, sequestered but constantly burning, a torment of heartache and loss so agonizing it was not possible to console, only suppress.

It could not heal, would never go away.

* * *

The afternoon sun now waning...

...Quell's body was laid to rest quietly, respectfully buried in a small clearing within the jungle. Ames and Kalo returned to the beach, both hoping possibly their companions would be looking for them and might have passed their way. Expectations diminished to disappointment—no tracks in the sand.

The man and girl decided to continue their search until sunset, make camp wherever they might be, and resume in the morning. Until they were certain, neither was willing to abandon hope that others had survived. They traveled several miles along the shoreline and shortly before sunset came upon an estuary.

There was the trimaran, beached, her sails ragged and torn, windblown fluttering strips of canvas. Both outriggers were broken off, but the triple hulls, half submerged in sand, were still intact. She rested aslant, tilted over the beach much the same as the first time the travelers laid eyes on her. Battered and scarred the defiant craft had withstood the storm's fury and refused to surrender to the treacherous sea. Now again, heaved by the watery mantle she was a castaway, flotsam banished with the storm tide, lying silent, still, and patient; but destined never to make the return voyage.

The pair halted, then approached slowly, hoping.

"Our boat," Kalo whispered nervously scanning the area, dreading, almost expecting to discover more dead. Involuntarily, subconsciously, her eyes searched the water's edge; and they moved closer. There were no footprints in the sand; nor were there any flopping fish.

His voice startled the silence. "Ahoy to the boat," and in a wink, two heads popped into view from behind the trimaran.

"Mr. Ames!"

"Nitana, Tere—" Kalo blurted, rising to the balls of her feet with thrilled disbelief; then darting a glance as though to assure him, *they are alive*. Finally able to hope again Ames smiled, and they ran to join the Renoloi. With waiting arms both women embraced the girl.

Tears of relief. "I am sorry," Kalo apologized, "a Renoloi warrior does not cry."

Beaming, holding her, Nitana leaned close wiping Kalo's cheeks with the side of a hand admitting, "I believe there are times when it is allowed." She quickly lowered her head wiping tears of her own, then still smiling, looked at the girl again.

"I agree," Kalo said, tears gathering anew; and she flung her arms around Nitana's neck.

"Others?" Ames inquired, placing a gentle hand on Kalo's shoulder, directing his question to Tere.

Shaking her head, "Not yet. We believed we might be the only survivors." With renewed hope she beamed, "I am so happy to know we are not."

Nitana rose as Tere spoke, tussling Kalo's hair then turning to Ames. "We thought it best to camp here tonight, and perhaps our fire would be seen."

Ames looked at Kalo. "Lots of driftwood. A big fire."

Elated, "Yes, a big fire!"

* * *

Hours later, the bonfire…

…A blistering, crackling cacophony illuminating the beach converting driftwood to saffron light, ocher flame and ash; its amber aurora visible for miles. The four sat quietly, resting, their foresight of stocking the trimaran with provisions and water providing recompense—the grasshopper and ant. Now fed and exhausted they were wearing down, sleep deprivation extracting its toll.

Leaning against the hull of the boat as Tere and Nitana drifted to sleep, retrospectively Ames observed. Kalo was seated solemnly beside him and was worn out, but resisted, struggling to stay awake. Her head drooped, chin to her chest, then suddenly jerked with a start, her eyes opening again. Ames rose, shuffled to the fire and piled on enough driftwood to provide hours of fuel, and after arranging the logs to his satisfaction flipped his poking stick into the flames and returned to his place beside the girl. Reseated, he leaned against the boat once more, gazed through tired eyes over the vast ocean, and sighed.

Another hour passed. Nitana and Tere slept without stirring as the young girl tried to remain awake beside her friend. At last, thoroughly spent, she slumped forward and slumber crowded upon her. Ames' arm gently enfolded her, guiding her over, laying her head in his lap. Weary, eyes fighting to remain focused, she looked up at him, his face worn, his soul exhausted. She began to protest, but he hushed her with a finger upon her lips.

"You sleep. I'll watch," he whispered.

"Will you wake me for second watch?" He nodded indicating he would; but she suspected he would not. Just before sleep overcame her, her head cradled in his lap, Kalo felt it; the intense, burning sorrow, a ragged tear cloistered within the fabric of his soul. *Tian, Reed.*

The tedium of night ticked away with long hours of waiting and the uncertainty of not knowing; hope diminishing, fading just as surely as the darkness would blend to greylight. The only sounds were sporadic breezes, cool and moist, with an occasional transient fluttering through trees. The fire still burned, steady now but diminished, no longer a boisterous crackle, rather constant and even, a beacon; only, *pop*, now and then. Last, the unending rhythm of water pushing ashore with the sea's continuum of gentle waves burbling onto the sand then whisking back to the mother, mysterious as the siren's song.

The sounds of the night absorbed within his soul, Ames sat quietly and thought, hoped, waited, and prayed. He did not move, fearful he may wake the frail girl lying curled next to his leg, her head cradled in his lap, her pillow. Finally, the soothing melancholy, solitude, night sounds and exhaustion blended magically within his head and he drifted to sleep. His final conscious, fleeting thought, drifting... *Reed, my friend, Tian, my love ...where are you?*

* * *

Bare feet padded with faltering irregularity…

…Heels leaving slight impressions and toes scuffing sand. From a far distance she had seen the amber glow of the signal fire and pursued it all night, following the coastline. Exhausted and injured she staggered into camp.

Her stumbling, uneven gait, out of harmony and inconsistent with the mood and rhythm of the night sounds instantly alerted Nitana's trained ear. The woman swept to her knees, bow drawn taut with a fluid motion that molded grace and warrior to a single concept. Nitana's fleet movement woke Tere and Kalo, also onto their feet, prepared. Sighting along the shaft of the arrow Nitana recognized the newcomer who stood slouched and misshapen, her shoulder humped in contortion, neck tilted and drooping to lessen the pain.

"—Seana!"

Nitana's voice promptly woke Ames, his eyes opening in time to see the woman crumple to the sand. Almost as soon as she had fallen the four were with her, surrounding and hovering to lend her aid and comfort.

"Gently, gently," Ames coached as they gingerly rolled the woman from her face onto her back. Kalo rose quickly and disappeared while Tere tenderly brushed sand and hair from the injured woman's face.

"Water," Seana murmured. Kalo appeared with a waterskin as the word was spoken. Ames noticed but didn't say anything, believing the girl had simply anticipated Seana's request; and holding the pouch so Seana could drink, Kalo's furtive glance drew his attention, but she said nothing. While she sipped the water Ames surveyed— primary medical assessment. When Seana finished drinking Kalo stepped back and Ames leaned forward focused on her left shoulder, her most obvious injury.

"Where do you hurt?"

"My shoulder."

"Anywhere else?" Weakly she indicated, *no*. He explained, "It's dislocated. I'm going to put it back in, and it's gonna hurt like hell when I do."

She coerced a feeble smile. "No worse than it does now."

Ames rose tractably taking her left hand, as unnoticed and carefully he planted his foot against her ribs below her armpit. Mischievously, to distract her he told her, "Don't count on it." Then the smile and a wink.

"I am…"

He jerked, and the —*pop*— sounded like pain —and she moaned. Without hesitating he gently lay her forearm across her belly as the three Renoloi, unsuspecting of his quick procedure, all winced when he acted. But none questioned him.

"Be still now," he told her removing his leather shirt and slicing it up the front with his knife, then cutting a wide strip from either side. Next, he gently tucked one strip under her arm and tied the knot securing a sling. Together they helped her sit up, he using the second strip as a wrap around her, below her breasts, thereby securely immobilizing her arm and shoulder. They carefully helped her to her feet.

A bit more comfortable, Seana grimaced, "It does not hurt so badly now."

Visibly impressed Nitana asked, "Where did you learn to do that?"

Plainly, "Dislocation—sling and swath—EMT-101." The Renoloi hadn't the vaguest inkling of what he meant and he considered explaining, then reconsidered deciding, "Not important. Just remember it." All assured they would as he slipped his cut-up shirt back on.

"Your shirt," Tere commented, believing it to be ruined.

Chest exposed, Ames tugged on its bottom inspecting it with satisfaction, then looked at her bumping his eyebrows. "Now it's a vest." They had never seen a vest before. And prefatorily changing the subject, "Seana, let's get you to the fire." The woman moved slowly, her pain no longer debilitating, but still persistent; and Ames was aware if there were torn ligaments or tendons it could be a long time before her injury might heal. As they mindfully seated Seana near the fire Kalo brought her food attentively kneeling alongside her. Ames mulled their plight; *circumstances could be better.*

Seana's eyes tallied as they scanned. "Reed, Tian, Quell?" Her eyes fixed on Kalo's. The girl remained silent.

"We are not certain," Nitana replied.

Not saying anything at first, Kalo looked up at Ames; then saddened, turned and told them, "Quell is dead." The Renoloi looked at her, then the man, then again the girl. "Mr. Ames and I found her." Ames confirmed the disclosure with a somber tip of his head.

Trembling, Seana touched Kalo's wrist. "Reed…Tian?"

"Unaccounted for," Ames quickly answered.

Seana turned to him. "So they could be alive?"

"Yes, but…" He hesitated, torn by the fear etched in her eyes, moved almost to tears. "Yes," he said at last.

Seana knew. "But you believe they are not."

Ames replied staunchly, "They could be alive." And looking down, pushing sand aside with his foot, to Seana, "Get some sleep; you need to rest." Focusing upon each in turn, he tried to smile but couldn't, then said, "At daybreak we search."

* * *

First light…

…Azure and clear; the bonfire vigil had not brought them in and the others held little hope of finding Tian and Reed alive. But without proof none were willing to forfeit them; today the search would begin.

The five gathered water and jerky from the trimaran, enough for several days. Marooned on the beach many miles beyond them, Seana had followed Ames' and Kalo's tracks; therefore, the travelers believed their best hope lie along the coast where none had yet been. That would be where they would search.

Pensive, Ames stood alongside the boat, his gaze wandering over the vast seascape; unending movement, the rise and fall of perpetual motion. Still weak but able to travel, Seana hobbled from behind him, her injured shoulder immobilized with the leather bandage restricting her breathing; however, determination compensated for that. As she shuffled closer the man turned with a smile and concern. "How do you feel?"

"Very sore, but much better than yesterday. Today I am not alone." Ames clearly grasped her meaning; life being difficult when isolated. Not responding, he chewed his lip, took a deep breath, then sighed. The others were approaching. Anxious, needing reassurance, to at least hope, Seana asked. "Do you believe they are alive?"

Slipping a careful arm around her waist he drew her a bit nearer, kissed her forehead, leaned close to her ear, and whispered, "There are always possibilities."

Able to hope, Seana smiled. "Yes... always."

The others joined them. "You're Tian's second, Nitana; what do you suggest?" Ames asked.

Agreeing, the woman replied, "True, I am her second; but you are her first. We follow you." Her remark surprised him. He hadn't realized their influence, the change he and Reed had already begun; and as his eyes traveled from Nitana, to Tere, to Kalo, and Seana, the validity of the 'Prophecy of the Strangers' was beginning to unfold. They were waiting.

Intent, "Nitana, Kalo, assume point. Tere and I will follow with Seana. Cover as much ground as you can and return at intervals to keep us informed." Concurring with his jungle savvy, Nitana smiled approvingly and Kalo offered a 'thumbs-up' as both whisked away flipping sand with their feet. Slipping his arm around her and wondering, Ames looked at Seana. "Where do you suppose the girl learned something like that?" referring to the hand gesture.

Seana was able to smile, a real smile. "Well, he is *just* Reed."

With that, they followed.

* * *

Traveling the shoreline...

...For several hours the trio followed the beach, a wide thoroughfare of sand laid forth by the ocean until it narrowed abruptly margined by nearly vertical cliffs and tangled trees and liana. The abutting landscape was overgrown, absorbed in lush undergrowth of bracken; and the terrain rose sharply, the thicket of jungle concealing ragged peaks shaded and woven within the greenery that crept over them then disappeared in unseen regions on the other side.

Mountains, volcanic in origin, jutted as sheer formations of obsidian, basalt and granulated lava, heaved up thousands of feet with their birth, towering stately and now mantled, reclaimed and assimilated as though untouched since the beginning of time. This was a beautiful place, the farthest reach of their journey across an unexplored world. But there were no birds; peaceful, quiet, deceiving. This was still a primitive world.

Periodically Nitana or Kalo would return from the jungle, from around the next bend or inlet along the water's edge, to report. Their news was repeatedly unencouraging but succinctly punctuated with hope; and again they would be gone pursuing their lost leader and Reed. Undeterred, unfaltering, they searched.

Hours linked in succession; the day grew longer.

Seana's injury taxed her strength, and the persistent pain tormented her until weary and hurting she asked for a moment's rest. Tere and Ames immediately stopped, gently helping her to sit down. Tere's eyes constantly searched the beach and jungle; Ames always listening, hoping to hear, *hey doc, I'm baaack.* But the voice and words were only in his head.

They sat quietly for a while, until Seana, having spent some time considering, finally spoke. "Mr. Ames, you and Tere should go on ahead and I will catch up later." Tere's expression was surprise. Ames' was annoyed.

"What?" Tere remarked, darting a glance to the man.

"Don't *even* think it," he scolded.

"But I am slowing you down." Neither responded, merely shaking their heads refusing her suggestion. "Please…"

"—No," he told her, "we will *not* leave you behind."

She writhed with the pain in her shoulder, and fighting back tears admitted, "I cannot go on." She looked down, away, in defeat.

Placing a hand on her cheek, turning her face to his, love in his words, "Then I will carry you." That said, he scooped her into his arms, lifting her as he rose to his feet.

Draping her right arm around his neck and offering an exhausted, grateful smile, she asked weakly, "Why?"

Seriously, earnestly, "Because you are my friend... and Reed is my friend." Without saying anything more she tenderly kissed him on the cheek and lay her head against him. And as the three continued down the beach, Ames carrying Seana, Tere walking alongside them, very softly... Seana cried.

* * *

An hour later...

...Fleet, rushing toward them, feet a smear of speed, not detouring, leaping over driftwood riprap, a gazelle in flight; then running again, sandspray at her heels Kalo intercepted the three. Breathless, her small chest heaving, bouncing with excitement, both body and words conveying their discovery; Ames and the women anticipating something of significance.

"In the sand," she blurted out, "footprints in the sand!"

"How many?"

"One."

"How far?"

"Two miles."

It was a brief two miles, with Kalo and Tere leading the way, joining Nitana where she waited patiently but nervous, kneeling, scrutinizing. Someone had walked the jungle's edge where it blended to sand with the beach, then stopped as though watching their backtrail, and finally gone inland following an obscure path.

When Ames got there he let Seana down lightly and crouched to study the spore. All were faint impressions; none clearly defined making it difficult to ascertain what the implications might be. Apparently, the individual had milled around for a while, as though considering, then followed the trail inland.

Nitana spoke first. "Too large for Tian." Ames looked from the tracks to the Renoloi with an introspective nod.

"But why would Reed go into the jungle," he wondered, "to get to higher ground? Certainly he'd know we would be searching along the shoreline."

"I do not know. This makes no sense."

Stepping forward alongside Kalo and Seana, Tere asked, "Do we follow?" first looking to Nitana, then Ames. Concomitantly, both agreed they should.

Quietly leading the way Nitana disappeared into the dense shrublayer. Tere followed her, and when Ames turned to help Seana she weakly waived him off with a hand indicating she could walk.

After Seana and Ames entered the jungle carefully threading their way along the thin trail, Kalo lingered a moment, then quickly knelt beside the tracks placing her fingers in one of the faint impressions; and inside, she felt it—*unfamiliar*, something she did not understand. Still wondering, she silently, almost invisibly followed her companions. Accustomed to moving unobtrusively, falling back, she widened the interval between them, a nymph blending within the emerald mood and flow of the jungle. First she was there —*blink*— she was not.

The group followed the trail for several miles, proceeding cautiously, alert to the slightest sound or atypical motion, the reality of unknown dangers looming in their every thought. This new territory, unexplored and unclaimed, could likely be dominion for their antagonist, the Night Hunter. Two bows and one spear against the arachnid armor of the obsidian horde would mean certain annihilation of their small team. Remnant voyagers transformed… Darwin's terminology, "Survival of the Fittest" …now the desperate few.

At last the dense undergrowth became so tangled Nitana resorted to crawling on hands and knees, examining every leaf and stem, brushing aside shed vegetation and humus with her hands; carefully probing, searching for sign. Her concentration was so focused on keeping the trail the others were compelled to watch over her, maintaining a guarded defense. The longer Nitana tracked, following the spore, the more entrenched her suspicions and conclusions. Reed did not have the ability to so carefully conceal his passage, nor would he try. A man in search of his companions would want to be found.

At length the team entered a clearing, very small, almost carved then compressed within the jungle's walls. There was no vegetation or grass within its confines, only a floor of black loam —and tracks— footprints forming a circle where someone had walked around and around. Carefully the four surveyed and puzzled.

Nitana, turning to Ames, said softly, "We will never find him; the jungle is too thick."

"Like a needle in a haystack," he agreed as he considered, then turned to Seana. "Call out," he whispered. Unsure, she hesitated; but the others all agreed, waiting.

"—Reed, Tian. Where are you?" disrupted the silence. There was no reply, only quiet. "Reed, Tian!" Ames raised a hand. Now they would wait.

Close by, easing through the understory she stopped, absorbed within the jungle's camouflage. Motionless, the silent Kalo detected a glimpse of movement within the foliage. Prepared, she moved unseen, unnoticed, drawing her bow full. Not making a sound the person crept closer to the clearing, watching the travelers intently. Kalo's eyes followed her target, so close she could reach out and touch it—thoracic spine, between the shoulder blades. From behind, Kalo's soft words interrupted the quiet.

"Who are you?"

The four in the clearing spun around and saw them both, the stranger captured at the jungle's edge, and Kalo, the girl, the Renoloi warrior, standing beyond, bow drawn, arrow ready for flight.

Back to her, not turning around, "I am Lent."

"Lent," Ames remarked. "You sent the note in the bottle?"

"Yes."

"Not a Renoloi." Nitana intimated with wonder.

"Mr. Ames..." Seana whispered, "*he* is like you."

CHAPTER EIGHT

Without speaking...

...Lent stepped forward, into the clearing. He was young, perhaps his mid-teens; dark, tanned by the sun, rawboned, sinew and muscle strengthened by the jungle. And he regarded the world through dark brown eyes filled with youth and wonder set beneath a shaggy mane of the same color hair. He wore a dingy old tee shirt that was full of holes as if chewed on by mice, and khaki shorts, frazzled and torn up the sides along the seams of the legs. In his hand, lowered at his side, he held a twibil; a ponderous battle-ax with an ornately engraved handle, medieval in design, its twin blades gleaming, broad, razor-sharp —tipped with a pike head.

"Your weapon," Kalo warned as the youth moved, her arrow aimed at his back. Lent released the ax allowing it to slip to the ground, walking forward, away, leaving it behind.

"I mean you no harm," he informed them collectively. Now unarmed, over his shoulder he peeked back at the girl. She, still cautious, lowered her bow, and he turned for the first time viewing her, and she him. "You move quietly," he admitted complimenting her. "I have spent my life in the jungle; still, I had no idea you were there, so close." Kalo studied him, said nothing.

"She is skilled," Nitana allowed recapturing Lent's attention.

"Indeed, very," and he grinned innocently with a congenial nod.

"Where are we?" Ames inquired, altering the mood and direction of their conversation. The youth seemed confused. "The name of this place," the man clarified.

"This is the Island." Ames' expression was blank, so Lent asked, "You don't know where you are?" He thought briefly, then inquired, "Where were you bound?"

"Here," Nitana said, "to help you."

Again he was puzzled, counting, "But there are only five of you."

"There were more when we began," she explained. "The journey was difficult and many were lost."

"Night Hunters?" he asked, suspecting. She nodded confirming his presumption. "I am sorry." Then directing his attention to Ames, "And the one on the beach?"

"You were watching?" Ames asked.

"Yes."

"She drowned. Our boat capsized in a storm."

"In a storm," the boy repeated; then almost disbelieving, ventured, "a circular storm?"

"Yes."

"The 'Hole in the Sky'," Lent whispered, astounded, gazing at each individually, "and you are alive." Smiling ear to ear, "You sailed into the core of the world—and you are alive. I knew it was possible, could be done; but they always refused."

"Sound advice. Avoid it," Ames granted. Then he asked, "They?"

"My people," Lent explained. "My village is not far. Come. I'll show you."

"Can we trust you?" Kalo asked from behind.

Lent turned studying her momentarily before answering. "You crossed the water to help unknown people, a difficult journey in-and-of itself. By your own admission many were sacrificed along the way —but still you came to help someone you did not even know." He drew a breath then asked, "Do you believe I would repay such kindness with treachery?"

"We believed you to be Renoloi," she confessed. "You are not."

"You are Renoloi?"

"Yes."

"That is an unusual name."

"Her name is Kalo," Ames explained. "Her people are called Renoloi." Turning, again the boy seemed confused. "Nitana, Tere, Seana," Ames introduced them in turn. "My name is Ames." Next he inquired, already suspecting, "Are *all* your people like you?"

"My tribe? Yes," Lent replied matter-of-fact, "but we have different names just as your people do."

"What is your tribe called?"

Lent shrugged considering, "We all know one another. It never seemed necessary to name our tribe." Contemplating, he busily scratched his head; and as he deliberated Kalo moved from behind him alongside her companions, curious, wanting to more carefully examine this unusual person. At length, after surveying each of the five, Lent asked Ames, "Are you Renoloi?"

"No, I'm a man; different than the Renoloi."

"Yes, I noticed." Ames grinned, but didn't respond. "I imagine then, my people are called man," Lent concluded.

"Men," Ames told him, "the plural is men."

"Men," he repeated, "I like that; perhaps we will be called men." Thinking, "Yes, you and I appear to be different than the Renoloi; their clothes are dissimilar, their mannerisms less..." undecided.

"Masculine," Ames volunteered.

"And their bodies are shaped differently," Lent continued, "they have bumps on their chests that we do not." He turned to Kalo with genuine naivete', "—except you;" he observed, "you don't have bumps."

Ames quickly interjected assuring, "She will." Snuffing a grin he explained, "She's young, and the bumps—breasts—develop as they become a little older."

Lent looked to Ames again, guiltless, interested, "Breasts. Why is that?"

"Long story," the man answered suppressing a smile and ending a conversation destined to become impossibly complicated. He abruptly changed the subject. "May we visit your village?"

"Of course." Then considerately offering, "One of yours is injured," stepping forward intending to assist Seana, who quickly withdrew.

"No—" she instantly rebuffed obviously anxious. Inherent mistrust of outsiders was natural and clearly defined in her expression. "Mr. Ames will help me." Without understanding herself why, she extended her hand to him and he stepped alongside her; his touch was reassuring. Seana knew Ames.

Lent halted realizing his mistake. "I am sorry; I did not mean to..." hesitating, feeling awkward, eyes darting about, glancing at his weapon nearby; then pointing, asking, "may I?" Ames nodded and Lent picked up the twibil. "My village is not far. Come. I'll show you," and he led, Nitana and Tere following, next Seana and Ames, and last Kalo.

As they walked, his arm around her waist lending support, Seana looked at him. "You are my friend," she whispered. "I trust you."

He wrinkled his nose and squeezed her gently. "I know," then turning again, watching the youth in the lead, to himself he thought, *this could be interesting.* Furtively keeping an eye on Lent, Kalo followed them... ever watchful, and silent.

* * *

A winding path, and new direction...

...Lent's village was a collective of dwellings loosely scattered throughout an expansive jungle basin surrounded on all fronts by lofty mountain peaks, most concealed beneath tangled vegetation. Thatch huts were dispersed in no particular order, appearing as roofed haystacks cast into every possible nook and cranny not already occupied by trees. Randomly arranged and cached, almost compacted beneath the dense canopy, the huts were interconnected by a labyrinth of narrow trails that served to create an irregular web of footpaths crisscrossing the valley basin. Were it not for their characteristic 'color of dead grass', a contrast to the jungle-green that set them apart making the dwellings distinguishable, they would have otherwise blended so well with the surroundings one could have followed any one of the trails and likely overlooked most of them.

The village was also plainly native, natural, except for out of place contrivances. There was a two-slice toaster shining chrome in the sun, a tipped-over wheelbarrow with a broken handle and flat tire sticking out of some bracken. There was an oak door with the knob still in place, now a footbridge crossing a creek; a stone statue—perhaps some Greek god—left standing along the trail for no particular reason, and a Martin birdhouse sitting atop a large rock. In this world, there were no birds.

As the small group approached the village, word of their arrival spread like ripples on a pond. Newcomers. And curiosity literally brought a crowd out of the woodwork. When Lent and the others arrived locals were everywhere, behind every tree, alongside every bush. This sort of occurrence was beyond a rarity, being truly unprecedented. These people, similar in appearance but with light color hair and bumps, were rumored to be from somewhere unknown to them. Lent's people characteristically shared common traits: none very old, all with hair tending to be dark, and all genetically masculine in appearance.

Lent guided the Renoloi and Ames to a small clearing within the wide-ranging territory of his village; not really so much a clearing as a breach within the trees, having been hacked open, cleared, and maintained. In the ground, located at one end, was a hollowed-out pit covered with a steel latticework grate for cooking, and sticking up almost everywhere were tree stumps now used for stools. This was one of several clear-cuts fashioned by the people where they could gather.

Resting the battle-ax against a stump and sitting down, he motioned the visitors to join him, and walking Seana to a stump Ames let her down easily, as discretely she squeezed his hand worried that he might abandon her. Without comment or gesture he sat on the ground leaning back casually against the stump touching her thigh, as Nitana and Tere seated themselves close by. However, Kalo, still suspicious, remained on her feet.

Forged with insatiable curiosity the young men drew nearer to their unusual visitors, intending no harm, but pushing, crowding in until their numbers and accumulating presence within the small enclosure bordered on claustrophobic, becoming spatially invasive. Brandishing an odd assortment of weapons like axes, swords, flails, spears, pitchforks, and hoes, they milled inquisitively, their weapons carried out of habit, simply part of everyday life.

They seemed compelled, longing to touch the Renoloi, but none willing to venture so brash a gesture; all hesitant yet inquisitive, not meaning to be offensive or inhospitable. It was a curious exchange, each marveling at the other, not quite certain what to make of one another. The Renoloi were familiar with Reed and Ames, but this time there were so many; and these young men had no idea a different kind of people also inhabited this world.

Their curiosity was understandable but a little too much, so finally Ames had to politely say something. "Please, Lent, ask your people to move back, just a little. I realize this is all new; but they're going to smother us pretty quick."

Looking from Nitana to Ames another young man turned motioning others away, apologizing, "Our behavior is inexcusable." Grateful, Nitana smiled. "You have come far and must be tired and hungry. Cord," he said, "bring them something to eat and drink." Obediently a younger boy in the crowd left as Nitana thanked them.

Still easing back, respectfully, "Kale. I am Kale —and you are welcome." Stopping as he spoke, pleased that this stranger might speak to him, the youth lightly stepped forward again. He wore a faded green polo shirt, blue jean cutoffs, and cowboy boots that at one time were polished brown but now were scuffed to raw leather.

"There will be time enough to get to know one another," Lent assured." With mutual agreement on both sides, incrementally the young men drifted into the jungle again, each in turn, offering his congenial smile of, *welcome.*

Eventually, only Lent and a few others remained in the clearing, sitting quietly until Cord returned with the food. To each of the strangers he offered a chunk of meat wrapped in a broad leaf, all more than willingly accepting. Bouncing it on his fingertips, Ames gingerly unwrapped his meal, still hot and steaming, just retrieved from a barbecue dugout in another clearing.

Taking a bite, "Chiqua," he announced flatly, a hint of disappointment leaking out with the word. Both pleased and amused, the women looked at him; and Nitana even grinned.

Curious, Lent inquired, "You have eaten Chiqua before?"

Looking up from his food, "Yeah, often." Seana sputtered with near-laughter poking him with her good elbow. Puzzled, Lent looked at Nitana.

"Chiqua is our staple," she explained with a teasing grin.

Beaming enthusiastically, "Ours too," he said, his white teeth flashing a broad smile. Ames feigned approval, but his stomach said, *oh great*. Chiqua, food; common ground, the seed of friendship germinated. Kalo sat down.

Again Cord appeared from the jungle, this time with others, all toting more food and two five-gallon Jeep cans—one red, the other army surplus, drab olive-green. The entire group was given odds-and-ends cups or mismatched glasses from an old cardboard box, and a second boy followed filling them from the red gas can. As the youth finished filling the last cup Tere took a quick, hearty drink from the chipped china cup she had been given. Her reaction was —instantaneous, simultaneous— choking and coughing, spitting liquid from her mouth, at the same time blowing it out her nose. Her sinuses burned and her eyes reddened as she puffed and fanned trying to suck in some air. Nitana and Kalo reacted —onto their feet. Ames, less reactionary and suspecting, took a sip from his Donald Duck figurine glass. He coughed then inhaled a deep draw to clear the flame and tears from his eyes.

"Whoa—shit!" he snorted, "one-twenty proof at least, Kentucky white lightning," smacking his lips, blinking his head back in place; squinting, sorting his vision until the blur went away, finally managing to ask, "where did you get that?"

Rascal grinning, Lent answered, "We distill it from yellow grain that grows on tall stalks. Makes you blink, doesn't it?"

"—Make you blink; it'll blow your shorts off." Still clearing his head Ames sucked in —sputter-laughed— puffed a good breath; then asked, "You've got a moonshine still?" blinking incredulously. "Where did you get the corn, and how did you learn to distill it?"

"We found a cloth sack full of grain, with a small book inside it," Kale explained. "The pictures were easy enough to understand so constructing the cooker wasn't too difficult; however we almost ran out of grain before we finally tried planting some. The seeds grew fine, so now we have plenty."

Enjoying their narrative and relaxing, Ames grinned. Nitana and Kalo, now assuming Tere would survive, sat down again. "Corn can be used for other things too," he told them sipping his shine.

"Really, like what?" Lent asked, surprised.

"Food. You can eat it."

Amazed, "It can be eaten?" Apparently that possibility had never occurred to them —after all, they already had Chiqua.

Reflective humor, Ames remarked under his breath, "Pilgrims."

"Pilgrims?" Kale inquired, interested.

"Just talking to myself, an analogy," Ames told him, "new people, in a new world."

"Yes," Lent concluded as he, Kale and the others arrived at the decision with a cooperative of smiles, "we are Pilgrims."

Looking up over his shoulder and winking at Seana, Ames agreed with them, "Yes indeed, you certainly are." Even though inadvertently coined, from that time on, Lent's people had a name. Another sip, then Ames asked, "Where did the sack of corn and book come from?"

Offhand, "The Accumulation," assuming his new friend might already have known. Ames' brow wrinkled, apparently not comprehending, and the bushy-hair youth explained, "The Accumulation, from beyond." Pausing to see if Ames grasped his meaning, then furthering, "This is the Island… from beyond."

"Yes," the man agreed, "you told us that before." But he still didn't understand.

A bit frustrated, "The same place we have found many things, our clothes, weapons," and pointing to the pit, "that grate," he explained.

Inside his head the light went *'on'* and Ames realized, *beyond.* His next question, "The Accumulation is here, on the island?" Lent bobbed an energetic affirmative. "Can we see it?"

"Sure," glancing at the sky, "but it's too late today." Then back to Ames, "It is on the other side of the island. The shortest way is over the mountains —half a day. Stay here tonight and we'll leave at dawn. Is that acceptable?" The travelers exchanged brief looks; they all were worn out and needed some rest, agreeing to leave at dawn. The Pilgrims were pleased. Lent grinned. "Good. Now, shall we imbibe of some brew?"

Curious to try it again, Tere willingly offered her china cup for a refill smiling as Cord topped it off, right to the brim. Holding her breath she chugged a big gulp, squeezed her eyes shut to flush the alcohol taste, and finally went, *"...Aaah."* Incredulous, Ames watched, expecting she might tip over, but she didn't; finally smacking her lips announcing, "Warm, all the way down."

Nitana was next, a big swallow, followed by Seana and Kalo. They all made peculiar wrinkled faces, then quaffed some more. Squinting fretfully Ames watched while they continued to drink the curious beverage more quickly than was prudent.

"You might want to go easy on that," he cautioned them collectively.

"It will help them sleep," Deet, another young man said. He was topped off with a dark blue New York Yankees baseball cap with half the bill broken —or cut off with pinking shears— frazzled as it was you really couldn't tell. Along with his scruffy old shirt and jeans he wore gray-brown canvas Nikes that should have been white.

Ames concurred, "No doubt." Tere emptied her cup and grinned sheepishly. Mildly amused, Ames told her, "New word for your vocabulary..." and a pause.

"What word is that?" she asked child-like.

"Hangover."

"Hangover?" Considering, "I am not familiar with hangover."

"You will be in the morning."

Hesitant Lent stood, then vacillating, almost timidly walked over to Kalo and knelt near her, seeming intrigued with her allure, ostensibly compelled, wanting to better know her. But the girl was wary, inherently a part of her nature, a defining aspect of who she was; and she allowed his proximity with guarded caution. Self-conscious, he had already hurt her feelings once; she was receptive but remained suspicious. Still seated, she pivoted gracefully to hear what he might have to say, prepared to listen, her way of learning.

Peripherally watchful, from where he and Seana sat together Ames listened surreptitiously. For a minute or two Lent didn't say anything, just remained kneeling as he looked at her, as though studying her, aware of their outward differences and curiously deciphering them within his head. The girl at first presented the pretense of casual disregard, but his persistent scrutiny eventually made her uncomfortable, almost like a specimen out of the laboratory. And at last, she made intentional eye contact crooking an eyebrow with an obligatory frown, so he would know, time to say something —or scram.

"I don't mean to bother you," he apologized bashfully. She didn't respond, waiting. Hushed words, "But we are different."

"Yes, you are clumsy in the jungle and I am quiet," she agreed coyly. Payback. Kalo had observed the interaction between Tian and Ames, and her comment caught his attention. He smiled ever so slightly deciding, *she'll be fine.*

Across the small clearing Lent was captivated by her wit and charm, but defended anyway, "Well, you had the drop on me." It was a feeble attempt, but the best he could do.

"Drop on you?" coquettish. *From small beginnings... acorns.*

"Yes," he explained scooting a bit closer, "it's an expression from the western paperbacks: Louis Lamour. The cowboys say that."

Puzzled she asked quizzically, "What are western paperbacks and cowboys?"

"Books of course, pages with words that tell stories; like the Marvel comic books —except without the pictures." Then lacking a better explanation, "Well, you'll see tomorrow in the Accumulation." Again his eyes drifted to her chest.

Annoyed, she asked, "Why do you look at me like that, at my chest?" and almost hurt, she snapped, "you said yourself, I have no bumps," her first twinge of self-consciousness. Even though she was still too young to understand, Kalo somehow sensed having bumps might be important, if not right now, at least some time in the future.

"No, the fetish," he replied cautiously reaching out and touching the tooth, caressing it, then turning it admiringly. "It is truly beautiful."

She said simply, "It is a dinosaur tooth," modesty compelling her to abate, even diminish, the accomplishment.

"Dinosaur tooth?" he wondered. "What's a dinosaur? I have never seen one."

"Great, large creatures," she informed; then curious, asked, "—you have never seen a dinosaur?" More amicable now, she smiled lithely elaborating a bit. "From a Tyrannosaurus Rex, commonly known as T-Rex, and possibly named in honor of a little paleontologist who discovered its fossils, but…" she paused, considering, then concluded, "I cannot be certain of that."

"Why not?"

She frowned. "My source of information is somewhat questionable." Eavesdropping, Ames almost laughed, and she glanced over her shoulder, then seeing him, grinned. He shrugged, as if to say, *don't look at me.*

Lent marveled. "Well, it certainly is beautiful; where did you find it?"

Nitana, who had been speaking with Deet, turned joining their conversation. "In the dinosaur's mouth." Her meaning being unclear to them, Lent and the Pilgrims looked at the bleary-eyed Nitana, she and Tere already showing effects of the one-twenty proof.

"The dinosaur's mouth?" Lent repeated.

Tere bobbing her head, both proud of the girl, Nitana explained drawing an imaginary bow with hand gestures. "One arrow, through the eye, into the brain. Dead T-Rex." She pushed playfully and Tere demonstrated by toppling from her stump sideways onto the ground.

Visibly impressed Lent asked Kalo, "You killed the dinosaur with one arrow?" Embarrassed, she bashfully admitted having done so. "That's remarkable."

Ames listened, pleased; she deserved recognition, the accolade. Tere struggled clumsily back onto her stump, however nearing intoxication the feat seemed more difficult than before. The distance must have increased.

Seriously Nitana interjected a final comment directing her words primarily to Lent, but making all aware. "Kalo may be small, but do not underestimate her. For as invisible as she is within the jungle, Lent; she is more deadly with a bow."

Gesturing, Tere mimicked, pretending her finger to be an arrow, popping herself in the eye, and giggled, "Dead eye." Giddy, both she and Nitana laughed comically.

Amused by their inebriated foolishness Ames cautioned, "You guys better slow down a bit with that hooch."

Tere waved him off with a hand. "We are fine. We are fine," and they snickered again.

"We are fine. We are fine," he mocked, and flourishing an, *all right then, don't listen to me,* smile, Ames looked up at Seana. She was grinning from ear to ear. "Does your shoulder still hurt?"

Bleary-eyed, "Not at all."

Chewing his lip, he winced. "That's what I was afraid of."

Bumping him playfully with her leg, "We are fine."

"Just what I need…" a resigned chuckle, "a bunch of swilling wenches," then shaking his head, *learn the hard way.* And the smile.

Having overheard, Seana tapped him lightly on the shoulder. "I do not know what swilling wenches is?"

"Yeah, I know," he admitted, "if I thought you did, I wouldn't have said it."

Spending the evening together, becoming better acquainted, and the more homespun they drank, the Renoloi's suspicions diminished. They told their hosts of their homeland, beyond the range of the Pilgrims and Night Hunters, where after the defeat of the Trogs, until recently there had been an interlude of peace. Lately though, unusual events had caused some to wonder if it was possible that some unforeseen change might be descending upon their land.

The Pilgrims related a similar story however with altered circumstances, nonetheless parallel in nature. Long ago the Night Hunters prowled the jungle with unremitting predation, until one day they suddenly vanished; and although the Pilgrims were never able to discover their origin, as time passed the enormous spiders were forgotten; out of sight, out of mind, a grave indiscretion. Then, plasma cold, unfeeling and relentless, the obsidian predators once again appeared —pestilence merely dormant and waiting; renewed savagery that drove them across the water, beyond their dominion of fangs and claws.

Different, but the same; the Renoloi and Pilgrims, separated by distance and circumstance, each previously unaware of the other's presence, were both struggling to carve a niche in a hostile, untamed and unexplored world. They had more in common than they knew. It was not random chance that brought them together. Although different, with a mutual bond they were destined to unite, the task before them... to survive in a primitive world.

* * *

Their frivolity and laughter...

...Eventually subsided as the whiskey's full effect settled upon them. Kalo, the smallest, was first to succumb. As she finished downing her third tin cup, her lips, and everything else, went numb. Stuporous, wavering and still sitting on the stump, the cup slipped from her fingers and plinked to the ground. Her eyelids drooped, closed, and refused to attempt the journey of opening again. She teetered precariously as Lent moved forward, and with Ames' unspoken permission took her into his arms then gently lay her on the ground. Childlike, she curled fetal; a kitten, a precious ball of young Renoloi warrior.

Nitana was not as lucky to tweak away so smoothly. The inverted axiom, what goes down sometimes must come back up, possessed a truth all its own. Speaking to Kale in a silly jumbled slur of indiscernible babble likely comprehensible only to herself, she stopped mid-sentence. Her expression betrayed unexpected distress and quickly turning her head she gushed icky splatter of projectile vomitus into the bushes, puke soup splashing the greenery and leaving it reeking. Appalled, when Tere saw that, she had a sudden-misery onset of her own, her stomach knotting then twisted sick like a worm doing a fishhook death-coil. She nearly lost it but swallowed hard holding the bubble, keeping it down. Anticipating, Deet watched Tere; *almost.*

Kale feigned sympathy for Nitana, who was still vomiting, asking pitifully, "What's the matter, feeling sick?" Leaning over and patting her gently on the back as she continued to retch, he watched the puddle, seemed to be studying as it grew. Then looking around and finally intentionally settling on Tere, he observed with devious innocence, "Look at all that Chiqua; what a waste," referring to the partially digested chunks of meat bobbling in the gastric stew at their feet.

Victim of her subconscious, Tere couldn't help herself, she just had to look; and when she did… her eyes involuntarily searching and finding them—chewed, miserable little bits of swimming meat being splattered in the growing puddle …it was all over. She managed one pitiful short groan then a gut-wrenching gag —and flush— up came her own dinner.

Amused, Kale shook his head woefully observing, "Drunkern' Cooter Brown." He and Deet exchanged mischievous looks and glanced at Ames as if to say, *imagine that.* Ames couldn't help but chuckle, and just about then —*thunk*— Seana's empty cup hit the top of his head. Going ashen her color faded, eyes rolling-back-white she tipped over crumpling onto him. He caught her as she wilted; being careful of her injured shoulder, and gently lay her 'to rest' on the ground. Kale and Deet, both guilty as sin and still smirking, likewise helped Nitana and Tere lie down.

Perhaps provoked by a self-conscious twinge of his own culpability, Ames chastised with good humor, "You guys are some cruel scalawags."

Suppressing a snicker Deet replied, "Guess we all learn the same way."

He agreed, "Some things never change."

* * *

Later that night…

…The much-needed laughter was a break from the hardships of their journey, soon to be a memory for each, a keepsake. All were asleep except three. Lent, Deet, and Ames relaxed in the small clearing near the glowing embers of the fire pit, their hushed, intermittent conversation only occasionally interrupted by rattling snores of intoxicated people, sleeping. For the women, a twenty-first birthday celebration of sorts; however, dawn would bring recompense for their over-indulgence.

Reticent, Ames lay upon the soft loam, feet to the fire, head propped against a stump. Although his body was idle, his mind was not. Haunting recollections crept in as invisible phantoms transforming the still of the night. Darkness, inseparable companion to loneliness stole around him, absorbed him with her opaque secrets; and doing so, dragged the nagging emptiness of despair along at her side.

He breathed slowly. The anguish returned; that inextinguishable ember of torment. Wrapping his arms, folding himself within, a vain attempt to quell the pain, squeeze it away; but it was still there. It would remain. *Tian, Reed, where are you?* And the festering, incessant fear he could no longer deny, *are you dead?* Appreciating the camouflage of night, it brought a tear to his eye, he hurt so god-awfully bad deep inside.

Lent shuffled to the fire pit, plinked in a few chunks of wood, moved back alongside Ames, and sat down again. Without facing his new friend the young man matter-of-factly began, "Do you want to talk about it?"

Attempting to conceal his surprise Ames quietly responded, "About what?"

Squaring with him, "I pretend to be simple and it serves me well at times; don't you agree?" Realizing the innocent dolt was a facade, a sham, Ames nodded without speaking. "But I am not stupid," he explained. "It's there in your expression; a look. Not so much *in* your eyes as from *behind* your eyes," thinking, then continuing, "from somewhere deep inside your soul. Something... the look is *troubled, turmoil.*" And he ventured a guess. "Are you searching for someone or something that is missing?"

Unsuspecting, Ames wondered how he could so wrongly have assessed the youth. Lent was no simpleton or inexperienced boyish prankster. Beside him sat a very intelligent, highly perceptive individual. "Why did you pretend to be so naïve earlier?"

Lent grinned. "Better to play the fool, than an arrow in your back lying dead in the jungle." Then seriously, "I apologize for the deception."

Deet interjected, "He leads, and we don't follow a fool."

The man's eyes skipped from one to the other as Lent asked, "Now, can we trust each other?" Ames nodded. Satisfied, Lent inquired, "Then how may I help?"

Tears tried to come but he pushed them back. "I don't know that you can..." a slow breath, and sigh, "if anyone can."

For a moment there was silence; then Lent whispered, "Two are missing."

"What did you say?" Ames' question flashed.

Not quite certain, Lent repeated the words. "Two are missing." Genuinely puzzled he explained, "I heard one of you say it."

Deet shook his head. "We didn't say anything."

Coercing a nervous grin, believing they may be gaming him, he insisted. "Yes, you did. One of you did."

"No... we didn't," Deet said solemnly.

Disconcerted, Lent whispered, "Two are missing. I heard it, inside my head." Then attempting to dismiss it as alcohol-induced, he decided, "Drank too much shine; time to slow down."

Offering no information, Ames suggested, "Let's get some sleep. It will be daylight soon." Intoxicated and tired, both Lent and Deet were soon asleep.

Later, Ames lay still, all alone in the darkness, thinking, *two are missing*, until exhaustion finally took him away.

* * *

Sunshine and misery...

...Morning arrived quiet and shuffling, their 'Humpty Dumpty' heads pounding from the night's residue, none moving quickly, all trying to put themselves together again. The Renoloi were hurting, hung-over, that place behind the eyes throbbing like something was in there thumping on over-ripe melons.

Seana walked tenderly, weaving across the clearing.

"You okay?" Ames asked gently.

"Hurts every time I step."

Fearing she may have reinjured it, he asked, "Your shoulder?"

"No," she groused, then winced, "my head." He watched as she faltered, suffering alcohol-retribution, expecting she would not soon forget this lesson.

"It'll go away in a few hours," he assured. Squinting, Seana looked at him wondering how she would ever survive that long.

"A few hours?" Nitana simpered trying to get up from the ground. Smiling with false sympathy, Ames shook a, *yes*. She moaned lying back down. "I will get up then."

"We are fine. We are fine," he teased.

"That is not funny."

"No rest for the wicked," he bantered reaching down and taking her by the hand, tugging easily. "Come on," coaxing her back up. Slowly, pathetically, she staggered to her feet, teetering and pained.

She protested. "But I feel so..." at a loss for the right word.

"Miserable?"

"Yes," she admitted barely able to look at him. Waking, the others were also stirring; and about then they all heard a gut-twisting sound,

Kalo huddled at the clearing's edge on her hands and knees. Gagging, she shivered and retched with the anguish of dry heaves.

Lent, perched on a stump and shaking his head empathetically, "No, Nitana, you feel bad." Then pointing to the pitiful girl not far away, he winced and said, "She—is miserable."

Her attention directed to Kalo, Nitana's lips curled to pre-vomit mode and she staggered to the bushes, sick again. Within a moment, Seana and Tere joined her all barfing to beat the band.

Perhaps it was the alcohol consumed the night before, or perhaps the spectacle and disgusting noise of their activity —whatever— the urge seized them as well, and Lent, Kale and Deet were quickly at the bushes with them. The women's sopranos, the Pilgrims' baritones, harmoniously consolidated creating an awful chorus.

Standing alone in the clearing center, staid, Ames scanned the whole bunch; their cacophonous din of liquid gushes, awful gagging and generally disgusting misery, "Pathetic," he mumbled, "just pitiful." But he couldn't contain an almost imperceptible and ever so slightly sadistic grin, prompting his sage counsel, "Sip whiskey... *never* chug it."

* * *

Penitence paid...

...The sun was high by the time the group finally got underway. The trail they climbed to the summit was not really so much a path as a ribbon of space allowing passage, able to push their way from one narrow opening to the next. Nor was the distance too far, however the grade was remarkably steep, ascending mountains that jutted almost vertically, their progress constantly hampered by an unending tangle of undergrowth, liana and vines. It took several hours, but by early afternoon they were at the top and traveling was easier, being more level terrain; but the jungle remained, verdant and crabgrass twisted. Tired and sobered with their ascent they pressed on steadily for a couple more miles.

"Soon now," Lent called back over a shoulder.

Following Nitana, Tere was third in line, trailed by Seana and Ames, with an arm around her helping her along; then Kalo and ten Pilgrims. Tere, casting a glimpse back to them, expounded the obvious, "Soon what?" No sooner had she said it than Lent climbed a gravelly incline and stopped at the top as they emerged into the open. The jungle was gone, as though a giant hand had scooped the tangle of greenery away.

Unexpected. They stood on a barren surface, an elevated plateau, built up as if heaved from the mishmash and smoothed over with granulated pumice and debris. The jungle lay forty feet beneath them, buried, silent and dead under a mountainous windswept plain of volcanic ash. Slate gray and gritty it crunched as it squeezed between their toes concealing ten million tangled trees that once were, and now were no more—nature's preparatory workshop of a petrified forest.

Miles away, to their right, a volcanic composite landform waft steam and acrid smoke in a thick drifting cloud that ascended in wind trails to the upper reaches of sky where it blended to haze with the limit of vision, then faded away. The plume.

Stark, the volcano transcended the landscape much like the overseer of a jungle graveyard, dredging recollections of Pompeii. Amber flow of blebby lava oozed from a side vent pushing lethargically down the cone's solidified mound continuing to create additional topography with artistic, liquid design. Steam rivulets floated up in translucent vapor winds from along the flow's winding path, then disappeared in the sunlight absorbed by the day; ghost-like fingers of tranquil illusion, drifting, rising precariously from an unsettled land… for this was still a primitive world.

Gathered together, catching their breath, they watched the volcanic activity. Liquid and orange, lava pulsed in rolling boils as it coursed down the sloping landform.

Seana observed, "It is beautiful."

Ames agreed, "Yes, it is; nature's power. Lent, how long has it been active?"

"Not long."

"Not long?"

"It was dormant until recently. We thought we might have to leave the island, but the activity subsided; so we decided to stay for now." Ames seemed to accept that as Lent rose to his feet. "It's not much farther. This way."

Within a short time the group had crossed the ash plain and arrived at the precipice of a cliff that dropped vertically for thousands of feet to a valley basin sprawling for many miles, eventually reaching out to the sea. And within the basin was the Accumulation, a virtual mountain, but not of stone.

There were:

Stoves and refrigerators, all rusted and old. A Harley Davidson frame without wheels or a seat, and televisions with broken screens that were piled on top of crushed computers. Vehicles spanning more than two hundred years of automotive progress created enormous heaps of scrap metal, literally millions of them... and more.

Scattered haphazardly stagecoaches, buggies and Viking ships with wood rotted away, were mixed in with countless missiles and tanks. Guns, personnel transports, artillery and aircraft were crammed among schools, churches, and ribbons of concrete interstate highway that lay inert and silent circling the blown-out aircraft carrier USS Enterprise... and more.

Clothes from the Goodwill were stacked in great rotting mounds near water-soaked boxes of Barbie dolls without arms, or with broken-off heads. Carousels and roller coasters with horses and benches thrown askew, were buried under billboards and a Buddha statue. Charred Roman chariots with broken tongues and spokes lay abandoned in huge shredded piles of books, magazines and newspapers alongside an Egyptian pyramid tipped onto its side. Dead lawnmowers were amassed as red, green and rust, and a single Lone Ranger action figure lay twisted and dead without his mask. Amidst all this were Legos, comic books, ten billion cell phones... and more.

There was:

The Chernobyl nuclear reactor, its half-life radiated away. Entire trains with locomotives, steam engines, Pullman, and boxcars and ribbons of rail lay like string in a pile. Seeming ready to launch, a space shuttle protruded from a city-sized jumble of houses with broken windows and shingled roofs torn apart. Built in the 1470's by Ivan the Great, the Kremlin's Cathedral of Assumption was now lost in the aggregate. Nuclear missiles mounted on overturned mobile launch racks leaned against Saint Peter's Basilica... and more.

Radio Flyer wagons and tricycles and bicycles with bent or missing wheels, a Daisy Red Ryder Western Carbine air rifle, and untold numbers of toys were crushed beneath the Eiffel Tower. Tarnished and twisted, entire skyscrapers listed gutted and burned with blown out window glass; and dwarfed by them, a solitary clapboard steeple and belfry from the mountain jutted out... and much more.

The Accumulation was a junkyard surpassing their wildest imagination, enormous beyond comprehension. It was gigantic, from a time and a place only Ames could appreciate. It was the Lost World of Atlantis one hundred-fold, from an insignificant liquid-blue planet and universe of long ago, now lost somewhere in the dark void of space. It was from Earth.

Lent beamed viewing a collectible dealer's treasure trove on display; smiling proudly, "Lot of stuff, huh?"

Speechless, Ames simply nodded.

In awe, "What are those things?" Nitana whispered.

Kale answered, "Too much to understand—the Accumulation."

"Where did it all come from?" she asked. Stabbing the ground with the toe of his boot, Kale shrugged his shoulders not able to say; so she turned to Lent.

Scanning, the youth's eyes surveyed the unbelievable conglomeration before them; then with measured words, solemnly he turned and faced her. "No one knows; but passed down through the years with folklore... some say the Accumulation was dragged through a hole in the sky."

* * *

That evening...

...The group made camp on a rise near the beach near where the mountain of accumulation poured into the sea and disappeared within the wet-green secrecy of the waterworld's opaque shroud. They had spent the waning hours of daylight wandering through the endless mass of discarded debris, an exploratory expedition of minimal consequence. The vastness of the junkyard was so immense it would require months, years to go through it all, even the accessible material, much less what was buried below. The Accumulation was incredible, enormous, seemingly endless... and More.

As Deet moved to the fire laying on more driftwood with one hand while carefully keeping his place in his new-found Marvel comic book with a finger of his other, Ames asked, "Find something interesting out there?"

He nodded and flipped it closed so Ames could see the cover. "Oh yes, always a new issue." Fastidiously he pointed them out, carefully indicating each caption as he read, " 'Captain America Special', 1 Jan. 1970, 25 c-line, king-size special edition. It includes three episodes. One: 'The Origin of Captain America'. Two: 'Midnight at Graymoor Castle'. And three: 'Bucky Barnes Captured!' " Pause. "It's by the Marvel Comic Group."

"I meant, in your pocket," Ames said, pointing to the bulge in Deet's bermuda shorts.

Wondering, Deet looked down inspecting himself, then realized, "Oh, that— no, that's just grain, seed." He reached into his pocket and produced a handful of corn.

"He always carries it with him," Lent explained from across the campfire. "He likes his shine, and since that time we almost ran out, he wants to be sure we always have seed for a new crop —in case we ever need it." Lent chuckled as he recalled, "The prospect of going without made him *re-eal* nervous."

Ames grinned. "Cornerstone in the foundation for 'AA'." Then to Deet, "Just don't let it sprout in there."

"I won't," he assured agreeably.

Beneath them the ground rumbled trembling perceptibly, the landscape rising ever so slightly then settling suddenly as it dropped back two inches, to where it was before. Seismic swells.

The topmost twenty stories of a leaning skyscraper two miles out in the Accumulation echoed a harsh concrete snap as it shifted and fractured. Like a tear through tight canvas, the sound of ripping concrete rang gritty and hollow over the trillions of tons of junkyard, and they all watched, waiting as it teetered, walls sliding over one another, crunching and grinding, then fell. The expectant, brief silence ended in a tremendous crash as the colossal structure smashed onto the pile breaking apart and crushing itself in a suffocating cloud of dust and hurtling fragments.

Shockwave. Another jolt swept underfoot.

The splatter of cement bits ricocheting and raining down onto the aggregate piles had just subsided with the dust cloud still rushing out, when, in the distance the volcano erupted spewing flame for its breath. Gagging superheated gas blasted billowing, black clouds with vaporizing heat venting liquefied magma froth that sprayed out in a fountainfall a thousand feet high. It was a pulsing, molten lightshow illuminating the sky with its amber glow.

Boiling up as a gushing fountain it splashed onto the composite landform, bubbling, burning insatiably, consuming everything it touched as it poured into the ocean below their line of sight. Dark waiting water exploded in blistering dense clouds of steam and violent sizzle cooling the molten lava in ever-increasing igneous rings that congealed as oppressive layers of obsidian glass.

Matted against the evening sky the eruption was beautiful, a horizon corona of molten yellow-orange heaved up from a jellied magma paintpot below, the sky darkening with inky sulphurous clouds as they fanned out shedding firefall ash and sparks of twinkling, wistfully spiraling orange-gray snow. Then, as the embers died, they quietly floated away. Nature's fury was awe-inspiring. Thousands of cubic yards of igneous pulsed in plasma blobs ejected with each succeeding eruption. And in the volcanic plume heat lightning etched crooked wires of silent light.

"We're in no immediate danger," Lent assured the nervous Renoloi. "The lava flows to the ocean on the other side of the island and the wind will carry the poisonous cloud out to sea, back toward the mainland." With that the women were a bit more at ease.

Without intentions of being an alarmist Ames suggested, "And if it goes pyroclastic? Volcanic activity is generally erratic, unpredictable at best; the entire island would be forfeit."

Lent agreed, knowing they should leave soon, "And us along with it." Both studied the volcano a moment longer before Ames spoke again.

"But as long as it's venting fluidly you're probably right; we should be okay for now." They all watched a while longer. It was beautiful, majestic. Then eventually, one by one, each settled in around the campfire and drifted to sleep.

* * *

Two hours later...

...Only Lent and Ames still remained awake. Observing the gleaming sword lying on the sand alongside Ames, its broad, swept blade reflecting the orange fairy dance of campfire flames; conversationally Lent inquired, "May I ask you something?"

From the flames to Lent, "Sure."

"Your sword, the one you found in the Accumulation today," directing the man's attention to the weapon, "why did you choose one that's broken?"

"Broken? It's not broken."

"It's crooked," the youth observed. "The blade is bent. There were so many, why not take one with a straight blade?"

Realizing, "It is supposed to be that way," the man explained. "It's a scimitar; very ancient, supple, lethal." *Recollections of, 'Ali Baba and the Forty Thieves,'* palming the weapon, examining it in the firelight. "Exceptionally sharp."

"That was why I asked. It seemed strange that it could be broken and yet, still have such an edge."

"Nimble, very swift," Ames whispered, then demonstrated twirling the sword before him creating illusive figure-eights as it sliced with swishing echoes; his hands and wrists lithely guiding and propelling the glistening steel creating a fluid wave of blade before him. Curiously drawn, Lent retrieved a finger-size stick of driftwood from the pile and flipped it toward him —and effortlessly the scimitar whisked the piece of wood in two.

Impressed, the youth conceded, "I see what you mean, graceful and deceptive." Then solidly laying a hand on his twibil, "But personally, I prefer the more direct approach," he remarked, imitating, *whack.*

"You, and Lizzy Borden."

Briefly Lent pondered the analogy, then bashfully admitted, "I don't know what that means." Ames offered no explanation, distracted, his thoughts focused. Hours earlier, when he had first seen the graceful, svelte weapon amid all the others... allured, it *seemed* right, *felt* right. For a moment he was still.

It was quiet for a while.

The distant volcano rumbled persistently pouring orange-melt from the vent, its intense heat and fury absorbed by the night. Paradoxically, above them space; quiet and vast with its majestic beauty self-evident in another display, stars. The night sky was splashed with shimmering, enigmatic sentinels, minutiae sentries, cold, constant and distant. They burned with white fire. Twinkling pinpoints of light, visible by the thousands, scattered amidst a milky blend of nebulae gasses; beauty beyond comparison, their mystery beyond definition, empty and lonely beyond description... so far away, and yet, the same was within him.

Tian, Reed... where are you? A shooting star streaked overhead ribboning a flash of meteoric blue-white trail. *Make a wish,* and he lay there silent, his heart aching, so awfully alone. His eyes teared until they were full; then his blink washed them away tracking wet trails from the corners and down his cheeks. It was dark. No one would see them. No one would know. He was alone.

"What did you wish for?" Lent asked taciturnly, his voice startling the man on the opposite side of their small encampment. Ames didn't respond, only lay still and wondered how Lent could have known. A moment more silent, then, "Tian, Reed. Two are missing." Turning over, shifting his body and rising onto his elbow, the youth peered at him and said, "The words I heard were yours." His voice sincere, his concern genuine, "Tian and Reed are your friends... and they are missing."

"Yes." Ames admitted. "Just before the trimaran capsized they went overboard." Lent said nothing, so Ames continued. "But they weren't washed ashore with the rest of us, so they must have drowned." He choked back tears, unwilling, still unable to accept what he knew he must. Very likely the two people closest to him, most important to him, were gone and not coming back.

With all of his being he vowed to resist the emptiness carving a hollow, ever-widening hole inside him; its relentless, nagging pain clawing and digging deeper with each passing hour. He would not believe they were gone until he knew for certain. But this was difficult; denial of logic, not part of his character. Then the thought —*for everything... there is a reason.*

A memory flash: on the cliff overlooking 'Black Water' with Tian, and she confronting her fear. *"Looks like a giant swamp,"* Reed's simplistic analysis, his uncanny ability to cut to the chase. They had faced it straightforward, head on, and somehow survived. Then somewhere else, not so clearly defined in his mind's eye; a room glowing red in the dark, dank, filled with the putrid stench of death, a woman's form on the floor. Then without warning, confusion and cascading bright sparks —and a burning blade in his chest bubbling blood with its fire. And more: evil gray eyes.

Pieces... pieces still missing.

"Mr. Ames, are you awake?" Lent's voice brought him back. "You were quiet for so long, I thought perhaps you fell asleep."

"No, just thinking." Then he asked, "Lent, have you ever heard of the Legends?"

"No, what are the Legends?"

"I wish I could answer that." His mood reflective, "I only wish I knew." Rolling onto his side he looked at the youth. "Somehow, some way, that's what this is all about."

Considering a moment, Lent finally commented, "I don't mean to be disrespectful, but you really aren't making much sense."

Ames grinned. "No offense taken. I imagine you're right." Then offhand he inquired, "Why did you send the note?"

"I don't know," he replied spontaneously causing the other's eyebrow to rise, telling doubt.

"You don't know?"

"Well…" Lent hesitated, then explained, "you will think me a fool."

Ames understood, having been there before. "Try me."

Reluctant, the youth admitted, "I had a strange dream."

"What kind of dream?" Interest piqued, sincere, "Tell me about it." Lent hesitated. "Please, it could be important." Still unsure, he focused intently upon the man. "Lent, please."

"Promise you won't laugh." Ames agreed and the boy took a breath then began. "It was a dream, but not like any I've ever had before." Considering, he told him, "This dream was real. Well, at least part of it must have been real."

"What do you mean?"

Uncertain, still not understanding himself, he related, "I had been scouting all day and returned to the village just as dark was coming on. Hunters had been seen close to our perimeter and people were being taken each night; so I took first watch and was near the springs, alone. It was very quiet, a long night; but I had a feeling something was going to happen." He thought carefully, remembering, "It seemed, no, felt uneasy… expectant almost, like a portent or premonition." He looked at Ames.

The man said nothing, waiting, so he continued. "When Moran relieved me I decided to stay with him; but not wanting to worry him I said nothing of my ill feelings. I told him if I should doze off to wake me; because as I said before, I was very tired. Eventually though, I must have fallen asleep, and dreamed. That's the only explanation that even makes any sense at all."

Recalling that night, his voice softening, mood changing, "I remember a shooting star streaking across the sky and going down in the jungle nearby. Only it didn't burn out; the glow remained... and from the jungle rode a Mystic."

Attention riveted, "A Mystic?"

"A ghost warrior, shining —no— glowing white, sitting atop a four-legged animal like those in the comic books." He interjected mechanically, "Specifically, 'Buffalo Bill, Classics Illustrated', Number 106, 15 c-line, 1953."

"Fifteen c-line?" Ames repeated, then realized, "Oh, fifteen-cents. Go on, please."

Lent, curious: "What is fifteen-cents?"

"Money. It's not important anymore." Brushing further explanation aside Ames entreated, "Tell me about your dream. What happened?"

The youth continued, "The animal was huge, with a flowing tail and hair along the top of its neck and ankles —and it had incredible, black solid feet."

"Fetlocks—and hooves—a horse."

"But twice the size of those pictured in the western comics that cowboys ride."

"Clydesdale, Percheron, Lippizaner," a quick breath, "go on, what else?" the man asked.

Lent looked back to the fire, recalling, "The rider was wearing shiny metal and glowed illuminating the springs. I'm not certain that he spoke, but I heard words in my head; and the voice told me to put the note into the green bottle and send it downstream."

"And? Go on."

Lent turned back to the man, paused as he thought, then answered, "That's all. The Mystic told me nothing more, just turned and rode into the jungle." Then reticently, "Well, not actually into the jungle, so much as *through* it... a ghost. Then he was gone."

"Can you remember anything else?"

Lent reluctantly admitted, "Yes... the strange part."

Ames said nothing, the obvious having already swept through his mind *—the strange part?*

Lent told him. "I know I must have fallen asleep, because when the Mystic turned and disappeared, I blinked —and it was already morning. Wanting to be sure I hadn't imagined the ghost warrior I asked Moran if he had seen him too; but he just looked at me strangely, shaking his head. And even after asking him several times and finally convincing him I was sincere, he still maintained that we had spent the night alone."

Lent looked into his cupped hands as though presenting a reenactment of what had transpired. "I sat there for a while trying to figure it out, to be sure in my own mind. Then I looked in my hand… and I was holding a little piece of rolled-up paper, and beside my leg was the green bottle." He looked from his opened palms to Ames.

Almost a whisper, Ames asked, "What did you do?"

A feeble grin. "I put the note in the bottle, broke a stick off to seal it, and threw it into the spring." He shrugged. "What would you have done?"

Ames, at a loss, raised his eyebrows presenting a quirky expression. "The same, I suppose."

Lent fingered his scraggle of matted hair. "There are some strange things going on in this world."

"No shit."

Pensively, Lent resigned himself to his own conclusion. "You know, a lot can happen with a hole in the sky."

Recalling Reed's analogy of the Bermuda Triangle, and now Lent's similar hypothesis, he asked, "Do you really believe that?"

"Well…" Lent began to respond; then he paused in thought, his gaze drawn away, followed by the hushed words, "there are always possibilities."

"—What?" Ames' question flashed as an involuntary outburst. "Why did you just say that?"

Perplexed, intent, the youth looked at him. "I don't know really. It was as if a voice, from a great distance, whispered to me." Not saying a word, Ames studied Lent until finally he made him nervous and the youth suggested, "Maybe we should go to sleep." They lay down with no further conversation.

Sleep taking him, John Ames wondered, his fleeting, fading thought… *pieces.*

* * *

Morning, a new day, unusual day...

...Nitana, Kale and Kalo stood abreast on the rise near the beach scanning the horizon with anxious eyes. Bewilderment drawn taut in their shared expressions, they couldn't comprehend it.

"How can it be?" Nitana whispered. Again, "How can it be?"

Kale was speechless, merely shaking his head.

Kalo's eyes narrowed —focused— felt a stirring inside. She was silent.

Behind them Seana woke and sat up, immediately being informed of the phenomenon by Nitana. "Wake Mr. Ames and the others."

"Mr. Ames, you must see this," the gravity and immediacy in her voice rousing him. Still groggy he looked, as confused and concerned, Seana pointed to the horizon. By now Lent and the others were rising, all of them singularly focused.

A new piece… *the Puzzle.*

Joining them, "It's not possible," Ames muttered, "just not possible."

For some time they all gazed and wondered, until finally Lent said it out loud. "What happened to the water?"

"Gone…" Tere murmured "…all gone."

Before them lay an unnatural landscape, the bottom of the sea. Dyed with the tinge of dark algae were vast rolling hills, open sprawling plains, and ragged mountains rife with crevasses and enormous trenches carved out in crooked ditches that meandered for miles in all directions. An unworldly phenomenon, all of it was covered with a tangle of knee-deep, matted, dry seaweed and kelp.

The ocean was gone.

The Island stood alone, an isolated sanctuary pinnacle towering high above the surrounding landscape, its sand beaches now dry and sloping down to the seafloor where it was absorbed within a ravel of brown-olive green and fractured mud base below. All around them was an unending valley basin of ocean bottom: rolling hills, jutting peaks and expansive level plains, yesterday submerged and concealed within a liquid world of green mystery, now more mysteriously exposed.

The mountain of debris on the island itself was dwarfed by what had been underwater. The conglomeration of the Accumulation deposited upon the island trailed to the seafloor then fanned out for miles and miles, enormous beyond comprehension. Complete cities were encapsulated within the incredible mass, the entirety cloaked with algae, seaweed and kelp that was wilting and crisping, all of it dying, drying in the sun.

The lost world of Atlantis one hundred-fold... and More.

Nitana turned to Ames. "The volcano?"

"Ten thousand volcanoes couldn't boil it away."

Kale offered, "Evaporated?"

Ames looked at him incredulously. "You're shitin' me—right?" Then plainly, "Not in millions of years."

And Lent, "The 'Hole in the Sky' must have sucked it away," improbable, illogical —but still, as good as the others.

Ames, again: "And we all slept blissfully through such a storm?" However thus far, even for him, only Lent's proposal, regardless how bizarre, could ever explain this; the inexplicable. Then a memory, the three of them on a sheer mountain ledge in the Forsaken Land—*four days of rain.*

As the group talked about it, trying to figure out what they should do, Ames walked quietly away. Kalo followed him. Now a short distance from the others the man and girl scanned the surreal landscape. Neither spoke.

He laid a gentle hand upon her shoulder, squeezed tenderly —and inside, Kalo felt it. Still there, more ardent and afflictive than before, growing; the unremitting smolder of corrosive pain dissolving his heart with anguish. *Tian, Reed.* But this time she sensed something more, the white heat of pure fire born of unyielding, unrelenting resolve; the ember that glows, then sparks, then bursts to the flame only death can extinguish. He bore the fury of frustration, and determination to know... the *need* to understand.

As he looked at her and she at him, eyes captured by the other, "We must. It is time," she whispered.

Solemnly he agreed, and bending down picked up the scimitar and scabbard looping it across his back by the sling. He turned, told Lent, "We're going to follow the beach around the island, back to the trimaran."

Their conversation interrupted by Ames' voice, Lent pivoted, facing the man. "To the trimaran?"

Nitana, Tere and Seana were instantly silent. They were ready. They would follow.

Not immediately understanding, Lent asked, "Why?"

Ames glanced at Kalo then focused on Seana, answering, "Something we must do."

Reoccurring words came to him, and Lent said, "Two are missing." Ames' nod was his reply, and the youth offered, "Then we will search in the opposite direction and meet you there." Briefly scanning the horizon, he surmised, "We'll be there around midday." That said, and Seana's, *thank you,* conveyed with a grateful smile, the Pilgrims and Renoloi parted company, all well aware this would be their final search for Tian and Reed. As the Pilgrims disappeared within the aggregate jumble of the Accumulation along the beach, the man and women watched.

A moment longer, then, "Nitana, Kalo —point."

They moved out.

* * *

Several hours later...

...Their reconnaissance a disappointment, spirits waned, morale beaten, the Renoloi neared the estuary and beached trimaran just as Lent and his group came into view from the other direction. As Nitana approached the stranded craft a short distance ahead of Kalo, her skilled eye captured the prints immediately. A hand signal from the Renoloi warrior alerted Kalo, *something important*, and the girl reeled and backtracked —full run— to get Ames, Seana and Tere. With her fleet approach the trio knew they had found something and they hurried to meet her.

As she arrived, "What is it?"

"I do not know," she replied breathlessly. "I believe though, we should hurry." In anxious minutes the four were within sight of Nitana, kneeling statuesque on the beach, trying to interpret; and as they drew nearer her bewilderment became obvious when she looked at Ames.

"This makes no sense," she said. Lent and his group were now approaching, but still in the distance.

Ames looked… and wondered.

During their absence the tide had washed the sand clean erasing the tracks they had made around the trimaran before setting out and leaving the craft. Now, before them was a smooth tan beach presenting an undisturbed table of sand —with one glaring exception. Apparently, before the water had vanished someone had called. Two sets of footprints were clearly visible circling the trimaran; and as Ames and the women pondered the tracks lined out in the sand, unable to decipher their meaning, Lent's group arrived, now all of them reunited and none able to make sense of it.

"What does this mean?" Tere finally asked turning to Ames. He had no answer. Seana and Nitana traded brief looks of the same question, then to Lent, who also had no conjecture to present.

Kalo looked at Ames. "We must," she whispered.

He agreed. "We're going back."

Lent: "To where?"

"To the beginning…" the man answered, "to the land of the Renoloi, to find the Legends." He drew a deep breath, exhaled a sigh. "For all of this, the Legends are the key. They hold the secret. And by God, I—will—find the Secret of the Legends."

"How will you get there?" Deet asked nervously.

Scanning the dry ocean floor, "Walk."

"But Mr. Ames," Deet insisted, "what if the water returns?"

Ames looked at the women, all prepared to stand by him; then again to Deet, "We drown."

"That being the case..." Lent interjected drawing everyone's attention, "then we all drown together." The decision was made. "Moran, go to the village and get everyone. We leave immediately."

"Right away." Ten steps, and he vanished within the jungle's verdant web.

Slowly, still considering, Lent, Ames and the others walked away, down the beach. Behind them, clearly defined in the sand were two sets of tracks emerging from the ocean, going directly to it then walking around the trimaran… then curiously, inexplicably returning back to the sea.

Small feet, work boots—children's, size twelve.

CHAPTER NINE

...And the Lord drove the sea back by a strong east wind all night, and made the sea dry land, and the waters were divided. And the people... went into the midst of the sea on dry ground... [in part]
(Exodus 14:21-22 RSV)

Ames, four Renoloi, Lent, a thousand Pilgrims...

...Before them, the vast empty space of a vanished sea; dry ground laden with a now-brittle mantle of seaweed. Time to go home. With a sweep of his arm the multitude followed Lent as he, Ames, and the Renoloi walked from the beach onto the ocean floor, without fanfare beginning their journey... bound for their destiny.

Feet crunching as they trudged through knee-deep kelp, Ames was no longer able to suppress a dry grin. "What?" Lent asked.

"Just thinking," the man told him. "Seems we started out rather low-key, anti-climactically, if you know what I mean."

Puzzled, the youth inquired, "What would you have done?"

As though considering, still walking, Ames decided, "Well, you might at least have said something like, *Pilgrims Hooo!*" Darting a glance and wink to Seana, figuring Lent probably wouldn't get the joke. Alongside them Lent mulled it over then guffawed comically.

"Of course," as he smiled broadly, " 'Zane Grey's, The Lost Wagon Train', Dell Comics, Number 583, ten c-line, 1954." He bopped himself on the forehead exhibiting a silly gesture of realization, agreeing, "What an excellent idea —drat!" Looking over a shoulder, "Well, too late now; but I'll certainly remember next time."

Incredulous, Ames sighed, "Good grief," and teasing he ruffled Lent's hair causing Seana to smile.

Deet called out, "Mr. Ames!" closing the gap between them.

Glancing back, "Yeah?"

"I've been wondering…"

Maintaining their brisk pace, "About what?"

"Were you really serious when you said, if the water returns, 'we drown'?" Deet's concern was gathered with the wrinkles across his forehead, shadowed from the bright sunlight by his bushy eyebrows and Yankees ball cap.

"Well," Ames mused, "that depends."

"On what?" a spontaneous reply. Deet was worried.

Poker-faced, "How long can you tread water?" Beside him, Seana grinned.

Deet, wading through and stepping over dead kelp, keeping pace with them, allowed the question some serious consideration, then fretting finally concluded, "Well, not *that* long."

Stone serious, "Damned shame," Ames mumbled.

Next to them, Nitana and Tere giggled as Seana playfully bumped Ames with her hip and remarked, "That sounds like something Reed would say."

Ames' smile evaporated. "He probably already has."

Suddenly quiet again.

* * *

Nights later…

…They approached the mainland, still some miles distant, their direction of travel the towering composite landform illuminated by the volcano's amber glow. The catalytic precipitant of a hasty launch was now shepherding their return. The sun had set, blotted by the horizon an hour earlier as the opaque blend of darkness rose quietly from the other horizon.

More than a crescent, the waning quarter moon hung low in the night sky beyond the flickering column of torches carried by the

Pilgrims. A winding procession of candle flames, they resembled trailing luminous bugs on a mantled seafloor bound for the volcano's soft light, still off in the distance pulsing and glimmering, providing a beacon. They pushed on. Ames was determined to return to the cove near the newly formed volcanic mountain's base before stopping again to rest, and all were keenly aware they were again entering the domain of the Night Hunters, dangerous territory; but none translated the thought into words. A cool night wind at their backs and dry seaweed scraping their legs with each step into the brittle tangle, they proceeded in unspeaking determination.

The flutter of yellow flames filling the air with a harvest odor of torch smoke, and cornflake-crunches of moving feet, were the predominant sensations, synthesized, recorded and assimilated within the scope of consciousness. Beyond those, the superficial, cached within the subconscious was that feeling and the voice inside warning, *beware*, danger is out there, where you cannot see, in the darkness. That disquieting intimation bedeviling each and every one of them pushed exhaustion aside, keeping it in check —maintaining— kept them alert. Still, they were physically drained, and only halfway home.

She could not see them yet, but inside, she knew. "They are coming," Kalo warned.

Heeding her words Ames raised a hand and the Pilgrim army halted, all eyes straining, watching. Between them and the volcano the distant seafloor began moving; black waves of glistening arachnid exoskeleton and skittering barbed legs. Hundreds of them —Night Hunters.

"Any ideas?" Lent asked shifting the ax in his hand, a firmer hold, a fighting grip. The man turned to respond, his footstep producing a crackle as withered kelp crunched brittly beneath him. He looked down, then swept his foot through the dry tangle.

"Fire and water," his focus traveling over the seafloor, studying the approaching horde, their vile trilling chatter just now perceptible as they came in a bounding flow. "Wind at our back," he thought aloud. Little by little his troubled aspect transformed to a sneer of determination.

"Well?" Lent asked again, betraying worry.

"Spread them out. Form a line as wide as possible." The youth signaled and unquestioning the Pilgrims formed a solitary rank spanning more than the width of the approaching swarm. A moment later the army was in formation, prepared to face their adversary, black waves of chitin armor moving over the seafloor.

Ames waited. The Night Hunters were getting close.

And in the morning watch the Lord in the pillar of fire and of cloud looked down upon the host... and discomfited the host... (Exodus 14:24)

Apprehensive, Lent finally asked, "And...?"

Lowering his torch into the tangled seaweed, resolve in his eyes, hate in his words, Ames answered, "Burn 'em."

First a flicker. Then flames.

Erupting from his feet, streaking forward on the wind burning seaweed and kelp, fire ate the dehydrated vegetation. Hundreds of Pilgrims did the same; the slender line of fire sweeping before them with incredible speed, a sidewinder of inferno consuming and growing in a widening gap, an ocher fire-snake uncoiling across the ocean floor. Quickly it became a field of fire, vaporous sheets of translucence possessed with insatiable hunger, devouring everything, eating the seafloor as it ran.

They waited. They watched.

Very close now, coming for them, the obsidian giants were a debauchery of gnashing chelicerae and clustered white-glowing eyes piercing the night, rushing them as a menagerie confusion of twenty-foot legs armed with ragged-hook claws and wire-barb hair in black killer bodies. And fangs... razor-sharp tips, anticipating ...already weeping venom.

Weaving in a zigzag progression they clamored over one another bounding with recoil strides like jet-black Slinkys running irregular ground punching holes in the kelp, ripping it to slivers of silage that twirled behind them as dusty chaff spun from the clatter and blur of black speed. Consumed by the scent of the quarry swept before them on the wind and frenzied with insanity's ravenous hunger, disregarding the fiery barrier in front of them; evil and dark they attacked their prey.

Having given up the advantage of concealment within the jungle canopy and the fortress protection of their subterranean burrows on the mainland, the arachnids were now exposed on the barren seafloor running open terrain with only darkness for an ally. This time, the battle would play out more evenly, neither side holding advantage. Here, the Renoloi and Pilgrims, endowed with intellect and weapons, faced the stimuli-driven ruthlessness and fangs of the arachnid horde in a panoramic coliseum of primitive world.

Shredded by claws and eclipsed by the rush, the seabed's dead vegetation swept beneath them with the swather's song like rotary blades slashing harvest away, then spewn to the wind as hayflakes raising a dust cloud behind them. They were a sinuous momentum of clattering chitin zigzagging side to side, black so dark they glistened of blue, intent on the feast and bound for the kill.

Eighty-foot bounds. Predators intent on slaughter scrambling over each other and on top of one another in frenzy and rush, their ragged legs propelling them in a blur of swept speed —disregarding all else— even the flames.

Unreasoning, attacking—

They plunged forward oblivious to the roaring windstorm of fire boiling fifty feet high, one-thousand-degree incineration that whipped through the night...

—Into the flames!

...Then mindless confusion and running ocher fire, a chaotic, blistering mixture of alizarin liquid and swirling yellow-orange light. Flashing everywhere dozens of Hunters burst wildly from the infernal fireline as screeching, flaming overgrown cooties trampling the charred seafloor, careening insanely, chattering scream-like howls into the night. Blazing oily boils blistering their hulls, wind-twisted fire gobbling them, it was chaos of commotion and conflagration of momentum —low running torpedoes— all burning up.

Fireballs streaking toward them—

Their burning legs were dropping off or twirling away in the dark, scores of spiders being consumed in terminal rush. Hulls split open —legs flying apart— they were stumbling then collapsing in flaming scorched shells and boiling hot blood splattering fiery rain!

Amazed, the warriors watched the bizarre onslaught. Unexplainable. Spectral. Unreal. No creature should possess such unnatural and reckless willful sacrifice, a spectacle contradictory to instinct, violating the laws of nature. Lunging into such an intense fire and inevitable death—even starvation could not incite such maniacal insanity; to explain this there had to be more. Prepared, the army waited for the Hunters emerging from the wall of flames, should any survive.

"Unreal," Lent murmured, standing ready to fight.

"No creature should do such a thing," Nitana said uneasily. "This is not right." Not quite believing, Ames did not reply.

—White noise of savagery and trilling, burning, chattering insanity of animalistic screams!

Being eaten by fire, more Hunters erupted from the blaze wound with phantasmal spirals of yellow-orange flame trailing boiling dark smoke. A bedlam of screeching, they wildly ran the charred seafloor trilling bizarre creature screams —racing whirlwinds of cackling firelight— then collapsing or exploding in splashes of gray flaming muck.

Apprehensively, Seana leaned closer touching his arm asking softly, "What does this mean?"

A sideways glance, then again to the front, "I don't know; but Nitana's right." Scanning the mile of fireline before them and the unceasing arachnid self-sacrifice, his hand adjusted the scimitar, twitched ever so slightly, and the blade revolved just a bit. Finally, he proposed, "It's almost as if they're being controlled… driven."

Inside, Kalo felt it. "Something absolutely evil," she whispered collaring his attention; then abruptly it was snatched away with Deet's alarm.

"They're getting through!"

Armed with axes, swords, flails, spears, hoes, pitchforks, and bows, the army was ready to take on the Hunters; their weapons honed flawlessly sharp. Shimmering steel reflected firelight the length of each edge; their nerves wired electric and frayed at the seam, muscles drawn and wound to sinew and stone. Waiting for them, the warriors stood fast as Night Hunters began finding their way through gaps in the flames.

By circling the fireline some avoided the infernal barrier; however their natural tendency to attack as a pack proved fatalistically flawed. Those already burning collided with the others —scrambling and ricocheting, lethality trailing flame— pandemonium rushing the Pilgrims as wild confusion and fire.

Desperately, warriors tried to keep track of them, the harsh contrast of sweeping firelight and darkness causing intense night blindness. Time and again, bright orange to pitch —and blurry white spots. Fateful eyes flashed selecting dark targets amid blinding fireballs scattering all directions beneath a waning quarter moon black.

A scream —*snap*.

Grabbed by his neck, then into the air, the youth swelled —a balloon— liquid and lifeless. And the horrific sudden-suction literally drained him away: eyes sucked inside his skull, face wrinkling, chest shriveling drawn onto the thorax, abdomen collapsing to the spine as his arms and legs seized and wrapped tightly around brittle bones. Vacuum-packed. Then the fangs let go. Discarded and dead. Wizened skeletal dry rot his remains shattered when they hit the ground, a mummified shell gone fragile and still, a parchment Pilgrim who would never go home.

From below an ax swooped through the darkness severing the Hunter's pedicel, dropping the posterior abdomen heavily to the seafloor as the connective stalk rotated pumping like an eggplant with a neck. Still cackling the legs and front half sprang into the air then toppled sideways. A second whack —howling eerie violent chatter— it collapsed.

Missing four legs and flailing franticly like a spinning beetle ripping scorched residue to a black charcoal cloud, another flung a Pilgrim aside as a second rushed in swinging—hard. Timed precisely his blade severed the head evacuating eight glowing-white eyes from a simple gray brain. Renouncing a fading drawn wail as its insides leaked out, the gigantic spider finally died.

And another. Reflecting firelight illuminated its shadowy silhouette as the Hunter made the breach closing in on its prey. Its speed was amazing, resembling a hovercraft thrashing black ground it skimmed the charred terrain so quickly it seemed to almost fly. Coming.

Nitana was ready, leading the target; Kalo alongside, her bowstring drawn tight. Within range now, each inhaled a deep breath, held it —and two powerful, *snaps*— as arrows flew into clustered night-vision eyes. Crumpling, driven to the burned seafloor the monstrous spider furrowed headlong, its legs collapsing then dragging limply behind until its posterior abdomen's momentum flipped it end over end and it slid to a halt on its back. Quivering, the legs contracted to the cephalothorax then slowly eased splaying outstretched and lax. Seemingly embarked upon a desperate search for reprieve from its fate, for a moment the eyes continued to glow as seeping dark blood oozed from two mortal wounds. It flowed over them blotting its pixel vision as the luminous glow faded, darkened, dull, then went out.

Far and wide dead arachnids littered the seafloor as others leaped over their carcasses, attacking indiscriminately, deranged, anything that moved. Hacking holes and ripping splattering chunks, resolutely Pilgrims took them. Standing their ground, Pilgrims defied the horde's intense savagery of claws and fangs wrapped in whirlwinds of fire. Determined, repelling them —flashes of steel— fast-moving violence. And still smoldering in bubbling-soup piles, the tally of fallen spiders and shriveled Pilgrims mounted, while above the rampant fray on the battleground, rising smoke veiled the sky with a cloak of dark, wafting silence.

The seaweed inferno and running bedlam of burning arachnids rendered their nocturnal vision useless. They were hunters gone blind. Spurred by instinct and evil the demented horde inexplicably began lashing out at one another; a maniacal slaughter of insanity on fire, burning hulks shrieking white noise of savagery dragging meteoric trails of flame-twisted smoke.

Too many to track, everywhere at once —fireflashes— leaping fireballs searing overhead —and nowhere— just dark patches of night. Sensory congestion was overwhelming, too much going on to sort it all out. Sweeping darkness —then light— in an unending mixture of confusion peppered with fractured collisions of sound and sight. Bright flashes —night-blindness— total chaos of raw mental images…

Motion: dark smears of obsidian —the clatter— and a glimpse of ragged black legs.

Fire: yellow-orange liquid wind streaming passed trailing rank vapors of burnt-garbage odor. Then above, to that side —and a streak over there— gone then reappearing again.

Dark: empty and black —can't see a thing— sick with the anticipation of danger and death.

Mindless eyes: glowing clusters of white —never blinking— then disappearing from sight.

Wind: glimmers of steel —cold air then heat— swishing closely enough to hear air sliced with each edge.

Smoke: invisible and thick, its taste in the air —burning the eyes— beyond the amber, dragged into the night.

Sound: crackling flames and hollow thwacks of things being cut —then running feet— pieces pelting the ground in the crowded blend of darkness —or, *snap, someone's dead.*

Fire: boiling and blinding, then things with no texture —just silhouettes— phantoms vanishing in the blink of an eye.

Smell: acrid and intense, with splattering blood —harvest bonfire's odor of burnt autumn leaves— ash and armpits soaked with sweat, and an indecipherable mixture of others.

Chaos: people everywhere —hair, more running feet— shards of calamity and scattering drops.

Too much confusion: cackling screams and mind-bending chatter —rushing claws— then quick slices of steel crunching chitin-based bone, fluttering winds and the flames, too dark even to see.

…And the sick hollow awareness of death barely an instant away.

Hunter coming down—

Its legs a grappling hook of eight ragged claws lunging at Ames and Seana, eyes locked on, fangs wide and coming at them. He reeled —the scimitar whirling overhead— a glimmer of firelight shimmering on steel —intercepting— piercing cackles and screams!

Clattering feet tearing the mishmash of burned kelp and black ash; eyes fixed on the giant spider Seana ducked. No time to move —but the scimitar was already there flashing through— she could sense it in the darkness.

The enormous spider was collapsing —again and again— the razor-edge slicing with blurs of gleaming motion, sweeping into the eyes sending them twirling overhead then disappearing somewhere. Finishing the monster he sidestepped shaving off four legs taking it to the ground —another through the neck— and last, to the stump of its head.

Seana was still crouched where she had been, the Night Hunter in pieces around them; that quickly it was over. Brandishing the weapon Ames winked, *nice sword;* then quickly surveying the battlefield and offering his hand he helped her to her feet.

Ames' words, loud and clear: "Stay close to the fire!"

Fiercely clenching the twibil in a raised, fisted hand, Lent signaled the Pilgrims, his voice carrying throughout the night. "Forward— follow the flames!"

For the first time they went on the offensive, into the Hunters, equaling them in combat and darkness. Inspired and advancing, the terms of engagement had finally shifted and balanced to center; and now the young army attacked!

A single footstep at a time, they moved forward, tense with the uncertainty of not knowing what the outcome might be; but instilled with commitment and determination to fight. Slowly but unwavering at first, each footfall succeeding the last, then more quickly and faster until altogether they were running… the Charge!

"—*Attack!*" an unseen warrior's battle cry rang courageously through the night. And with that single bolstering word, almost nine hundred young Pilgrims swarmed over a charred seafloor of black flaking ash.

Avoiding burning spiders and fractured hulls strewn upon the seafloor like the smoldering ruins of blown-out tanks at the Battle at Kursk, the army launched their assault into the midst of the horde. Their weapons reflecting fire-steel in the dark, the army rushed headlong into the Hunters; and with courage of conviction they swept viciously laying waste a swath through the monstrous horde scattering them on swift feet of determination with fleet wings of blade.

Severed in the dark, splintered legs flew like harvested bamboo or crooked black sticks flying into the night, disjointed hulls collapsing like immense oily vases, all of them left scattered in gray blood on charred, darkened ground. Shimmering blades cut savagely, chopping and ripping, hacking spiders with echoes of muck dismembering chelicerae, pedipalps and fangs among scattered clusters of white eyes now gone dull. Sliced cephalothoraxes and abdomens were cratered with blade wounds draining jelly-soup puddles that oozed onto the ash, later to congeal and tomorrow dry in the sun.

Warrior battle cries overpowered all else instilling them with a rush of courage they had not known before, even drowning out the surreal, trilling chatter of the empty-minded loathsome arachnids.

And still they charged on, following the fire.

Conflict raged. Dying valiantly Pilgrims went down taking their enemies with them, screams lancing over a battlefield charred with ribbons of flame —cries from here, there and beyond— lost somewhere in the darkness. Relentlessly, doggedly, inflicting considerable losses they forged an anvil of mortality through the savage black horde.

Then, as if swept up suddenly in a wind, the confrontation abruptly ended when the Hunters veered off and fled resembling an unnumbered flock of blackbirds changing directions in the sky. As quickly as they had come, they ran, shredding blackened kelp, seeking security again within the jungle's shroud of ecliptic darkness, their pouring black, wicked commotion rolling over the seabottom as opaque waves pursuing the obscurity of unseen horizon beyond the illumination of flames.

Never before had the dark killers been bested on a foray; and were they thinking creatures capable of evaluating, or endowed with rationale, they might contemplate the defeat and learn. But their involuntary interpretation of the event precluded any such analysis. Simply put, this was nothing more than predatory misfortune; the prey got away.

Still, as before, they were hungry. And mindlessly driven by the impulse of instinct, soon again, veiled by a raven moon and disguised within the sable cloak of arboreal canopy, inveterate within their element… they would return.

They were Night Hunters.

* * *

Dwindling flames…

…And wisps of dark smoke, the fire had run its course devouring the seafloor, her tawny mantle now ashen and black. Ramparts of scorched jutting landscape spanned the miles burned hours earlier, with all surface life now swept away. Behind them lay a wasteland charred and darkened wafting cerulean willows in black smoke that drifted then congealed as a haze.

As far as the eye could see, the terrain lay littered with carcasses of exoskeleton armor venting trailing fingers of smoke. Scattered everywhere, silent and still after violent collisions of life and death, were crumpled arachnid hulls lying tangled and twisted. And among the hollow shells of villainy lay others, Pilgrims whom bequest the most precious gift they could offer, those who willingly sacrificed themselves so that others might live. Like untold conflicts past and forgotten with time, this battle had ended and many were lost, but not forgotten.

For those who believed, their souls were Beyond.

* * *

Dawn was creeping from below...

...Rising to meet them. Only a few more miles. Lent and the others were finally approaching the cove at the base of the volcano that now towered mountainous, obsidian and basaltic on top of their buried village. They were exhausted from the forced march of the journey, hunger and thirst, waned adrenaline withdrawals after the rush, and those lost along the way. These circumstances and emotions combined and coagulated within them fashioning a mixture of feelings and stress that consumed energy with a consistent metabolic hunger, and drained it away. Despite overwhelming fatigue, nearing the point of collapse, they pushed on. Heads down, heaviness in their footsteps, they carried their weapons lowered, blades layered with congealed dark blood.

Still they marched, trudging along.

Bone tired, moving slowly, Lent surveyed their random formations. More than ever before, within he sensed the stirring of pride. His Pilgrims had fought with honor and courage and prevailed. True, many had fallen during the conflict; but predictably, that was the outcome in most struggles. With this battle had dawned the realization the Hunters would no longer control the night. In the open, beyond their camouflage of jungle they were vulnerable, and their weakness could be exploited. The arachnids survived by instinct. His people survived through adaptive learning, evolution—survival of the fittest.

As he looked across the ranks at Ames, the man's tired eyes met his, and Lent wondered whom this stranger, this friend really was. Where had he come from and what purpose was there in him being here. For so long Lent's people had believed they were alone in the jungle; then one night that all changed with a dream… and a note in a bottle. The youth would not accept coincidence, a random chance of fate. Surely there must be more.

And who were his companions, the Renoloi, who were so different than Ames and himself, yet also, so much the same. Lent was still young, inexperienced in many ways, but eager to learn; and he respected the man for both his courage and dedication to his companions. Lent was still unaware, unable to grasp the connection. Although many Pilgrims had offered to assist Seana she steadfastly refused, always turning to Ames; and each time they asked the man why, he offered the same answer, one they could not appreciate— *because Reed is my friend.*

Walking slowly together, Seana weakly looked up to Ames; and noticing him watching Lent she squeezed him lovingly. He glanced down without saying anything, and they kept moving. She looked across to Lent and their eyes met, his white teeth flashing a contrast below the shaggy hair; and together they smiled.

His ingratiating manner and silly grin captivated Nitana and Tere, and unable to help themselves, they smiled as well momentarily washing exhausted expressions away. The silent Kalo observed, always very careful, invariably suspicious. She did not smile, but almost did… then looked away.

Encouraged and pleased Lent perceived he was winning her confidence. No matter how slowly each bit of rapport was a token of progress, she now being more receptive, even the tiniest bit. The others were more open, more at ease, and talked more freely; but with Kalo there was always guarded suspicion. Somehow he would find a way to win her trust; but it would take time. She was different.

Accepting that realization, again he temporarily put aside his effort at friendship and was taken in transition of thought. For now, exhaustion born of exertion and satisfaction born with their victory returned, precluded Kalo. A heartening warmth welling within, he surveyed the ranks and was content, proud of his people. They had done well, fought well, decisively had won the battle. That much was true. But in the trees and the darkness the Night Hunters were still out there.

Lent had no way of knowing... the war had not even begun.

CHAPTER TEN

Weary, draggin'-ass tired…

…The Pilgrim army finally arrived at the cove where the trimaran had been harbored, and ascending from the seafloor they climbed up to the beach. The strip of sand bore remarkable likeness to a war zone, fifty yards wide. Along the waterline, forty feet high, an ungodly wall of entangled dead spiders evidenced their frantic but futile attempt to escape the volcano's fury. Their unwillingness to enter the ocean cost them hundreds as they clamored on top of one another and died en masse at the water's edge. The destruction on the beach and hillsides reeked of timber burn and sulfuric blast, charred and glazed over, exposed to temperatures of molten two-thousand-degree rock.

For miles in any direction the landscape lay barren waste, flattened and cinder-burned, all the way to the volcano's igneous face; then reaching beyond, everything destroyed for many miles more. What was once lush green plateau now lay ashes and dead, a purifying fire-harvest that consumed millions of emerald trees now supplanted with charred, black jutting stumps. Incredible though it was, the jungle's obliteration was surpassed and overshadowed, even eclipsed by the carnage on the beachhead—D-Day intense and horrendously gory.

With careful scrutiny the raisin-like skeletal remains of the nine Renoloi who died there could be located; but their shriveled presence was unfairly diminished by the decomposing hulls of arachnids that had fallen. Grossly rank and putrid the scent of slaughter wafted a clinging smog among hundreds of giant spiders that lay collapsed and hollow, in death their shells no less empty than they had been in life. The soulless creatures were scorched and burned, some mutilated until they were almost unrecognizable, all of them lying in a congealed lake of unmalleable ectoplasm blood.

Scattered among the corpses were innumerable fragmented blobs that were one night careening skyrockets of lava bombs. Now, partially flattened, the cooled projectile firefall lay extruded obsidian marbles in silica-glass cratered sand. The beach was covered with them and the exposed seafloor was littered with pieces of splatter formed when the cold water fractured them creating black, glittery glass pebbles. Sparkling obsidian was everywhere. They were beautiful melted marbles... and cold.

Completely burned, the driftwood riprap wall was reduced to gray-powder ash and charcoal collar-ringed pieces. And with first impressions it seemed everything on the beach was destroyed; but upon closer examination there could be found innocuous objects that were passed over, somehow left untouched by the holocaust of flames. There were two Folgers coffee cans, flakes of styrofoam that at one time was an ice chest, burnt fifty-five-gallon drums now mostly rusted and crushed, a drum set, broken lamp, and two sizable, scorched wooden crates still tightly hasped and secured with steel strapping tape.

With exhaustion coagulating syrup-thick and pushing mid-winter lethargic through their veins, the travelers settled onto every available nook and cranny of unoccupied sand. The hazards of sleep deprivation now bordering precariously on delirium, they were too tired to continue any longer. Plopping down wherever they could, in less time than it took to arrange their sleeping quarters, one by one they promptly drifted to sleep. Whether curled with others or sprawled full length, the Pilgrim army settled in for several hours of down time. Much needed rest.

Lent propped himself against a vacant cephalothorax, legs spread and dead tired. Without comment he observed as Ames secured a little niche of sand, then Seana, Nitana, Tere and Kalo all snuggled around him forming a webbed nest of warm bodies. He couldn't help but smile, quietly contemplating the connection that he was not yet able to translate; however, it was not so far away as he perceived. His fleeting thought, watching them... still, serene, huddled, and secure ...as his eyelids closed and the smile faded to slumbering unconsciousness—*they seem so much to belong together, a part of one another.* And with that, everything was quiet.

Sleep.

* * *

Sunlight, eyes fluttering, open...

...He lay still, the Renoloi piled upon him; arms, legs and heads all pillowed in a cluster, having not yet awakened. Daylight half spent and the sun's warmth and healing rays seeping into sore, strained muscles with therapeutic balm; it felt good. The past hours of needed sleep were golden, more valued than troy ounce. Four long days still ahead—their return to the land of the Renoloi.

While Ames waited quietly for them to wake, he studied each in turn.

Tere. So engaging, her enthusiastic zest for life and dedication to her companions—the image framed within his mind's eye as she scaled the mast to the crow's nest; her laughter, feline agility and grace. She had come from their homeland determined and eager, now dismayed and perhaps disillusioned with their hardships.

Nitana. Tian's second; mature, serious, considerate—fearless and unrelenting in her loyalty to both leader and people, willing to die if necessary, without reservation. Beauty and courage molded into the perfect warrior, Tian's wisdom clearly self-evident in her selection.

Seana. More precious to Reed than she could ever know—and for that reason alone Ames had committed her care to himself. Yet, more than that, aside from Tian, the Renoloi he knew best, and loved.

And finally, Kalo. The silent one; the girl who had embarked on an odyssey of growing without being aware—the pure face of innocence gone now, evaporated with their ordeal, defined instead with experience and stress, life having taken its toll. The journey had transformed her in unseen ways. Kalo the girl, who had been, was no more. Now Kalo, a young woman, a warrior returned. But there was more in her story, things he could not appreciate… an unknown conversation in the cabin of the trimaran. *"Perhaps you have begun a journey, a journey that others will follow. Today you are a Renoloi warrior… beyond that lies your destiny."*

As he looked upon the four of them, earnestly Ames tried; but the more he tried, the stronger his heart pulled him back. *Tian, Reed… where are you?* The penance of being alone, emptiness flooding his soul pouring black and hollow into a void lying somewhere within, sequestered in fire where nothing could reach it… the whirlwind hall of cold, aching loss.

Pain sneaked up and got stuck in his throat pushing a sour taste that filled his eyes until they teared, and he choked on a swallow. Involuntarily shivers chilled him with burning cold and an ache that numbed to his heels. The twisted nausea wrest inside his chest as a sickening lump that made his hands tremble; so he inhaled a deep sigh, tried to breathe it away. A futile attempt.

Alone with his thoughts the pain had again captured him, and his soul leaked tired tears that dripped to his cheeks. Very quietly, he sighed, *Tian, Reed…* and slowly his gaze was drawn skyward to where he perceived Heaven might be. "Please," he whispered, pleading, hoping, praying somewhere in the silence… Someone might hear him.

A gentle hand caressed his, and squeezed. He turned to her.

"Are you all right?" Seana asked.

Sniffling a runny nose, "I was just thinking."

With those words she knew, tears flooding her eyes as her emotions came loose, and folding into his arms Seana cried too. He held her, agonizing, knowing her need, tears briefly cleansing and trying to soothe the pain in her heart. Determined, willing his consciousness to petrified stone he summoned resolve from within. He had to be strong. But this time, it was very, *very* difficult.

After a while her trembling subsided a little, and stroking her head, brushing hair from her face then tucking it behind her ear, he comforted, "It's okay. It will be all right." Their shared loss was their common bond, and he gently caressed her cheek. But now, no matter how he defied the feeling, that hollow vexation consuming his soul crept insidiously within him. The anguish would not go away. The fire would never go out.

From behind, small hands lay upon them both and Kalo's hushed voice consoled, "Do not cry. They are not dead."

Seana and Ames, unaware she had awakened and startled by her presence quickly turned with wondering, questioning faces. "How can you be so certain?" Seana asked petulantly, her words sharpened along the edge.

Not offended; feeling, understanding, the girl patiently answered, "There is a reason."

"But how can you *know*?"

Plainly, seriously, Kalo answered, "Inside, I feel it... because I believe."

* * *

Soon...

...Pilgrims were stirring, none knowing what might lie ahead, but all willing to find out, prepared to finish the journey. Their homeland was gone, now sealed for an eternity beneath a towering volcanic mountain. They knew it was time to move on to a new place awaiting their arrival... the land of the Renoloi.

Lent asked, "You ready?" preparing to move them out.

Ames, brushing off sand, looked over the cove again, believing they would never return to this place; and as he checked one last time his attention was strangely, unexplainably drawn, awareness finally dawning as he halted abruptly. "No, wait—" thinking, "—the forest for the trees."

"The what?" Lent asked following his eyes. "It's all ashes," taking in the battered beach and scorched forest of stumps as far as one could see. "There aren't any trees."

"There is a reason —not just the trimaran, something more." Then quickly turning he said, "Break them open."

"Break what open?"

"The crates," Ames told him pointing out the rough lumber containers.

Waiting. Resting partially submerged in the sand were two large wooden crates, hasped and sealed. Still there.

The travelers immediately converging upon them, curious, Lent inserted the pike tip of his twibil beneath a steel-tape strap; and turning the blade, applying firm lifting pressure, it snapped easily in two. He promptly cut the remaining straps while others hacked off the hasps then pried the side panels apart revealing its contents. They were solidly packed in individual pressboard boxes, two dozen per crate, signified with indelible markings stenciled with flat-black faded paint, block lettering four inches high: M2A1. Taking several from the stacks the Pilgrims quickly opened them—Christmas presents of unknown origin on a war-ravaged strip of sand.

Intrigued and having no idea what the strange thing might be, Kale removed the first from its shipping package inspecting it. Three-cylinder tank group with a valve at the bottom, mounted together on a harnessed backpack with a dark snake of flexible hose and trigger operated gun-group with suppressor nozzle. It was spray-painted military issue, drab olive-green.

Kale: "What is it?"

"Flame thrower—from World War II. Kale, help me get this on." The youth eagerly lifted and held the queer contraption as Ames harnessed it onto his back. Once mounted, he prepared to demonstrate unscrewing the ignition shield, a nozzle device at the end of the barrel; next, inserting an ignition cylinder, a flame producing cartridge, and finally, screwing the shield back on. Last, he turned the valve handle charging the line.

The weapon seemed operable; and anticipating, with a broad sweep of his arm he motioned for them to clear a path. "Get back— everyone move away." They scurried aside. A moment's more tense psychological preparation considering an explosive worst-case scenario, finger on the fuel valve trigger... he squeezed.

Ocher jetstream of napalm hosed an inferno of splatter-incineration that boiled black-orange in its wake. Churlish opaque smoke and molasses-like flames billowed with sooty fire-lace clouds engulfing everything it touched in sticky-jell blaze. The air dried —an arid hot flash— sucked up with the flames into a jettisoning whirlwind of mankind's destruction; long since past, but not forgotten.

Releasing the trigger valve he wiped beads of sweat from his brow, then relieved, plainly announced, "Whew, it works."

Hushed amazement passed over the crowd until, unable to come up with anything more profound, "Ingenious," Lent finally said, realizing the weapon's usefulness. "The Hunters."

Ames beamed, "Forty-eight flame throwers," giving notice, "now we kick spider ass —and take names."

Clenching his fist with a gush of enthusiasm, Lent agreed, "Yeah, we kick spider ass..." then tractably admitted, "—whatever that means."

In minutes the crates were empty, the weapons passed among the Pilgrims, and with their new weaponry and no reason to delay longer, they were ready to go.

With a forward sweeping arm, a "Pilgrims Ho-oo!" and a dash of raised eyebrow, Lent's indelible mischievous grin started them moving. "This time I didn't forget," passing Ames and leading them out; then talking to himself, "Does have a nice ring to it," his voice quickly drifting beyond hearing.

Standing alongside with the Renoloi as Pilgrims filed passed, Ames surveyed the beach one last time, viewing the carnage and devastation, finally realizing why the dwarfs had so carefully directed them, sent them. He looked at Kalo suspecting she knew, as he acceded gratefully, *P.T. Barnum, Wilson... wherever you are, thank you.* And wondering, in the back of his mind he thought he heard, *you're welcome,* but believed he must have imagined it, although it made him blink twice.

Listening carefully, Kalo stood beside him. Always silent.

They followed the Pilgrims.

* * *

Days later, familiar terrain...

...Single-file they traveled the meandering trail shadowing the cliffs abutting the lowland and river. From somewhere within the canopy their approach was observed, inciting a sentry's whistle. Anticipating, quickening her pace, Nitana answered returning a solitary note.

The procession continued as wraith-like, appearing from the understory Renoloi warriors materialized from within the camouflage of greenery and joined the caravan of Pilgrim army, following along, interspersed among their ranks. Silently the two peoples blended without conversation continuing toward the village and the end of their journey.

The Pilgrims were unanimously surprised and impressed with the stealth of the Renoloi. Phantasms, able to move so invisibly, so gracefully; to be so close, yet remain unseen, mere footsteps away, within reach of delivering a fatal blow. This people knew the jungle—its mood, its breath, its life and being. More than a part of their world, they were one with it.

Eyes darting here and there, walking just ahead of Ames and Seana as he followed Nitana and Kalo, Lent tried time and again to locate the silent, waiting warriors before they would move revealing their presence. Repeatedly he was unable to. One after the other Renoloi would materialize within arm's reach of him offering a cautious brief smile or curious look, then wait motionlessly again eventually joining the procession somewhere farther back in line.

While Pilgrims stepped solidly, heel to toe —thumping, making noise— pushing flora aside with their arms and bodies, and rustling leaves; the Renoloi floated, wisps of warrior, seeming never to touch anything. They possessed the allure of an evaporating heartbeat with wondering eyes. Obviously, visibly apparent, the tribes were diametrically different.

"Like ghosts," Lent murmured.

Amused, Nitana darted a glance and wry smile to Kalo; then over a shoulder to Lent, "Yes," she confirmed cordially.

Another woman appeared alongside the trail, so close Lent's arm brushed against her as he stepped passed. He reacted with a start, jumping instantly beyond and away from her. *Very—impressive,* he admitted.

With monotone objectivity, and without a smile Kalo told him, "They are Renoloi warriors." Eyes wide with fascination, the youth said nothing more.

Shortly—

They entered the village where Tondra stood waiting. Her first words to Nitana: "Tian—the others?" Sensing something wrong, but not waiting for an answer and seeing Lent as he and more Pilgrims filed into view, "Who are they?"

Nitana stopped before her. "I will explain all that I am able."

Tondra turned to Ames, he taking her by the arm, "Lent and his people. Tian is missing," his involuntary sigh and demeanor speaking volumes. "Let's go to the meeting circle and we will explain."

She nodded, then authoritatively, "Nemuk,[13] Ronto, help Seana." Immediately the women stepped forward to assist their injured friend, intending to escort her to her hut.

"No please, I wish to go to the circle."

Understanding, Tondra conceded and they began in that direction, again ordering others as they proceeded, "They are hungry and thirsty. Food and water," then a pause, watching Pilgrims still filing in behind them, speculating, "quite a lot."

Stepping alongside her and extending his hand in friendship, "I'm Lent."

Tondra studied him momentarily; then continuing at a brisk walk turned again to Nitana and Ames, not quite sure what to make of him. "Lent... the note in the bottle?"

"One and the same," Ames replied as both shook their heads.

Accepting his hand, "I am Tondra." He grinned with his doltish pretense causing her eyes to snap the unspoken question to Nitana and Ames; their reply —peculiar, smart smiles. A bit more at ease she told him, "You are welcome here, as are all your people," perhaps emphasizing, *all*, more than the other words.

From the dense foliage—

Along the path that led to the meeting circle small eyes were watching each and every stranger coming in. A small heart was pounding furiously with anxiety and anticipation; concerned, desperately worried... *but he had said so.*

Within the clearing—

They assembled reticently, nervously, as children scurried about offering Chiqua to those who were hungry; and all of them were. With this homecoming there was no celebration. In spite of the newcomers, sadness was pervasive; friends were lost.

It was a curious exchange, Renoloi and Pilgrims all staring at one another, hesitant at first but gradually intermingling, trying to initiate friendship. At length, small conversations emerged, very succinct and abrupt to begin, but in time expanding as both people became more at ease and suspicions receded. By the time the Chiqua was eaten there hummed a constant drone of dialogue and interaction among small groups, all being eager, fed with curiosity and wanting to know those who were different than themselves.

Some time ago the Renoloi had befriended two strangers who had inexplicably emerged from the jungle. The same just happened again.

Ames and Reed were now accepted as no less than their own, and to the Renoloi, the only difference this time—there were so many new names to learn. As for the Pilgrims, their exposure to Nitana, Seana, Tere and Kalo, accompanied by Ames, had already moved them beyond the most difficult obstacle, mistrust. They could foresee no reason their people would be any different. The journey had been long and hard and they had fought side by side, their struggle to survive binding them without them realizing it. But beyond the hardships and dangers they had overcome, there was another reason... known only to one.

Many years earlier a small girl and her mother read of mysterious things that had been and were yet to be in the land of the Renoloi, the girl's mother from time to time pointing out what she believed to be important, passages that her child should commit to memory. The young girl, confident in her mother's wisdom, learned all she was able and tucked those lessons away, believing the time would come when that knowledge would serve her well. The girl was correct. Her name was Tian.

Many years before, she had been there, looked upon words chiseled in stone and inlaid with gold; cavernous walls of elusive mystery and wisdom, beyond her ability to comprehend. Those were the Inscriptions of the Sacred Temple, truly magnificent in and of themselves; but only a small part of what was sequestered there— more, much more, things the Renoloi could not understand. Magic.

When she was a small girl, inside those mountains Tian had studied the Legends, over and over... very carefully. But today, she was missing.

The meeting circle—

Now, almost routine, having developed a sense of security in being near to one another and with what they had been through; Ames, Seana, Nitana, Tere and Kalo sat together. And as usual, by this time almost habit as well; Lent, Kale and Deet sat with them. Tondra, wanting to know of their expedition, joined them. For almost an hour, Nitana recounted what happened, sequential events, since the group left their village, her recollection telling enough to transfix the attention of all who could hear —and impeccable— accurate to the most intricate or innocuous detail.

During the narration Tondra and the Renoloi listened intently; this was a matter of utmost importance. Lita and Denen were known and accepted to be lost; however, with less than irrefutable proof, Tian and Reed were *missing*. Regardless how improbable the likelihood of them being alive, Tondra refused to acquiesce to their deaths.

After Nitana's account was concluded, Tondra and others began with their questions. Many questions. It was late afternoon and the inquiry would continue for hours, details, clarification of many things.

Ames sat quietly involving himself in the discussion only when asked, apart from that, allowing others to speak. He had been there, already knew. He was preoccupied, still though, his senses were keenly attuned. Sitting beside Tere, Seana briefly slumped in a doze, worn with fatigue and the nagging pain in her shoulder. Kalo, as always, sat motionless, listening.

From the bushes—

There came a meek little sound from behind them, near the clearing's periphery. Lithely Kalo glanced at Ames and both inconspicuously rose and stepped to the shrublayer undergrowth. Kneeling side by side, each with a hand carefully pushing fern fronds aside, they found her.

The man looked down, stricken; a bitter lump of scrambled emotions lodged thick in his throat. Overwhelmed with empathy he said nothing. Huddled within the tangled greenery, curled fetal, in unrealized, unknown depths of despair's darkest clutches, wet shriveled thumb poked desperately into her mouth, she hid miserable and small. Reed's special one.

Afraid to cry again in front of the others the child had secreted herself, all alone with her misery. Her grubby wet little face was covered with dirt, tears, and a runny nose… from waiting, from hiding for so long. Her grief-stricken little eyes bespoke the loss only her appearance could evoke.

"Where is my Uncle Reed?" her small words pleaded —piercing— then drawing hot wire through their hearts. Kalo and Ames were both speechless. "I waited for him right here. I saw. I watched them all." Her sobs supped away with her breath. "I looked and I looked, but I did not see him…" and she cried, "where is my Uncle Reed?"

Ames opened his mouth, but words would not come, and Kalo's eyes were already tearing. The man tried to answer but couldn't, aware his lips were moving but his heart stopped the sound. *How could they have forgotten?*

The child scampered from the dirt onto his lap and desperately flung her arms around his neck. This friend—he—was her last ray of hope. For a moment she clung to him and continued sobbing with the trembling heaves only a child can manage. But finally Jade mounted her tiny courage, drew back just a little, wiped her soaked cheeks and runny nose and asked, pleading for his help one last time.

As bravely as she had ever been able, she asked, "Where is my Uncle Reed?" then waited expectantly, hopeful. A child's analogy: *my mother left and did not come back... but Uncle Reed did; he had to, he absolutely promised.*

Kalo couldn't stand anymore. Her heart ripped in two. Even though others who overheard were beginning to gather around them, she trembled, and cried. With all they'd been through, they had completely forgotten the day Reed had absolutely promised.

"*Pleeease...* where is my Uncle Reed?" her pitiful plea, words that wrenched his heart in pieces.

He tried again to speak, but choked; knowing Jade's world was about to be shredded by the villainous transgression of reality. Uncle Remus, Jack and the Beanstalk, and all the rest, obliterated in one fell swoop. Kalo, torn desperately inside, lay her head against them embracing both; her heartfelt, most sincere effort, the most she could do to help them get through this. But she knew there were no words in any world to describe how much—how deeply this would hurt.

"Sweetheart," Ames whispered, "Uncle Reed—Uncle Reed... is missing."

Terror swept over her pale small face stabbing despair in her heart. Shaking her head, her eyes fixed on his face, her brain absorbing his words but reacting with pain, she sobbed, denying. Her frail chest heaved a violent gasp, tiny fingers clutching his shoulders with lost confusion; she involuntarily stammered, "Oh no, oh no, oh no..."

Eyes wild with panic and desperation —flashing everywhere— across the people now gathered around them, trying to find him, "Oh no, oh no, oh no..." but he still was not there. One final sob of hysterical bewilderment —chaos— her heart shattered in pieces as her eyes filled with tears that ran down her face, hair and dirt matted against it. "Oh no, oh no, oh no —*ple-eease...*"

Then frantically to Kalo, who could do nothing; then someone, —anyone. Jade let go of the man sliding aimlessly from his knee, wringing her fragile hands together, "Oh no, oh no, oh no..." backing away from them all.

Ames reached for her, but she was too quick moving beyond his grasp. "Oh no, oh no, oh no..." and in a heartbeat she turned and vanished in the undergrowth —a swish of leaves. The last, pitiful sounds they all heard, "Oh no, my Uncle Reed... *oh noooo...*"

Wiping her eyes, Kalo looked at him. "I will find her." A tip of his head and she was gone, absorbed within the green.

So overwhelmed he couldn't get up, Ames turned his face to the ground. A solitary drop of salt-water, a tear, spattered on his bare foot dredging an axiom from a world long ago. Realizing now he had been so absorbed with his own self-pity that others had been neglected... including a small child. Overwhelmed, on her own... all alone.

He sighed and thought, *I had no shoes, and complained... until I met a man who had no feet.* An old Persian proverb, he did not know who said it; but now, as then, it was still true. Inside his head, in his heart, in his soul, the fading, excruciating echo of loss even he could not comprehend, *Oh no, oh noo... oh noooo...*

* * *

Not too long after...

...The sun on its way to the horizon, Kalo returned from the jungle, meeting him at the edge of the clearing.

"Did you find her?" Shaking her head Kalo indicated she had. "Where?"

"Hiding among some ferns, alongside the trail near the cliffs." Then quickly, "Come, I will show you."

"No, I'll find her," he told her, "and try to explain what happened."

"But she is well hidden..." then understanding, she directed, explaining, "—where the trail turns sharply from the escarpment to the right."

He left the village.

Following the escarpment, moments later Ames quit running, slowing to a walk and moving more carefully, listening. The rush of whitewater below was fading, the mood of quiet returning. His bare feet padded silently upon the soft humus loam and his concentration became focused, attuned to the world surrounding him. He kept moving, slowly, closed his eyes, the Renoloi way. Listening, ahead, nearby, a fragile whimper; six more steps and he knelt, hands gently prying fronds aside. A child's eyes and pitiful, grubby face peered up at him.

Whispered: "I'm here, Jade."

"But my Uncle…" her words broken with heaving gasps of supping, "…Reed is not." Her heart and faith were destroyed. "He absolutely—promised me." And she cried again.

"I know, Sweetheart," as he reached for her, taking her small curled body into his arms. Even though he tried to hold back the tears they still leaked out with his heart, his soul commiserated to a raveled knot. A deep sigh, and he tried to continue. "I know Reed absolutely promised." Tenderly he drew the child to his chest and she lay her head upon his shoulder wrapping her frail arms around his neck; she, needing so desperately to be held. He held her gently, caressing, and yet unable to soothe her pain. First, her mother had gone away and not come back, and now… 'Uncle Reed'.

Forlorned, she sobbed weakly, "Where is my Uncle Reed?"

A deep slow breath, and softly, "There was a terrible storm at sea," he tried to explain; then, "I don't know. I just don't know," was all he could manage.

Jade trembled, and cried… and the man held her. For a very long time he knelt motionlessly, holding the child… and she cried. Every so often he would gently, lovingly run his hand from her head, down, pat her back, comfort ever so softly… and let her cry.

Inside, pain turned and wound. Two who were lost, because two others were lost. They were all alone in a world neither could yet understand, a very small child and a stranger, this man. *I had no shoes…* Finally, Ames could take no more, and holding Jade, he began to cry. He trembled and cried, this time not for himself, but for her *...a man who had no feet.*

At length, Jade rubbed her cheeks and runny nose, and lovingly, caring, wiped the tears from his face. "You are crying," she observed with innocent curiosity, concerned.

"Yes," he whispered, looking away.

"Do you miss Uncle Reed too?" He nodded; a brief laugh of hopeless sorrow, eyes bleary and red. Jade puzzled a moment and finally mustered her courage, tiny and incomprehensive of an overwhelming circumstance, waiting patiently, until slowly, finally, he looked her in the eye.

"Yes, Sweetheart."

"Would Uncle Reed ever lie to me?" she asked, her world dangling on a thread, a single response. Child logic.

"No," he assured. "Uncle Reed would *never* lie to you, not *ever*—but..."

Gently touching his cheek she asked, "If he promised, would Uncle Reed keep his promise?"

Tears again gliding down his face, Ames nodded. "With every ounce of his soul," he said softly, "to his very last breath, he would keep his promise."

Again, the child lovingly wiped the man's tears. "Do not cry," she said sweetly, "then Uncle Reed will come back. He absolutely promised." And she managed a fleeting smile... a tiny child, 'Thumbelina' courage.

* * *

Sunset...

...Together on the rimrock at the crater of the collapsed mountain range of the Legends, the sheathed scimitar on the ground beside him, Ames held Jade in his lap. Very quiet. Two who were lost, because two others were lost. With heartfelt love and sympathy he silently prayed, *she can't take anymore tragedy; please don't let her suffer anymore. She is too small.*

Not a sound, unobtrusively Kalo approached from the path along the cliffs, without speaking sitting down beside them. He glanced at her and she smiled, a smile of hope; then saddened, she looked at Jade, exhausted, asleep in his arms. Kalo leaned her head against the man's shoulder and gently kissed Jade's head; then looking over the expansive crater of the destroyed temple and collapsed mountains beyond, she contemplated. Inner reflection.

After a long while Kalo observed pensively, "There is a reason." He did not respond, only gazed over the mountain range toward the lingering sun, holding a weary, lost child who desperately needed assurance she was not alone in a primitive world.

Kalo turned, looked at him and Jade; and as her heart went out to them, her mind went deeper within, her destiny unfolding one day at a time... one step at a time. Inside, she felt it.

Studying him, "This is your place... and Tian's," she said at length. Her words surprised him; but he did not respond. "You came here often and would sit here, where we sit now." Scanning the surrounding area Kalo laid a hand upon the granite surface of the rimrock. Still not answering the man looked at her, and after a while the girl repeated, "This is your place... and Tian's."

"Yes," he admitted, "how did you know?"

"I can feel it." Closing her eyes, "Inside, I feel it... because I believe." Drifting away, entranced, a fragment of destiny, a spiraling ribbon, one step at a time. Eyes closed, she lay a hand upon him, going within, destiny drawing her... only a fragment.

From Kalo Tian's voice emanated; the Renoloi leader spoke. *"I love you, John."* Next, she mimicked his voice. *"I love you too. I always will."* Then again, Tian's, *"We must wait until sunset."*

Astounded, Ames touched her. "What did you say?"

Kalo instantly came back, blinked twice.

"What did you say?" he asked a second time.

The girl looked at him, unaware, puzzled. "I do not know." She had no idea what had just happened; but as surely as he was sitting beside her, holding a bewildered, lonely child, Ames had witnessed her transcend, to somewhere unknown... somewhere Beyond.

I had no shoes, and complained...
...Until I met a man who had no feet.

* * *

Later...

...The sun having gone down, now sequestered with a world's rotational journey; the three remained together. Huddled with the simplicity of innocence Jade and Kalo slept cuddled together on the rimrock at the mountain range of the Legends. Silently Ames sat beside them; watchful, very quiet, thinking of all that had happened, mulling things over in his mind: *pieces... the Puzzle. What did it mean?*

Exhaustion stealing upon him as emptiness turned within him, he was searching for answers cloistered beyond reach. *What did it all mean?* The ache. Tian, Reed, Jade, and himself. Their bond. Those who were lost. Fatigue born from frustration of not understanding, creeping from behind somewhere, and inside somewhere.

Finally, he drifted away. Slumber.

It *might* have been real...

...The Dream.

In the darkness—eerie, an unnatural glowing, red darkness illuminating the murky haze. And a sudden shimmering flash of movement with a hollow, awful sound; something going down, falling to the ground, the floor... a concrete floor.

Then eyes—saddened and fading away amidst a tangle of hair. Listless with vacancy she was closing her eyes, dying in his arms and he was helpless but to watch as blood ran onto his hands from the mortal wound... the hilt of a sword glimmering before him.

Into the darkness again—spectral, banshee eyes, gray and evil, moving closer, and closer. They were watching him, crawling and lurking everywhere, glaring and making sounds. —No, not the eyes, the sounds were evil and empty, resonant in his brain; but not from the eyes. Somewhere else, something else; hollow, uncaring sounds, the echoes of emptiness, evil for evil's own sake, empty and dead, a soulless void. Hideous and unfulfilled, they were the sounds of hate and spite… wonton and unworldly laughter.

Someone standing there—towering evil and dreadful, formidable and dark, the faceless specter of death. And the sphere, shimmering… and waiting.

Sudden explosion—hurtling fragments of pain; sparks in his vision and evaporating scatter-white spots. Darkness crowding in. Smith standing over him drooling satisfaction and jubilation —and the sword—and the fire— the blade slicing his heart; then clearing and blending in an aurora of red… and fire in his chest.

—Brilliant White Light!

Sparkling starbursts around him—dazzling, scintillating, hovering and swirling as the breath of a wind. He could see the Light… the eyes. Their beauty was unequaled and warm... safe. The Light was beautiful, radiant… everywhere. Beyond cradling hands flashed tumult and noise… chaos! But he was secure, and a voice called his name... Tian, calling his name.

Then growing swells of rhythmic noise—above him were unshod hooves and fetlocks of powerful, mighty steeds. Of course —White Riders to battle— to Battle!

Shapes and shadows rising up—ghosts of the darkness with red glowing eyes; it was all so unclear, obscured and confused. And Red.

Conflict—bloodspray and scatter, the violence of war reaching out beyond the horizon; but he was secure and safe within the Light, protected from the holocaust and destruction.

Everywhere, there was Light... and the Face, the perfect Smile. Wisdom… and Love.

—Boom!— startled awake.

Shaken, momentarily confused, Ames sat upright not knowing where he was; images evaporating, his mind scrambling trying to sort them all out. Just darkness.

A piece of… *the Puzzle*. Pieces still missing.

They were lying together, Kalo and Jade. The child was snuggled within the young girl's protective arms; two small beings in a powerful, primitive world. Their shared love and the Renoloi bond lent them peace within the night's shroud of mystery. And as he watched them sleeping together, mystery moved one step further...

To where reality and the dream world merge, that place, where faith becomes reality,

...Just a single step beyond.

Ames looked from the small sleeping Renoloi, to the mountains of the Legends, shrouded in darkness. Inner whisperings, their intuitive allure and the key secreted somewhere within.

Meteoric —luminous flash through the night— a shooting star streaking from heaven and the mystery of space. The green-white flare arced downward in a twisted-tight streak toward the ruins of the Sacred Temple; then halted hovering momentarily, pulsating strangely like a glowing ember of exquisite light. Until again descending, ever so slowly, wistfully, an illusion of scintillating wind within starlight, it came to rest within the temple ruins, just out of sight.

Filled with wonder Ames silently rose to his feet, wanting to know, he had to find out; but hesitated, looking down upon the two fast asleep on the rimrock. *For just a few moments, they will be fine.* Again, he turned toward the ruins, drawn to the mystery and light.

Only a moment later, perhaps a bit more: he cautiously peered from the cover of fractured boulders into the clearing the explosion created when the temple was destroyed. There, unbelievable and majestic was a ghost rider and mount, a Centurion and incredible, unworldly white steed. Both were luminescent, purest white, glowing with radiant effervescence and shimmering light, their vision enhancing the enclosure with reflective moonlight glow.

The Animal was massive and muscled; the perfection of symmetry, pawing impatiently with ponderous unshod hooves that shed sparks when they struck. The Percheron's neck, breast, point of shoulders and thighs were extraordinarily thick rippling intense strength with every movement it made. Its forelock and mane lay full, draped and curled around alert pointed ears at the pole and swept in a wave upon its neck. Its withers, back and shoulders gleamed, pristine and smooth with summer slick sheen. Its tail long and flowing almost touching the ground swished gracefully in a blend of beauty from unknown origins, forged of beauty and grace.

Restless, it tugged impatiently and high-spirited in the woven satin headstall with a hackamore, so it didn't taste cold metal in its mouth. The creature's eyes were large and round, the virtue and color of aquamarine. It was purest white, unbounded and powerful, possessed of the unicorn's spirit and grandeur; a fury of hooves with the soul of The Lamb.

Mounted bareback the rider was a Roman Centurion with a breastplate cuirass of lorica segmentata armor, tasseled helmet and visor concealing the face; a leader of thousands, follower of One, a warrior of biblical times. Garbed in a cape of flowing linen with tassets and sandals, in the rider's waistband of wide harness leather was braced a broad scabbard and mighty battle sword; straight as a beam of sunlight, sharp as the limit of creativity and forged in the benediction of mankind. Incredible beyond words, shimmering, silent and awe-inspiring, the legionnaire remained mounted, identity concealed in a shroud of mystery and light.

Within the armor dwelt the heartbeat of honor, the soul of a dream, the breath of spring flowers, and the Love from Beyond. Mythical, visionary, intangible, yet very, very real; from where reality and the dream world merge…

…A Warrior from Time.

Ames sensed the ghost rider was aware of his presence, awaiting him; so he rose slowly and reverently approached the white warrior sitting straight and still upon the animal's back. The horse was restless, neck bowed, head down, pawing impatiently; intent, a fervent spirit awaiting the phantom's command, yearning to be spurred to action and free to fly once again. Ames neared the apparition overwhelmed with its radiance, awed with its majesty and beauty.

Uncertain, carefully he approached.

Unspoken words, heard only in his mind: *"Come, John."*

The voice was coarse and garbled, disguised; and without speaking the man slowly moved a bit closer. Sparkling like starlight, the vision was a translucent texture of vision, shimmering with minutiae pulsars and quasars, glittering pinpoint starbursts of light. It was beautiful, incredible.

"Come forward. I bid you no harm."

He complied, stepping before the rider, not knowing what to expect, wanting so much, so desperately to touch the apparition. But he was afraid. Surely such a being would be untouchable by man. From somewhere he could hear music, a song...

Very faint, as though sung by a choir, from a place far, far away; the music was so beautiful, and seemed familiar somehow,

...Seemed so familiar.

"I bring a dispatch of importance," the rider advised in a voice disguised with warbled, coarse words.

"You talk to me without speaking." And more softly, "Who are you?"

Flipping its head restlessly, the animal pawed and backstepped with a solid gait; and the rider brought it forward once more, alongside Ames.

"I am the breath of tomorrow... the wind of consciousness delineating and separating thoughts of good and evil, defining who you are and will be. I am the juncture of mortality and immortality. I am a Mystic."

Overwhelmed, but still unable to resist the impulse, Ames had to reach out, to touch the magnificent steed. "Are you real?" he murmured; and as he did, his hand slipped gently through the vision before him. It was intangible, seemed unreal. Perhaps it only existed in his mind. He could not touch it.

The Centurion spoke. *"Reality is possessed of many dimensions."* The man looked up at the Mystic, whose identity was concealed within the helmet. Ames said nothing. Then, in a subdued, more compassionate voice, the rider asked, *"Do you believe?"*

Captured, fascinated and transfixed with the incomprehensible vision before him, Ames' heart felt warmth. A whisper: "Yes."

"Then, John... I am real."

As the words touched him, his hand delicately stroked the horse's mane and powerfully muscled neck. Turning its magnificent head the Percheron nuzzled him affectionately and nickered into his chest unintentionally pushing him back a step. Astonished, he was speechless. Then he remembered Kalo's words: *"Because I believe"* and a smile welled from within; so simple, yet so profound, *because I Believe.*

Not knowing what to say, he asked, "Why are you here?" His brain was raveled, an inarticulate knot. "What do you want of me?"

"A dispatch," the white warrior replied warmly leaning forward, tendering a message rolled up like a small scroll and sealed with wax. Ames accepted the piece of paper, gazed upon it, and began to pry the wax seal with his thumbnail intending to unroll it. But his attention was drawn again to the Mystic as the rider continued, *"You must hurry, John. Find the Secret of the Legends,"* straightening upon the Percheron's back, sitting upright again, *"the juncture is near."*

"The juncture..." Ames inquired respectfully, "what does that mean?"

Serenely the Mystic told him, *"That answer is forbidden."*

"But how can I find—I don't even know where to begin."

Raising a hand the rider silenced him. *"John, follow your heart, and the stars. More than that, I cannot reveal."*

Reluctantly, "But, I'm only a man, why me?" he appealed, as he, without realizing, tucked the scroll into the back pocket of his jeans.

"That decision was made long ago."

"What do you mean?"

"I cannot interfere," the ghost warrior replied calmly.

"But..."

"—John," the Mystic interrupted, *"you must."* Sitting tall, scanning the surrounding countryside, indicating with a sweeping arm, the rider told him, *"Very soon, all that is... will be no more."*

"But..." self-doubt. At a loss for words, how could he explain; how could he possibly accomplish such a task without any idea where to begin? He began to speak again then hesitated; and looking up to the ghost rider he finally realized—said, "You seem familiar. I know you, don't I?"

"Yes, John." The voice was softer, less disguised, the warmth of the Mystic's words flowing from within the cloak of helmet. Slowly the vision raised a hand. *"When it is time..."*

—Shaking,

Something shaking him, harshly, abruptly, interrupting his thoughts, the shimmering vision vanishing like a zephyr of wind.

—Shaking,

Something shaking him again, more fervently, almost violently, a small hand. Inside his brain, another voice, hushed in whisper—very urgent.

"What is it?" he mumbled in groggy half-sleep, still not completely aware of his surroundings.

"Mr. Ames, wake up—please," Kalo's desperate words finally sinking in.

Opening his eyes, seeing her face mere inches from his own; tense, fear in her eyes. "Kalo?" he mumbled. "Kalo, what is it? What's wrong?" he managed to ask, finally waking, becoming aware. Jade lie still, peacefully sleeping next to them. Kalo was scanning the darkness with frightened eyes, terror etched upon her face.

They three were at the rimrock.

"What is it?" he asked again. "What's wrong?"

Darkness all around them, the girl's eyes met his. "Mr. Ames..." her desperate whisper, *"they are in the trees!"*

PART IV

CHAPTER ELEVEN

It began a long time ago…

…On an insignificant liquid-blue planet: the sixth sub-level.

"It is time for harvest." Smith bellowed vicious laughter, and plunged the sword down —into Ames.

The man was helpless except to watch, a vision of surreal slow-motion, the gleaming blade slicing through his tattered shirt and into his chest. His mind racing through a million memories…

…All that had happened. And the whisper, *"There is a reason."*

His face flushed and he wanted to vomit, vision clouding, beginning to blur. He could see the blade but the room was fading, darkness creeping closer. Still grasping the laser in his fisted hand, he tried to bring it up to fire; but his hand wouldn't move, his finger could not obey.

"And now…" Smith anticipated greedily, "now you shall die." And he plunged the sword at Ames again…

—Then, Light all around him!

The Being was White Flame with Blinding Fury,

All Powerful, All Knowing,

…Brilliant White Light!

Beyond the Light he thought he saw movement, but it was all so unclear. And Smith seemed to be changing. Growing larger. Growing taller. Wild with rage, Smith roared and hunched his huge shoulders ripping both coat sleeves up the seams. Then grabbing his chest, he tore the coat and shirt off and flung them away. He swung with his sword —again and again.

It all seemed so cloudy, distorted.

Ames lay dying on the floor, his thoughts drifting away. Everything just mists of confusion. Was this really happening?

In his mind he thought he could see them arriving, white riders on horseback —and a dark army below. So many there were on both fronts he couldn't count them, but certainly more than millions, the armies going on forever, beyond the horizon. Riding bareback — were they angels?— robed in white with broadswords drawn. And there was blood spraying from wounds and splashing upon the world forming an incredible sea of red littered with endless lost souls from all of history.

The last great battle,

Armageddon,

God's Day of Judgment.

All the things he imagined… and sounds fading away.

His eyes closing, dying, lost somewhere in the realm where reality and the dream world merge, that place where faith becomes reality… and reality just a single step beyond. He was drifting, lost in the dreams of eternity. And in his mind serenity was calling, a tunnel of light guiding him, spiraling onward forever and ever, floating into mists of nebulae, being drawn away into the arms of the universe.

So beautiful… the angels sang a mellifluous song.

And gossamer winds of ethereal color: all the beautiful colors, the incredible beauty of Creation. It was there, waiting… the realm of Beyond. Viewing its immeasurable majesty, longing to be part of it, wanting never to go back. But he felt something more, so very deeply inside, calling his name, someone calling his name…

—Brilliant, incredible, sparkling light was everywhere

…And God smiled.

The portal of the geodesic sphere closed as it began to sparkle like fairy dust. Scintillating minutiae, shimmering rainbow colors,

Whisking trails of starlight,

A shrill whine —*pop*— it was gone.

—And at that precise instant…

The geodesic sphere and solitary occupant within propelled through time to a future awaiting his arrival within the crater of the temple ruins and the collapsed mountain range of the Legends.

…Shatter-flash of ripping destruction swept over the face of the world, an incredible wave of exploding landscape —speeding forth, flashing out— ground splintering and blasted away. The Earth quaked in upheaval and volcanic eruption scattering mountains and landscape to shards of oblivion. Thundering, rattling, pounding, a surging pulse-wave swell of blinding, rushing, boiling incineration and nonpareil detonation-burn of vaporous fireflash white light...

—The world exploded with Cataclysmic Finality!—

…And blue-white fire of luminous gas flashed a liquid storm into the atmosphere pouring inferno, brimstone and firefall upon the wretchedness of mankind. Hurtled shreds of what had been were swept up in gagging, suffocating, particulate clouds —all of it— an entire world consumed in planetary destruction.

* * *

As the riders encircling Smith…

…Began closing in upon him, he roared gutturally and primal, a banshee's howl, eyes flashing hate, jaws dripping saliva. Reeling, twisting, contorted and struggling he lashed out savagely as the white riders surrounding him created a ring of horseflesh, armor and mighty broadswords.

Through the drool on his chest his blotchy, bruised-looking skin glistened as he clawed frantically in villainy and blind rage. But the Percherons held steady, a solid barrier of horseflesh and hooves Smith could not penetrate. There was no escape, no way to get through.

A roar of futile exasperation with despise in his spectral eyes, now yellow-gray and evil, meld within the carcass of absolute evil, Smith slammed into the mighty horses time and again, refusing submission.

But with each solid step the riders drew nearer, converging, choking freedom away. He bayed letting a horrendous god-hating moan, a lament of disdain echoing rabid frustration above the encompassing explosions of shatter-white fire and splintering earthscape.

Confusion and chaos were omnipresent. Ripping destruction continued everywhere, overwhelming, enhanced and amplified by a spiteful, drawn reverberating wail.

The Mystics encircling Smith began wrapping him with the gleaming length of massive chain, binding him tightly, taking him down within the golden bonds, sealing him within. They pulled tighter, and tighter. Then the riders on either side of the Centurion passed their end of the chain back to their commander. It was almost complete.

Desperate, knowing the inevitable result once the circle was complete, Smith coiled and with a wivern's power sprang into the air trying to leap over the Mystics. But more sudden than reflex, gleaming broadswords swept overhead with their outstretched arms creating a canopy of starflash-shield, a prison of powerful blade and shimmering white light. Slamming face-first into the barrier he was decisively stopped, falling solidly to the ground.

Above him swirled shimmering quasars, pulsars, and minutiae embers of glittering light; beautiful tornadic whirlwinds of mystical starlight twinkling like fairy dust... so confining and pure. And still the song.

Finally, the Centurion, with an end in each hand brought them together. The chain fused, connected. The links intertwined and interlocked. The circle was complete.

He screamed. Chipped boxer's teeth and stub of cigar, he roared. His ripping claws were ineffectual, a struggle he could not win, was preordained to lose. Even still, consumed with defiance and disproportionate hatred of absolute evil, Smith fought and resisted to the very last. He screamed again —and roared— unwilling to submit. He would never yield. Overcome with frustration he cried, then growled and wailed and cried, again and again... and went down.

He was bound securely within the golden chain as it sizzled with a smoldering burn cauterizing his discolored flesh. And still he shrieked and howled until finally his loathsome, cursing tongue stilled, spilled out and went slack, the stub of cigar dangling from the panting, puffing jaws of defeat seeping vitriol of saliva and exhaustion. Wickedness blinked hatred one more time, and at last, narrow yellow-gray eyes rolled-back-white in his head... then closed.

Brilliant, sparkling light was everywhere!

And they rejoiced, and sang such a wonderful song.

They were so beautiful.

* * *

Finally, confusion diminished, subsided...

...Whirling then spiraling, a fragmented existence of wind and soul absorbed within the vast emptiness of perpetual cold and dark... and the vacancy of space. Then fading away, the day of Armageddon drawing to a close; and with that day all recorded history of mankind's endeavors and existence was ending. It was now a place of darkness enveloped with loss, slumber of absence, and silence.

* * *

Then I saw an angel standing in the sun, and with a loud voice he called to all the birds that fly in midheaven, "Come, gather for the great supper of God, to eat the flesh of kings, the flesh of captains, the flesh of mighty men, the flesh of horses and their riders, and the flesh of all men, both free and slave, both small and great." (Rev 19: 17-18 RSV)

* * *

Tick, tick, tick...

...Unhurried, uninterrupted, there was solitude. Satan was chained, taken down, and would remain imprisoned. The world that had been was completely still.

One Thousand Years.

For that time everything was very, very quiet. In the shaded darkness of an eclipsed sun and blood-red moon there was sadness and emptiness draped in the winnowing twilight of between now and then. And eventually… Once Again.

* * *

Then the saga continued…

…The ancient battleground lay barren and dead, no vegetation, no life; everything was completely still. As far as the horizon, then beyond, it was a desolate land cratered and scarred with wounds that would never heal, from a battle long since past, an empty wasteland of crumbled mountains and fractured landscape torn apart in a cataclysm of upheaval... now forsaken and abandoned.

Millions of skeletal remains long ago gleaned of flesh in a carrion feast littered the terrain as far as sight would allow. Countless disjointed, dismembered bones were strewn in random disarray and heaped in crumbling, ungodly piles, now all picked clean of every fragment of meat. This was a dead land, destined to never again know the nourishment of even microscopic life, absolved with war, purified in fire.

Now and forever this place would remain a land cursed and cast off, eternally shaded with the eerie, unnatural violet corona of a veiled sun, and always eclipsed by a blood-red moon. Both still low, near the horizon, their prophetic alliance casting long blue-black shadows of sadness and desolation upon the 'War Land of Armageddon'.

It was all very quiet here, unearthly and unnatural.

Even the great slab of stone bound with a massive golden chain and held fast with a pure, Holy Seal seemed absorbed within the interlude of time and forfeiture. The silence of absence was deafening, the intense feeling of sadness and loss ubiquitous, overwhelming emptiness absorbed within every grain of sand and particle of dust swept along with a cold incessant wind. This place would always remain forsaken, and cursed, hallowed from this time forth only by a frigid, desolate... *Relentless Wind.*

* * *

And when the thousand years are ended, Satan will be loosed from his prison and will come out to deceive the nations... *[in part]* **(Rev. 20: 7-8 RSV)**

From the distant reaches of Heaven...

...They came, moving slowly, none relishing the journey. Their return. Untold mounted centuries molded to unnumbered legions, the army of angels arrived quietly and solemnly, led by their tribune the Centurion Mystic. Bound by their Leader, the Word of God, they were obliged to perform their duty.

One thousand years had passed.

Finally, the Mystic Army arrived and assembled. Warriors in white robes and armor mounted on magnificent Percheron horseflesh encircled the ponderous stone slab held fast with a golden chain and Holy Seal. The great army waited in formations that seemed endless, innumerable legions that spanned the desolate battleground, and then beyond. They were awe-inspiring, incredible, luminescent spirits; beings of virtue who fought —warred— in the name of justice and righteousness, riding shimmering, powerful steeds.

The Command came down. ***REMOVE THE SEAL.***

Dutifully the Centurion obeyed, with un-spurred heels nudging the mount from the front line of the ranks. The horse stepped forward proudly, then capturing its scent, stopped at the chained slab where it snorted and pawed. Sadly the Centurion drew the broadsword, raised it overhead, and with a deft, precise blow the seal on the chain was severed in an incredible starburst of clear splashing light. The impact of the blade flung both ends of the chain aside and off the ponderous stone slab; and momentarily the chain glowed, luminesced, then diminished as it faded, turned to dust... and was gone.

Now, only the dust remained. The dust was real.

With a gentle tug on the satin reins the Percheron backstepped returning to the forward rank. Throwing its head, the animal bowed its neck and pawed snorting impatiently, then nickered and stood obediently awaiting the rider's next command.

Again, there was silence. Even the wind stilled, anticipating, waiting.

Expectation… a breath of regret, and knowing what must be.

Almost negligibly at first, the stone slab shifted, moved, and then began to slide with a hollow grind of grit-echo sound. Clawed fingertips prodded from below then dragged the slab a bit further creating a crack between the lid and lightless, vile black prison chamber below. Long, taloned, wretched fingers pried themselves into the crack and pulled the slab again, enough this time for the forelimbs to push through. Evil fumes wafted from the murky depths rising in miasma trails of sickening stench and putrefaction of vacant soul. Firmly this time, the fingers seized the lid and pushed it powerfully with an empty, grinding, sliding-concrete sound.

From the darkness, yellow-gray eyes peered out.

Grinding the cigar between his teeth he breathed taking in odors of sensory perception, satiating, inhaling the long-awaited taste of freedom. Hideously his misshapen head poked forth with hate and loathing, and his narrow, crooked lips opened, mouth covered with the filmy paste of decay and drool of despise. Then slowly he emerged wearing moldy, tattered rags that were once a uniform; and with the insidious slither of a malignant, creeping cancer, Smith crawled from the blackness of his tomb into the blood-red ecliptic light of the defiled land of Armageddon.

Vile and narrow, his eyes surveyed the surrounding Mystic Army contemptuously with indelible hatred, slowly turning in tight circles. Around and around he sidestepped, scheming, staring them down, glowering as he moved, shedding the ragged clothes as he did. Beneath the filth his skin looked bruised and blotchy, and in some places scaled, its color going to magenta. At length he finally stopped, eyes fixed, glaring at the Centurion as he rose standing erect on his strangely shaped legs.

Attention grimly focused, his words slurred with a wicked hiss, "We shall meet again," and with that menacing omen Smith — Satan— whirled and vanished as he leaped into the air absorbed in the sound of beating wings and blood-red ecliptic darkness.

"Yes. We shall," the Centurion confirmed reticently.

A warrior alongside the Mystic leader respectfully inquired, *"What will he do now?"*

"Prepare for war," the Centurion replied sadly.

The warrior asked a second question. *"Where is he bound?"*

The Centurion's answer, a solitary word: *"Revenge.*

CHAPTER TWELVE

"Mr. Ames," her desperate whisper, *"they are in the trees!"*

Now awake and aware of his surroundings; they were together on the rimrock at the crater rim. With her face so close to his, in the darkness it had taken a minute to sort it out; but now he could sense her worry as she studied the jungle one hundred yards away, where the treeline abruptly ended and the irregular face of the rimrock margin began.

In the pitch-dark awareness instilled fear; and thinking the name made him shiver. *Night Hunters.* They were out there lurking, sleek adroit killers using both darkness and the jungle's camouflage to proficiently accomplish that end.

Moving lightly, his hand felt along the surface and touched it, retrieving the sheathed scimitar then ever so quietly tucking it in his waistband. Scanning the darkness and treeline, scarcely breathing he sensed the protracted sliding of metallic tenor as he eased the sword from the scabbard; now armed with anticipation and the swept razor edge blade. Kalo, crouching virtually undetectably next to him, reached over her shoulder, withdrew an arrow with two fingers and silently set it to her bow.

But Ames knew that in spite of her extraordinary skill and his own ability to fight, they would most likely both die here this night. The arachnids were pack hunters, and regardless how many they managed to take down there would still be too many; and being more than a mile from the village, any possible help from others would not be in time. Help would arrive but most surely would be too late.

Tian's omen occurred to him, recalling the Tyrannosaur crossing from the Forsaken Land. *Something is wrong, John... very wrong.*

Dinosaurs suddenly appearing where they had never been before: something wrong. And now the most wicked, proficient and savagely venomous killers darkness had ever conceived and unleashed upon a people; more than something wrong... much more.

Although he couldn't see them, he knew they were there; night-vision eyes watching and waiting, gathering for the attack. Kalo had said so, and by now he knew not to doubt her. Even though she was still young, Kalo was growing into someone Ames was not yet able to appreciate and might never understand. But priority's edict was first they survive this night, and that too, at present, seemed improbable.

Finally, he looked down upon Jade, already hopelessly bewildered with the loss of both her mother and Reed. She was too vulnerable; too emotionally torn to manage any more tragedy in a world she was far too small to comprehend. After hours of crying she had finally curled and fallen asleep, helpless and dependent upon him and the girl for her very survival. With immeasurable sadness for the tiny child, and apprehensive with their present dilemma, Ames gingerly slipped his left hand under her picking her up. She curled more tightly when he touched her, a subconscious reflex, something inherent in us all, the need to be touched, and sometimes, held.

She willingly snuggled to him sleepily laying her head upon his left shoulder, draping her tiny arms around his neck as he lovingly kissed her on the cheek. Soft, her warm smooth skin, damp hair, and vulnerability emanated innocence and helplessness reminding him of another whom once was able to joyfully bubble the words, 'piggyback, piggyback' —but now, was forever lost. Drawn with regret Ames looked from Jade's small sleeping face into the darkness surrounding them, danger lurking therein.

He had no idea how he and Kalo alone could possibly manage, but somehow, someway, they must. Then and there, with all his soul he solemnly resolved, *no little girl, it is not a good day to die.*

Ahead of them—

Glimmers of motion, obsidian flashes; before he even realized, Kalo's arrow was already bound, and by the time he heard the resonant, *twang,* of her bowstring the arrow was punching through eight clustered eyes and into a skull. All he was really aware of was the skittering sound of claws running the rimrock and a scraping, colliding noise of something that went to the ground.

With a supple fluid motion the young Renoloi drew a second arrow —into the night, into another— then the trilling shriek of the scream. He could see nothing in the intense darkness; *how could she?* It was then he realized that she was just as blind as he, her sight as limited as his own; but still she took the Hunters when one by one they came. Powers just awakening, simply explained with the words—*inside I feel it... because I believe.*

Kalo whispered, "They are coming, all together now," as she rose from her crouch, onto her feet. Time to fight —or die.

Another arrow vanished, sinking unseen in cephalothorax eyes. Ames stood, precious sleeping cargo cradled in his left arm and an exquisitely honed blade of razor death in the right.

Scraping clatter in the darkness betrayed their claws on the rimrock as sporadic shapes of splattered ink rushed from the tangled-black jungle canopy. Again and again Kalo sent feathered harbingers whisking into them; her skill and accuracy incredible, firing without sight, visualizing targets, warrior instinct focusing her senses with intensity beyond explanation. Her destiny unfolding, one step at a time.

She acted, reacted and fought superbly. No longer tethered by limitations of size and strength, now she was driven, compelled by an innate consciousness beyond awareness, a singular Renoloi warrior empowered by a kinship of reckoning. Her movements were unseen speed in the darkness, her energy beyond intense, to the limits of extreme. Inside she felt it, growing intrinsically, an unfathomable power meld with unmeasured defiance: a fragment, a step, the chrysalis of her destiny… the warrior to be.

Ames leaped toward the jaws of a Hunter slicing whirls of figure-eights that carved through fangs and pedipalps letting gray sticky muck. Ducking then moving, he leaped and spun in midair as the razor edge slashed through eight more clustered orbs in the blink of an eye scattering them like glowing marbles that bounced away on the rimrock. The Hunter howled a maniacal shriek that bawled out as a cry before the next swipe cut its cephalothorax head in half.

—White noise of savagery, and trilling, chattering animalistic screams!

Gray slop still splattering the ground, the man reeled hacking into the next—another strike taking four ragged legs, put the deadly giant down.

Side by side, man and girl fought defiantly as the ravenous Hunters rushed them, gasping quick breaths in flashes of motion, their arrows and blade withstanding venom and fangs. Time after time Kalo let fly, her targets tumbling as the scimitar twirled, their tally mounting leaking ugly gray blood.

But as quickly as one set of eyes went out, two more appeared. Next to her Ames fought relentlessly, slicing with unyielding determination, carcasses piling up around them; severed legs, chelicerae, pedipalps, fangs, obsidian cephalothoraxes and heavy posterior abdomens scattering upon the rimrock.

Then, a racket of cackling and screeching, the pack came as a swarm. It was darkness and speed and confusion and muck.

With more already dead than they could count, adrenaline drove them. Moving furiously, hearts pounding and chests heaving they were skip-images of smeared speed, intensity and obstinate aggression drenched with sweat that flicked away in the dark. Dodging —duck, roll and sidestep— and avoiding —get up, get away— as the monsters came in; then striking back with the power and force that only the most desperate fight for survival could induce. Seconds passed with uncompromising regularity shaping minutes that seemed forever—too long. But the man and girl would fight to the end. Two against hundreds —impossible odds— each refusing to abandon the other —side by side— committed with resolve and pledged to the death.

Still the Hunters kept coming.

White noise of savagery. Cackling railing echoes that lanced through the dark, the monstrous spiders attacked screaming their chilling ungodly howls. Seemingly everywhere, they were blue-dark venom and death concealed by the night —a glimpse there, then there— no more than evaporating shadows. Ames realized some had circled beyond them and gone into the crater, coming up from behind. All around them, too close —no place to fall back— trying to get them from all sides now.

He reeled, fighting back-to-back with Kalo, the scimitar whirling as Hunters scrambled from the crater onto the rimrock; slashing and slicing, keeping them back. Together the man and girl stood and fought, and together they killed —one giant killer, the next— amid the shrieking screams and clamor of the onslaught they slaughtered with the rush of adrenaline and survival. But sheer numbers overwhelmed them.

Legs wide —overhead— fangs intent on Jade. Ames leaped aside narrowly saving her from twenty inches of death that locked with yellow-poison spray, his blade slashing through the black demon as the head fell away. The Hunter splat solidly then slid back down to the crater below, and for an instant longer, asleep in his arm his small cargo was still alive.

A Hunter was almost upon her as Kalo reached to her quiver —empty— "I am out of arrows!"

Eyes flashing back, clutching one end of the bow she swung with all her might clobbering it between the eyes. Staggered, the creature chattered pain with its yowl of surprise, then reared onto its hind legs towering over her, a monster with treacherous fangs—and those bale-hook claws!

Glowing white without blinking, it absorbed her image and reflected it back through its prismatic eyes as it loomed above her, its abdomen shining as much as it reeked with the black oily sheen and stiff bristling hairs. Forelegs clawing darkness, fangs opening to penetrate her neck, wretched and malevolent, salivating, glaring down upon her—tensed, preparing to leap…

—Silence,

Sound stopped; a world distorted then still in stop-motion imagery, one blink at a time.

Peripherally she saw him coming from the side and behind, shielding Jade with an arm. Ames was beside her, tense as wound strands of sinew and courage, eyes wide with determination and terror. Reeling to save her he spun with the sword, sweat on his face and flung from his hair, the glimmering steel, *swooshing,* flicking blood from its edge, slicing then sinking in chitin; a blur of razorblade sword now their only defense.

—Time standing still,

All noise and sensation suspended; side by side against impossible odds...

—Blink,

...Inside, Kalo felt it —from above— her eyes sweeping to the night sky as the canopy exploded —shattering brilliance and luminous fire— *light was everywhere!* Dazzling starlight explosions illuminated the rimrock, a firestorm of intense sparkling flame washing the jungle in sudden whiteflash. Around them a world of surreal motion glowed —daylight at midnight— darkness was gone, the entire crater bathed in *White Fire and Vengeance!*

Seeing the vision, awestruck, she blinked...

...Magnificent—Incredible—Unbelievable!

Massive unshod hooves were galloping down from the firmament pounding explosions of fire in the darkness of sky. Muscular and broad, the strapping white steed's enormous chest and flanks rippled with ethereal strength, the cadence and pulse of symmetry and might. Bound for the captives on the rimrock the great Percheron scattered boiling nebulae clouds as it came, its flowing alabaster fetlocks trailing flames through the night.

Focused and intense, its eyes were aquamarine burning with fury and anger; nostrils flared snorting crimson breaths of rage and reprieve. Its astonishing speed tossed its mane and tail like silky white strands of willowing flame splashed through with nebulae stars, streaming in waves of luminescent hoarfrost and wind. Possessed with the intense awesome flow of an ocean enveloped within supernatural horseflesh, it stampeded from the sky whinnying an intrepid neigh of deliverance.

—Blink,

Indomitable, the luminous warrior wore a tasseled helmet and visor and Roman cuirass breastplate of splendid lorica segmentata armor —riding hard— with lungs full of night sky. Unparalleled, dispatched with an edict from somewhere unknown, the vision was bound for two who were vital and would not survive. Born with intent that was faithful and true, gleaming brilliantly with holy dominion and armored with unfailing valor —an incoming shooting star of bright, burning light— a zealot ghost rider from the realm of unknown...

...The Mystic appeared from a starburst of Light!

—Blink,

Conveyed with the mysterious power of the Legends, to abrogate an evil coming forth from the past, the phantom spurred the steed with sandals and bare feet brandishing a fiery broadsword, a burning blade of pure light. An avenging luminescent flame, the Mystic's weapon was honed with divine fiery power —coming for them, snared on the rim of the crater— the rimrock glowing brilliant, like daylight! —Dazzling! —Blinding!

—Blink,

They were surrounded. The Hunters had them —but they suddenly stopped in their tracks— still clamoring and pushing forward, but hesitating, confused. Climbing on top of and creeping over one another the giant arachnids seemed to be confounded and stunned by the light. Illuminated, the jungle and rimrock glowed increasingly brighter and brighter, now almost eerily radiant, the warrior streaking down like a star from above.

Driven by external stimuli with unreasoning brains, the gigantic spiders involuntarily looked up like a mob of cretin defects with sparkling night-vision eyes, struck blind, reflecting the glare. They all watched it —boiling, burning fire— like a meteor coming in. Curious, some even rose onto their hind legs delicately scratching the sky, perhaps trying to get a little closer look; a crowd of dark tangled dimwits just waiting, as though waving, their fangs dripping venom, seeming to wonder what this oddity might be. They just stood there, their eyes glowing, all blinded by the light…

—Blink,

A second longer, the flash coming in,

…*Clash-Clatter!*

Thundering unshod hooves crashed upon the face of the rimrock landing between the trapped people and arachnid horde —*granite exploding!*— scattering starlight and flames in a supernatural rush of incredible ripping force —*splattering yellow-blue fire!* Blasts of fiery rock and blizzard-shard spray searing through the jumbled Hunters the same instant —*the shockwave splashed out!*

Pandemonium and death flashed through them—battered by flames—and they went nuts like blind cooties pounded by stunning starbursts and incinerating light! Incredible boils of explosive blue-white starlight and flame slammed them with a tidal wall of sparkling fire and a windstorm of death. Torched, arachnids burst into fire. Yellow-orange—seething heat—a blue-ocher wash of extreme melting spray!

Frothing inferno splashed through their tangled chitin like methane's indigo-saffron hot winds flashing across a stagnant quagmire, the rush of flames billowing as it boiled: hollow, guttural roars of a medieval dragon snorting unworldly fire. Detonating, bursting flames everywhere —completely encircling the three hostages— an explosive wall of vapor-rush and yellow-blue—then orange blaze!

Crazed, melting where they were, dead where they stood, Hunters were engulfed like boiled-over gigantic bugs dripping opaque oil and bubbles of flame.

—Then, *rush!*

They fled scrambling with insanity and the deranged uncertainty of terminal velocity. Run till you die —every direction, every possible means— dissolving, sprinting and leaping chased by insidious tongues of horrible scorching fire. Dashing, burning tumbleweeds, they raced across the rimrock propelled by a hundred different winds. Seeking the dark, they were cockroaches racing blindly from a bundled mob —get out of the way— colliding, bouncing off one another, falling then jumping back up.

—Incoming fireball!

One knocked another down trampling it; another leapfrogged from its back. Springing back onto its legs —now all eight were on fire— charring, flaking, crackling and splitting, it couldn't move; it was falling apart. Everything at once, everywhere at once —ocher, blue-yellow and fire— being eaten alive by horrific melting heat.

—White noise of savagery, and trilling, gurgling, dissolving animalistic screams!

On brittle burning legs they banged into each other and ricocheted off things. All across the granite face, from the rim of the crater to the jungle understory ran fiery pinball-wizards of rush hour death.

Frantic, confused, darting one way then the other, one's blistering shell bubbled fiery thick-clinging molasses that ran down its sides until icky-gray blood squirted from the joints where its legs were attached—all eight bursting in flame, swirling whirlwinds of fire. Crackling and melting, guard hairs snapping off as spark-twirling bits, the Hunter fled blindly, deranged —front legs shattering— going down in a crush of hot blob. Hitting hard and ripping, the posterior abdomen popped and skidded dragging scalding sludge, the creature wailing its horrific puking scream, retching boiled-up globs that stuck to the ground.

Sprinting —a low-runner— scrambling in circles and burning so furiously it was completely engulfed; twenty feet of baton twirler's flame, running crazy, winding itself up, forming tighter and tighter loops —until *zoom*— the boiling ball of fire-spider shot straight up —a skyrocket— launched from the rimrock one hundred feet high. And it exploded up there as a violent cloud of yellow-blue flame and scattering gray mustard-froth.

Another—

Cracking and weakening, its blebby shell started falling apart as the arachnid careened trying to outrun the flames. Two legs broke and spun off tearing a hole in its side squirting like sizzling weird alien blood. Screeching wildly the Hunter made one final leap —then a scream— splitting apart along the length of its back, the front half hurling away and its remaining legs shooting out like catapulted burnt sticks. The frisbee head skipped over the granite face then splashed into another crossing its path. Already on fire the hit spider exploded in a twirling-liquid boil of flame; targeted military armor taken out by a rocket-propelled grenade.

—Tongues of scattering flame, bedlam's holocaust roars; fire was everywhere!

Speechless, empty bow in hand Kalo witnessed the unbelievable; it just seemed too incredible. Holding the tiny sleeping Jade, Ames stood awestruck and overwhelmed, the scimitar dripping blood. Chattering dying-screams were echoing around them so intensely and horrific they could almost feel them as Hunters wailed and howled drawn with the torture of burning alive —then rupture explosions— the screams vanishing mid-sound.

Death burning far and wide, a landscape ablaze…
Smell—fetid, scorched ectoplasmic blood,
Taste—burnt and raw that clings in the throat,
Sound—screeching cackles, with death in their trills,
Feeling—choking, restrictive, confining, closing in,
Sight—yellow-blue fire and chaotic confusion,
…The rimrock gone wild!

Onto its hind legs, hooves raking fire, the mighty Percheron reared and neighed silhouetted by flame. Gleaming of starfire, majestically and powerfully, the Centurion wielded the broadsword overhead…

…Incredible—a Warrior of Mystery—and Light!

Stunned by the vision's power and strength Kalo and Ames stood dumbstruck and watched, while spellbound with wonder, their eyes then beheld the remarkable, astonishing Power from Beyond.

Held high, blinding and radiant the broadsword burned with bursts of starfire and crystal-clear light. Then with a mighty sweeping arm the Mystic brought the sword down—a shattering—*crackling*—razor-of-flame flashing a swath with the blade!

—*"Fly!"* the warrior commanded.

Snorting crimson and rage the Percheron neighed and bolted — into the fire and into the fray. Rider and horse pounded across the rimrock splashing vitriolic starburst clouds from its hooves, plowing over and trampling burning Night Hunters as they charged into the onrushing confusion of fiery obsidian crush.

Undaunted, fearless, unequalled by the foe, with unrealized power the Mystic's sword flashed out with another shattering—*crackling*—razor-of-flame hurling fireball spiders as scattered molten hulls. Arachnids were split open or shredded as the brilliant warring zealot sliced through them with a blade wielded so sure, so deft and precise that it manifest a flame of pure razor light.

A thundering fireflash, the rider swept through the night and opened the way, pitching arachnids through the dark in flames and disarray. Boiling spider infernos flew then tumbled aside clearing a path for the captives.

Seemingly within a heartbeat the surreal vision was at the jungle's edge and the mount stopped, reared and neighed. Ethereal and incredible, the broadsword again swept a shattering—*crackling*—razor-of-flame as the Centurion, in one astonishing swipe, cleared a swath through the jungle fifty feet wide penetrating hundreds of feet deep, tearing entire trees out with their roots, flinging them into the sky. Hurling away the gigantic ancients burst into flames trailing twisted green vines and catapulting great clods of dirt, igniting the jungle along both sides of the path.

An escape route to safety, alizarin skies rimmed in *pillars of fire!* —*"Run!"* the Mystic commanded.

Both girl and man sprinted headlong crossing the rimrock to the jungle, the girl fleet as a cat and the man at her heels carrying the small sleeping child. As they approached the treeline horse and rider backstepped allowing them passage because the canopy was still filled with them; from beyond the flames, in the dark, more Hunters were coming. Impending danger was very near; but even still, Kalo had to stop. So unbelievable, such a warrior, beyond her imaginings, her destiny unfolding, one step at a time… she had to know.

Eyes filled with wonder, words telling faith, she whispered, "Who are you?"

Rearing, the Percheron pawed as the Centurion Mystic looked down upon her, and with a coarse disguised voice answered, *"Inside, you feel it. You already know."* In a blend of pulchritude and muscle the imposing mount reeled and whinnied, the warrior preparing to battle the arachnids, now very close.

"Go now, both of you," drawing the reins *"—Run!"* And with the word the mighty Percheron reared again then neighed, raking fiery sparks, strafing the sky.

Without question Kalo and Ames fled along the wide, opened pathway rimmed on both sides with fiercely burning trees; and as they ran, from behind them shook the crackling thunder of explosion— radiant, crystal-clear, dynamic angelic fire. The Mystic's sword flashed celestial shattering flame —resonating lightning— quasars, pulsars and starbursts…

…A weapon of *Vengeance,*
   And Power,
     And Light!

In seconds the fugitives neared the end of the protective corridor carved through the jungle, darkness ahead of them, confusion behind. Kalo sensed it; cloistered in opaque and flickering shadows they were there, in the canopy —tree limbs being torn with the rush of gouging claws— Night Hunters, the attack, coming down.

Still running, Ames glanced over his shoulder realizing the fires still burned but the light had vanished; the Mystic was gone —and the Hunters were close— claws shredding bark on the branches around them, at their heels, just behind them. Then from the dark…

"—Hose 'em Pilgrims!"

…Lent's voice sang out as twenty jetstreams of liquid-orange flame washed the trees splashing waves of bright scattering fire. Through the understory and into the canopy, flame thrower blasts ignited opaque shapes with napalm's dissolving, incendiary death. Treetops and branches rattled confused commotion and creature-screams as Lent and confederates emerged from the thick and dark of the jungle's tangled night. His face reflecting orange in the firelight, Lent's grin beamed like Lieutenant Rip Masters in an old episode of 'Rin-Tin-Tin'. Coming to their aid, the cavalry had arrived.

Illuminated by sporadic bursts from Pilgrim firefighters, Renoloi archers showered arrows into the denizens above as the forest floor came alive with warriors in attack. Now united, Renoloi and Pilgrim stood defiantly juxtaposed, courageously side by side, against their mutual enemy. From now on, together they would fight the speed and savage fangs of a black mindless horde; their battle of survival in a primitive world.

Treetops alive with death—

Smeared obsidian and fire, arachnids vaulted through the limbs, some colliding as explosions and firefall, rupturing on impact then raining down as dripping liquid flame. Others bound frantically from branch to branch, breaking apart and shedding burning chunks like crackling firestick torches falling down through the branches.

The warriors stood fast. Taut, senses alive, muscles flexed, waiting—a rushing of claws and the warning cry, "Incoming!"

Targeted overhead with the sounds of split-wind, arrows intercepted the sleek demons as they weaved through the limbs then dashed down at them. Just as quickly as they came, they were taking them out.

Another shadow—

The sudden, *smack*, of the arrow sinking deep on the shaft in its head, and the ensuing sounds of the Hunter as it fell. In a flurry of leaves and snapping branches the arachnid tumbled then flopped on the jungle floor causing its guts to slosh with liquid echoes inside. Slowly its eight tense legs splayed and relaxed. Another killer lay dead.

A Hunter leaped from the trees, the young Pilgrim a heartbeat below; unflinching, palms sweating, squeezing the trigger spraying fire in the white eyes and black ugly face drenching the spider in a wash of bright flame. Then moving, a blitzkrieg of speed, Renoloi and Pilgrims scattered from underneath as the gigantic spider splashed in a liquid-hot fall that shattered its legs.

Still another slammed down, its melting posterior flattening when it struck, then waterballooned springing back up, splitting open—erupting—a firesplash of gray flaming froth that swirled out and plashed back onto it as bubbling-hot burning foam.

Fire raping the trees, arachnids were scrambling to the uppermost reaches of the canopy wailing garbled, fading chatter while others vainly raced imminent death on the limbs until their bizarre bone-chilling moans climaxed when they died. More than a hundred were afire, snagging on branches, yowling terminal puking gasps, or dropping like flaming bugs in the night falling out of the sky. Beaten, the giant spiders abruptly abandoned their attack and fled for the darkness beyond the burning jungle and rimrock; and like a moving wave of black sin, the canopy swayed as they left.

Watching the horde flee and glaring at those lying about, not a shred of remorse, Ames said, "Let's make sure they're all dead."

* * *

Soon after, the arachnids were gone...

...Having left many hung up in the branches or smoldering on the forest floor; and eventually the fires began subsiding as they burned themselves out. Quiet returning, the mood of the jungle; safe again to breathe, the skirmish was past.

Looking around they took it all in: scorched ground, charred trees, and the smell of burning dead. No one talked as they milled among the dwindling small fires illuminating the corridor of bizarre destruction and carnage. The jungle canopy was tattered and torn, opened with wounds of scattered crown fire and crooked arthritic fingers of blackened branches that let starlight peer through. Gray miasma trails wafting up through the foliage dissipated silently, withering away. The hush of wind now rustled green and charred, and empty spaces.

Not speaking, Lent stepped forward walking into the wide corridor where trees had once been. It was now a clearcut, an exposed thoroughfare reaching out to the rimrock. Both sides were lined with huge smoldering trees that still crackled and sporadically popped flaking embers that floated wraith-like to the ground.

Stepping slowly and seeming to study the gnarled ancients on either side, absorbed with disbelief, the youth stumbled falling into a hole. Quickly springing to his feet and finding himself in an excavation, he brushed himself off and puzzled, listening as remnant bits of dirt trickled in. Wondering, he stood there, in a hole five feet deep, a root-system crater—until realization sank in. Torn out somehow… a tree had been there.

Ames extended a hand, and as he pulled the youth from the hole their eyes met. Lent's expression asked, but the man couldn't explain; and they walked on. Moving closer to the rimrock, side by side Lent and Kalo tread carefully, with Ames, still carrying the sleeping Jade, a step or two behind.

Quietly others followed, eventually arriving at the jungle's edge.

Over the granite landscape, all the way to the rimrock, were smoldering, dark leaking mounds, random tangled piles of dead. Night Hunters. Burnt, wafting stench, some were cut apart with savage gashes and sliced-open wounds. Others were broken in pieces that lay everywhere. Unbelievable carnage. Dozens, or hundreds, too may to count; arachnids oozed puddles of thick ectoplasm-blood.

Lent looked at Kalo, and then again looked around at an ephemeral vision of happenstance strewn upon the granite face. As Ames and others approached from behind none of them spoke, in awe, telling amazement.

Finally, softly Lent whispered to the girl, "How did you, the two of you, do all this… and set the jungle on fire?" Turning, he studied her, then back to Ames. Neither answered.

Quietly, "I ran out of arrows," Kalo admitted.

"I can imagine," he said plainly, still looking around, trying to figure it out. Stepping alongside them, Ames somberly took in the landscape, to the crater's rim.

Turning to Ames, "Was it real?" Kalo whispered.

"It seemed real," he said uncertainly, "but…" He didn't know what to say.

Lent, misunderstanding her question and assuming both might be experiencing posttraumatic shock, interpolated the obvious. "What do you mean? Of course it was real." Then with an open hand indicating the dead arachnids, "Look at 'em. They're all over the place."

"Not them," Kalo told him then hesitated, saying no more.

Puzzled, he turned to Ames. "What then? What is she talking about?"

"Nothing, Lent," he replied succinctly. Then more subdued, still not quite believing himself he repeated softly, "Nothing," and the quiet of his voice awakened a small, sleeping child, drawing his attention as she stirred then yawned groggily in his arm.

Jade innocently rubbed her eyes with tiny fisted hands and sheepishly offered a bashful grin when she noticed his face so close to her own. "I was very sleepy," she professed, "but I am awake now, and I feel better." Ames' smile emanated love and a growing attachment for her as she curiously looked at the carcasses of the Night Hunters, and at length simply surmised, "Lot of dead bugs."

"Yes, Sweetheart," Ames agreed, "a lot of dead bugs."

Noticing Kalo standing next to them, Jade reached out to her with both arms, wanting to be taken; and when he handed her to Kalo the child snuggled within the girl's arms. Kalo turned and began walking away, holding Jade; and the child earnestly inquired, "Has my Uncle Reed come back yet?"

Softly: "No honey, not yet."

"He will," she told Kalo. "He absolutely promised."

"I know he did."

Then Jade plainly announced, "Uncle Reed is with Tian."

Attributing it to, 'child's imagination', Kalo disregarded the disclosure at first; then wondering, aware no one had told her that Reed and Tian had been on the boom together, asked, "How do you know that?"

"While I was sleeping an angel told me," Jade replied, reflecting a child's simple acceptance.

Kalo smiled incredulously and inquired, "Was she a pretty angel?"

"Oh yes," the child answered, and their conversation drifted off with their distance.

And as Ames watched the two of them, Kalo carrying Jade, slowly walking away, he realized, the tiny child who had already suffered more than anyone else, who was too vulnerable to manage anymore tragedy, simply too small, not strong enough to endure anymore pain... had slept through it all.

Chance or Providence? Looking up to the stars, to Heaven, he knew,

> *Someone was listening.*
> *Someone had heard him.*
> *Someone was there.*

* * *

Inconspicuously...

...Lent quietly walked farther onto the granite face, away from the others, toward the rimrock and crater. He stood silently for a moment, alone, looking down and considering. Saying nothing, he simply stood there, looking down; until finally, he knelt. Ames saw him, followed, and without speaking crouched beside him. Visibly moved Lent looked from the ground to the man, then again to the solid granite upon which they were kneeling.

Before them was an impression four inches deep cratered into the granite. A hoofprint; massive, unshod. And turning his head Lent could clearly trace their path —tracks— ragged, ruptured holes shattered into the stone, all the way across the barren surface to the jungle's edge where a corridor, a swath bordered on both sides with smoldering trees, entered the forest.

Blinking with reverent persuasion and wonder, Lent carefully touched the broken pieces of rock lying around the edge of the hoof impression, and raised his hand displaying a finger for Ames. Sparkling, glittering, crystal-clear dust upon his fingertip.

Uncertain, Ames reached into the hoofprint lightly drawing three fingers through the track; and withdrawing his hand, rubbing his fingers and thumb together, he could feel it. Then looking at Lent he whispered, "It came from my dream."

The youth did not smile, nor did he frown, his countenance simply conveyed wonder. But he *did* believe.

At last Ames breathed a deep sigh and both rose to their feet, looked around. Still not understanding Ames quietly said, "Let's go," and turning, they headed toward the village.

Walking away, thinking, he was compelled. A final look back at the massive hoofprints shattered in the granite, and rubbing the glittery, pure dust between his fingers...

It all seemed very real,

    But then again, perhaps,

        ...It was only *a Dream.*

CHAPTER THIRTEEN

Sitting cross-legged…

…Scrawling circles in the dirt with a stick, he mumbled, "Zap me with the wizard's wand." Then looking around, " 'Toto, I've a feeling we're not in Kansas anymore'." Reed wasn't expecting a reply, not involved in conversation, simply his way of putting in words what he'd been trying to figure out for some time now. *Where are we, and how did we get here?* He looked at Tian lying beside him, sleeping fitfully, not really resting, exhaustion and illness taking its toll.

Something was wrong, and he didn't know what. No smile today. His eyes betrayed worry, reflective, subdued; time to be serious, and he was concerned. Impasse did that to him. Despite his resilience and ability to adapt, things here were problematic. As Alice would say, *curiouser and curiouser,* and he grumbled, "Yeah, fuck the white rabbit."

Pieces… *the Puzzle.*

This was a beautiful world, but not their own; their familiar jungle of gnarled chlorophyll-green trees was gone. It all had disappeared, evaporated somehow on the way to this place. Here and now. He viewed an enchanted forest. 'Hobbit land'.

Here craggy granite mountains, incredible rock columns and massive spires jutted from the landscape, climbing stately and towering loftily thousands of feet above, their summits absorbed and obscured within an overcast sky of achromatic shades, congealed dove gray. The meandering valley basin, a landscape of dense meadows, lay dormant and pure, fingered with trickling brooks of clear water rushing in riffles filling pools and lagoons then continuing on, going to somewhere unknown, to regions never before seen by anyone's eyes.

Always moving, flowing easily. Perhaps just around the next bend or beyond the next rise a tributary might gather and pond creating backwater providing foothold and nourishment for rushes, cattail bogs, camass, pampas grass stands and others garbed in unusual ornamental colors, swaying gently, pushed by breezes of new design.

Violets, blues, reds and yellows, phenomenal fluorescent displays interspersed in casual array, this world was absorbed in drenching warmth of vivid color captured and revealed in flowering blooms. Tulips, hyacinths, four-o'clocks, azaleas, daffodils, morning glories, asters, roses, and a thousand others grew lush, oversized and gorgeous, bursting from a carpet of fringed phacelia.

The marshes were bordered with runs of emerald grasses: fescue, darnel, crested wheat, timothy and sorghum, anchored solidly upon nodes in mineral-rich loam as dark as anthracite. The understory and shrub layer were thick with plants of all shape and kind, and the herb layer and forest floor saturated with ferns, mosses, lichens and enormous woodland mushrooms. Glens and hollows rose to the rolling foothills adorned with forests of oak, walnut, hickory, weeping willow, sycamore, maple, aspen, and countless others; each proudly brandishing its cloak of color, bold, bright, and beautiful. The colors of autumn.

Sequestered within this waiting world were small ones, microorganisms and single cells: amoebas, flagella and others. Insects scampered in limitless variety: ants, beetles and bugs—to butterflies. Fish, reptiles and amphibians filled water and fields, from perch and trout, snakes, chameleons and lizards, to turtles and frogs. An abundance of life; replenished supply. And scattered throughout the meadows bordering the wetland marshes grew flowering shrubs, fruit bearing bushes and trees: willows, dogwood, chokecherry, plum, elderberry and currant, along with a multitude of others.

But here, in this world, there were no birds.

Farther up the ragged slopes, above the color of the changing seasons, grew conifers: Douglas fir, Scotch, lodgepole, ponderosa, white and jack pine, Sitka and blue spruce, and larch not yet having gone to yellow. The evergreens stood proud and strong scaling the steep inclines of the mountains, columns and spires, and clung tenaciously to the irregular contour of the timberline where barren rock stood alone veiled in a cloak of snow, and silence, and cloud.

For all its beauty and color, unusual by what we might know, fluorescence of blues, reds, violets, yellows and greens blended softly within the texture of others. This place was truly beautiful; and it might be the perfect world were it not for a few minor imperfections. Tian and Reed were lost, the two of them completely alone, somewhere they could not fathom. Pristine. Uncharted.

Also, more than inconsequential, but less than monumental, this land possessed two singular oddities. It was always overcast; the sun never shined. Nor did it ever set; one day, immeasurably long, that somehow simply refused to end. Reed summed it axiomatically and succinctly; same day—different shit.

He impatiently squirmed stretching his legs, getting a bit more comfortable. Tapping his bare heels together three times he grinned with pretentious derision; then did it again and muttered, " 'There's no place like home. There's no place like home'." He reflected, "Christ, I'm losing my mind. Stupid bullshit."

"What did you say?" Tian asked, weary, waking but not rested.

Turning with an oblique glance, "Oh nothing, Babe; just being stupid." Forcing a smile, pushing the pain aside she sat up weakly beside him when he asked, "How do you feel?"

"Very bad," she admitted. "It hurts today."

"Frickin' mushrooms," a half-hearted mumble. "I'm really sorry. I didn't know they'd make you so sick."

"It was not your fault, Reed."

"But I should have…"

"—No," she insisted grimacing; then managed a thin smile, "you and John have become a part of our lives, and at times we forget we are different." Squeezing his hand gently, love evident in her words, "I am Renoloi and you are not, even though we forget that sometimes."

"Still, I should have found something else," fondly brushing hair from her face with a careful hand. "Shouldn't have eaten those mushrooms."

"Reed…" she let it go, her gaze traveling over the unfamiliar, unusual landscape, ushered by subconscious impulse. Homing instinct.

He sighed; concession and concern regarding their situation to be deteriorating, certainly not getting better—*she's worse now than before*. He grinned, a facade.

Tian, seeing the trouble in his eyes, placated with the quieting nature of a woman's words. "We will be all right. We have come this far, have we not? We are still alive and still together, even after so many days being here." Scooting closer she snuggled against him for security, someone to lean on.

"So many days," he repeated pensively. "How can you tell? It's always overcast, a gray afternoon. Talk about seasonal affective disorder —and the sun never sets. Fuckit. Just—plain—fuckit."

"I know," she said, softly and supportive. Then changing subjects attempting to lighten the mood. "What were you doing before?"

"Before—when?"

"Bumping your heels together when you said, 'No place like home'."

"Oh that," as he smiled the 'stupid' smile, "just foolishness from a long time ago. A fairytale story about a girl named Dorothy who got herself whizzed off in a tornado, sorta like us."

"A story? Is it an interesting story?"

"Well for crying in the soup, 'course it is."

She asked, "Is Bloody Bones in it?"

"No," he reluctantly admitted naturally assuming the narrative quality would be diminished without his fabled and trustworthy monster, Bloody Bones.

"Then you must tell me the story."

"Really?" he asked, "even *without* Bloody Bones in it?"

Slapping him playfully on the arm, her spirits a bit lighter, "Yes, *especially* without Bloody Bones in it."

Reed realized, offering a hangdog expression, "Oh—don't be disrespectful about Bloody Bones," he chastised pompously, "that's *totally* uncalled for." Tian grinned. "I'm not kiddin' you now; so don't be smiling."

"Very well, I am sorry." But not really.

"That's better," he teased, rising to his knees slinging the pulse laser across his back. "Ready to go?" getting on his feet, then with a strong solid arm, helping her up. Standing she hesitated, unsteady. "Can you walk?" protectively slipping an arm around her waist. A nod. "Okay then, I'll tell you all about Wiz and The Dorothy on the way."

Slowly they resumed their journey, Reed relating each delicious morsel of the timeless classic as they proceeded, his somewhat modified interpretation an entertaining version all its own. Pleasurable fodder, keeping their minds occupied; Reed was truly a gifted storyteller.

* * *

The Renoloi village…

…Exhaustion settling in, hurting and sore, they were fatigued, muscles aching with waning adrenaline-energy. Together they milled on the path in front of Tian's hut near one of the night fires scattered throughout the village, a precautionary measure with the advent of Hunters in this region. It had never happened before; until now, Night Hunters were unknown here and no one understood why the adroit assassins might so suddenly appear at this particular time. They opted to speculate, chose to believe, it was chance, and not by design.

"Did we lose anyone?" Lent asked.

Nitana: "All Renoloi are accounted for."

"No casualties," Kale advised.

Pleased, Lent grinned. "We're getting pretty good at this night combat —firefight." A bob of his head, he scratched his mop of dark hair and said it again, "Firefight. Good expression; I like it."

"That's not original," Ames told him, "it was coined long ago."

"And how would you know that?" Deet asked defensively on Lent's behalf.

"I read books," a spontaneous, fabricated reply.

Hand in his pocket, "I still like it," Deet decided aligning with Lent as he unconsciously fondled his stash of corn kernels.

"So do I," Ames agreed, then continued, "—but a word of caution; don't underestimate the Hunters." Lent's side-glance showed he agreed. Observing Deet's hand in his pocket, Ames couldn't resist. "And don't do that too long either; it'll make you go blind." Gullibly Deet jerked his hand from his pocket scattering a sprinkling of corn at his feet. He promptly knelt and began recapturing the escaped kernels, now a precious commodity, seed stock. Not understanding how handling corn kernels could possibly affect his eyesight he looked up at Ames. The man bounced his eyebrows and grinned, but didn't explain.

"Could they have followed us when we returned?" Nitana wondered.

"Possibly," Ames admitted.

Lent asked incredulously, "You mean the Hunters have never been here before?"

"Not until now," she told him,

Kale: "That's strange."

"No stranger than the dinosaur crossing the river from the Forsaken Land," Nitana considered, referring to the Tyrannosaur Kalo killed at the meeting circle not so long ago.

"Forsaken Land?" Deet joined the discussion, ball cap cocked sideways, still on his knees collecting corn.

Nitana, Ames and Kalo immediately traded peculiar glances. "Yes, the Forsaken Land," Kalo explained, "where T-Rex and other great beasts roam."

Lent, again: "Really?"

"I would not lie," Kalo fired back with a tinge of irritation. "Across the river the land is harsh, and many of the dinosaurs there are even larger than the Night Hunters." Ames listened.

"No kidding. Are they all dangerous?" he queried; then assured, "—and I don't mean to imply you would tell me a lie; this is just new to us."

Now more placid, her tone instructional, informative, "Some, like T-Rex, are very dangerous —but generally, they are not." All three Pilgrims shook their heads.

"The Forsaken Land, and dinosaurs..." Lent contemplated admitting, "we've never heard of them."

"But we are familiar with Chiqua," Deet chimed in rising to his feet.

"We are all familiar with Chiqua," Kalo replied wryly.

Not interrupting, still listening, Ames thought, *segregated world.*

"We are all tired," Nitana said drawing their dialogue to an end. "We should get some rest now." As Nitana and the Pilgrims ambled away on the path, Kalo lingered outside Tian's hut with Ames. She wanted to speak privately.

Alone now.

Beneath a canopy of night sky freckled with scintillating pinpoints of stars, and beyond the amber glow of flickering night fires, lie the secrets... secrets wrapped in divine mystery.

Cautiously Kalo stepped forward and took Ames' hand with her own, looking into his eyes, and then beyond, to a soul weary and torn, struggling in the dregs of confusion… into the chamber of loss. With her touch, secretly, she crept into the darkness of the room that sequestered the pain. It was there. Inside, she could feel it. She assured softly, "We will find them."

"I know."

She sensed it, could feel it, the doubt. "You must believe."

"It's difficult," he said solemnly, studying her face. Then he became aware her hand was quivering, and looking more closely realized her entire body was trembling. She seemed almost entranced. He asked, "What are you doing?"

Closing her eyes, still holding his hand, she whispered, "A gift —but only for this night— so you may rest. Your soul is weary and difficulties still must be overcome. The conflict is yet to come." Still trembling, eyes closed, entranced, she revealed, "You long so for Tian and Reed; it tortures your heart. But this night you shall have peace."

And with her words... *Inside, he felt it; the pain slipped away.*

Suddenly, with a convulsive heave Kalo fell backward breaking their grasp as she collapsed onto the path. At once Ames knelt to help her; but she instantly stopped him with an opened hand and the command, *"No!"* Then her eyes blinked open and she looked up apologetically, almost in tears. "I am sorry. I did not mean to yell."

"You remember—" he blurted out; then more softly, "that you yelled."

Puzzled, "Yes. I do."

"Anything more than that?"

"No, only that I yelled," she said thoughtfully slowly rising to her feet, brushing herself off. Then continuing conversationally, "You should get some sleep; this night you will rest."

Unexpecting, suspicious, "How do you know that?"

Confused, she reticently answered, "I am not sure."

Eyes riveted upon hers he urged, "Kalo, think. Try to remember," she, gazing distantly into his eyes. Then again, "Kalo, try to remember. Who told you?" He waited...

A minute elapsed, very long, seemingly forever.

...Finally, she whispered, "The Mystic, the Mystic told me." Then without saying anything more the young girl turned and walked away... down the path.

He let her go. And watching her moving into the darkness, intermittently illuminated by the scattered campfires of night watch, Ames believed that somehow, she, a young Renoloi warrior, was the key to it all... the solution to a problem wound tightly within a puzzle cloistered within the mountains of the Legends. But what he did not realize, had no way of knowing, drawn by destiny, Kalo was indeed the key... to something more, much More.

Beyond imaginings.

* * *

Before dawn…

…They crouched in the underbrush near the path opposite Tian's hut; then leaning forward a bit pushing bracken aside, carefully they peered out. Not too far away, a campfire alongside the path and two sentries: Renoloi and Pilgrim sitting together, facing the other direction, dark silhouettes in the amber glow of the small fire. Intermittent crackles and an occasional pop spitting embers that sent wood-spark up with winding wisps of evaporating smoke, were the only sounds frustrating the quiet of night. Beyond the sentry post was another night fire, but too distant, of no immediate concern. The pair exchanged glances and a nod. The time was right.

Whispered words: "Wait here." A final check to make sure the coast was clear, and quickly he rustled from the bushes and scampered across the open ground of the path. At Tian's hut —*ssst*, the door went up and he was inside, out of sight. The door closed behind him.

On the stone couch Ames lay sound asleep, not stirring, not moving a muscle, not even a twitch. His chest rose and fell with peaceful regularity, the rhythm of nature's healing power and its precious medicine, balm for his heart. Kalo's predicate words of peace and reprieve, a brief respite from the torment, for one single night —the Gift— to unlace the knot in his soul.

Within the confines of the small hut the burglar stepped confidently and quietly, intent on his objective. Moving stealthily to the wall opposite where the man lay sleeping the intruder crouched running a hand down the wall to the floor. Small fingers probed into the crack and carefully withdrew the gray antimagnetic envelope containing a two-inch disc. Palming the data CD he smiled with satisfaction, his twinkling eyes reflecting the dim illumination of the sepulcher's flame.

Without a sound he removed the disc from the envelope and examined it carefully, intently. Then casting a compassionate glance to the sleeping man, he wrinkled his pudgy nose, rubbed a thumb over the disc, and blinked twice, altering data. Confidently the small burglar snugged the disc back into the envelope and folded the flap sealing it closed, then tucked it into his shirt pocket, sleeves rolled up to the elbows—flannel, red and blue.

"Sleep well, Mr. Ames," the hushed words of his benevolent benefactor; and —*ssst,* he was gone, into the night.

* * *

It was late when he finally woke...

...Feeling revitalized, better than he had for a long time. Today there were no aching muscles or knots of stress devising pain that crawled from his back, through his neck into the brainstem, then hanging there throbbing and nagging. He lay easy, relaxed, and closed his eyes again. The black leather cover of the stone couch felt comforting and soft as his face pressed upon it. But he was not tired; his mind was alert. It was time to get up. With fisted hands he reached out and stretched full, then turned and swung his legs sitting upright, and pushing the fleeting traces of grogginess from his eyes with his palms, finally scratched his nose. He felt good, restored.

Ames padded across the floor, and as the door rose stepped outside onto the path. Standing a short distance away, Seana and Kalo were talking; and for a moment he observed presuming that by now her injured shoulder would have mended more than it had. Rather than having regained the use of her left arm her condition suggested her health was deteriorating and she appeared more listless and haggard, her vitality and strength emaciating with each succeeding day. He suspected the tapeworm of infectious emptiness was culpable, not the injury itself; her only medicine, panacea, was Reed. And Ames was acutely aware; two were still missing.

Speaking with Seana, Kalo's alert eye spied him the moment her head turned obliquely; the unheard swish of her hair with the breeze that fluffed it away from her cheek exposing her ear just a bit, and her fleeting but loving smile. The hardships they had endured and survived together, was their bond; their trust in one another forged with the power and strength of the fetish she wore. When Seana noticed Kalo's attention distracted by the man's presence she also turned, and seeing him, both walked to meet him. This man, who was once a stranger, was now their strength. He was their friend.

"How do you feel today, Seana?" his first words, revealing concern.

"Better. I feel better today."

Ames, skeptically, "Really?" Kalo said nothing, but believed her no more than he did.

Seana relented, "Perhaps then, not better, but no worse either."

"'Bout the same."

"Yes," she admitted, "it is still stiff and at times the muscles become tight, and that makes my side ache." Listening, Ames nodded as she hesitated then finally asked, "You do still believe it will heal, do you not?"

"Yes, there's no physiological or medical reason why it shouldn't. Just be careful not to bump it; and gently exercise so it doesn't tighten up." Then he cautioned, "Don't overdo it though."

"I will be careful."

"How do you feel, Mr. Ames?" Kalo inquired.

A smile. "Rested," his straightforward answer —and she knew precisely what he meant. She beamed offering a reciprocal smile —and he knew precisely what she meant. Changing the subject, not wishing to pursue it further, conversationally, Ames inquired, "And why is it I find the two of you here at the doorstep this morning?"

Seana told him, "We were discussing your visitor." She paused, waiting; but he offered no reply.

"Is there something we should know?" Kalo asked.

"Visitor..." darting a puzzled look from one to the other, "what visitor?"

Kalo pointed to the ground near his foot. "Your visitor."

"I had no visitor," —then he saw it. Beside him, near the edge of the path was an indentation in the soil, clearly visible someone had recently stepped there. Wondering, he knelt lightly tracing the outline with his finger; a work boot—children's size twelve. Looking up to the Renoloi his voice softened. "But I had no visitor," his words spreading contagion; now three of them wondering.

"Good morning," Lent called out, approaching on the path. Ames quickly rose as Seana turned to greet Lent. Kalo, as well, pivoted to welcome him, and doing so, with a furtive glance observed Ames discretely place his foot upon the impression of the boot, pressing down with his heel, grinding, wiping it out. 'Good mornings' completed and smiles all around, with the exception of Kalo who was still leery, Lent commented with boyish enthusiasm, "It is a beautiful day today, is—it—not?"

"Yes it is," Ames' cheerful, orchestrated response, "too nice a day to spend here in the village." Offhand, "Let's go for a walk," he suggested.

"Good idea," Lent agreed, "where to?"

"The cliffs," Seana said, joining in.

"To the cliffs it is then," and walking more slowly than usual, Lent allowed Seana to set the pace as they headed to the precipice. Kalo lingered briefly unobtrusively eyeing the ground; no other impressions in the vicinity, only the one. A partial outline was still barely visible, just the edge at the ball of the print where Ames had missed. Discretely, as she spun around she stepped on it again with her small foot, completely wiping it out.

In this primitive world, as Alice would say, "Curiouser and curiouser."

* * *

Ambling along the path…

…The small band came upon Nitana, Ronto and Tere listening as Kale and Deet were bending Tondra's ear. The pair was rambling vivid with particulars, waxing nostalgic as they enthusiastically reminisced rehashing their perilous adventures of hair-twisting encounters with Night Hunters and other such denizens of the netherworld and darker side.

Occasionally Tondra dubiously glanced at one of the others when suspicion warranted the Pilgrims' recollection might be a bit more grandiose than the facts and the truth in the matter, and with each glimpse of inquisition there was an almost imperceptible nod or quick smirk indicating it was. Nevertheless, Tondra's easy smile was incentive enough for the Pilgrims to keep their narration moving, and growing, and entertaining.

However, beleaguered after listening to them for less than a minute and well acquainted with their prattle, Lent curtly inferred with a comment tossed to Ames. "Fertilizer for the corn." The man chuckled; but the Renoloi didn't get it and Kale and Deet kept right on rambling.

Ames inquired, "Where did you learn an expression like that?"

Lent grinned lightly. "Comic books of course." Then joking, " 'Marvel Group Britannica'." Indicating Kale and Deet, he added, "But those two have read a lot more of 'em than I have," strongly emphasizing the word, 'lot'. The group milled another minute or so until Lent finally asked the captive Renoloi, "Tondra, we're on our way to the cliffs; would you care to join us?"

Her immediate reply was, "Immensely," as they started again with Nitana, Ronto and Tere gladly joining them politely attempting a graceful exit. However, not wishing to be left behind and their narration unfinished, Kale and Deet tagged along. The group of eight became ten.

Looking quickly over a shoulder Lent said, "I knew it." Ames smirked; but Seana's expression asked, *what?* so Lent cordially explained, "Sure gonna miss that shine. At least after they've been imbibing they pass out, and—shut—up." He sighed, "Those two idiots will be wide awake for hours." Kale and Deet paid him no mind, pestering, following, bending Tondra's ear and tugging at her arm ever so gently when they thought she may have missed something; persistent, talking as they walked.

"Tondra," Lent wisecracked, "if they get on your nerves too much just go ahead and bitch-slap 'em if you're a mind to. I've certainly thought about it often enough. They'll make you go crazy."

Tondra just smiled, not sure what that meant.

* * *

Still searching...

...They wandered endlessly upon the valley basin, following a fingerling brook. The meandering stream wound like a watery ribbon through lush green meadows embracing niches overgrown with flowers of spectacular pigment. All around them was a blossoming world of incredible color and visual delight. The reds were so brilliant they welled with a pulse and heartbeat; orange so vibrant as to defy ecological balance, offsetting equilibrium. Yellows and saffrons seemed like they burst from the sun; greens so intense they tasted clean and sweet. And the blues were so deeply absorbing they floated like waves. Violets abound with their intrigue born of mystery and magic —and flourescents shimmered wild and fiery, sprayed and glowing throughout the flowering landscape.

The meadows were glorious and pristine, woven then gently laid at the bases of towering, dark granitic columns, wound and twisted spires, and ragged mountains that jutted almost vertically then disappeared somewhere within the impenetrable ceiling of clouds. This world was truly beautiful, absorbed within the silence of calm and the still of empty quiet; the sensation of looking around... *waiting*.

They were completely alone in a land of deciduous trees painted the colors of autumn.

His arm carefully snugged around her and gently supporting her weight, Tian's long flaxen hair quivered in gossamer waves with every step she endured. But with each passing hour her strength was slipping away, so they trudged on. The pain was more than a nagging irritation now, even the slightest movement twist electrifying knots inside her. Reed was quiet, his concern gathered within and hidden there. Very worried, but she must not know.

A misstep. She faltered and he squeezed just a little tighter holding her up. As she turned her head her tired eyes met his, and the indelible smile. "Thank you," she murmured. He wrinkled his nose answering without speaking. Several steps more, then an intense spasm seized her and she slumped weakly clutching her stomach. They stopped.

A minute or more passed before the pain subsided and the Renoloi was able to draw in a breath; then again she breathed, very slowly, raising her head to nod indicating she was able to go on. Outwardly Reed presented calm concern, but within churned the vexing blade of apprehension. The toxic effect of the mushrooms was becoming apparent, seeping through her body. Time was running out.

Languid, they began walking again. "Reed, do you believe we are lost?"

"Lost," he repeated drawing a lackluster grin, "I don't think we're even on the same planet anymore." Then he asked, "Has anyone ever told you that you have a penchant for understatements?"

"Yes," she said plainly, "you have told me that before."

Her reference to the Trogs tugged a memory, a half-hearted diversion, and he managed a chuckle amused with her sincerity and innocence. "Tian, I was being facetious." She seemed puzzled as she glanced up, so he explained, "I was kidding. It was a joke."

Their conversation distracted her from the pain and her eyes brightened a bit. "I understand… like Mr. Wrinkle."

Miffed: "Don't you guys ever forget anything?"

Serious: "I try not to; but sometimes I do forget things."

"Well for Pete's sake, do me a favor and just forget about Mr. Wrinkle, okay?"

"I will do that—for you," and she tried to smile. They continued quietly for a while, Reed always in step with her, his arm securely around her lending support.

At length, as though he had been deliberating and now putting it into words, he mumbled, "Tell me the Bermuda Triangle isn't real."

Pained, limping along, "Bermuda Triangle?" He had spoken of it before, on the trimaran.

Realizing he had said it out loud and looking around as they walked, Reed began. "Yeah, once upon a time, back on our world there was a place, an expanse of ocean located between three points of landfall: Puerto Rico, Florida and the Bermuda Islands. The area covered a half-million square miles and roughly resembled a triangle —thus, Bermuda Triangle, its most commonly recognized of several names. Some of the others were 'Graveyard of the Atlantic', 'Triangle of Death', 'Hoodoo Sea', 'Devil's Triangle', and so on; you get the general idea."

He continued, "It really wasn't all that unusual—in fact—actually it was just another ordinary expanse of water ranging from a few thousand feet, to thirty thousand feet deep in the immense undersea canyon called the Puerto Rico Trench. But within the Triangle, on the ocean bottom, lay a range of limestone mountains honeycombed with a labyrinth of caves that created intense underwater currents powerful enough to drag ships inside them, never to be seen again. Another interesting aspect was the fact that the seafloor, in many places was quicksand."

"Quicksand?" she repeated, then remembering paralleled, "black water?"

"Yep," he confirmed, an analogy familiar to her. They passed beneath the swaying branches of a weeping willow, avoided a clump of hastas with oversized leaves thriving in the shade beneath it, and continued on. "Anyway, the average water depth of the Triangle was about eighteen thousand feet —deep water— deep enough to make it very difficult to locate ships and planes that went down."

Tian puzzled, "Ships and planes?"

"Large boats—very big," he explained.

"Like the one in the storm?"

"Exactly. And planes... more difficult to describe," he told her, then elucidated, "magic machines that could fly." Lacking a less technical explanation he let it go at that.

"Really..." amazed, "your people could fly?"

Reed smiled, almost sadly. "Oh yeah, they could fly, and a lot more, things you could not even begin to imagine." They hobbled on a moment before he finally added, hinting regret, "And they pissed it all away... screwed it up with war." War, she understood.

"Please go on," she encouraged.

He sighed pushing sadness aside, his mood changing, informative again. "—Anyway, as I was saying, the Bermuda Triangle seemed pretty much to be just an ordinary slice of ocean, 'cept some strange things happened there. And people being people, predisposed to exaggeration by nature, probably embellished and distorted the occurrences blowing them out of proportion, if you know what I mean."

"Yes. I try not to do that."

He chuckled, "So I've noticed," then continued. "Altogether there were probably a-hundred-fifty or two hundred known occurrences within the Triangle: ships sinking, planes going down —stuff like that— and more than a thousand lives lost. Most people attributed those incidents to the mundane, natural causes and so forth. Plausible enough." He shrugged, "Generally commonplace in nature or origin, resulting from nothing out of the ordinary, nothing more than mechanical failure, human error, stupidity; things like that."

He moved his hand slightly readjusting his grip around her waist as they walked. "In 1492 a guy named Christopher Columbus, a sailor, recorded strange lights in the night sky." Reed grinned as he explained, "Scientists attributed that to a meteor —but hell, there's no way to ever know."

"Meteor?"

"Shooting star." She understood and he went on. "Columbus also experienced discrepancies with compass readings, and that was accounted for with variations between celestial and magnetic north." Glancing at her he realized she didn't understand. "I don't even know how to explain that, so don't worry about it. Likely this world exhibits the same anomaly." They stopped momentarily, both watching a small harmless garter snake as it crossed in front of them, wriggling along as it furrowed through the grass.

They continued and he went on. "Later on, there were other stories of radio communications that were garbled or distorted, some even lost entirely, and for no apparent reason, possibly causing experienced pilots and navigators to get lost when they shouldn't have. The government dismissed most of those cases well enough to at least lend them some credibility. Generally, they'd claim they were nothing more than prosaic accidents, commonplace mishaps, ordinary or not." Then reflecting, "Yeah, 'Big Brother'[14] government *never* lied."

Making their way around a thicket of grapevines before he offered another perspective, "Then, on the other hand there were those who believed mysterious forces were at work, strange dabblings, perhaps something supernatural or extraordinary was amiss there that no one knew anything about. They believed there was more to the Triangle phenomenon than anyone knew —or was telling. Some folks told weird tales of UFOs from other worlds bringing aliens to and from the lost city of Atlantis, human abductions, and a bunch of other folklore cough-syrup-thick with dripping suspense and sinister plots —some really strange, and the rest verging precariously on completely bizarre."

"UFOs, aliens? Reed, these things I do not understand."

He grinned, perhaps amused with such fantasy. "UFOs, Tian… spaceships and flying saucers transporting aliens, little green men with ray guns zipping hither and yon throughout the galaxies, taking prisoners and demanding in squeaky little voices, 'Take me to your leader'," his glib reply. The very thought of it ludicrous, ridiculous —after all…

The gist of his mockery eluding her, Tian puzzled, "Reed, you really make no sense at times. How can that have anything to do with us?" Faltering, she missed a step, and flexing his arm he instantly steadied her preventing her from falling. More carefully and slowly they continued and Tian finished what she had begun to say. "You speak of UFOs and little green men, but I do not understand what that has to do with us." Watching the ground, stepping softly, she considered then remarked, "After all, we have no little green men," and looking at him "—only P.T. Barnum and 'Just Plain' Wilson... little gray men."

That quibble of technical trivia not having occurred to him, he reluctantly admitted, "Babe, you do have a trenchant flair when making a point. Must be some new kind of feminist logic."

She drew a painful breath, exhaled slowly, then replied sincerely, "No Reed, not really, just common sense. I know nothing of feminist logic. I am a Renoloi."

"Yeah, whatever," but he wasn't so sure. Resuming their discussion, "Anyway, the Bermuda Triangle had to be something more than myth and nonsense, but I don't know that anyone ever figured out just exactly what." Stepping over a copse of black-eyed Susan's and pansies, "Invariably there were two constants in all the bizarre stories: one, strange violent storms with waterspouts that could tear ships apart, and two, the 'Hole in the Sky'."

"The hole in the sky?"

"Yeah," considering, "some people believed it was some kind of mysterious corridor or wormhole linking different worlds, connecting unknown places, or a time warp between parallel dimensions, a tear in the fabric of time." As they walked he scanned the strange landscape around them and sighed. "Who really knows what was going on back then. Couldn't believe anybody. None of 'em had an ounce of truth in 'em. The government even lied about Area 51. Hell, it was all just stupid. Dumb-bastard greedy politico all chronically infected with their self-important, elitist 'better than thou' attitudes —and the mega-corporations weren't any better. Buncha' self-serving, money-grubbing stupid twits."

"Took the bureaucrats a while to put it all together; but they eventually succeeded. Yeah, the idealistic liberal's hidden agenda; they used the term benefit recipients, but what it was really about was creating an entire class of generational parasites dependant on the government, too lazy to work, all suckling the welfare teat at the expense of those who were productive. Redistribution of wealth; what an unholy, socialist crock of shit."

"And they just had to keep preaching that Global Community, New World Order bullshit —but that could never work, never happen; too many self-serving people involved."

"One of the two unique traits inherent in mankind, was the intrinsic desire to be free. It just couldn't be suppressed. So inevitably it all ended in war. They were so stupid. Yeah, it was all just stupid." Then he was quiet for a moment, until finally considering just how lost they really might be. "Hell, for all I know, right now we could be in the twilight zone." Pensive, a sigh.

"Reed," she said gently, not wanting to be excluded.

"Yeah?"

Glancing up, "I know nothing of the things you are speaking of."

"Yeah, I know—sorry," he apologized, "forgot about the Renoloi factor."

Not understanding that she asked, "If you feel so much of what you told me is untrue, why do you still think the Bermuda Triangle was real?"

Serious, he looked at her. "The circular storm we sailed into — and that hole in the sky— they were real, weren't they?"

"Yes," she had to admit, again watching the ground.

"And the ghost ship, that strange dead ship that shouldn't have been there..." They stopped. She looked at him. "...you saw it too, didn't you?"

Whispered: "Yes."

Soberly, almost carefully, "That *same ship* vanished in the Bermuda Triangle."

"But Reed, how can that be?"

"Your guess is as good as mine," he admitted, "so... we'll just have to keep looking."

"What are we looking for?"

"I don't really know." Determined, he looked around again. "But finding myself at a loss for a more plausible explanation, regardless how outlandish it may seem, we're going back the same way we got here. Even if it was only a figment of our imaginations, something that wasn't even real, it *was* a circular storm... and a 'Hole in the Sky'."

Pieces... *the Puzzle.*

* * *

Following the jungle path until...

...They entered a clearing on a point at the summit of the escarpment; eight of the ten gathered near a very large boulder, some sitting, some standing. Quiet conversation. Kalo and Ames walked to a mound at the brink of the precipice and sat down together.

Silent, neither of them spoke for a while. Companioned with thought, Ames reflected opening his scrapbook of memories. To his right, not far off the trail was the place where it all began. Within the web of jungle remained the abandoned wreckage of a geodesic sphere, and a pool at the base of a bluff; his first encounter with warm, enchanting hazel eyes that kindled a dormant ember within to the flame of enduring love.

Before him lay a harsh and barren land entwined in quagmires of evil and reproach. Unforgiving. The Forsaken Land was no longer the domain of the Trogs; the hulking behemoths had been defeated in a confrontation foretold many generations before it happened.

Now the arid region beyond the river again lay inert and dehydrated, awaiting monsoon and an ensuing resurrection. And with the resurgence the craggy landscape once again would change overnight to a world of swamp and forest, an unexplainable transformation, something that should not be. With the rains would come T-Rex and the reemergence of the mighty reptiles roaming the lands on ponderous feet, traipsing heavily upon swampland appropriately named 'Vanishing Valley'. The Forsaken Land was hostile, misunderstood, mysterious... and More.

Below and to the left was the floodplain bordering the river; the lowland abutted the stair-step formations of the ridges, where one day not so long ago a decisive battle, Renoloi against Trog, was fought. A lush emerald land once torn and saturated in scarlet, consecrated with blood, was now healed in chlorophyll-green. One afternoon, on that field of battle beneath ancient, gnarled trees, the 'Prophecy of the Strangers' became very real.

Behind him and to the left, beyond the ridges and escarpment was an aggregate of small, gray-tan stone huts from where they had come, the Renoloi village. It was home, where Tian, Seana, and all the others stood together, their undying devotion to one another their bond. It was just a small village, its people endowed with conviction to persevere, determined to carve a niche and somehow survive.

And the most haunting image, one final photo in the scrapbook; a mile to his right, beyond the geodesic sphere, where the trail and jungle ended abruptly, was the rimrock and crater of the destroyed temple. And beyond that, a mountain range that for an unknown reason collapsed one dark night, and in doing so buried the answers to so many questions; vexing, disquieting, and still unanswered, in a strange world seemingly filled with mystery. Within those mountains, sequestered somewhere, lost in a primitive world… lay the Secret of the Legends.

Approaching from behind, Seana spoke. "The two of you, sitting so quietly over here." Turning her head Kalo presented a taciturn smile.

"Just thinking, Seana," Ames replied warmly, his gaze still to the front, eyes scanning the vast emptiness of the Forsaken Land.

Seana began, "I do not mean to intrude, but the Pilgrims talk so much," she confessed, "a little peace and quiet would be nice."

"Not at all," the man obliged, "certainly, join us," rising and offering his hand; and as he did, Kalo desperately grasped his arm with a hand.

"It is coming," her fatidic warning drawn with anxiety.

Startled, "—What?" But he hadn't time to say anything more.

Beneath them, from somewhere deep within the tectonic plate came rumbling echoes caused by reverberations of mounting pressure. Ever so slightly the landscape shuddered with foreboding harmonic tremors; while unfelt, slowly building, a groundswell pushed from far below, lifting subterranean pressure inching up and moving the precipice virtually imperceptibly.

Then shivering guttural rumbles, preemptive foreshocks forewarning...

…The Quake.

Suddenly a loud, *crack,* and the entire precipice vaulted violently tossing them up —then contracted— dropping from beneath them leaving them stranded in midair. Falling, unstrung limp puppets they tumbled to the ground as the escarpment began vibrating and rattling, scattering them like jostled pebbles upon its agitated face. Increasing, the noise and quavering grew more volatile, upheaval pounding with the pulse and intensity of bass drums hammering rolls of deafening thunder, continuously surging beneath them.

The monstrous boulder was spewn from the ground then slammed down thunderously as those near it scattered and ran. Rolling and wavering unevenly upon the jostled surface it ground and turned up onto an end —paused, teetered— then went the rest of the way over. Again it rolled up, onto an end —paused— like an enormous oblong egg of momentum without direction on a heaving, rattling tabletop. Until finally it turned, rolled and crunched down near the edge of the cliff.

Brittle cracking sounds. Still vibrating, its weight and bulk splintered the rim of the precipice releasing ten thousand yards of rock. Crumbling, the brink of the cliff broke apart and collapsed in a fall of boulders and rockslide that cascaded away with sharp earsplitting crashes —sliding, tumbling— going into the canyon and whitewater below.

Frightened and grabbing one another the ten were repeatedly bounced and thrown, the fear in their voices being absorbed within the confusion of boil and congestion of sound. Tossed randomly they stumbled and fell on the heaving surface, a roller coaster trampoline of staggering bodies and vibrating, skittering stones, scattering dust and chaos and wide-eyed apprehension.

Huge gnarled trees surrounding the clearing swayed uncontrollably as their massive limbs heaved to-and-fro listing like masts in a seastorm. Thick green branches snapped off shooting brittle-rip barks through a backdrop of mean-angry rumble; then they fell like chlorophyll torches with sticks and leaves following twirling down. Wrenching, creaking groans —then *craa-ack*— huge treetrunks splintered as ragged shredding tears crawled from their roots up into the limbs.

With the incessant quaking spasms, the towering behemoths began unearthing exposing their tangled root systems, then suddenly snapped apart like mud fists with twisted fingers ripping up great wads of dirt. And finally uprooting, boiling up from the ground the ancients shivered and leaned, then collapsed shattering on the escarpment sloshing showers of quivering confetti and leaves. Skyscrapers of forest shuddering, spewing up, collapsing, crashing, splintering and splashing debris of emerald waves with branches scattering foliage.

As the precipice rattled hairline fractures ran the granite then cracked with abrasive, explosive noise. And from somewhere else came a deep rumbling growl resembling guttural haunting echoes —then another heaving sudden-shudder and the chaos of swarming tremors. Everything vibrating, shattering, quaking. It was deafening, pervasive, terrifying confusion.

—Until suddenly it stopped.

First, the subsiding clatter of pebbles—momentum evaporating away. Next, the quieting swishes of rustling leaves—sturdy limbs and softly floating wisps on trees that survived.

Stunned by the unexpected sudden-hush they got up and just stood there; then a quick visual accounting confirmed no one was injured. And last, nervously they looked around.

Everything still. The calm, that eerie silence preempting the strike. Then one by one each realized it was, *the pause,* inhale a deep breath, followed by that awful, sickening feeling of, *uh-oh, it is coming.*

Beneath them the substrata had shifted as it heaved, then cracked unlocking fissures that splintered and ran opening pathways that snapped revealing trace-lines of veins for the pressurized molten magma that surged pushing, pulsing and oozing. Prying fingers of unrelenting liquid fire crawled as it seeped with extraordinary force, melting broken rock and fusing the seam while the buried caldera of dissolving froth crept forth, climbing, always upward with spiderweb-fingers that kept gathering strength.

Those on the precipice could not hear the incredible pressure; but they knew. That sixth sense of awareness, they could almost feel it, waiting. It was coming. Deep below the molten cauldron ocean boiled and expanded with mounting intensity. Blind, yellow-orange snakes of probing, slithering fluid fingers searching, the molten magma squeezed from crevice to crevice seeking out a passageway to the barren wasteland above.

Lying deep underground the solid sheet of tectonic plate had fractured during the quake then recompressed as the stratum settled again. But now, even the crust's intense weight was unable to completely seal the rift along the fault line; and there it remained, submerged, and now structurally weakened.

A fracture, the fissure, a crevice; the vent.

And thirty miles distance from the ten on the escarpment, upon the arid bench in the parched rolling topography of the Forsaken Land, the vent opened. Magma exploded into the crevice, tracing it up then blasting the crust and surface away with twisting force and a windstorm of light...

—Pulsing, pushing, heaving and rushing,

—Frothing, erupting, flaming and roaring,

—Molten spray of waterwings and fire,

...Volcano!

Explosion after explosion pounded slamming into the sky, hurling great slabs of stone and voluminous dark smoke that rocketed in liquefied fire and gagging thunderous clouds of black ash gushing dripping-hot muck. The pressure and discharge explosions were so intense that immense wedges of landscape were hurled spinning and melting, thousands of feet high. Superheated temperatures propelling ejecta were so extreme that massive blocks of granite were dissolved and absorbed in vaporizing twenty-two-hundred-degree fire, and the screaming boil of eruption so opaque it spewed miles into the sky before spreading out then dumping hot black rain and steaming wet ash.

The fireflash of eruption and superheated air swept over the dryland in a desiccating pulse of blistering shockwave and sweltering wind like a boiling, speeding tsunami setting miles of landscape afire. Rocketing skyward the fountainfall flare was so intense and incredible it began blotting the horizon with a liquefied smear of gagging black cloud carried aloft in the wind.

Thunderously roaring, blasting fire and light of belching molten lava, slowly the composite landform began to form, and to rise. Slopping vermilion waves fell splashing around the vent spreading flames with their touch, then poured out rolling over everything in their path washing the Forsaken Land with rivers of fire.

Overhead murky clouds laden with ash and steam unfolded as pouring smog that crawled across the azure sky like an impenetrable dark cloak smearing daylight away. Building to a black mushroom tower the clouds churned and piled with the intensity of viscous heat and asphyxiating particulate flakes beckoning their companion phenomenon of silent lightning.

Splashing atmosphere apart, ragged flashes burned invisible holes with ripping white light as firebolts sliced trails through the volcanic soup. Then vanishing and abandoning electrically charged embers they left burning, whirling June bugs of afterglow that careened as they died like gently floating waifs until their fires went out. Succeeding each megavolt flare the churning, viscid atmosphere instantaneously collapsed reclaiming the void with resonating thunderous collisions in a teeming opaque and twilight sky.

Molten globs of lava hurling from the vent resembled screeching rockets that soared into the shroud of mushroom sky above the volcano then reappeared as lava bombs falling like pulsing meteors trailing windswept flames, twisted smoke trails and bright light.

Solemnly, apprehensive, those gathered on the trembling escarpment watched the commanding spectacle of the volcano's birth. Inspired by its power and majesty they witnessed its growth, from infancy to adolescence, and beyond, amassing maturity. All the while, not one of them spoke.

With the volcano's eruption the tremors gradually diminished. And even though the village lay miles beyond the range of plummeting ejecta and lava bombs, and the river separating their homeland from the Forsaken Land afforded a protective buffer from the scattered fires, the gravity of this occurrence could not be overlooked or diminished. What they assumed was a seismically inactive and geologically stable region was now known to be otherwise. Beneath them was a subterranean fault overriding an unmeasured caldera. The ground where they stood concealed an unpredictable, boiling cauldron, a primitive recipe and cataclysmic disaster in the making.

From the escarpment they watched the natural world's fatidic Fourth of July, lightning's wizard-fingers flashing and ripping awakening resonant thunder while meteoric lava bombs streaked from the plume. Nature's transcendental lightshow in prophetic display.

Standing in a mild rain of clinging feathery-gray volcanic ash of damp sticky snowfall, watching the erupting volcano, Lent insisted, "We can't stay here. It's too dangerous."

Tense, no one said anything until Ames finally spoke. "I'm not leaving."

"Why?" Lent couldn't understand his unwillingness to go.

"The Legends," the man answered soberly. "The Legends are the key, and I will stay here and find them."

Not knowing the complexity of the dilemma, "Then let's get them and get out."

"Can't."

"Why not?"

Eyes fixed on the volcano's amber spray, mind focused upon a vanishing point along the darkening horizon, Ames told him, "I don't know where they are," then more softly, "or even what they are."

"You don't know?"

"Buried," Tondra murmured, "beneath the collapsed mountain range."

"Buried?" He looked at her. Then turning again to the man, "Buried… under mountains of rock? How…" he asked, his persistence becoming annoying, "then how can you ever hope to find them?"

Agonizing Ames turned clenching his fists, his voice hard with exasperation, "I—don't—know!"

Silent, watching him intently, Kalo's subliminal thought—*your pocket.*

Consciously unaware, in a gesture of frustration Ames jammed both hands into the back pockets of his Levis, and his fingertips touched it. *The dream...* at the crater, in the mystery of the moment he had completely forgotten *...it must have been real.*

Very carefully, between two fingertips he withdrew a rolled piece of paper, flattened from sitting on it. For a moment he just looked at it; then his eyes found Kalo and without speaking she stepped forward, both their smiles welling from deeply within. Having no idea what this was about, the eight watched curiously as the man and girl tenderly, intently, unrolled and opened... a miniature scroll.

Aloud, Ames read:
> *"Alpha and Omega reformation... mettled.*
> *Galactic composition replenished... begun.*
> *Time captured, an hourglass... trickled away.*
> *The amalgamate turbidity... unsettled.*
> *Legends sleep within the throat of... the dragon.*
> *Shall rise to the Light, invoked... the last day."*

The Riddle.

He held the answer in his hand.

No one spoke. No one knew what it meant. But the cause was worth the risk.

Almost reverently, frightened but determined, Nitana stepped forward. "We follow you," she told him.

It was then Ames remembered something from a dream. *The juncture is near. Follow your heart and the stars. Very soon, all that is... will be no more.*

A piece of... *the Puzzle.*

CHAPTER FOURTEEN

And when the thousand years are ended, Satan will be loosed from his prison and will come out to deceive the nations which are at the four corners of the earth, that is, Gog and Magog[15], to gather them for battle; their number is like the sand of the sea.
(Rev. 20:7-8 RSV)

Narrow yellow-gray eyes…

…Scanned a ravaged world below, with unabridged contempt for the multitude of shimmering Mystics assembled there upon the scarred landscape that once had been a beautiful planet of blue and green. The timeline of Earth had run its course and drawn to a close with the conflict of Armageddon. Now the battleland stood testament to an undeniable universal axiom; the single constant, now, as always, was *change*.

To him his thwarted effort was not so much failure as a missed opportunity; *misjudged, miscalculated, it almost worked.* Evaluating, conniving, and surmising; *the deception would have succeeded were it not for Ames.*

Free again—

In the ecliptic darkness of a blood-red sky Satan glided upon invisible layers of atmosphere, scheming. A wivern, his eyes were yellow-gray, loathsome and seething with anger as sharp and penetrating as his fangs. It was time.

After so long inside, to be loose again was exhilarating, and that freedom replenished his strength. He roared. How special, extraordinary, to be complete, supreme, remarkable, absolutely evil. Himself again.

"Come my minions!"

The scream, drawn and empty, beckoned those who would follow and was acknowledged by chattering ghouls, the shapeless souls of a forgotten, banished army. Heeding the call, the amorphous beings emerged from concealment within cracks and crevices among jutting crags of wasteland on the blue planet. For so long the Dark Forces had awaited their master's command to arise, and now having been summoned they would willingly follow.

Their time had arrived; time to rise up from hiding and the lethargy of slumber. It was time for change, and like wraiths, opaque wisps of motion and shadow they emerged from everywhere, their tally a swarm of untold numbers, more than the grains of sand; immeasurable, innumerable, and evil. One thousand years had passed, a long time to wait. Finally, the millennium was over.

Satan had summoned… and they answered his call.

The Dark Ones—

A black storm, cloudy and bleak, they oozed and flowed into a blood-red sky gathering en masse with sin-filled red-glowing eyes and saturating wickedness inside them. Cast off in years long since forgotten as the dregs of humanity, the Dark Forces now emerged to strew emptiness and despair, inflict pain, wreak sorrow and unleash relentless vile plagues upon a far distant land. Boiling and screeching with goblin howls, horrid moans, and unworldly shrieks of hideous laughter, the Dark Ones flocked in whirlwinds of nefarious wanton villainy.

Visions of shadow, flowing liquid and dark as long trailing wisps of amorphous beings, they swept through the sky as it blended to black. Spanning the horizons east to west and north to south were whirling winds of commotion and evil as the dark army amassed and marshaled to an incredible cloud. The firmament churned blasphemously and ecliptic, blotted and filled with an ungodly chatter of despise, squeals of laughter, and howls of anticipation. The time for revenge had finally arrived and their raucous numbers shifted with boils of confusion like banshee flocks on the wing and monstrous, spiteful, obsidian thunderhead clouds.

The Dark Forces swarmed—

Trailing as winds of neglect the shadow of destruction and sorrow followed him tumbling and rolling in acrobatics of flight, until they converged and congealed as glutinous murk. A blended cloud of confusion blackening the surreal violet skies over the wasteland of Armageddon, they cried out for vengeance with hostile shrieks of anger, vulgarity, lechery and wickedness. Howling delight, fury and despise, they maligned and defamed all righteousness with screams for revenge wound inextricably within the fabric of cloud. The shadow of malady, ruin and sorrow, pathetic and black they followed until…

…In the blink of an eye, Satan and the Dark Forces were gone.

Below, on the battleland—

The legions of white warriors had somberly watched the pompous charade in the blood-red ecliptic darkness of a twilight-world's sky. The Mystics had not intervened to quell the unholy uprising. It was written, forbidden.

Possibly most of mankind considered Armageddon to be the conclusion of all that would be; but in truth, it was only a page of a chapter in the binding of eternity. The incredible army of Mystics on their powerful Percheron mounts remained silent, and ready. As far as the eye could see, spanning the devastation that was Armageddon, the warriors had watched quietly. They were obedient, patient and resolute, armed with conviction... and brilliant white Light.

At length, *"Revenge,"* the white rider contemplated as he looked to his leader again.

And the Centurion turned and disclosed, *"Only a battle was won. Now the war has begun."*

* * *

Out there…

…In the endless regions of space the Dark Forces pursued his heinous persona like a flowing black cloak with a glimmering sandstorm of red-glowing eyes. Altered images of darkness, forlorned in villainy, they propelled onward through the expanse and vacuum of space. At his heels the dark cloud followed as shadowing wraiths and swirling visions of motion trailing his presence in twisted strands of obscurity within the shroud of his eminence.

Absorbed within the cosmic emptiness Satan and his army soared, seemingly nothing more than an indefinable floating smear on dark canvas. Their black-hearted presence wound spiraling through the void; and camouflaged within that darkness, wicked yellow-gray eyes scanned, perhaps for something at the fringe of imagination, on the very edge.

Still screeching a cacophonous heckle and hideous discordant cackle they flashed through the vacancy of space without uttering a sound. The unparalleled emptiness within them, and surrounding them, engulfed their multitudes and absorbed all vestige of noise as their nefarious presence swept across the universe in an opaque whirlwind-tempest of transcendental imagery. With no atmosphere to convey sound there was none, only cold and dark emptiness, vast and bleak silence… and the stellar winds of rushing red eyes.

* * *

Far ahead…

…On the brink of time and periphery of space lay an unknown, unexplored region within the territory of no return. Out there somewhere, was the boundary, a horizon waiting silently and magnetic… and drawing them in.

At the edge of eternity and dawn of tomorrow it loomed winding the space-time continuum to an immense vortex beyond the limits of comprehension. Too intense and incredible to imagine, it revolves where time and space collide destroying one another within its gravitational field. It was out there, waiting for them, expecting them. Invisible and gigantic, remarkable and awesome, the gaping jaws of oblivion.

Caught up within the gravitational cosmic winds, Satan and his whirling phantasmagoria propelled ever onward toward the anomaly's horizon. Manifest in a malevolent cloud of spiraling strands, the murky, twisting apparition of Satan and whizzing sands of red-glowing eyes had embarked on a journey from the netherworld to oblivion, and beyond, into the lair of the Lion, the passageway to forever... where the mythical Lion roars.

The Black Hole remains.

Then suddenly, the horizon—

Pouring and rushing blistering jetstreams of light, a climactic cascade of confusion and chaos without sound. From everywhere they came, broken planets whirling as fragments and duststorm flashing past, winds of particulate shards exploding, recompressing and detonating again and again. Stars rupturing in twisted veins of luminous gas, expanding upon themselves then colliding and splashing with unbelievable, indescribable flames; continuously reigniting, perpetually exploding, pure cataclysmic fusion and light. All of it searing into a helix of oblivion at the farthest reaches, on the most remote fringe... where time and space collide.

Everywhere was liquid gaseous confusion, fusion in its purest form; everything ravaged and dismantled as scattered calamity, swallowed from space and into the throat of the black hole. It swirled sizzling and plummeting at the speed of light, disappearing to somewhere on the other side, a place that might be only a dream... a figment of the imagination.

Within that matrix turbulence and holocaust pitch Satan and his Dark Forces traveled through time and space concurrently, jettisoned forward to where time warps and space folds. Deeper and deeper into the gravitational draw they went amid the winding apocalypse of colliding stars and exploding debris burning far and near within the void.

Chaos was omnipresent —the winds of oblivion— a conflagration of explosive, gaseous disorder and particulate confusion cascading in perpetual waterfall flashes. Everything —all of it— pouring and streaking in the same direction, to a vanishing point somewhere ahead. It was a continuous stream of liquid light created by countless melted stars and galaxies poured into a funnel so black it absorbed everything. Nothing would escape... not even light.

Such tremendous cataclysm: the confusion, destruction, and reformation. Stars exploding then imploding again and again... unending cycles.

Fifteen billion years!

—And the Rush—

An incomprehensible surging torrent of blinding cataclysm erupting from the other side —exploding trillions of planets, stars and galaxies all at the same instant— too much to envision, unimaginable, incredible beyond description...

The 'Big Bang'!

—And the black hole was gone,

...An Entire Universe Was Born!

Satan and the Dark Forces had arrived.

* * *

The next day...

...The volcanic mountain, breathing ebony and orange, loomed above the landscape like an overseer of basalt and obsidian glass; a bubbling cauldron still given to intermittently grumble every now and then, but no longer spraying the powerful waterfall of ejecta. Through an overcast of murky volcanic plume and confused particulate sky, heat lightning ribboned glimmering flashes that danced in the clouds as Kalo and Ames stood abreast on the escarpment overlooking the Forsaken Land. Where there had been arid bench of open dryland before, now in the distance a towering composite mountain of volcanic basalt stood. The intense eruptions subsided during the night, and now less active and glossed with an ebony sheen, the massive landform issued steam and sulfuric fumes, a belching smokestack from an industrial revolution of a different kind.

Still weeping flows, the newborn mountain fed sluggish oxbow rivers of molten blebby lava that trailed from the cone basin, numerous sidevents and fissures, as warm dismal drizzle fell in gray-brown rain saturating a landscape of pale ash. Nature's rhythm and consistency, soaking them in a tepid wash the color of dun. Barefoot, standing side by side ankle deep in soggy volcanic ash they were unable to suppress the urge of curling their toes and sloshing a bit. Neither spoke.

Preoccupied. His mind was elsewhere, not thinking of the landform, plume, overcast, lightning, rain—or even the ash. Reflecting. Turning it over again, a piece of parchment and an allegory, a parable riddle.

Two on a cliff.... the answer on a scroll, in his hand.

"I don't know what it means," he whispered, discouraged.

"Nor do I," Kalo's admissive words. Then looking from the volcano to Ames, she offered her hand. "Come. Perhaps if we walk and think about it."

Unable to suppress the grin he took her hand and shrugged, "Yeah, okay." Leisurely they began following the escarpment trail going in the direction of the rimrock and Legend Mountains, and he asked, "Walking helps you think, does it?" Looking up obliquely, her eyes bright, expression pert but sincere, she nodded a, *yes*. A chuckle and, "What the hell kid, whatever helps." Then teasing, he let go of her hand and playfully tousled her hair.

Not really irritated, but making him aware, she swatted his hand away admonishing, "You should not call me kid."

As much surprised as amused, "Why not?"

"Because I am a Renoloi warrior," her eyes narrowing, feigning defiance.

"That's true," he agreed, "but I'm still a lot bigger than you; so just mind your P's and Q's or I'll tip you upside down."

She thought about that, and after a few more steps admitted, "I have no idea what that means." He mussed her hair a second time and she slapped his hand again. Friends.

Leaving the trail—

Shortly they arrived at the rimrock and crater, and emerging into the open on the granite ridge, anticipating, they prepared themselves emotionally; images still vivid, intricate, and clear in their minds.

But as they stepped into the open and looked around, the aftermath of carnage they expected was not there.

There were no empty hulls of dead spiders, no charred, smoldering trees, no exposed corridor leading into the jungle where gnarled giants had been snatched from the ground by the roots opening a pathway. The rimrock appeared untouched, unscathed, as though nothing had happened there, as if it were healed and renewed overnight.

Before them were undulating jungle and a bare granite floor just as it had been the day before, only now covered with several inches of gray, sodden ash. Amazed and bewildered they looked at one another, then again over the rimrock. This made no sense.

Softly, Kalo said, "This cannot be."

"Did we imagine it?" Ames wondered, putting their thoughts in words.

"It was real," she insisted refusing to believe otherwise, as cautiously they stepped forward moving onto the rimrock.

Still looking around and taking her hand, "Well, maybe we'd better start walking," half-heartedly trying to lighten the mood. She glanced up, no reply.

Moving tentatively, he stepped in something; so they stopped and knelt, he gently pushing the ash aside. Before them, shattered deeply into the granite was an impression, a hoofprint —massive, unshod— traced with glittery, sparkling dust.

He carefully, almost reverently ran his fingers along the rim of the track transferring shimmering dust to his fingertips. They could see it; he could feel it. Still silent, still kneeling, both looked at the hoofprint again; and as they watched, before their eyes the hoofprint began sealing itself closed, winnowing and gathering, refilling... until the impression was gone, all traces of it fading away. Slowly Ames turned his hand so they both could see—dust on his fingertips. Sparkling, glittering like starlight... the dust remained.

Kalo's voice quivered, "It was real, all real," her eyes welling with tears, "but I do not understand," she murmured as she scooted closer burying her face in his chest. Himself unable to understand what it meant, Ames shivered a bit and drew a deep breath, let it out with a sigh; and he held her.

After a few moments Kalo peered meekly from his chest, embarrassed. He was not looking at her, rather scanning the crater and beyond, to the collapsed mountains of the Legends.

"I am sorry," she apologized unassumingly, "I should not have cried."

At length Ames looked down warmly, kissed her tenderly on the forehead and told her, "Hush... even angels cry." He waited as she wiped her cheeks with the palms of her hands and sniffled once or twice. Then he asked, "Ready to go?"

Girlish, she nodded eagerly inquiring, "Where to?"

Ames, looking again toward the collapsed mountain range, "Out there." Drawing a deep breath, "The answer is out there." Rising to their feet, "Time to find it."

Standing alongside him, "We are true friends," Kalo told him.

He agreed, "Till death do us part," tousling her hair again as they began walking; and for a third time she swatted his hand.

Now Kalo smiled. "No, much longer than that," she disclosed. But he didn't understand what she really meant.

The Puzzle.

* * *

From the rimrock...

...Together they went into the collapsed mountain range, walking for hours, not really knowing what they were searching for, a cave or crevasse perhaps; then again, maybe something else entirely, anything out of the ordinary, something unusual, out of place.

The granite formations created an irregular topography of jutting outcroppings, massive slabs, boulder batholiths and enormous slides of granular decomposed granite. The pair climbed over prominences and crossed rockslides pushing gravelly waves of loose debris downslope with their footsteps. They squeezed between building-sized stones and through myriad cracks and crevasses created long ago in what was evidently an earthquake of severe magnitude, or some other unknown cataclysmic upheaval.

Eventually they found themselves following a gorge rimmed on both sides with sheer cliffs and piles of broken rocks deposited along the base of the vertical walls. The winding canyon floor was a dry riverbed of sand, smooth gravel and rounded eroded stones. They proceeded quietly stepping from one of the larger stones to the next, constantly scanning the perpendicular rock walls. Occasionally one or the other would spy a shallow indentation or pocket in the cliffs pointing it out to the other; but each time they turned out to be nothing more than superficial erosion impressions, none leading to an underground passageway.

Their search continued until late afternoon and waning daylight. The volcanic cloud, reaching out for many miles across the sky, now drifted heavily as a dreary blanket overhead causing an impending premature nightfall. At length they stopped and sat down to rest among a scatter of rocks that had broken loose and fallen near the cliff wall, then later snagged several large driftwood logs creating a logjam of sorts. As the two settled side by side Ames elevated his tired feet upon a rock in front of him, and sighed.

"Are your feet sore?"

Casting a glance with his fleeting smile, "No, not really," and wiggling his toes, "just helping the old circulation." He crossed his legs flexing and wriggling his toes again as Kalo mimicked his posture propping her feet up next to his.

"Circulation?" she queried.

"Blood flow, good circulation helps prevent varicose veins as we get older."

She frowned. "I do not know varicose veins."

Chuckling, he commented, "Doesn't matter. Not likely you'll ever have to worry about it. It's an affliction of the lethargic couch potato, and the Renoloi lifestyle is anything but sedentary." Then considering, "That is... unless the Pilgrims found a flat-screen TV in the Accumulation and stashed it somewhere." Offering her a mock serious expression, "That could be our undoing."

She puzzled a minute then professed, "You are as bad as Reed sometimes."

Ames smiled with his, "Thank you," and as the smile faded, the girl knew.

"I am sorry. I did not mean to remind you…"

"—It's okay," waving it off. Then more subdued, "It's okay." Looking away, along the length of canyon, he drew a deep breath and was suddenly quiet. Memories. A moment passed and he blinked pushing tears back inside, to the room where he kept them. Aware she had said the wrong thing Kalo was at a loss for words, even though she knew no words could lessen his pain. So she waited silently, in case he wanted to talk, needed a friend. She would be there to listen. She was learning.

Suddenly from behind them, in the distance, imposing footfalls on the dry riverbed, the crushing sound of gravel crunching against larger rocks. Hollow clatter ricocheted back and forth between the canyon walls; echoes skipping toward them —then overhead— then continuing beyond until the sounds faded somewhere farther off. Another clatter; bouncing along the vertical walls —here and there and back again— skimming from layered strata, reverberating above and around them.

Ponderous footsteps; something very large was coming. Smaller rocks pinged and splattered as elephantine feet trudged along, larger stones squashed solidly into the riverbed compacted by eighty-five short tons of bulk. Closer, just around the last bend. Coming.

Two chipmunks on a ledge, Kalo and Ames vanished from where they lounged only seconds before. Both swiftly out of sight, avoiding detection they disappeared within the camouflage of the logjam near the canyon wall. Out of harm's way, both peered cautiously, watching, waiting.

A moment later, sixty feet above, half the distance to the canyon's summit, the animal's head appeared. Next, the long slender neck— and one more step—the massive body thundered into view. A Brachiosaur rounded the bend trodding on leather-tough, treetrunk legs supporting its enormous weight and trailing an immense swaying, supple tail. Lackadaisically, surveying the world as it proceeded, it ambled with a deliberate gait following the riverbed with measured, ground eating strides.

Ducking her head under the taut bowstring Kalo slipped the bow from her back and began reaching to the quiver. A touch of his left hand on her shoulder, and she darting him a glance as he shook his head, *no*. Still, she silently watched the magnificent dinosaur pass, not noticing them. Ames' right hand eased from the scimitar pommel.

The towering reptile's movements were poetic with symmetry and fluid with grace. Its head and neck almost flowed with a swan's ease of motion as its body swayed back and forth with the undulating rhythm of an ancient wooden-hulled ship, in cadence with each thundering footfall. Docile by nature and aggressive only when provoked, it plodded along the dry riverbed, a gentle giant of epic proportion.

As it sauntered on by, "Herbivore," Ames whispered, "not a meat eater." Bow in hand, Kalo began to rise from hiding; but he stopped her with a hand. "Where you going?"

"We will follow it."

"What for?"

"It has crossed from the Forsaken Land." Then stepping away, pursuing the Brachiosaur, which was already rounding the next canyon bend, she summoned without looking back, "Come."

He must have had curiosity for breakfast. He followed.

Maintaining a safe interval between themselves and the Brachiosaurus the two trailed the animal for a mile or more, weaving through rock and riprap along the canyon wall and staying only close enough to keep it in sight. A routine precaution, and by now a habit, Ames glanced over a shoulder checking their backtrail —then a flash of green and his heart skipped a beat. Less than one hundred yards behind them, a Tyrannosaur was swiftly approaching, tracking, appeared to be stalking them, intent on their movement.

A terror-thick swallow stuck in his throat and sudden, instantaneous anxiety squeezed nervous sweat in his armpits, more trickling down his back. Immediately he snatched Kalo's wrist yanking her to the canyon wall —down— among some sizable scattered boulders. Still partially exposed but nowhere better to hide, both lay flat. To run would be foolish, sure to be quickly overtaken; to fight, plain stupid, very likely fatal. Two against T-Rex, would be an absurd endeavor.

The only choice, "Meat eater..." he breathed, "remain perfectly still."

They lay facedown and flat on the ground between two boulders, nerves frayed as an old nylon rope and scarcely even breathing, both wringing salty-wet with perspiration. Its yellow-green eyes searching for movement, with an avian strut the Tyrannosaur slowed as it neared their hiding place. Stepping almost on top of them its toes dug gristling track impressions in the river gravel and moist dirt.

Looming over Kalo it craned its ungainly head, sideways slightly for a better look. Blinking slowly, pupils readjusting, it leaned forward rising up on its toes like a drooling toothy-jawed lizard-chicken searching for worms and scouting for bugs. From two inches above her head, throaty guttural deep gurgles and breathing in her hair; a swish of its massive neck, turning its cumbersome head it snorted hot breath and mucus on them trying to decipher what each was. Two unfamiliar scents masked by the odor of algae and mud. Both of them lay flat and perfectly still among the rocks, iron acumen, possessed of presence of mind—*don't move a muscle.*

With one foot the awesome reptile stepped almost lightly upon a smaller boulder, laid its disproportionately large head alongside another and pushed it aside with its powerful, thickset neck. The ponderous rock moved five or six feet with a sliding, crushing-gravel sound as dirt and debris mounded in front of it and poured over Ames' legs partially burying them, scooting him across the damp ground.

Quivering with involuntary trembles but knowing not to run, neither man nor girl moved. Both remained completely still, the dinosaur overshadowing them, snorting, exhaling rank sticky puffs of hot breath down their backs. Unsure what the two curious prostrate objects were and unable to flush them to flight, the Tyrannosaur inspected them a moment longer; then assuming they must be something other than prey, rose, standing erect again as it scanned the surrounding rocks. No movement.

It lost interest, and when the predator stepped over the man to leave the clawed outer toe of its right foot landed four inches from Kalo's ashen, petrified face. As it moved the keratin-sheathed toe dug a furrow six inches deep and six inches wide into the gravel and soft dirt, its weight compressing and squeezing mud and rocks out of the impression, against her face, literally moving her head aside. Dirt pushed up in her face filling her nostrils with the pungent earthy odors of moist ground, fresh-water algae and fish. She gasped—tried not to breathe—shuddering in sync with the vibrating tremors of quaking ground beneath her as the dinosaur took another step —and the foot was gone. The Tyrannosaur moseyed on.

With knots of fear and tension winding themselves out and adrenaline trembles waxing their arteries, for a very long minute neither person moved; then the sudden-rush of relief gradually ebbing away. Slowly, very carefully and still shaking, Ames rose to his knees and peered over the boulder. The Tyrannosaur had already covered fifty yards and was moving away, the curiosities no longer of interest. It did not look back.

Sour emotion and tension still stuck in his throat, he finally managed to sputter, *"Shi-iit."* Still trembling, tinged pale and shaken, Kalo pushed herself up onto her knees and innocently lifted her skirt for a peek —just to be sure. Ames noticed and asked, "What are you doing?"

Immodest simplicity: "Looking to see if I wet myself."

"—Kalo." Her candor embarrassed him; but now that she had brought it up, he was unable to constrain himself —just had to do it— a furtive glimpse to the crotch of his jeans—*whew, I'm okay; no wet spot.* Still holding her skirt with both hands Kalo saw him, and as he looked up their eyes met, snickering then giggling, and finally laughing; nervous, silly, flushing relief. It was all right, because they were friends.

After brushing the dirt off and getting their wits about them Kalo told him, "We must go now."

"Where to?"

Matter-of-fact, surprised he need ask, "After the dinosaurs," and she started out again.

A frown. "We almost get eaten and now we're going back for more," he groused shaking his head. "Go figure."

Turning, Kalo stopped and faced him. "You really are as bad as Reed sometimes." But this time she grinned. "If we hurry we can still catch them," and wasting no more time she was on her way, him at her side.

* * *

Shortly the canyon ended…

…Opening to a sprawling mountain plateau. The dry riverbed wound its way down gently sloping terrain with both canyon walls parting, receding, and eventually blending within the rolling topography of what was once a vast, high mountain plain. Small rock formations jutted here and there from the open land of crested wheat grass and irregular, winding windrows creating scattered runs of rye. Sparsely strewn across the land were acacia trees reminiscent of another world; savanna, the South African Serengeti plains.

Kalo and Ames stood together surveying the region before them. Both were spellbound, not with the expansive plateau, rather with the dinosaurs traversing its face. There were hundreds of them, thousands, all journeying in the same direction, toward the horizon and an unknown destination, a migration of mysterious, incredible proportion.

Apatosaurus, Diplodocus, Pterosaurs, Stegosaurus, Dimetrodon, Styracosaurus, Iguanodons, Tyrannosaurs, Coelophysis, Deinonychus, Velociraptors, Ornithomimus, Troodons and Triceratops; too many to count, too varied to identify them all. From the immense mega-dinosaurs of the eighty-ton Brachiosaurus to the smallest miniatures, the chicken-sized two-foot tall Compsognathus, entire herds intermingled lumbering along, all disregarding the others. Herbivores and carnivores crowded together following shared trails, raising thick clouds of dust. The magnificence of natural wonder, hundreds of them, thousands.

"My God, what's going on?" Ames wondered as he beheld the spectacle. "What are they doing?"

"Final Migration."

"What?" But she didn't respond. Her eyes were misty, glazed, her visage, *somewhere else*, almost entranced. "Kalo…" Her expression still vacant, he touched her with just one finger, and she blinked—*here and now*. Intrigued, he noticed but didn't mention it.

"What does final migration mean?" she asked intently.

Surprised by her question involuntarily his mind digressed, to Earth, the age of dinosaurs… a poignant end of their kind. Considering her question he asked, "How do you know that?"

Looking at him, voice calm and sincere, her eyes placid, "I do not know how I know; I just know."

Pressing her, wanting and needing a better explanation, "But how, Kalo?"

"I heard the words, spoken very softly, from far away." Inside, she felt warmth, and a smile; then she explained, "Because I believe."

CHAPTER FIFTEEN

Meanwhile…

…Two of them lost, trying to get home.

"Lord, this is a beautiful place," Reed observed conversationally as they stopped briefly, helping Tian sit down on a small boulder, its pockmarked surface half-covered with a mantle of tightly woven liverwort, a cushion on which she could rest. Having spoken very little for the past few hours, she had never complained; but he knew she was in pain, the padded stone the most he could offer. Every so often she had even managed a feeble smile; but her tired eyes revealed she was losing ground, the pain becoming unbearable. Reed knew she wouldn't be able to continue much longer, and still, they were just as lost as when they first arrived here.

Here, he contemplated, *where the hell is here?* Tian sat bent over with both arms wrapped around her abdomen, squeezing, trying to lessen the pain as Reed gently rubbed her back working her kidneys and lumbar region; circular motions of soothing pressure to lessen her discomfort. Alternating palm compression and kneading her skin with his fingertips, he manipulated the muscles to get the blood circulating and make them relax, work out the knots. He could feel her trembling. Sitting on the stone, curled fetal, she was crying. It was that bad now, and likely to get worse.

Stupid mushrooms, he thought looking upon her, his eyes tearing a bit; that frustrating feeling of wanting to help, but there was nothing he could do. The burning sensation of saltwater and sorrow made him blink as a teardrop stole onto his cheek and he had to look away before her heart-wrenching misery made him cry. *Think of something —anything,* his eyes fogging, wouldn't focus on their surroundings. *Think of something —anything,* on the trimaran, something Kalo said —*because I must be brave, and I was frightened.* And what Tondra told Jade —*you must be brave; you are a Renoloi.* The image of the child's desperation flashed through his mind's eye; *Jade—fuck!—wrong thing to think of,* unable to stop the ricochet of words in his head. *Renoloi warriors do not cry.* Then somehow his brain and mouth got confused, sniffling, exhaling a sigh, his brain spoke, his mouth moved, and he said, "Fuckit, we all cry."

Her attention drawn by his unexpected words, Tian looked up, her face wet with tears, eyes red, her expression drawn with anguish. She muttered, "I am sorry, Reed." Taking a shallow breath, "I did not mean to cry." Then she looked down and curled tightly again.

Tenderly slipping an arm around her Reed knelt close, kissed her on the cheek and whispered into her hair. "Don't tell me you're sorry. You don't *ever* have to apologize to me—for anything—*not ever.*" Turning to him she looked into his eyes. "We're gonna make it," he assured softly, his eyes narrowing with resolve. "Somehow, we *are* going to get back home." Then forcing a false smile of resiliency he concluded, "Like I always say, she ain't over till the fat lady sings —and so far, the bitch hasn't made a sound." Tian couldn't help it, just a wee, tiny smile. Her reaction encouraging, he grinned. "That's my girl."

"We can go now," she told him.

Carefully slipping an arm around her waist he helped her up again; next, looked at her and nodded asking the question, "You okay?"

"Yes." Easily they set out once more, one step at a time. And as they walked Tian inquired, "Reed…"

Looking around, "Yeah, Babe?"

"Why does the fat lady sing?"

Instant smile. "Oh, well, that's a long story," he confessed, "but I'd be happy to tell it to you."

Distracted from the pain again, she darted him a glance and said, "Long story?" Then, "Somehow that is not at all surprising; but you already know that of course."

"Really," genuinely surprised, and actually a bit puzzled, "how come?"

Almost playfully, "Because, after all..." she told him, "you are, *just* Reed."

He chuckled. "Well hell, it could be worse. You could be stuck here with me —and I could be frickin' boring."

Continuing on they paralleled a small brook walking past several snowball bushes blooming in various colors, and approaching a small grove of blossoming magnolia trees the pair roused flocks of viceroys, swallowtails and monarch butterflies to flight. Rising suddenly, lissome bustling breezes composed of lacewings tailored in yellow and orange and trimmed in black, a fluttering cloud of delicacy in motion, lithe fairies of the insect world. With split-open feather pillow confusion, thousands of individuals whirled together creating a single entity of shifting commotion that rolled through the air as a frittering swarm. Incredibly beautiful, all around them the dainty, tiny creatures mounted upon papery wings flitted above a wonderland of flowers, and color, and life.

Not too far away... all alone, was a small leafless tree, its fragile branches withered and barren, mostly drifting to the left as though bent with the wind. And on one of the misshapen branches, hanging upside-down, was a beautiful, precious tiger swallowtail butterfly, all by itself. It spread its wings a time or two, but did not take to flight.

Reed noticed, but said nothing; he had Tian to worry about, so they moved on.

* * *

Another place...

...Standing together, side by side. Before them, regal, majestic creatures. Final Migration. Kalo and Ames wondering, *what did that mean?*

* * *

Walking together, in step...

...An arm around her lending support, concerned Reed cast a side-glance at Tian. He had never realized before, but now, she seemed so small, almost frail. The Renoloi was not very tall, only twice the length of her flaxen hair, her waist so tiny his hands could easily close around it. And her body was toned, muscular and fit; but still, every bit bespeaking effeminacy. Much more than her stature, such a small woman possessed of such demanding responsibility; to keep her people from harm, to simply survive, surely much more than most others could ever have managed. Tian was a paradox, a paragon molded within the being of a Renoloi leader.

The whirlwind of butterflies behind them now, resettling in the blooming magnolia trees; again Reed surveyed the surreal beauty of the valley basin lying before them. Towering mountains, monolithic granite columns and spires rising majestically and silent to a congealed overcast of pallid cloud; winding emerald meadows and vales ribboned a carpet at their bases where wild flowers flourished with saturating, dazzling colors even brighter than rainbows. And trees: warm beauty, pristine glory, a vibrant canvas enveloping the hillsides. The colors of autumn.

"Strange place," his impromptu remark.

Without looking up, "Yes," Tian agreed, "and very beautiful."

As they continued the man observed, "All the deciduous trees have turned to fall colors," recollecting, "just like Sunday afternoon drives along the river in the Midwest when we were kids. Autumn was beautiful there," remembering a childhood that now seemed an eternity ago; those unrealized precious memories, very special, irreplaceable. Pieces of life.

"The Midwest?"

His reminiscence drew a brief smile and he replied, "Just a place, a long time ago." Tian accepted that as explanation enough and they hobbled along a moment longer while Reed thought to himself. At length he casually observed, "Yet here, at the same time, we have grass as green as emerald and zillions of wildflowers in bloom; springtime. Butterflies gathered in migration swarms; autumn. It's as though the flora and fauna don't know what season it is."

"Seasons?" Tian asked.

"Spring, summer, autumn and winter. In some places the seasons change from very warm, long days, to very brief, cold days; and plants and animals react accordingly, being very active or hibernating, and so forth. It's sorta complicated to explain."

"That does not happen in the jungle."

"Yeah, I know, only in temperate regions," he said as they ambled along the creek that now settled, opening to marshland overgrown with common milkweed weeping white cream, tawny cattails and clustered panicle stands of fluorescent-blue pampas grass. A carpenter frog jumped from a small flat stone, *kerplunk*, the riffling commotion scattering a school of minnows. Both looked down at the frog bobbing in floating posture on the water's surface.

Turning again, curiously Tian inquired, "Reed, during the summer, where you are from, how long were the days?"

Understanding, he smiled; then scanning the countryside once more answered, "Shoot, nowhere near as long as this one. This is just *strange*." Then he admitted, "But, Lord, this is a beautiful place."

Very slowly, they continued; a piece of... *the Puzzle*.

* * *

They sat on high ground, an overlook...

...The sprawling plateau of savanna before them, watching as the colossal creatures moved heavily, single-file processions converging creating seemingly endless columns across the grassland plain, all going toward the horizon. The dinosaur migration continued.

Taciturn, Kalo and Ames observed for some time, neither saying much; an occasional comment now and then, but no more than that. The spectacle of the final journey for so many magnificent creatures was more than awe-inspiring, almost sad in a way. Icons, paragons of an animal kingdom traversing the final mile; their common bond of kinship.

Champions, soon their namesake destined to become a footnote in the pages of history and to be recorded in ledgers by future generations as prehistoric. Certainly not forgotten, but diminished somehow, pictures and words unable to instill within the mind's eye their true splendor and grace. The grandeur of an era, an epic, waning away, a primitive world trodding the path to cataclysmic change.

"They are so beautiful," Kalo whispered at last.

"Indeed. Dinosaur. 'Terrible Lizard'," Ames commented.

A side-glance, "Not so terrible," she remarked. "They are only creatures struggling to survive, very large, some frightening perhaps; but not so different than ourselves."

"I know. I didn't mean it like that. It was only a figure of speech, a metaphor, not to be taken literally. Such powerful animals, and yet, perhaps no less vulnerable than ourselves." Agitation was evident in the texture of his voice and the tenor of his words. Sitting upon the ground he drew his legs to his chest wrapping his arms around them and rested his chin on his knees, eyes vacantly scanning the countryside. He exhaled frustration and sadness, then inhaled conviction.

"What is it?" the girl questioned earnestly. There was no reply and she allowed a moment before prodding further. "We are friends, are we not?" Still no reply. Already knowing, she told him, "The dinosaur migration is not what troubles you."

Turning his head to the side and laying a cheekbone upon his knees, a tear tracked from the corner of his eye, glided briefly, then dripped away, absorbed silently but expeditiously by the faded blue of his worn-out jeans. "I'm sorry," he said, "I didn't mean to be curt with you." Then forcing a smile, "Yes, we are friends."

"I will listen…" with genuine regard, "that is, if you wish to talk."

Not moving his head, he reached out tenderly and stroked her cheek with the back of his hand brushing hair from her face with a finger. His smile this time guileless, honest, and he admitted, "I don't know what it means."

"The riddle?"

"Yes, that… and other things." He began to say more, then hesitated, words travelling through his mind.

"The juncture is near. Follow your heart, and the stars," Kalo whispered. "Very soon, all that is… will be no more."

Intrigued, but this time not really surprised, "How did you know that?" he asked.

"I heard you say it."

"No, I didn't say anything," he told her, "but that is what I was thinking just now." Wondering, raising his head from his knees, "Are you psychic, clairvoyant?"

A frown. "I do not understand those words."

"Can you hear my thoughts, read my mind?"

Her legs crossed, sitting Indian fashion beside him, the girl fidgeted kneading her slender thighs with nervous fingers. Apologetic, anxious, "I do not mean to do it." She paused then explained, "I do not try to hear your words when you do not say them but…"

"—No, no; it's all right." Unoffended, then ascertaining, "You *can* read my thoughts."

Hesitant, she confessed, "At times, when your heart speaks clearly, or you feel very strongly, I do not hear what you do not say, but I can sense it. Inside, I can feel it."

His words measured, thoughts focused, looking intently into her eyes, "Tell me, what am I thinking?"

Demurely, "Please…" she pleaded, almost ashamed, "do not ask me that."

"Kalo…"

Hesitant: "You long for Tian, think of Reed, almost all the time." She looked away, then into her lap and went on, "Your heart has been opened, cut with a blade. They are your greatest concern." She stopped.

"And?"

Returning her eyes to his, she asked, "Will you still be my friend if I answer?"

"Yes, of course, always."

"But they are your thoughts," she insisted, "they should belong only to you."

He smiled. "Then I'll share them with you."

The girl closed her eyes, breathed deeply, slowly, transcended. "Tian and Reed are missing, gone forever."

Next— "The Mystic, magnificent, beauty..." suddenly she frowned, "confusion, disorder, emotions colliding into white light."

Then— "The volcano, fire of orange and yellow..." her brow wrinkled, "black of the night."

And— "The throat of the dragon, sleeping, breathing." Still closed, her eyelids fluttered briefly.

And last— she murmured the hushed words, "The riddle." Opening her eyes again she told him, "You are thinking many things."

Almost disbelieving, "Yes," he admitted, then asked, "do you know the solution to the riddle?"

Shaking her head soberly, "No, only you know that."

"What do you mean?"

"Only you possess the answer to the riddle."

Frustration evident, his voice wired and tense, "That's the problem; I don't know the answer." Aggravated, running his fingers through his hair, "I can't figure it out —and I don't know if I even care anymore."

"You do care," she insisted placing her small hand on his arm, "everything depends on you." Her voice softer now, reassuring, "The answer lies within. You must lead, and we will follow." The young warrior smiled warmly then calmly told him, "Clear your mind of the confusion and torment; only then will the answer come." She blinked twice. "Tian and Reed are alive. I know they are. I can feel it. I believe, and you must believe. Greater than all of us... there are always possibilities."

A Power mystical and magic within her... the ember of destiny. Only a spark, just the briefest glimmer, preordained long ago... one day to become the Flame.

* * *

Just a little tug...

...Recentering the pulse laser on his back by adjusting the leather strap across his chest, Reed scanned the valley basin. *Lost.*

Great mountains and columns and spires ascending into the overcast above, and a pristine valley of emerald beauty flecked with blossoming color rivaling the halo of rainbows before him; and trees, the rich, earthy blend of autumn.

They were alone.

He knelt beside Tian, more than concerned now, their situation verging on critical, almost to desperation. "We have to keep moving." The facade was gone, evaporated with their dire circumstances. Very serious now, perhaps life and death.

Sitting on the ground, propped up with an arm, Tian looked at him weakly and nodded. Her eyes bloodshot with scarlet-veined sclera, she was fatigued beyond the limits of her stamina, exhausted. Her strength was virtually gone now and every movement was an intense struggle defying the pain. Perspiring profusely, face ashen, her hair no longer flowed wistfully, now adhered matted and damp as tangled strands that clung to her forehead and cheeks. Sickness and fevered sweats had depleted the blush from her face and the hazel sparkle was drained from her eyes. The healthy bronze color and tone of her skin was now pallid with acute pain and pale with illness, wrenching shivers and shakes. She was nearing convulsions. Time was running out.

Her leather skirt and top were stained with rings of evaporated body salt that formed irregular white crystalline lines along the wrinkled-dry edges rimming the wet leather. But mostly her clothes were damp with perspiration clinging tightly as a second layer of sleek black. She was so ill she tried not to move. Even taking a breath hurt, gnawed inside; but in spite of the pain, the sickness, the suffering, she offered her hand. "Reed, please help me up. We have to get home."

On her feet again, and Reed at her side, the woman ventured a step. Wavering, she did it again. Then confusion and dizziness clouded her eyes *—the rush—* swimming flashes swished through her head —*faint*— white spots of silent explosions sparking out — *then floating*— fading to black.

It was cold all around her in the hollow, dark place where she lost consciousness and slumped to the ground... ground that seemed so far, far away. It was quiet there, only echoes and sounds... garbled noises. No, not just strange noises, words, *Tian, Tian...* from far away, calling her name. *Can you hear me?* Her friend's voice; so she opened her eyes... and Reed was there, cradling her head.

"I am so tired, Reed," she mumbled. "I do not feel well."

"I know."

Not quite so distorted and fuzzy, his words seemed clearer now. Coming back, *into the light*, she drooped a cold hand upon his forearm. Her head still spinning, swimming in circles, her insides twisted with nauseating knots, she weakly murmured, "Reed... you go on ahead. I will catch up."

"What? Don't *even* think it," he scolded gently.

"But I am slowing you down." He didn't respond, shaking his head in refusal. "Please..."

"—No," he told her; then more softly, "I will *not* leave you behind."

She writhed with pain, and fighting back tears admitted, "I cannot go on." She looked down, away, in defeat.

Placing a hand on her cheek, turning her face to his, love in his words, "Then I will carry you." That said, he scooped her into his arms, lifting her as he rose to his feet.

Draping her right arm around his neck and offering an exhausted, grateful smile, weakly she asked, "Why?"

Seriously, earnestly, "Because you are my friend... and John is my friend." Without saying anything more she tenderly kissed him on the cheek and lay her head against him. And as they continued through the valley basin, Reed carrying her, very softly... Tian cried.

Worlds apart... within its texture and intent, a glimpse of very real, genuine Love,

    ...The *true* meaning of life.

CHAPTER SIXTEEN

Dinosaurs…

…Still filing across the savanna before them, methodical, heavy, labored strides; and the sun going down on Legend Range. Evening's chill moving in.

"Better make a fire. We'll camp here tonight."

Surprised, nervous, "No, we must return to the village."

He looked at the girl sitting beside him, "Why?" then over the grassland before them, "the answer is here, within these mountains, not in the village."

"No, we must not sleep here," she insisted, her eyes searching the lengthening shadows as though their trespass would offend something or someone unseen. "This land is sacred. This is Holy Ground."

Ames nodded solemnly. "I know." He looked away, over the plateau again, considering a moment before he spoke. Quiet, pensive, almost reverently he said, "No one will mind," drawing a deep breath, "please, help me gather some sticks. Just a small campfire," then pointing, he indicated a level space to their right that was backed by a rock face overlooking the valley, "by that ledge."

"You are certain no one will mind?"

"It's all right," he assured warmly, "no one will mind."

Soon after, they were nestled against the craggy granite face, delicate fingertips of campfire skittering within the stones of the fire circle. Sheltered from the wind by the rock wall at their backs and toes warmed by orange heat radiated with the flames, Kalo snuggled within the arm around her. She drifted to sleep.

Looking upon her he couldn't help but wonder; such an unusual young girl possessed with faith enough to challenge a world. When he brushed the hair from her face with a ginger caress she stirred just a bit, curled closer, then was still again, sound asleep.

Dark now, a sky full of stars above him and an enigma before him, he gazed into the night and listened. He imagined he could hear footsteps of the great reptiles crossing the plateau; but of course that was not possible, they were miles away.

As he looked to the night sky scattered with stars visible through the broken clouds of drifting ash, he realized the distance, in light years, to some of those stars was millions of years; but those stars were there. Though nothing more than mere pinpoints of light on an endless canvas of pitch drawn from one horizon to the other, he was sure that those stars were burning suns of fusion.

He knew the dinosaurs were down there trodding upon the savanna. He could not see them, couldn't hear them; but he knew. And he knew the stars were out there, glimmering pinpoints of light from distances so vast he could not really comprehend. He knew those things simply because he believed.

With his thoughts of the great emptiness of space—out there— returned another emptiness, the void of loss nagging within. His brow furrowed with determination; but again the recollection of Tian and Reed stole in, and the thought, *two are missing*. He looked at Kalo curled within his arm, wishing he possessed her faith. To be endowed with such a gift would be invaluable in troubled times like these; strength to persevere, stay the course to its end. Such a young girl with such infallible inner courage, so much more than she seemed to be; what was it she told him? *'Clear your mind of the confusion and torment. Only then, will the answer come.'*

Pieces.

'Clear your mind. Follow your heart and the stars.' In the darkness of a primitive world Ames looked up at the sky: very cold, very distant, only pinpoints of light. It was time to think, time to reflect. His eyelids grew heavy, and fluttering, began to close, ever so slowly,

A Puzzle, a fragment, a *Vision of Dream.*

Hushed words, from a distant place…

…Tian said, *'Something yet Unfinished.'*

He was in the Complex sublevel again with Alex and Kristina; naked corpses piled in gruesome tangled mounds, piquant brine of coagulated blood and the clinging taste of copper sultry in the air. The last corridor —and '666', the mark of the beast— where Smith waited, the essence of pure evil.

In the darkness—eerie, an unnatural glowing, red darkness illuminating the murky haze. And a sudden shimmering flash of movement with a hollow, awful sound; something going down, falling to the ground, the floor… a concrete floor.

Then eyes—saddened and fading away amidst a tangle of hair. Listless with vacancy she was closing her eyes, dying in his arms. Blood on the floor… Kristina was dead, slain by the sword.

Into the darkness again—spectral, banshee eyes, gray and evil, moving closer, and closer. They were watching him, crawling and lurking everywhere, glaring and making sounds. —No, not the eyes; somewhere else, something else.

Noise—metallic collisions ringing of empty despair showering sparks through the gloom, and the stench of death thick in his nostrils. A sinister red glow and fiery blue sparks as they fought near her body —and laughter, hideous and unfulfilled, the sounds of hate and spite… wanton and unworldly laughter.

Whirlwind momentum—whizzing solid and dark, a mass of concrete coming at his head.

The pulse laser—a whine and flash then white sparks of shattering explosion and pain. Sticky and warm, there was blood in his mouth and a flame in his chest.

Standing over him—towering evil and dreadful, formidable and dark, the faceless specter of death drooling satisfaction and jubilation —and the sword, and the fire— the blade slicing his heart.

Wind tunnel confusion.

Deafening wind whisking him away; then more gently, blending to silence, the universe unfolding, drawing him to forever. It was all so beautiful, the incredible purity of colors: blues, greens, golds, violets... and quiet. Never wanting to return, encompassed within the embrace of serenity and peace; but someone was calling him back, calling him home. Tian... more precious than life itself ...his reason for living.

Softly, Tian said, *'Something yet Unfinished.'*
—Brilliant White Light!

Sparkling starbursts around him—dazzling, scintillating, hovering and swirling as the breath of a wind. He could see the Light... the eyes. Their beauty was unequaled, and warm... safe. The Light was beautiful, radiant... everywhere. Beyond cradling hands flashed tumult and noise... chaos! But he was secure, and a voice called his name... Tian, calling his name.

Emanating warmth, shimmering, incredible, the Light smiled. Unconditional Love. Everlasting Truth. Limitless Wisdom. The Face. And the Smile. The Light said, 'Farewell.'

Then...

...*"John,"* the disguised voice said coarsely, *"listen carefully."*

Not awake and thinking Kalo had spoken, he looked down at her, still curled within his arm. Then quickly he glanced at the small campfire that a moment ago was burning with a warm, steady flame. Now it was only embers and ashes. Again he looked at Kalo; but she was gone.

He was alone.

"John," the hoarse voice repeated, *"I am here."* He heard the words clearly that time and searching, rose on one knee. Then a glow from the darkness, and not far away, standing there, was the shimmering vision of the Centurion Mystic holding the Percheron by the reins.

The great horse impatiently pawed the rocky ground startling sparks with its hoof as it elegantly flipped its regal head, nickered, then shook its powerful neck. It was the portrait of majesty with rippling muscles and white glowing mane. The Mystic, standing silently before it, let loose the reins, and with a hand stroked its nose and cheek. The animal quieted and the ghost warrior quartered and turned toward the man advising with garbled words, *"The juncture is near."*

Filled with wonder, Ames momentarily did not reply; then at length, he respectfully inquired, "Where is Kalo?"

Moving closer to him, *"My words are for you alone,"* the warrior informed warmly.

Eyes wide, absorbing every detail of the surreal vision before him, he swallowed and confessed, "I can't figure out the riddle."

From inside the helmet green eyes looked upon the man kneeling on the ground, and the Mystic assured, *"When it is time, you shall know."*

As Ames viewed the legionnaire, his mind was captured with the warrior's shimmering translucence and sparkling beauty. Standing quietly now, placid and obedient the mount waited patiently for the white rider. Studying them, Ames realized background objects were visible through the Centurion and animal, both ghostly translucid apparitions, both shimmering with starlight beyond beauty; scintillating starbursts of quasars, flashing pulsars and glittering minutiae of starfire explosions all around and within them. And the Mystic was speaking to him without words, an invincible warrior and mount. He believed, once he even touched the magnificent Percheron... somewhere in a dream.

Can you tell me what it is I must do? he thought.

"It is forbidden." The Centurion spoke in a garbled, feigned voice. *"Very soon, all that is... will be no more."* A rush of cool night breeze swept over the land. *"Do you remember John, from a time in the past... Four Winds of destruction and twelve children in the school yard?"*

"Yes," his concentration fixed upon the vision, "I remember."

The warrior recited,

"This is why I speak to them in parables, because seeing they do not see, and hearing they do not hear, nor do they understand." *(Matt. 13:13 RSV)*

The Mystic turned slowly, walked with measured steps to the steed gathering the reins and turned to the man again.

"But blessed are your eyes, for they see, and your ears, for they hear. Truly, I say to you, many prophets and righteous men longed

to see what you see, and did not see it, and to hear what you hear, and did not hear it." (Matt. 13:16-17 RSV)

"John, clear your mind of the confusion and torment. Only then, will the answer come." The Centurion affectionately stroked the Percheron's cheek, patted its thickset muscled neck; then grasping its mane at the withers, swung gracefully upon the animal's bare back. Without stirring Ames watched. Mounted again and gazing down upon him the warrior revealed, *"The answer lies within. Bring forth the Secret with the keys to a three-lock box."*

"The keys to a three-lock box," nearly inaudibly, repeating the apparition's words. The Mystic drew upon the reins turning the Percheron. "—Wait," Ames pleaded. Halting, the rider turned back and looked upon him amenably. Then more softly, almost cautiously Ames whispered, "I know you, don't I?"

The disguised voice: *"Yes."*

Uncertain if he even dare ask, but with no other way —he simply had to. "Please…" he murmured so quietly only a vision could hear, "tell me. Who are you?"

"When the moon is full." Unseen by the man, inside the helmet concealing the identity, was a smile that was warm, and the love of green eyes. Then reining the Percheron, *"Remember, John… follow your heart, and the stars,"* and in an astonishing splash of starlight the warrior was gone.

Gazing at the darkened space where an instant before the vision had been, misty-eyed he muttered, "The breath of tomorrow, the wind of consciousness… who you are, and will be …the juncture of mortality and immortality."

"Who are you talking to?" Kalo asked from behind him.

Turning, he found her curled upon the ground where she had been before. "No one," he said quietly, "only to myself."

Brushing hair from her face, groggy she asked, "Would you please put a few more sticks on the fire?" then curling kitten-like, "my feet are getting cold."

Without speaking Ames scooted nearer rubbing her shoulders and back with a hand as he scooped a few twigs from their cache and carefully laid them on the bed of radiant embers. Waiting a moment until the flames sprouted again, he continued to knead the girl's back to warm her; and when the small fire rekindled, Kalo, still snuggled beside him, rubbed her legs together relishing its radiated heat. She peeked up smiling a, *thank you,* then curled more tightly.

He nodded a, *welcome.* "Now go back to sleep."

"And you?" a girlish inquiry, her eyes already closed.

Stroking her hair tenderly, looking to the sky, "In a little while," he answered. Quietly he sat there studying the stars peering down through holes in the broken cloud of volcanic ash. "First, I just need some time to think."

Kalo, drifting again to sleep... smiled.

* * *

From the darkness out there...

...Vile black winds of the netherworld emerged, descending. Spectral eyes of jaundiced yellow-gray observed the small planet below. Virgin territory... a primitive world.

His gaze fixed intently upon the dim amber glow masked within an overhanging cloud of poisonous sulfuric gas and a mountain of ash that trailed away with the wind. The grin curled configuring a menacing sneer. Contemplating. Scheming.

Through drifting holes in the congealed overcast, barren land was visible below peering up through clouds that shed gray-brown snowflakes drenched with sulphurous steam. Still stirring silent lightning, the composite landform stood solid and igneous encircling the cone basin as it ladled boiled-orange melt fed by magma fields far below. Now wafting lethal gasses and steam into a night sky, it was a volcano just resting.

Moving opaque and raven, the flow of malevolence swept down from the past as he glided easily upon the wind composing an evil symphony inside his head. Absorbing minute samplings of the environment below, salivating he relished it, the sweet taste of revenge.

Blacker than pitch in the core of a hole the Dark Ones followed their steward, their countless aggregate comprised of the lost godless souls of mankind's dregs and riffraff. They were the cast-offs, forever unwashed and eternally unclean, the adherents of Hell; and through a portentous sky they blotted out starlight with their innumerable multitudes like a black storm of shapeless amorphous shadows rolling across the emptiness of night.

They came like night waves on an ocean from the abyss and squalor of a time long ago; a billowing wind of sordid whirling commotion glowing hollow and dead in a sandstorm of luminous red eyes. Drawn from the bowels of the netherworld by their master's beckon, wherever he would lead, Satan's army would follow, an incredible conglomeration of mindless phantasmagoria intent on dispersing wretchedness, affliction and waste upon this land.

An itinerant whirlwind of opaque despair dropping down through the ash clouds, he and his Dark Forces came in. The lightless wave of motion circled twice around the volcanic mountain with its obsidian rifts and crevasses offering security of refuge, then hovered and descended alighting as a sinuous black fog. Amid fissures created by the molten rock and froth and miasma of simmering bubbles, the Dark Ones settled like a locust swarm upon a raven landscape. Crawling en masse for a moment they formed great squirming mounds of black maggots; and slithering, eventually quieted colonizing the composite landform until it was entirely engulfed then smothered beneath their glowing red eyes.

Finally, seeking hiding, the ebony army oozed slipping into cracks and crevasses among over-boil cliffs and wave-like slides; and the scuttle of brittle and vile voices subsided as they were absorbed within the darkness and shadows. Shimmering fields of scarlet sand specks, their glowing eyes blinking out, all movement upon the volcanic mountain diminished, then stilled.

Powerful whooshing-pulses in the night air, coming down from the sky, he descended. Yellow-gray eyes surveying and wrinkled lips drooling saliva, he sought out a deep chasm, the very darkest abyss. First there was the sound of pumping and hovering preceding the muffled flutter of wings spreading wide as he floated gracefully into the blackness below. Next, for a moment there was no sound, the volcano ominously boiling amber and lava and emitting a spiraling windtrail of miasma steam.

Complete quiet. Silence.

Then from somewhere below, a thought-stopping howl and the echo of a sickening moan that trailed; out of the bowels of the chasm came a blood-curdling groan, and a roar—long, drawn, soul-chilling and anguished. From the very core of darkness the crevasse walls reverberated echoing a wail of hollow emptiness and absolute hatred that railed into the night sky… across the Forsaken Land.

Miles away, in the village, startled Renoloi and Pilgrims exchanged troubled looks wondering what wild animal could bellow such an outcry that would cut so supernaturally and bone-chillingly disrupt the quiet of night. No creature or beast known to any of them had ever before wailed such an unworldly growl, so wanting, so antagonistic, so hungry.

While across the river, in the very darkest abyss, at the base of the volcano's composite landform, within the depths of the chasm…

Shape-shifting…

…Iridescent magenta, to bruised-looking and blotchy, to human skin and a perfectly tailored military uniform.

Transforming…

…Grotesque and distorted, to pockmarked face with a fat porous nose and deep-sunken evil gray eyes.

Changing…

…Ragged fangs, to stained chipped boxer's teeth clenching a stub of cigar, and stubble-gray hair.

And then…

…With the solid crushing footfalls of spit-polished boots upon stone, grinding three hundred pounds of bulk and at least as much vengeance and hate, from the chasm's corridor of Darkness and Shadow, Smith stepped forward…

…And into their lives.

CHAPTER SEVENTEEN

The next morning…

…Gathered at the meeting circle they ate with little conversation; the haunting recollection still lingering, but no one wanting to broach the subject straight-forward. They all knew it would eventually come up —and finally, it did.

"This is foolish," Lent admitted flatly, "we all heard it and no one wants to talk about it." Biting off another mouthful of Chiqua he frowned, trying to chew his aggravation away.

"True," Tere admitted, "but it was not like any animal I have heard before." Her glance passing from one to the next, she asked, "Have any of you ever heard such a scream?" Kale, Deet and Ronto uneasily shook admissions of, *no*.

Ronto asked the Pilgrims, "The Night Hunters are here now; could they scream so horribly?"

Taking another bite Lent responded, "They make queer chattering sounds, but I've never heard 'em roar like that."

Tere nodded then told him, "Do not speak with your mouth full. It is impolite."

Unprepared for that, and somewhat embarrassed, but wishing to avoid an argument, "I apologize," he said. When he did, the 'p' in apologize pursed his lips enough so he spit a bit of meat onto his knee. Quickly dipping his head and covering his mouth with one hand, he retrieved the speck of meat with the other, popped it back into his mouth and continued chewing.

Almost maternally she said, "*That*, is precisely why you should not talk with food in you mouth." She frowned; the Renoloi would not tolerate such display of bad manners. Ronto grinned. Neither Kale nor Deet said anything; however, both were definitely listening.

Now, his ego offended, Lent finally managed a swallow; then in an overt, almost defiant gesture, scrutinized his knee locating another bit of meat, perhaps though, only imaginary. Meticulously he plucked it from his thigh with thumb and forefinger, popped it into his mouth, and making deliberate eye contact with Tere said, *"Excuuuse me,"* one of those macho, 'how dare you' things. Although his words bespoke rebellion, his eyes betrayed, *boy, these Renoloi sure are bossy.*

Candlesnuffer extinguishing a flame, Ronto interrupted derailing any further argument. "Has anyone seen Kalo today, or Mr. Ames?" Distracted, both Tere and Lent indicated they had not; however, Kale, still chewing, raised his hand with an extended index finger.

Pretentiously he swallowed hard so they all could see, then said, "They went into the Legend Mountains yesterday and have not returned yet." Tere grinned—*Pilgrims are manageable.*

Concerned, Ronto asked Kale, "They stayed overnight in the mountain range?"

"Yeah; so?"

Now Tere grew serious. "But that is forbidden."

"Legend Range is Holy Ground," Ronto explained. "No one may spend the night there."

Lent: "Well, shit happens."

Instantly darted glances askance by both Renoloi, Tere threw a quick retort. "—And where did you learn that?"

Stopped mid-bite, Lent's mouth retreated from the Chiqua, but of course, only because it was easier to speak when it wasn't full of food, manners be hanged. He told Tere, "I was talking to Mr. Ames and…"

"—Talking to Mr. Ames," both Renoloi chimed in unison; then trading disapproving looks and concluding at the same time, "that figures."

"What's that supposed to mean?" Deet asked, having finished eating and fondling his corn again, an incessant habit of his.

Both women again, almost sarcastically: "Men."

Just then, Tondra and Nitana approached on the path, running. "Mr. Ames is not here with you this morning?" Tondra asked as they arrived, both disappointed and concerned.

"No," Lent replied, "what's wrong?"

"Seana is worse today," Nitana told them, "we need Mr. Ames."

"He and Kalo have not returned from Legend Range," Tere advised the Renoloi leader and second.

Surprised, "They stayed overnight in Legend Mountains?" Tondra asked. Tere nodded. "But Kalo knows better than to do such a thing."

"Seana…" Nitana reminded then volunteered, "I will find them."

"I will go with you," Tere offered.

Lent: "Me too; I'll get my twibil."

The quick-witted Tere, not one to allow opportunity to escape un-seized —had to knock— asking with mock sincerity, "We will be traveling quickly; are you sure you will be able to maintain our pace?"

Lent threw back a playful insult of his own. "If you miss a step, it will be your own fault when I run over the top of your little bottom." By the time he finished saying it, he was already on his way to get his weapon and beyond hearing distance of any possible rebuttal.

* * *

Running…

…Nitana, Tere and Lent were soon crossing the crater plain of the temple bound for the craggy landscape of Legend Range just beyond. Three foxes of fluid momentum —two fair, one dark— swift on their feet and sure in their purpose, covering miles with athletic grace and ground eating speed. They were undaunted by the fact the mountain range spanned many miles, all rugged terrain, and within the maze the formations could conceal someone although they may not be far away.

After several hours of searching the trio finally stopped on a ridgetop to catch their breath. All three were well-seasoned and honed for endurance, but were also aware the likelihood of finding two of their own within such a vast labyrinth of canyons, rimrock and winding crevasses was an effort in futility. Instinctively, Kalo was accomplished at traversing all nature of terrain without leaving any trace of her presence; and Ames, having gleaned many of their skills from Tian, was nearly as undetectable as the young warrior. There would be no sign of either even if the trio did intercept their trail; so it was likely the only way to locate them would be a violation of all Renoloi precepts.

Still panting and peering from beneath his hair Lent asked, "Why don't we call for them?" Neither Renoloi responded. "Well," he persisted, "we'll never find them in these rocks unless we do."

Tere studied him briefly; then to Nitana, "He is right this time."

Slighted again. "This time?" Looking at Nitana he asked, "Why don't you want to call for them?"

"Noise draws predators, Lent."

"Yes," he agreed, "and it also attracts attention from great distances and a lot of places we'll never be able to search any other way." Pushing sweaty hair out of his face he asked, "Which makes more sense, continuing searching quietly until Seana's so sick we may not be able to help her, or make some noise and have a better chance of finding them?"

Prudence dictating the latter, the Renoloi acquiesced *"—Kaloooo,"* she called at the top of her lungs. Lent and Tere joined in. The combination of their voices sent echoes ringing through the afternoon sky, and even before the ricochets subsided two figures appeared atop a rock outcropping not more than a mile away.

The reply, *"Heerre,"* Kalo waving both arms above her head. Shortly the group of three became five as they met in a draw. "You called out?" the girl remarked dubiously.

"It is important or we would not have done so," Nitana told her.

Ames immediately asked, "What's wrong?"

"Seana is worse." She needed say no more. That quickly they were moving —and no one would stop until they were home.

* * *

Seana tossed fitfully…

…On the leather-covered stone couch in her hut, trying to rest, but unable. Matted with sweat her hair was pasted to the side of her face, her skin ashen and damp with fever. She was very ill. Drawn and sunken, her eyes had the listless gaze of unmistakable sickness evidenced with encircling dark rings, and she ineffectually licked her parched lips with her tongue; but her mouth was too dry and they stuck together making it just that much more exasperating. Her injured shoulder was noticeably swollen, endemic and throbbing, even the slightest movement wrenching sparks of pain. The Renoloi was not getting well; her condition was deteriorating again.

Tondra and Ronto had been at Seana's bedside since the others left to search for Ames and Kalo. That was hours ago, morning, and it was growing dark now. Having spent the day fretting over the woman both were weary with the badgering apprehension of not knowing how to help. Again Tondra dipped the Chiqua chamois in the bowl, loosely wrung it out, then dabbed Seana's forehead and mouth with the soothing cool water. Try to make her more comfortable was all they could do.

Breathing labored, "Where is Mr. Ames?" Seana asked.

"He should be here soon," Ronto consoled, "I am certain by now Nitana has found him." Seana licked her lips again as Tondra squeezed the chamois dribbling more water on them.

"Thank you," she murmured, her mouth moistened again.

"It is almost dark," Ronto worried, no louder than a whisper, directing her concern to Tondra.

"They will come," Tondra assured.

And even as she said it —*ssst*— the door rose. Breathing hard Ames entered followed by Nitana and the others, and stepping forward sat beside Seana.

Without speaking he laid a hand on her forehead, next her cheek, then methodically examined her surveying from head to foot. His first observation was her labored, rapid, panting respirations. Applying delicate thumb pressure against her cheek, viewing the sclera of her eye—*no apparent jaundice.* Squeezing a fingertip he checked the nail—*capillary refill three seconds, poor.* Ears—*okay,* and massaging the neck and jaw...

"Open your mouth, Seana," a medical tone. The woman complied without question. *Lymph nodes, adenoids and tonsils—all right.* And avoiding the obviously swollen left shoulder and arm, palpating her other armpit—*no swelling.* Taking her right wrist in his hand he asked, "Where does it hurt?"

"My shoulder." Her pulse was weak and thready. He applied gentle pressure on each quadrant of her abdomen, asking each time, in turn, if it hurt. Four times she said no. Continuing down, pubis synthesis, pelvis, thighs, buttocks, legs, feet—and survey completed. Leaning back, he considered momentarily.

"What is wrong with her?" Ronto asked anxiously.

Shaking his head he admitted, "I'm not sure; could be infection or febrile reaction."

"But her shoulder," Tondra observed, "is so swollen."

Turning, addressing her, "True, but that's not what's making her so ill. The swelling is symptomatic of her immune system's inability to ward off some type of infection. I'm convinced of that now."

"What does that mean?"

Scratching his chin he explained, "Simply, her shoulder hasn't been able to heal because something else is making her sick. I believe her injury is being aggravated by an infection of some kind."

Kalo asked, "What can we do for her?"

"She's burning up with fever. All we can do is lower her core temperature and monitor her condition."

"We have been trying to keep her cool," Ronto told him presenting the chamois and bowl of water.

"We'll need more than that," he replied. "Mud. We'll pack her in mud and keep it moist." Turning to the others he explained, "Evaporation should bring her fever down."

Soon, with the help of Lent and Kale, the Renoloi had Seana blanketed in mud with sufficient waterskins leaned against the wall to keep the mudpack soaked for several hours. Crowded within her hut the small group lingered until her labored respirations finally began to subside and she was able to breathe more easily again. Her body temperature under control, she was finally able to rest, tired eyes closing.

Tondra and Ronto appeared exhausted.

Able to smile again, Ames commended, "You did well, and you've had a long day; why don't you both get some rest too."

As they and the others began milling in the direction of the door Seana's eyes fluttered, opening, and she immediately asked of Ames, "Are you going to leave me?"

At her side, looking down upon her, "No," he reassured, "I'm staying. I'll be right here with you."

"As will I," Kalo volunteered. Seana squeezed his hand offering a fragile, loving smile, and comforted again she closed her eyes.

Nitana darted a side-glance to Kale and he nodded. She spoke. "Kale and I will return to relieve you." Ames thanked them as the door rose and the others left.

One seated on either side of the stone couch, Kalo and Ames remained watching over Seana... because they were friends.

* * *

Long hours of waiting...
...The final night slipped away.

* * *

Three hours until sunrise...

...Within the humble, small, gray-tan hut the pair sat reticently watching over Seana, not leaving her bedside. Committed with the bond of friendship and their word, Kalo and Ames kept the mudpack moist so it could work its healing magic. Although both were spent from their trek in Legend Range the day before, and their vigil tending to Seana, neither would sleep until they knew she would be all right.

Catching a moment's rest, Kalo, sitting beside him on the edge of the stone couch, leaned against the man. Illuminated in the sepulcher's dim light his eyes slowly closed as his head drooped then quickly jerked back, waking again. Recovering and blinking he checked to be sure Seana was still resting peacefully, then sheepishly looked at Kalo.

She smiled warmth and admiration for this stranger who was not an enemy. "I am very tired also," she confessed.

"I wasn't falling asleep," he said. The girl affectionately grinned.

A hand pressed upon his back. "I am feeling better now," Seana whispered. Their voices had awakened her.

Turning, "You sure?" he asked.

Her eyes had recaptured their sparkle and her cheeks once again were flush with color. "Yes, however I am a little cold."

The man beamed with satisfaction, "That's good. Let's get you cleaned up."

It took some time to scrub her clean and culminated with the leather couch cover full of mud and tied knapsack-fashion in one corner, a sizable puddle in a second, and Seana slipping into a clean skirt and top in a third corner. By the time Kalo finished helping Seana dress Ames was already soundly asleep in the fourth corner of her dwelling.

Examining Seana in her fresh clothes, "Back to bed now," Kalo said, her most authoritative, motherly tone. Without argument, but rejecting the bed, Seana lay on the floor beside the man and snuggled against him. Understanding, Kalo willingly joined them, and soon the three were nestled together and fast asleep.

This stranger who was not an enemy... was family.

* * *

Two hours until sunrise…

…The pitch of night was broken only with scattered holes in the ash cloud as it dissipated somewhat allowing pinpoints of distant, glimmering starlight to peer through. Vast, the empty silence of space kept them, minutiae diamonds, the solace of heaven. The mood of this night was cool and hushed with only an occasional rustle of leaves, intermittent wind brushing gently through the understory and canopy. All seemed tranquil from the sentry post high in the tree.

Vigilant eyes scanned the village below, watching over those asleep in their homes. It would be a while until dawn, with the scattered night fires along the path dwindling, from time-to-time a, *pop,* of knotted wood consumed by simmering flames. The acrid scent of rising wood smoke lingered a moment then whisked away with the faint breeze.

It had been a quiet night... very quiet.

Suddenly, the sounds of rushing claws gripping bark, and *—snap, snap—* two sentries were dead.

Once more everything was quiet... too quiet.

Clustered night-vision eyes peered from the dark as the Hunters inched forward. Lethal, adroit, and black, the treetops gathered the sneaking arachnid horde on limbs absorbed within a camouflage of dark and green. With each passing moment clusters of white eyes glowing ghostly and evil, crept closer with the stealth of the panther and venom of vipers. Stalking, cold and relentless, cloaked in chain mail of chitin and possessed with the mindless obsession of instinct; clawed, grasping toes piercing coarse bark... one step at a time. Ratchet ragged legs sheathed in barbs of glimmering obsidian blade, under cover of darkness... the Hunters moved in.

Below—

Small stone huts lining both sides, they followed the wide footpath on their way to Seana's hut. Nitana and Kale passed a night fire exchanging silent greetings with the Renoloi and Pilgrim sentries, a wave of the hand and continuing on. Rounding the curve their feet padded noiselessly upon the packed, damp ground, and both proceeded speaking only in whispers abiding by an intuitive, unwritten law of the jungle; always move quietly, lest you move not at all. To either it would be no less than sacrilege to violate such an inborn perspective of their way of life. Loud noises had no place in the realm of the night.

Above—

Prismatic composition of arthropod eyes studied the specimens, watching them, tracking them, crouching, moving closer... one step at a time.

Below—

—*Ssst.* The door to Seana's dwelling rose. Nitana and Kale entered, and stepped out of sight.

Faintly illuminated in the sepulcher's glow Nitana surveyed the interior of Seana's hut. The stone couch behind the sepulcher was bare. In the far corner the cover still rested securely tied, a cumbersome knapsack of leather soaked through and stuffed full of mud. To the left, another corner, a latent puddle evaporating in moisture rings with coagulating mud in its center. Glancing to the right she and Kale found them, sleeping together, snuggled on the floor, a compressed wad of bodies and trust. Looking at Nitana, Kale grinned affectionately, as if to say, *imagine that.* Nitana smiled.

"Seana must be better," she whispered. Her voice woke Kalo somewhere within the tangle of arms and legs on the floor.

"Yes," Kalo whispered back, "her fever broke a while ago." A hand in the pile moved as she began prying herself free, and her movement caused the others to also stir. Slowly the three waking people unwound, extricating themselves and lethargically sitting up. Kneeling, Nitana and Kale joined them on the floor.

"You feel better, Seana?" Kale asked.

Rubbing her eyes with her right hand, but still favoring her left arm again secured with the sling and swath, "Yes," she answered blinking drowsiness away, "my shoulder still hurts, but not as much as before."

As they spoke, Kalo's attention was distracted, drawn, by what sounded like scratching on the thick roof of the hut. The others hadn't heard it and she made no mention of it; and from within the dwelling, she wasn't certain what the noise was. But once alerted, unobtrusively she continued listening, her attention travelling back and forth between the others' conversation, and something else.

Rising again and moving to the sepulcher Nitana passed a hand over the flame and it intensified lending more light to the interior of the home. After further chitchat and deciding Seana did, in fact, seem to be on the mend, the mood of the small group lightened.

"Seana, are you hungry?" Kale asked.

Eagerly, "Yes, very."

Kale beamed, "I have some jerky in my hut. I'll get it for you," and as Kale stepped to the doorway and it began to rise...

...*Ssst*...

...Night air sweeping under the rising door, into the room, and instantly the young Renoloi sensed it. Inside, Kalo felt it. She knew what it was —and she screamed,

"—Kale, get away from the door!"

CHAPTER EIGHTEEN

In a wonderland of flowers…

…And color and life, frail words, "Reed, I am too heavy; put me down and I will walk."

Pressing a cheek against her head, her hair damp and clinging with perspiration, he assured, "I've had puppies that weighed as much as you." But he was tired; they had been many hours now without rest. Stubbing his toe on a rock he stumbled missing a step, then continued walking. "You're not heavy."

The meandering valley basin with its lush meadows and wetland marshes interspersed with looming granitic columns and twisted spires ended less than a mile in front of them. There, contiguous and awe-inspiring, rose an immense range of mountains that reached to the cloud layer and then unseen, beyond. Powerfully the geologic formations climbed in stairstep escarpments of sheer cliffs and intense rock faces glittering black and gray with feldspar, mica and quartz. Somewhere high above were snow-capped peaks towering silent and sovereign, surely beyond their meager ability ever to climb.

This range of mountains was more incredible than any he had ever before seen, seeming almost alive, breathing the lofty reaches of pristine air miles above, intimidating with strength and structure he could not imagine, impenetrable beyond his comprehension, and transcending the limits of tectonic creation. To climb them would be impossible. The weary man knew they would have to go around, and viewing the vast chain of mountains he dared not even speculate how long such a journey might take. But aside from all else he knew, and resolved, they had to try.

Studying the landscape as he approached, Reed searched for an acceptable passage. Along the foothills abutting the sheer formations the rolling topography was clothed in hardwoods, thickets of blooming chokecherry, magnolia, caragana, buffalo berry, currant, and scattered small saplings.

If he could not climb over these remarkable peaks, then he must go around; there was no alternative. Tian's waning life was literally in his hands. For her and his friend he would give every ounce of his strength, his loyalty, his being, committing himself to the endeavor. Lest he should die, he would not fail them. Hope against hope, possibly on the other side of these mountains, perhaps many miles yet distant, out there, somewhere, lay his destination. Although exhausted he would go on somehow, searching, and find it... a mysterious circular storm, and a hole in the sky.

Stumbling along he gazed sadly upon the stricken woman he carried in his arms. They were lost in a world with a day that was endless. *Take a step... take another.* Somber, with devotion of love from the depths of his soul, inside him was a solitary reoccurring prayer. *Please... she needs to get home.*

Slowly Reed made his way from the valley; the bounty of flora it boast, swept from a kaleidoscope of pigment and vibrant mangle of color, didn't matter. The spectacular beauty of this enchanted world no longer interested him, nor did the fauna: butterflies, frogs, dragonflies, and myriad small creatures that skittered around him. Determined, his mind was singularly focused, their circumstances now to the point of desperation, only sheer willpower keeping him going.

One step after another; from the meadowland, upward and into the wooded foothills of the confused forests of autumn. His chest heaved with the added burden of climbing toward the climactic jutting mountains; but he continued on, persevered, until finally he arrived at the base. Without stopping he began trailing around them, pushing himself to his limit. *Take a step... take another.*

Beyond the point of reflection, the man was now so absorbed with survival his mind allowed no time to consider what might have been, and should have been… obvious. For all the times he had looked upon the hardwoods and wondered, the simple conclusion had been proudly proclaimed from each and every branch. But Reed, no different than most others, had tried to recover a deeper significance, some meaning perhaps more mysterious and unworldly. And in doing so, like the others, had overlooked, or disregarded a very simple piece of… *the Puzzle.*

It had never occurred to him; the hardwood trees, the guardians, sentinels of nature… already knew. Trees, the color of autumn; were preparing for change, far beyond the change of seasons... a cataclysmic transformation.

After following the mountain's sheer face for some time, finally, he had to rest. Reed stopped beneath a sprawling oak with twisted limbs splaying apart like gnarled arms flaunting clustered leaves the shape of hands, brittle and dyed a crackling brown. Tenderly he laid Tian upon the ground veiled with layers of moss and lichen. Its soft porosity and spongy texture would afford her some comfort.

She offered a tired smile of appreciation drawing her hand the length of his arm as he let her go, and last, clasped his fingertips and squeezed, an expression of love. She released his hand as he stepped away and sat down under the oak. The laser sling had by now rubbed his shoulder sore and he removed it and laid the weapon in his lap.

"You are exhausted," she said, almost a whisper.

"No, just a little tired," but his eyes answered otherwise. "I just need to rest for a few minutes; then we'll go." Tian nodded, but knew they were both spent, their chances now minimal. They talked and rested, and talked a bit longer. They were friends.

High above the two people, from the uppermost reaches in the canopy of the oak, eyes were watching, studying them with prismatic composition. Easing down through the limbs, claws penetrating bark, step by step, creeping nearer—eight clustered eyes, glistening obsidian chitin, and fangs weeping venom… the Hunter moved in.

A heinous dark predator, the creature inched closer, its posterior abdomen quivering and vibrating with its quest for the prey. Coiled with tension and malevolence it prepared for the strike, cat-like and ready, wound taut, rigid, bale-hook claws sinking into the branch. *Snap*— oak bark torn loose.

Instantly alerted by a noise that did not belong, Tian's eyes flashed upward, into the tree. *"—Reed!"*

The sound of rushing claws gripping bark —tearing it loose— and a blur of dark speed pouring down through the limbs as a smeared vision of motion. Posterior abdomen and cephalothorax a fleeting sheen of obsidian, lethal claws shredding wood slivers, clustered white glowing eyes, bristling pedipalps wide, and shaggy chelicerae with penetrating fangs poised for the strike. Thirty feet away...

Realization of her scream —the warning and reflex action— his head turning and looking up in an eye-blink, reacting. The man reached for the pulse laser lying across his lap. Black death coming —flying down through the branches— feel the steel of the weapon, finger touching the trigger. Twenty feet...

The arachnid leaping, claws fixed, a nefarious black parachute — out of the oak. Concentration focused, eyes locked on target, weapon rising, coming up. Lightless confusion and a cloud of motion —night-vision eyes, pedipalps, fangs weeping venom. Ten feet...

—A whine and the flash!

...A blinding blast of white light splattering and blowing through the Hunter shredding chitin to slivers and a vapor of guts; the creature's momentum instantly stopped —slammed backward, exploding in midair— hurling the arachnid straight up and twirling it over.

—Thwack,

The dead spider catapulted into an overhanging limb then fell like a jellyfish with dangling tentacles —out of the tree— landing directly on top of the man, a pile of lifeless arthropod leaking ectoplasm of viscous, mustard-gray blood.

Scrambling frantically to him, "Reed, are you all right?"

From beneath the collapsed Night Hunter, "Yeah..." and squirming, wedging himself free, unmistakably shaken he squeezed from under the dead spider, "I'm okay." Terror-stricken and trembling Tian helped drag him out instantly checking to be sure that he was, in fact, uninjured. "It's all right," he assured. "Missed me."

Then gravely, "No, Reed; it did not miss." She saw the gash and puncture-mark in his right leg oozing a coagulating pool of blood laced with venom in the hole. The wound went deeply into muscle, seeping dark wine-red venous blood and a telltale oily residue of neurotoxin. He had been envenomed, bitten in the strike. Tenderly she turned his leg to examine his injury more closely, and when she did...

"—Oh—fuck—that hurts!" It was bad. Without wasting time, Tian cupped his calf in both hands and compressed the muscle squeezing a gush of blood out onto her hands. "Shit," he protested, "what are you doing?"

"Trying to draw as much poison out as I can." Forcefully kneading his leg and squeezing again, "Just lie still and be quiet." She did it again then ordered, "Give me your knife."

Without arguing he complied, then nervously admonished, "Don't be cutting no X in my leg, Tian. That's just cowboy-and-indians bullshit." Ignoring him, she sliced the leg of his jeans to his hip; then cutting a cross notch, tore the pant leg away. "My Levis—" appalled.

"They are worn out anyway. Shut up." She was stone cold serious, and he didn't argue. Slicing the denim lengthwise again, she made two long strips and bandaged the wound as best she could, wrapping it securely and tying the knot constrictingly tight.

"It's just a scratch," he told her brandishing a false smile. Finally, she looked up from the wound. There were tears in her eyes —and he knew. "Come here," he said quietly. Tian scooted forward on her knees, and they hugged. "I've got to get you home." And more softly, words into her ear, "We are *not* going to die." Rubbing her back lightly, he allowed her to cry a moment, then murmured, "We better get going."

Leaning back, she wiped her cheeks, coerced a feeble smile and nodded. She rose, and extending him a helping hand managed to get him to his feet. After taking a few steps, "I'm sorry I can't carry you anymore," he apologized.

Squeezing him even more tightly, Tian looked at him. "I love you, Reed."

His smile said more than the words. "Yeah, right back at ya, Babe." Both limping, helping one another, they hobbled on.

Moments later—

Mumbling conversationally with himself, Reed was rambling incoherently and beginning to perspire profusely. Seeping insidiously within his bloodstream, the neurotoxin was manifesting symptoms of its presence. His words were unintelligible.

"What did you say?" Tian asked, not able to understand him.

More clearly now, "Nothing; just talking to myself."

"About what?"

"How could a Night Hunter be here?" he wondered, "—wherever, 'here' is."

"That also occurred to me; and I do not know." Her left arm around him, Tian reached up with her right and caressed his cheek. "How do you feel?"

"Fine," his quick response. She knew better but didn't contradict him. He began mumbling again manifesting signs of delirium. "I'm fine, you're fine, everybody's fine, fine, fine…"

"Stop please," she urged. Drawing his attention, he looked at her. Chewing her bottom lip she told him, "You have a fever. The poison is in your bloodstream."

"Sorry," he said plainly, "I know things are bad; but we will get home one way or another." Tian smiled at his determination; but it evanesced when he said, "If only we had a bomb, we could blow ourselves out of here." Presenting a fatuous grin, "Lint—that's the ticket," and looking at her, again reverting to irrational, meaningless babble. "Yeah, a bellybutton lint-bomb would do it. Bellybutton lint is highly volatile you know." Then elaborating, constructing within his mind, "Collect up a big wad, stuff it in a baby food jar, poke a hole in the lid, stick a fuse in the sucker…"

He stumbled onto a knee, then straining, regained his feet, staggering now. "Yeah, a lint-bomb…" recapturing his train of thought and continuing, "wrap the whole works with duct tape, and —*kaboom!*" He gestured, throwing up his free, left arm overhead in a sweeping arc, fingers spread wide. He glanced at Tian, his color ashen, eyes listless with vacancy, and his nonsense to him, very serious. "Only one problem though," dropping the arm to his side, he sighed, "can you guess what it is?"

Almost to tears with worry, "No, I cannot guess. Would you please quit talking; you are scaring me."

Ignoring her request, now in a world of his own. "Even with a whole shit-load of friends it still takes forever to collect enough lint."

"Reed, please…" and as she pleaded he tripped again, going to the ground in a heap and dragging her with him. Scared and stricken herself, Tian pulled managing to roll him over onto his back. With dirt on his face his eyes rolled-back-white, losing consciousness. His arms flailed ineffectually, limp and helpless. His muscle coordination was succumbing to the toxin being absorbed within his body, as involuntary muscular tremors set in with his failing nervous system.

"Reed—" she screamed into his face. No response. In desperation she slapped him. *"Reed!"*

Blinking, his eyes swam back down but couldn't remain focused, wavering as he whispered, "It's all right, Tian." Then, smiling, a far away smile, "It doesn't hurt anymore."

Her eyes flashed to the wound. His leg was severely swollen and transmuting, purple to black, with gangrene necrosis lurking in the wings. "Reed, listen to me," she cried in desperate frustration, slapping his face again. She screamed into his face. *"Reed, please!"*

Awareness fading, "Tian…" an incoherent response.

Their faces only inches apart, tears in her eyes, Tian pleaded with him, "You must get up or we will die. Please try to get up," she sobbed. "Please, do it for me." Her teardrop fell onto his cheek trickling into his eye. "Please—"

Reed looked at her; mumbled…

Green eyes blinked; their tears intermingled. Coming back, returning, trying to stay with her, cognizant again, "Fuu—uck, my leg hurts," he complained with hushed words. Then drawing a slow breath, concentrating on the deep hazel of her eyes so near to his own, he softly said, "The difference between success and failure, is getting up one more time than you fall." He groaned, and painfully rolling onto his side began to push himself from the ground. His voice gritted with determination, "I don't remember…" pushing himself up, "who said that…" a little more, Tian moving back so he could rise, "but, they were right…" almost onto his feet, "and I am getting up now." Standing, then faltering, he teetered and collapsed again, flaccid upon the ground.

"Reed!—" Instantly she was beside him.

A wet rag, lying on his back. "I'm sorry. I can't get up." He swallowed hard. "My legs won't move." The paralyzing effect of the neurotoxin was exacting its toll having effectively diminished his muscular control.

Overwrought, leaning over her fallen friend, Tian sobbed. And as she cried, little by little anger seeped in; took purchase… and determination took hold. Even though frail with sickness and petite in size, she avowed, monumental in courage, "Then Reed, if you cannot get up for me, I will get up for you."

That said, angered with frustration, chest heaving with resolve, soul fraught with the flame of defiance; she forced herself onto her feet, hobbled to his head, and bending over painfully clasped his hands with hers. Pulling as she rose, she staggered backward dragging his outstretched body across the ground, one step at a time. *Take a step… take another.* One foot behind the other, digging her heels into the ground, pulling with all her might, she dragged her friend.

Her chest heaved with electrifying pain. Her shoulders strained with adrenaline fire. Her back ached with tension's extremes. The valor of undying loyalty traced through her eyes and torment scrawled on her face, the intrepid Renoloi struggled, defying impossible odds. *Take a step... take another.* But in spite of her most sincere, heart wrenching, most valiant effort, quickly her foot slipped and she stumbled, falling, writhing in pain, lying by Reed's head.

"You go on ahead," he whispered, "I'll catch up later."

Drawn with pain and frustration she screamed, "*No!* I will not leave you —*not ever!*" And sobbing, "You are my friend." Then more gently, caressing, Tian tenderly brushed his forehead and cheek with an open hand, her face wet with tears and the realization of hopelessness. More softly now, her words telling love so very deep within her heart… "I am here. You are not alone. We are in this together."

Helpless, looking up to her Reed recalled those very words, words he himself had spoken to a terrified Renoloi on the trimaran, at the end of the boom in a violent green sea with an unworldly whirlpool stirred by a hole in the sky. Truly, they were friends.

"But if you stay with me, we'll both die."

Shaking her head, she refused. "No. We are in this together."

Tears welled in his eyes then dripped back toward his ears. He blinked twice—shifted his head a bit more to the side trying to make himself more comfortable. "We're gonna die," he conceded, "and I still have no idea where we even are." Irritated with the futility of their plight he tried to scoot himself sideways with his elbows. "—And the bitch of it is, this ground is hard as a rock."

It showed in her eyes, puzzled. Tian suspected the venom in his system. "It is only your imagination."

"Imagination my ass," trying to turn onto his side.

"Reed, the ground is not hard; it is very soft," leaning forward to help him, cradling his head with her hand, "you must have a stone under your head." Then lifting his head to brush away the suspect rock, her other hand pushing aside some soil... bumped something solid ...and very hard.

Curious. "Something is under your head. Let me help you move a little." With their combined efforts Reed moved enough so Tian could see something; and kneeling beside him, with a cupped hand she gingerly pushed a little more loam aside revealing a slightly protruding stone.

Stunned, bewildered, Tian saw what it was—a flat, circular, alabaster stone... embossed with the raised, solid gold symbol,

A/Ω

CHAPTER NINETEEN

Night air…

…Sweeping under the rising door, into the room, and she screamed, *"—Kale, get away from the door!"*

Startled, puzzled, the door still rising, Kale turned and looked at Kalo just as wicked black fangs stabbed into his neck —instantly swelling— sealing the entrance with liquid-stretch bloat. Grotesquely inflated, he was a dull goldfish bowl of tightly drawn skin, his tissue and organs dissolving inside, torso and limbs distended with the liquefied translucence of water-filled latex. Life draining from his eyes, he was stuck blocking the doorway as death took him with locked, hollow fangs.

Then suction. Caving in and wrinkling, his chest compressed then collapsed—face, arms and legs shriveling, his cowboy boots dropping to the floor. Crumpling and crinkling his skin drew tightly upon his bones until nothing remained but a skeletal raisin — wizened— vacuum-packed. And from the Hunter's lecherous fangs Kale hung dehydrated, processed, and dead.

The creature flung his husk onto the footpath outside then glowered from the doorstep chattering virulent delight; a mindless demon with heinous glowing-white eyes, bristling pedipalps, groping chelicerae —and venomous twenty-inch fangs. *Slit*— Nitana's arrow lanced through its eyes catapulting it back and over, and just outside the door it quivered and died.

A Renoloi's scream dispatched alarm through the village —then silence— snuffed with near-instant death. Another Hunter. All of them moving now, bounding limb to limb, claws rattling branches as they rushed from the canopy like a malevolent swarm of black spider monkeys. The attack.

From somewhere in the darkness came the war cry…

"—*Night Hunters!*"

…And warriors responded, out into the night.

Holding his ground, jettisoning boiling wings of fire into overhead branches, a Pilgrim defiantly drenched the onslaught of killers. Leaves crinkling, limbs burning, trees bursting in flame, he encircled himself within splattering waves of napalm, torching everything it touched.

Then more flame throwers, confusion, commotion—

Molasses-sticky fire splashing through foliage, the trees erupted in frantic insanity and soaked animalistic screams, night-vision eyes scrambling like whirling rockets of flame. Burning Hunters careened through the branches flicking trails of dripping fire swirling spirals of black smoke and soot. Asphyxiating, cooking and charring outside and bubbling within, they ran until they ruptured in explosions of rank flaming froth.

Alongside the Pilgrim, Jena never saw it coming —from behind— just a glimmer of lethal speed. Out of the pitch backdrop its licentious fangs speared through her ribs below her breasts — injected— no time even to scream. Astonishment inscribed in her eyes, her chest expanded with grotesque bosoms, arms and legs filling until her fingertips burst spraying cream-colored liquid from ten-finger-nozzles.

Turning, the Pilgrim saw Jena being hoisted from the ground, watching horrified as the gigantic spider reared and clawed raising her lifeless body still clasped in its scissoring jaws; his skin crawling, throat tightening holding the gag. Then a second demon came over the first —no choice— he squeezed torching all three. Both monsters and the dead Renoloi went up in a seething dark orange wash of cackling, lashing inferno —colliding and cracking— melting in a fiery tangle of broken hulls, crisp legs and bubbling white eyes.

The huts—

Throughout the village bronze doors were rising with an outpouring of warriors; arrows flying, flame throwers launching perditious dragon-tongues of spiraling hellfire into overhanging limbs. The Pilgrims and Renoloi were ready to fight. Suddenly everywhere, people were running the ground beneath fast-moving shadows that streaked overhead, the night highlighted by splattering amber flames eating darkness and trees—pernicious and orange, devouring anything they touched.

Above—

Trilling insanity railed through the canopy as arrows hissed from below aimed at glimpses of black and splotches of dark sheen. Blistering washes of bright fire and flames dripping from charred limbs illuminated the village in undulant light, while wild mindless nocturnal eyes searched targeting prey. Then the Night Hunters launched an all-out attack; claws fixed, legs splayed, fangs wide filled with venom—and the warriors fought back.

—White noise of savagery, and caterwauling animalistic screams!

Shredding bark from the limb the Hunter lunged for the Pilgrim —his ax intercepting, mid-swing coming up— its fangs finding his chest as the slicing edge opened the fiend with mustard-gray splatter. Injected and swelling he went down beneath the monstrous spider —stretched then *squeezed*— bursting a wet cloud —both dead— a pile in a puddle.

With uncertainty just beyond the threshold, Ames scooped the scimitar from the floor looping the scabbard across his back, offering a hand to Seana helping her up. Ahead of them, arrows nocked and ready, Nitana went outside, Kalo a step behind, both into the dark. Moving around the dead arachnid and onto the footpath Nitana scanned the trees, as the younger warrior, covering her back perceived the unseen. Instantly Kalo reeled and let fly toward the roof of the hut —into its mouth, out the top of its head— spitting an impact crunch that skipped like a wraith in the shadows. The Hunter crouched on the roof quivered as it slobbered, hunching rigid as it wavered and convulsed.

Alerted by the sound of Kalo's bowstring, Nitana spun around in time to see the glowing eyes fading as its legs began buckling; then the girl glaring defiantly at the arachnid, still there, wobbling but not quite down, realizing the young warrior a single footstep away had just saved her life. The creature shuddered one ugly terminal heave then crumpled limply onto the roof and slid from its blind falling heavily to the ground. Eyes dimmer, then out.

Backlit in the doorway, Ames and Seana witnessed Kalo's supernal prowess, both aware she couldn't possibly have seen or heard the Hunter. Even still they couldn't explain it; it was dark and had happened so quickly. Exchanging expressions of wonder neither spoke; but remembering the intense darkness on the rimrock Ames knew she possessed more than ability, where depraved and deranged spiders went down.

Tondra and Deet were hurrying along the path when a Hunter leaped from an overhanging limb. But it was no match for their skill and teamwork, she fearlessly taking it head-on, thrusting her lance between its fangs and jaws into the pipe of its neck effectively immobilizing its head. With a single deft swipe Deet's cavalry saber amputated four legs toppling the ghoul on the foot trail, leaving it ineffectively flailing as its severed legs gouged clawmarks in the dirt.

Without so much as a flinch, Tondra yanked her spear from its mouth opening a hole pumping gray-bubble globs, then finished it with a second unfeeling stab dead center in its bright sparkling eyes. Beaten and dying and pinned to the ground, all eight wretched orbs seemed to watch miserably as the speartip crunched through them making a gristling-ugly, queasing sound. And with a decisive, vengeful twist of her weapon inside its head, the Hunter groaned a pathetic whine, contracted its fangs ejecting a feeble piss of venom, then shuddered and died.

A cry from the darkness—another warrior down.

Avoiding crackling branches and flame-ravaged foliage arachnids sprang through the canopy as glistening flashes of black, then leaped and attacked like clawed grappling-hook monsters pouncing out of the night. The treetops trilled with white noise of savagery —and chattering, burning, evil animalistic screams!

Darkness and fire. Erupting from whore-winds of smoke, napalm splashed through the trees washing the ancients with incendiary flame and black ravaging boil that clung to whatever it touched.

Cackling rabid screams. Torched with jellied-liquid fire, limbs dripped yellow waterfall flames sending death with the spoil of swirling blistered air and dark sooty smoke that rose with the heat in the night.

Ocher-boil and death. In the trees and burning branches, beneath a pitch-dark sky of villainous pandemonium and glimmering white eyes, they set the greenery of jungle afire.

On the path—

Spear clutched with both hands Tondra and Deet caught up with them outside Seana's hut as he constantly scanned and she breathlessly reported, "They are everywhere," all of them tense, watching for danger.

Running toward them a Pilgrim stopped abruptly squeezing twisted-liquid flames, igniting an arachnid on a low hanging branch where it had been lying in wait. Springing sideways in a burst of yellow-red fire, it rushed to the end of the limb trying to jump to the other side of the path. Leaping overhead —lighting up the dark— blinded within the savagery of flames, the Hunter sailed like a fireball with eight shredding legs; burning, crackling and shooting bright sparks. Then the skyrocket arachnid exploded —and the rockets red glare, spider bursting in air, gave proof through the night, it was no longer there— a fiery skyflash of detonation flame and evaporating cloud, it vanished as a, *whoomph,* in the night!

From below the six witnessed the bizarre spider-fireworks display, Tondra expressing what each of them knew. "There is too much cover; we must get to open ground."

"The rimrock," Ames said, "get everyone to the crater."

Kalo reeled —her bowstring's *snap*— somewhere out there the arrow slicing through its eyes. From the distant canopy's woven darkness spiked green-stick cracks of broken branches and scattering leaves shaken loose; something falling. More limbs snapping, then hesitation, just the briefest silence, and resuming, crunching and clattering sounds as it tumbled down through the limbs. Finally, they caught a glimpse of its exoskeleton reflecting firelight from burning trees; able to see the Night Hunter just before it struck the forest floor. She was a warrior of instinct; another lay dead.

Amazed, Tondra and Deet looked at one another, just a beat; but it was too dangerous for anymore than that. All around them shrilled eerie, keening screeches like banshees railing in the night, trailed by barbaric echoes of hollow white noise and chattering animalistic screams.

"Everyone to the rimrock!" Lent yelled. "Pass it on."

Farther down the path, "Everyone to the rimrock," someone repeated.

Surrounded by puddles of dripping fire and burning arboreal light, the Pilgrims and Renoloi were ready. A stalwart determined army in a primitive world, armed with flame throwers, flails, spears, bows, battle-axes, pitchforks, unusual swords and an unorthodox collection of weapons, they were forged with the conviction to survive. From two previously separate lives, somehow they would persevere; very different people now united to an army that would fight its way through the jungle, bound for the rimrock, to the open ground of the crater.

"—*Warriors ho!*" Lent's voice sounded. Twibil in hand, prepared to fight for their lives, he led them into the jungle.

The Pilgrims created a defensive corridor igniting both sides of the trail with spiraling flames churning smudge-black smoke shedding the acrid, stick-in-your-throat taste of destruction and the raw, bitter scent of fire-scorched trees. And with each hurried step along the burning passageway, flanking warriors watched for the cold-blooded killers held at bay by the flames, lurking just out of reach.

Hundreds of them—

Avoiding burning limbs, Hunters crawled the canopy as raven shadows and glimmers of exoskeleton in a blend of opaque swaying treetops and burnt empty spaces. To those below on the path it seemed the whole world was torn with chattering villainy and aroused with malevolent howls… and alive with black fire, and green.

Moving quickly—

Shielded within the army's perimeter, but terrified and silent, the small ones obediently ran the trail in the direction of the escarpment, their path and the darkness ahead illuminated with ochre flames of Pilgrims lacing the trees with searing guttural bursts of suppression fire. Out there and overhead insane howling monsters shrieked deranged madness as splashing waves of flame left them sizzling, smoldering and dead in a jungle being eaten by fire.

All around them, perhaps imaginary, maybe real, peering through whorls of smoke and fire watching eyes fashioned surreal and evil images within the napalm showers that dripped from the limbs like burning waterfalls of hot summer rain. Twigs and leaves incinerated in the updrafts crackled as they spun skyward then fanned out with the wind, until finally descending as tumbling embers resembling crisp popping snowflakes glimmering a bright drifting orange. And just beyond the inferno, wicked prismatic eyes of mindless composite imagery watched from every corner of the darkness, mirroring the conflagration and reflecting it back.

Running the trail—

In spite of the barrier of burning jungle continuing attacks were vicious and daring, the arachnids still setting upon them in twos or packs of three. Consumed with the primal urge of hunter proclivity and seemingly compelled by an insatiable madness, the adroit killers oftentimes even disregarded the flames. Most caught fire and died, but some, ruthlessly spurred by stimuli-driven instinct, did manage to get through. Unnaturally and unexplainably, they wouldn't quit coming.

Following them on the trail, three Hunters dashed beneath some overhanging limbs of dripping napalm instantly setting one aflame in a flush of whirlwind fire and blistering froth. Frantic it screamed and veered off —through the understory, clawing back up a tree then into the canopy— where seconds later it vaporized in a boil of explosion and flame.

The others took a Renoloi defending the rear flank, one sinking its fangs in her abdomen, the second severing her arm at the shoulder. Instantly both were savagely all over her, her cry stopping mid-scream as she swelled retching and kicking, gushing crimson from her missing arm's shredded flap —as a courageous Pilgrim and Renoloi counterattacked.

Fangs stabbing through his head, another Pilgrim was snatched so ferociously his torso snapped loose and was flung through the air knocking a Renoloi to the ground. The decapitated body landed dead weight spurting blood from the neck, and puzzled momentarily the Night Hunter stalled as it searched for its lost prey —until four sudden arrows punched holes in its face. Ratcheting and wobbling one final step, the trembling monster collapsed leaking a queer dying moan.

Leaping, a Hunter missed as the Pilgrim sidestepped and swung cleaving a gash with his pickax; but within the confines of the narrow passageway, on its way down the spider hooked a claw in his thigh near his groin. Startled by the strike the young warrior looked down, both legs soaking with blood. Going into hemorrhagic shock, he gasped but didn't scream, and in a valiant act of defiance killed his nemesis burying his pickax dead center in its ugly, vile eyes. His stare again traveled to his pulsing femoral artery, realization setting in; he was bleeding to death. And to the backtrail: two more coming. With resolute defiance he made his final stand, bravely heaving his weapon and watching as it hacked into one; and that quickly the other was upon him.

Lent, leading them—

Arriving at the escarpment the warriors continued following the cliff trail constantly washing the jungle with protective walls of fire. Courageously and determined, fighting as they went, they fashioned a tunnel of fire forging their way toward the open ground of the rimrock and the mountain range beyond.

Snapping treetrunks with sizzling unbearable heat, churning wildfire devoured liana and trees on both sides of the trail in ragged winds of ravenous noise. Expelling eerie hisses the cyclone helixes snaked upward through the branches as twisted flame-devil-dance that penetrated the treetops illuminating the sky and shedding blistering showers of exploding-hot sparks —while constantly on the move, they followed the winding corridor through burning tornadoes of anger and unforgiving blaze.

Brave, small dirty bare feet on hazardous ground—

The children were hustled along the narrow footpath like a covey of scurrying hatchlings shielded within a safeguard of vigilant warriors. Mindful of what they'd been taught, the young ones did exactly as instructed, stopping when ordered and running when told, not questioning their guardians. No crying, no whimpers, not so much as a sound; instilled in each and every one were the lessons of survival in a primitive world. Hurrying together, they leaped over charred fallen branches and avoided simmering puddles of fire barely a step off the trail. Once cool and soft the ground now reeked of timberburn, humidity and steam, cooking duff and loam to hardpack of baked-solid cake. With flames ravaging the jungle around them and fire dripping from nearby limbs, screams bled from the surrounding darkness as images of claws and fangs filled their heads —because beyond the pillars of fire, death lurked a single footstep away.

Somewhere back there—

Tracking them, mimicking their flight along the trail, the arachnids closed in. Leaping on a Pilgrim at the rear flank the Hunter took him down gouging the length of his back—no time even to turn and fight. He fell face-first snuffing his scream with a mouthful of dirt as deviant hypodermics penetrated both ears spiking into his head—then queezed into his brain. But the Hunter didn't inject him; instead it savagely peeled back his scalp and gnawed through his skull. Tearing loose a final chunk of bone and trilling victoriously the monstrous vermin reared shrieking madness, its wild eyes glaring with villainy; and hunkering again it began feeding—a banquet of oatmeal mush.

Leapfrogging, three arachnids vaulted passed the oatmeal Hunter; but the laggard jumped too high grazing overhanging burning limbs. Instantly wrapped in flames its frenzied chatter of chase blurted out in macabre lunatic bawls as it skimmed franticly —low-runner-rush— trying to outrun the fire. Spun with the energy of cooking inside, the once flagging spider quickly overtook the others bounding on top of and overrunning them, the burner's tailflame sweeping both in the flash —that quickly all three were engulfed. Screeching insanely, destined to detonate and self-destruct, the trio of monstrous cretins propelled maniacally along the corridor.

With the jungle ablaze on both sides of the path, the two Renoloi now bringing up the rear saw the berserk flaming spiders blasting toward them at an impossible speed. Knowing they couldn't outrun them both warriors stopped, stood fast —ready, lances braced— intending to sacrifice themselves so those ahead would have time to reach the open ground of the rimrock, now, not far ahead.

Coming at them…

—Flying fireballs of searing chitin and wind-whistle legs,

—Chelicerae flailing, fangs squirting venom and fire, jaws gnashing, puking bubbles and froth of vomited boil and viscous gray muck,

—Clustered white eyes boiling blind, scorching black, popping out of their heads,

—Skyrockets screeching shrill animalistic horror,

…Lances ready, unafraid to die.

Clattering legs, whirling blurs of fire and speed —screaming they sprang, they flew!— trilling yellow-orange hellish flames, the passageway filled with dervish fire devils of death, the canopy and trees lining the corridor a boil of black smoke with flames in the wind. Coming at them, three soaring balls of wildfire…

—*Poomph, phoomph, whoomph!*

…Rupturing fireflashes of explosion, they vaporized as shreds and hot splatters of juice, their shattered hulls twirling, ricocheting then tumbling and piling atop one another blocking the trail allowing no more to pursue along the path.

Stunned, too frightened even to speak, the warriors looked at one another in astonished disbelief—then involuntary trembles of relief. With a final look at the fiery barricade they quickly ran to catch up with the others, both perhaps believing someone unseen had lent them a hand.

* * *

Ninety minutes until sunrise…

…Warriors poured from the jungle onto the rimrock immediately fanning out forming ranks, anticipating imminent attack.

"—Seana, Tere," Tondra called out, "take the children behind the battleline." They quickly guided the young ones through the battery of warriors, hurrying them onto the open landscape, away from the burning jungle.

Alongside Ames, Lent signaled, "Keep going—fall back!" and almost seven hundred Pilgrims and half that many Renoloi pushed into the crater in the direction of the temple ruins. Walking backward, eyes fixed on the conflagration of forest, Lent expressed the misgiving badgering them both. "Why haven't they attacked?"

A quick side-glance, then again to the trees, "I don't know." Ames turned, urging, "Keep moving—keep moving!"

Covering ground swiftly, the army crossed the crater plain with some fighters carrying the smallest children who couldn't keep up. Behind them the jungle fire spread as sinuous sheets of bright boiling swells spewing scalding smoke with a corona of amber halo. Illuminating the crater basin with waves of orange light, the scene was reminiscent of a time sadly gone with the wind, when Scarlett and Rhett watched Atlanta burning in the South.

Flattened with the explosion of the Sacred Temple months earlier, the crater's surface now lay an uneven barren plain eliminating the advantage of concealment so coveted by the Hunters. On this battlefield the terms of engagement should play out more evenly; armed warriors opposing arachnid fangs.

Hurrying, almost to the temple ruins and constantly watching their backs, from somewhere within the ranks, the alarm. *"They're coming!"*

All turned to face the enemy. Pilgrim and Renoloi were united, molded to a single entity, a force of obligatory solidarity, prepared to make their stand. Determined eyes focused with the gravity of resolve and unyielding courage needed to prevail, to survive, to dominate and keep this primitive world. Regardless of the outcome they would engage their common enemy, if necessary to the last warrior. They had no choice. Born of necessity and ingrained within each soul was a ramification of design; now, as in times long since past... was the concept of war.

The enemy—

In the predawn darkness they swarmed from the rimrock onto the tableland in a rushing cascade as sleek and dark as the death in their fangs. Chattering animalistic war cries pregnant with despair and the blackness of netherworld misery, they advanced as clattering claws and night-vision eyes clustered evil and white. The obsidian horde forayed.

Now on the gritty plain, as heinous as the black of their hulls, the Hunters were coming. Hundreds, thousands of them were closing on the makeshift army, sweeping back and forth with the deviating, rhythmic pumping locomotion of stampeding wildebeests on the African plains.

Black leaping momentum. Bounding, devouring ground at breakneck speed they were a hoarwave of insanity wrapped in glistening obsidian shrieking a sonata of eerie cackles. Unfeeling and unconscionable, mindlessly they rushed onward with instincts that were skewered in the blindness of hysteria and consumed with the malediction of Hell.

The arachnids attacked...

"—Flame throwers!"

...Dark waves of evil colliding with ocher waves of flame; the front line was splashing fire and chitin exploding wildly —yellow-orange in the night!

Napalm sizzled from twenty sweeping nozzles in long liquid crescents milking petroleum-char and suffocating smoke that roared to a firewall forty feet high. Drenched in flames —burning, blinded— still rushing forward and piling over one another, lost in the wash of infernal fireflash they hadn't time to veer off. Pushed with the sound of bellowing growls whorlfire swept through hundreds of them, searing then melting them, the flash pouring over and around them, hot splatter beneath them.

—White noise burning savagely, and heat-smothered chattering animalistic screams!

Soaked with napalm as they plunged headlong into the horrific wall of incineration, those forward detonated almost instantly in the fiery wash while others farther back scattered, burning alive in confusion and flames. They were crazed running fireballs, smears of melting motion —dying— demented visions of death. Wild eyes popping like champagne corks, they were burning bubbly-heads and a bedlam of tortured trilling howls shrieking strange gargled noises of puked-up plasma froth. Turbulence. Pandemonium. All of it fused in a flashdance of yellow-orange and speed.

Flashing legs —running— a forest of fiery bamboo, the murderous spiders hunkered with low-runner-rush. Seemingly unstoppable, they were no more than blurs of spiraling flametrails, disorder and noise. The battlefront was acrid with the stench of petroleum fire, charred hulls, burned blood, and saturation smoke. Splashed confusion caused visual chaos flashing all directions, going too fast and happening too quickly —mind-bending— too much all at once. Everything moving and melting; mixed together as indecipherable clouds of black and flames, white eyes and speed, weapons and people, and smoke and screams. Scattering explosions of dark and fire flaring over and over —the chaos of war!

Coming—

Bursting from the firewall —crackling— a Hunter plunged headlong into the front line of warriors —then a bonfire explosion— shredding chitin and seething foam splattering nearby warriors with flaming froth.

Another spider erupted from the inferno —a whorl of fire— completely engulfed. Leaping over the battleline, its ragged legs were coming apart like disintegrating fiery limbs —soaring seventy feet— still on fire, going down —and the crash— plashing cascading flame. Spider after spider rushed from the firewall then exploded, and time and again warriors were injured and killed.

Signaling, Ames yelled, "Fall back—fall back; get away from the flames!" Escaping the withering heat the army quickly retreated beyond the temple ruins, to the rocky ground bordering the collapsed mountain range.

"—Move, move!" Lent ordered. "Let's go, let's go!"

Brandishing the cavalry saber in one hand, the other jammed in his pocket fondling kernels of corn, Deet glanced back at the violent fires as he came alongside Lent muttering, "Serious warpath shit, huh?"

Darting daggers, then back to the wall of flames, Lent warned, "Deet, you really need to give up those western comic books." He hadn't the time. "Let's go —move, move!"

The army continued onto Legend Range.

* * *

Miles from the choleric conflict...

...In the quiet of the jungle and obscurity of night, a solitary glimmer of grey predawn light. Scintillating, mysterious; twinkling moonbeams upon a glistening sphere, a shimmering ball of polyhedral lattice and polycarbonate sheet embedded with metallic-flake. Months ago it had been taken from the crater and cached in a secluded niche of this primitive world.

Now sheltered by thick limbs overgrown with hanging liana and enfolded within a verdant cloak of bracken cozily nudged all around by large pulpy mushrooms, it rested undisturbed. The geodesic sphere seemed out of place, geometrically beautiful and symmetrical, the world around it prehistoric, and emerald green.

Very quiet here... in cold storage.

Until the gnarled ancients trembled, just the smallest bit at first, with reverberations that were triggered from below. Almost undetectably the vibrations traveled along their root systems and shimmied through the trunks to the larger limbs, then finally to the outer branches where the leaves rustled the flutter of quaking aspen in a breeze.

Quiet again... momentarily.

Next a stronger tremor, and the forest floor relented, shifting and opening with an almost imperceptible crack that ran directly underneath the geodesic sphere. This time the mammoth trees swayed heavily, those nearest the time machine tilting aside and partially uprooting as their tenacious buried fingers loosened from the ground. Listing, the enormous ancients draping tentacle liana leaned apart revealing a small clearing, with the geodesic sphere in its center.

Quiet again… momentarily.

—Then a solid abrasive jolt!

Head pounding, grating, the landscape vibrated furiously as tremors twisted more forcefully and the ground opened wider exposing a rift beneath the sparkling sphere. Quavering, the jungle shook tipping the leaning giants onto others colliding with tantrums of shattering limbs, then in slow-motion toppling, also taking them to the forest floor. Bounding and quaking, the ponderous weight of the falling ancients caused even more to uproot with wrenching, creaking moans of shredding green-stick fracture as fibrous tears crawled up their trunks ripping them apart with splintering snaps. Then more shockwaves, causing the canopy to sway forcefully as though taken suddenly in a gale.

Vibrating, the geodesic time sphere skittered upon the jungle floor, shifting, moving and shaking as the quake endured releasing twisted energy of spiraling jolts from below. The ground heaved and fractured more violently; then a thunderous sudden, *craack,* startled the terrain prying the stratum apart. With the upheaval the breach widened expelling a breath of pent seismic pressure in a cloud of spewn rock and dust. Like a tear through tight cloth, tracing a path beneath the time machine the forest floor came apart and the sphere started sinking, then slid deeper, and deeper, disappearing into the crevasse. Now only dust in a settling cloud.

Geometrically beautiful and symmetrical, a shimmering ball… out of cold storage …out of sight.

With the shift in the tectonic plate a crack in the world opened, then grew. Severing undergrowth it widened to a crevasse, splintering terrain as it crawled through the jungle with the hollow ring of fractured chasm. Crunching, cracking and shattering granite, it exposed a wandering rift tracing a ragged course. Toppling trees, it opened the ground like a burrowing sidewinder of tectonic force that tore through rock and shred the forest floor with an invisible knife blade of subterranean might, carving a path through the jungle, always moving in the direction of the collapsed mountain range.

Until suddenly it was quiet again… momentarily.

Greylight moonbeams, wafting filigree dust, drifting, floating gently along the rotating shafts of ethereal light. *Something yet Unfinished.*

* * *

The Pilgrim and Renoloi army…

…Pushed farther onto Legend Range warding off repetitious attacks by the raven horde, the young warriors engaging the adroit killers allowing those carrying children time to move farther into the foothills. After each counterassault they would quickly fall back preparing for the next foray, and as they withdrew the number of casualties grew, the irregular landscape of the foothills littered with smoldering hulls and many fallen warriors; defining their advance were dead from both sides. Valiant fighters killed and drained by the Hunters were discarded wizened and brittle among extruded granite rocks on the field of battle. But there were many more lifeless, melted spiders.

An arachnid lunged as a Pilgrim squeezed the trigger valve of the flame thrower he shouldered, but discharged only sputtering squirts of fire that splattered ineffectively upon the ground. It was empty and the Hunter took him with a gory mechanical, *snap,* its fangs piercing his neck with a gush of dissolving acidic injection. Swelled and stretched—immediately dead. Clustered eyes glared venomously as the killer swilled its victim through its embedded needle-fang straws, the bloated Pilgrim deflating and shrinking, collapsing and shriveling, the creature engorging and not stopping until the carcass was dry.

Uncaring, the Hunter flicked the raisin aside looking for another, fangs working, weeping yellow venom. Two arrows whisked into its throat slicing out through the back of its head, and its glowering eyes dimmed as the invertebrate creature collapsed regurgitating juice on the ground.

"Most of the flame throwers are empty," Lent yelled to Ames above the chattering warbles of Hunters skirting the fireline's perimeters and attacking from their flanks.

One leaped —Ames ducked— narrowly missing as the scimitar sliced all the way through. Down. Determination etched with his glance and defined in his words, "Then we'll fight with whatever we have."

Standing nearby Deet asked, "What is *that*?"

Vaguely illuminated by the dwindling puddles of burning napalm on the scorched battlefield, moving slowly and barely discernable, in the distance was a ponderous reptilian shape. Having abandoned the Forsaken Land it now lumbered across the plain, hunched over, trodding laboriously on powerful hind legs, its massive head carried low.

"T-Rex," Kalo fired to Deet, immediately recognizing the unmistakable outline in the predawn light.

Still hacking into a dying Hunter until it finally stayed down, Deet yelled back, "Well ain't that special?" Then firmly planting a foot on the spider's cephalothorax, he stabbed it in its eyes one final time, twisting forcefully, and satisfied, withdrew the dripping saber and sardonically said, "There spider; play dead."

Eyes drawn from the battle, Ames watched the Tyrannosaur crossing the open terrain. "What is it doing here?" he wondered aloud.

Near him Kalo answered, "A straggler, separated from the migration." Another Hunter bounding in, she spun and let fly taking it out, the gigantic spider shrieking and collapsing on a jutting shaft of stone that snagged its abdomen letting a glutinous pour like molasses oozing out.

* * *

In the jungle, the tremor reawakening…

…Crawling, then marching through the ground like a boil of thunder expelling trees with their roots. First creaking, then tearing, the towering behemoths teetered and fell with ground-crunching crashes of splintering branches splashing showers of leaves. Rumbling, the seism persisted slicing a widening crack through the bedrock, fracturing and shattering granite with the sound of ripping, brittle thunder. Until soon the rift fault had snaked its way to the rimrock where it inexplicably splintered in twenty divergent directions resembling etching claws that furrowed into the crater bound for Legend Range.

* * *

A climactic, nine-point jolt…

…Thrust up, the entire world seemed to roar with waves of subterranean seismic pressure.

"*—Earthquake!*" a Pilgrim screamed.

Quavering formations fractured shedding vast slabs from high ledges releasing tumbling rock with crushing, suffocating weight. Boulders bounded and rolled as they scattered and bounced a trampoline dance of trembling foothills and mountains being shaken in the fray. Surging then snapped by incredible pressure, sheets of strata growled deep resonant bellows thrusting slabs up through the ground. Extreme forces splintered and heaved, belching up and collapsing, pulling solid rock apart with the destructive power of intense burrowing waves. And uplifting again, then suddenly falling, the noise roared beyond deafening, like solid booming thunder and the clamor of rusty freight trains rushing inside their heads.

People and spiders were tossed with the fury of a careening roller coaster gone wild—lurching, battered from side to side and rushing downhill at rigid, impossible speeds. Stumbling then getting back up, those carrying terrified children clung to each other trying to withstand the dynamic pounding shockwaves, the furor teeth-slamming and untamed, jarring and jolting, wild enough to make jaws clench resisting the force, and eyes narrow like a blast of wind in the face.

Staggered and falling, the turbid upheaval overwhelmed the arachnids and they fled haphazardly, some stumbling in scattered puddles of still-burning napalm; then again onto their legs, crazed and confused, enveloped in flames.

Far and wide violent disorder and pandemonium swept the battleground as dissonance from the depths boiled to the surface like chaos of deep churning thunder, everything jarred and being torn with upheaval and the roar of fracturing landscape. Trembling and shifting the craggy foothills began breaking apart spawning falling rock and dust devil swarms wrapped with savage, biting sand. Confused by the quake, their attack unexpectedly delayed, the Hunters ran aimlessly and wild screaming their strange, strident chatter while the young army seized the opportunity to distance themselves, hurrying farther onto Legend Range.

Approaching the fray and still unnoticed by the arachnids, the dinosaur slowly continued its overdue migration; just a dim silhouette crossing a tattered, war-ravaged plain. A final sudden vehement jolt, and as abruptly as it began the quake subsided, then stopped.

Quiet again... momentarily; the world seeming strangely too quiet somehow.

T-Rex plodded on. Whispers almost... floating on the wind reeking of petroleum fumes, wafting unseen across the battleground as though quietly following the smoke drift with that unsettling sensation of premonition …impending sadness in the air.

In the Forsaken Land—

Across the river creeping lava began overflowing the landform; liquid-red with anger, orange of power, yellow of fire, and pale of pure heat. Unseen, somewhere below, lifting the squalid desolation of the Forsaken Land ever so slightly, it was gathering strength in a cauldron of bubble and boil. All of it seething. In the depths frothing magma and incredible pressures were churning and breathing — then without warning, violently bursting into the vent, the monster awakened from sleep.

Erupting again, heaving ash-laden clouds and roiling bright flame volcanic spray split the composite dome with a fountain of perdition and fire. Ground-rattling, soaring, skyrocketing boils of molten rock spew blackened fumes with pulse-pounding blasts of noxious poisons and superheated gas. Two thousand degrees of oracle fire and liquid light propelled a mountainous rile of suffocation, ejecta and steam in a monumental volcanic plume.

The crater plain—

Now almost directly between the Night Hunters and army, the dinosaur stopped and watched the black horde. Next, it seemed to survey the people; then finally it turned sluggishly and viewed the volcanic eruption in the Forsaken Land. Some distance from the Renoloi and Pilgrims, and posing no immediate threat to them, the Tyrannosaur drew Ames' attention.

There is a reason, he thought, something he did not yet comprehend. Mystified, he watched the dinosaur—*for everything... there is a reason.*

Causing the ground beneath them to tremble, the erupting mountain many miles beyond the river pushed its cloud of tainted, waterlogged ash into the sky forming a canopy for distant thunder. Within the growing volcanic smog wizard-fingers of lightning quickly appeared flashing quiet fury, highlighting dark places with intermittent flickering light. Here and there, skimming energy fashioned electrical vaults as the charges shimmered with silent screams dancing pirouettes of fire.

Standing in the darkness, in a panorama of ambiguity and the unexplained, Ames viewed a battlefield of smoldering corpses and dwindling flame. Empty hulls and valiant warriors lost in the melee lay random and lifeless on the ground. Beyond the river a volcano was erupting, churning evil in its heart and boiling amber from its throat. In the distance, on the crater basin and foothills confused Night Hunters skittered with the deranged insanity of clouded instinct. And closer, waiting, was a solitary Tyrannosaur lost from the migrating herds.

Upon an overlook with his people, Ames wondered what it all meant... standing on Holy Ground.

* * *

One hour until sunrise…

...With an indolent pace the dinosaur resumed its trek across the litter of dead, crossing directly between the man and volcano. Having taken less than seven steps it halted and turned again, looking away from Ames, as though searching the darkness. Then it roared.

During the moments of relative calm the Hunters had recouped and sorted their befuddled instincts; and now they saw it and rushed the Tyrannosaur in a black wave of penetrating fangs and clamoring bale-hook claws.

Quickly overtaking the dinosaur two pounced upon it —then four. Sweeping its pendulous tail the mighty Tyrannosaurus spun scattering a dozen or more, then with remarkable speed raked others with its feet. It lunged and gnashed crushing one clinging to its breast with its powerful jaws and potent six-inch incisors, and reeled tossing others away as they crawled up its neck and onto its head. But there were too many of them.

Another pounced on the dinosaur's back, then one onto its face, and with speed and poison buried a fang in its eye forcing a bubble of vitreous humor from the hole in the cornea as the needle-sharp point bore through and into the brain. Pushing acid inside its skull the Hunter envenomed the giant reptile causing it to jerk violently hurling the arachnid aside; and now mortally wounded with the severed fang still impaled in its head, again the Tyrannosaur roared.

From his vantage point Ames watched the gruesome, climactic struggle while a dozen more black demons leaped voraciously upon the injured dinosaur. The animal's overriding brow swelled grotesquely as colloid fluid drained from its torn eye onto its face. Still more Hunters swarmed upon it and it struggled even more defiantly —a bite to its throat, its neck bloated; another to its flank, its side swelled. But still it refused to succumb, crunching the demonic spiders with tremendous bites, crushing their armor with its powerful jaws, breaking them apart with its ponderous flailing tail; raking, trampling and squashing them with its herculean hind legs.

The villain, now the victim; the bizarre, esoteric life and death struggle silhouetted by the distant volcano, captured Ames, held him. Attention riveted, transfixed with visual imagery of a primitive world, he stood there, taking it all in.

Beside him, the silent Kalo watched.

His eyes and mind absorbed the intense, cabalistic vision. In the distance, pulsing and rumbling, a volcano blasting liquid fire into a darkened sky of ash plume. Above it, heat lightning etching lines of white flame through congealed brackish clouds leaving floating embers that eventually burned out. Before him, the incredible, surreal struggle of the Tyrannosaur withstanding an unbelievable onslaught of the unconscionable killers upon a fractured barren plain... and between them, casualties on the ground.

In the opaque darkness they were images broken with flickering illumination of scattered firelight. An unmeasured, terminal, fateful struggle... and soon, coming dawn and greylight.

Beside him, the silent Kalo watched.

Ames' eyes traveled from one to the other absorbing—dinosaur... volcano. Time and again focusing—dinosaur, volcano...

—Meteoric flash!

…Streaking through the overcast of congealed volcanic plume, across the dark sky, going down somewhere within Legend Range. Ethereal white light. Flame from afar.

A notion swept through his mind and seemed ridiculous even as he thought, *make a wish*. Then, comprehension —*no*— *the schoolhouse, the children... follow your heart and the stars.* His eyes skipped to the volcanic eruption. *The Riddle... Legends sleep within the throat of the dragon.*

In the Forsaken Land, the volcano breathed rivers of lava and fire. Closer, Night Hunters overpowering the Tyrannosaur, the massive animal finally collapsing beneath the savagery of their attack. Going down, the dinosaur roared. A volcanic fire-breathing cloud spraying fountains of flame and soot five miles high, the plume churning above and beyond.

Kalo could see it: realization. "Mr. Ames, what is it?"

Finally, he knew, his words measured and clear, "The Legends… of course …Kalo, I know where *they* are." Turning and pointing in the direction, "Kalo, take the children into the mountains."

"Only the children?"

"The Renoloi—and Pilgrims—everyone!" In his eyes burned the light, and a smile.

"Right away," she said ardently, instantly whirling and ordering others, "this way—quickly now—run!"

* * *

Overwhelmed, Tian stammered…

…"Reed, we are not lost. I know where we are," eyes wide with wonder and relief, engulfed in collisions of emotions —and tears— happiness and hope. Kneeling beside him, looking into his eyes, her fingers reverently touching it, stroking the alabaster marker embedded in the ground, she whispered, "Reed... *I know where we are.*"

"Now whose imagination is haywire?" he asked with near-resignation; unconvinced, but still curious,

"No," she insisted. And drawn, her gaze traveled from the embossed stone to the sheer mountain face forty feet away. Before them stood a vertical wall of dark glittering granite: quartz, mica, feldspar... and More. Captured by its immense structural power and unparalleled jutting strength, Tian solemnly viewed the geologic formation with deference.

Wondering, but quiet, Reed watched as she struggled to her feet, and faltering, staggering, one step at a time, hobbled to the rock face. Respectfully she forced herself to stand up straight before it, her mind focused, eyes studying its texture, its power, its beauty,

A piece of... *the Puzzle*. Part of... *the Secret*.

"What are you doing?" Reed asked. "It's solid rock," his voice becoming hoarse.

Turning, Tian looked at him; then without speaking, faced the escarpment again... and stepped into the mountain, vanishing from sight.

"What the—this can't be real."

"It is real," she assured reappearing from within the mountain wall. "It is very real."

Still drawn with pain Tian limped toward him, then stopped and turned facing the escarpment. Standing somberly, placing her palms together she raised her arms above her head, then apart to either side in wide sweeping arcs, then down to her sides. Then together again, as if to pray.

Before her the facade of sheer mountainside concealing an extraordinary passage dissolved, evaporated, fading away... wafting, glittery minutiae of starlight dust and glimmering sunbeams floating down, shimmering embers settling upon the ground, sparkling, clear, pure ...the dust remained. And revealed before them was an incredible cavern opening resembling a natural amphitheater... the passageway to Legend Mountain.

"A hologram?" Reed muttered; then he coughed violently, his breathing becoming difficult.

"More," Tian told him without looking back, "much more," gazing upon the immense cavern before them, "it is the truth of all tomorrows and the inscription of all yesterdays. It is the way to the Secret of the Legends."

"The Legends—how can—Legend Mountain collapsed into…" stopping he realized, coughing again, more hoarsely this time. Then with a difficult breath, "Aw man… perpetually overcast sky, a single day that never ends; columns, mountains and spires …it's electromagnetic. It's not a sky; they're supporting a ceiling. We're inside. That's why the trees don't know what season it is, there is no season." He coughed, wheezing, crowing, a barking cough, now almost gasping for air. "We're not on a world… we're inside one."

"More, Reed; much more—but now we must hurry; there is little time left." With notable difficulty, but ignoring the pain, Tian hobbled to him, his breathing by now acute, labored; and kneeling beside him, "Reed, what is wrong?"

Now in respiratory distress, nearly gasping, "Just having a—little trouble—breathing." Stridor onset.

"Reed…" realizing the severity of his problem, "your lips, beneath your eyes, you are turning blue." The venom had made its way into his lungs and she knew within minutes he would die.

"It's called…" he wheezed gulping air, "cyanosis. I can't breathe." Eyes rolling back, he slumped onto his side.

And as he said it, she knew. "We must get inside the mountain. The Legends are Magic." He did not respond. Tian glanced at the mouth of the cave, then back to him. "The Legends can save you." He didn't move.

Panic. "Reed, listen to me. Do not close your eyes. You must stay awake!" Nothing. Frightened and trembling she forced herself to her feet seizing him by both wrists and tried to drag him to the cavern behind her; but in her weakened condition, in spite of her most determined effort, his dead weight was more than she could manage.

Overwrought, "Reed, please— do not go to sleep!" Again she tried to drag him, and again she failed. She slipped and fell, got back up, tried to pull him again, went down again. Boiling angry frustration, desperate, she told him, "Please, Reed, do not die!" She tried to get up but faltered, writhing with razors of pain. Drawing another deep breath, unsteady, willing herself up and finally regaining her feet then straining with all her might, trying to pull him, "We have found the passageway." Staggering a step, the pain slicing inside, she stumbled and tripped.

Pain wrenched a tangle of fire inside her; but once more she forced herself to rise and pulled with all her might, trying to drag him. Crying. Angry. Her face contorted, straining until she could tolerate it no longer—another sharp knife, and she fell. Frustrated, pounding her fists on the ground, "We are so close."

Finally, as Tian tried to stand again an excruciating knot seized her chest ripping through her abdomen doubling her over with an agonizing, tortuous moan. She collapsed beside him, debilitated, unable to help him, herself trembling with pain and panting for air. Pleading, she murmured, "Oh God, please —*please*— do not let my friend die."

Frustration of futility churned with the vivid razors in her guts as tears welled up then slipped free when she blinked, and crying ever so softly, completely exhausted, she closed her hazel eyes...

As the world seemed to pause, so very quiet and still,

Until less than a breath, just a zephyr of wind,

The faintest scuffling from near the base of the sheer rock face,

...And from a burrow concealed among some bushes a walking stick popped out, followed by P.T. Barnum. Quick as a wink he stooped and brushed the dirt from the knees of his bibs, then scampered to a clump of shrubbery nearby and began rummaging around.

Shortly a voice chastised from the hole, "You're going to get us in trouble. It's forbidden to interfere," and elbowing his way out Wilson emerged, gray as life and just as quizzical.

From the bushes P.T. replied, "If we do, I'll just blame it on you —after all, we are identical."

"Oh that's rich," Wilson threw back brushing his hands clean and stomping in Tian and Reed's direction, casting the other a petulant glance.

Busy poking about Barnum ignored his twin, responding, "She found the entrance; that was the intent of design."

Wilson reached the two people; squatted beside them.

Opening slowly, Tian's eyes conveyed her pain inside, and the gratitude in her heart. A weak voice: "P.T.?"

"No, I'm 'Just Plain' Wilson," he replied contritely tenderly moving her hair from her eyes; then indicating over his shoulder with a thumb, "he's P.T. Barnum. He got the good name."

"Wilson sounds wonderful to me."

The dwarf's gaze fixed on her tired eyes; then blinking twice, he smiled. Without further delay he laid a pudgy hand upon Reed's shoulder. "Reed," he said, "can you hear me?"

Eyes fluttering, still lying on his side, "Yeah," he replied almost inarticulately, more hoarse than breath. "What is this, some kind of game?"

"Absolutely not," Wilson assured scratching his chin thoughtfully before confiding, "we are vulnerable when the matrix is in the mix."

Reed tried to move but couldn't, and frustrated, coughed as he said, "That doesn't make any sense."

"I didn't suppose it would," the dwarf admitted.

Thirty feet away Barnum rummaged, short arms and stubby fingers probing the bushes until he found what he was looking for, a plant similar in appearance to the bloodroot. Abruptly he yanked the plant —flower, stem, roots and all— from the ground, allowing time enough for appraisal and wrinkling his nose with satisfaction. He brushed some of the dirt from the fleshy legume rootstalk and without fanfare scampered to a copse of large mushrooms selecting a portly amanita. Quickly pinching the stalk off at the ground he palmed it and scurried to the others. Enroute, he reiterated defensively, "Well, she did find the entrance."

Over a shoulder Wilson conceded, "I know—I know."

Joining them, Barnum, still holding the mushroom in his left hand, stuffed the crooked carrot-like bloodroot into his mouth, indifferent to the moist clumps of soil still stuck to it, or the deep red sap that dribbled down his chin. Presenting quite an exhibition he chewed industriously.

His breathing constricted, dubiously watching the other dwarf, Reed asked, "Wilson, what's going on?"

Evading, "Goodness, we thought you two would never get here; so glad to see you."

"You didn't answer my question." Inhaling hoarsely, "What is going…" coughing.

Again the dwarf didn't respond, instead nervously darted a glance to his twin. "How are you doing, P.T.?"

Speaking through his mouthful and sputtering bits of masticated root, "Fine, fine." With that, he spit the soggy wad into his right hand, and with the mushroom still in his left, cupped them and screwed his palms together squashing and mixing the mulch and mushroom. Tian and Reed both watched, and watched.

Reed winced. "P.T.—*that*—is disgusting."

Looking up from his hands, still kneading the concoction, P.T. grinned mischievously. "Isn't it though." Then rhetorically, kneeling next to Reed he cautioned almost whimsically, "Boys and girls, don't try this at home."[16]

Curious, Tian observed quietly as Reed managed, "P.T. Barnum, you are a perverted little midget." P.T. grinned.

Hovering over his shoulder, a bit anxious, "How are you doing?" Wilson inquired again.

Parting his hands, palms still cupped together the little man inspected his potpourri and smiled broadly. "Just right." Then offering the potion to Reed, ordered, "Here."

"Here what?"

"Eat it."

"—Eat it my ass! You had that shit in your mouth and there's no telling where…" he coughed fitfully, coarsely, a barking cough; then catching his breath, "and that mushroom you just squashed in your grubby little hand was an amanita. They're deadly poisonous."

"Oh do tell, and I recall, once upon a time when a med student put poison in some coffee and the chicory caused a chemical reaction that cured someone's cold."

Reed remembered the museum. "How can you know that?"

Disregarding the question, "No time to explain," P.T. said.

"Oh yeah, well for your information, they executed that guy."

"That was his choice," Wilson interjected.

Studying them, puzzled, "—And how do you guys even know that kind of stuff?"

Throwing his question away Wilson told him, "Just eat it, or in two more minutes you *will* be dead." Quiet, Tian watched as P.T. squatted alongside and held the concoction in front of Reed's mouth.

"Aren't you supposed to pack it on the wound and wrap it with a bandage or something? You know —so it draws out the poison."

"Nah," P.T. answered, "that doesn't work; you gotta eat it."

Wilson warned, "Reed, the toxin has spread to your lungs."

Stalling, "What is it anyway?" aware Wilson was probably telling the truth.

P.T. grinned. "If you'd spent more time studying in Botany and less time chasing girls, you'd know the answer to that." Then sighing whimsically and wrinkling his nose, "But in all honesty, you really don't want to know."

Reed tried to withdraw, protesting, "It smells like spit and has dirt and slimy shit all over it."

Barnum wheedled, "Quit being so finicky; what about your last girlfriend at Montana Tech?"

"How do you know stuff like that?" Making feeble excuses and delaying, "I can't..."

"—That's not important," and P.T. pushed his opened palms against Reed's mouth forcing the mulch in. The man almost gagged and tried to spit it out.

"Reed," Tian cried weakly, *"just—eat—it!"* Her sudden unexpected outburst snatched his attention. "Please... for me," and all protest evaporated. His eyes on hers, his mouth moved. He began to chew, making a face. Drawn with pain she watched; then forcing a frail smile, and softer words, "Swallow it." He gulped, and the concoction went down. Without question, Reed trusted Tian. He knew her. She was his friend.

Wilson turned to Tian. "It will take a minute; now we'll wait."

Making a contorted face with the awful aftertaste, Reed said to the back of Wilson's head, "You still haven't answered my question."

Darting a glance over his shoulder, "What question was that?" innocently feigning forgetfulness, but entirely aware.

"What…" a hoarse cough, "is going—on?" a swallow. Both twins ignored him again focusing on Tian. Irritated he mumbled, "Okay, just go ahead and ignore me, even after you fed me that nasty shit," coughing again but eventually calming down. "Well then maybe… you can at least tell me what the two of you are doing here? And don't tell me you just happened by."

Glancing back, "No indeed," Wilson replied straightforward; then again to Tian as he smiled warmly looking into her eyes, "Someone was listening."

* * *

On Legend Range…

…Forty minutes until sunrise, Lent sounded the alarm. "They're coming!"

"That rock wall," Ames said to Kalo, "—through there."

Nodding, leading the others to the crevasse, "Follow me."

Turning to confront the Hunters and shouting over a shoulder, "Take them to the top of the hill." Answering with a wave Kalo hurried the people prodding each with a hand on their back, into the passageway of the vertical escarpment; while filling a gap in the line Ames surveyed the length of their ranks twirling the scimitar, its song slicing wind. Whirling figure-eights before him, the blade glistened mysteriously reflecting predawn's grey light. Eyes back to the front, a deep breath of resolve.

Packs were everywhere, zigzagging wildebeests coming for them. Imminent.

In line, the hundred-foot escarpment at their backs, standing beside him Lent braced his twibil and looked at the man. Methodically, almost rhythmically he palmed the handle rotating the ax's ponderous dual blades; then back to the enemy. Ready.

Ames recalled being here once before, standing in this very place not so long ago. With a flick of his wrist he swept the scimitar near the ground mimicking swiping through legs; then coldly, "Let's make 'em walk lopsided."

From beneath his shaggy dark hair the youth glared at the approaching arachnids, and simply, soberly replied, "Why let 'em walk at all?"

—White noise of savagery, and trilling, chattering animalistic screams!

Closing in, Night Hunters rushed and leaped, obsidian and fangs engaging courage and blade; weapons flashing time after time, the gigantic spiders steadfastly held at bay. Unable to circle behind the fighters positioned with the vertical wall at their backs, each attack was met with a fusillade of arrows and abhorrent blows of one on one confrontation. Two hundred strong, the Renoloi and Pilgrims stood their ground against twenty times their number, allowing the others time to go through the escarpment passageway.

Fangs flashed recklessly. Razor edges fought back. Trills of howling spiders and screams of dying warriors ricocheted stridently up the overseer of rock face overshadowing the bloodthirsty conflict below. Slashing blades in the dark carving vicious and deep; dark blood in the wind, the monsters just kept coming time and again.

A Hunter snatched him from the ground, its hypodermics sinking in as a second Pilgrim fearlessly charged and dove underneath it whacking through the creature's legs. Another fighter sprang from the ranks hacking a hole in the cretin's side letting gushing gray bubbles; the Hunter downed with the dead warrior still clutched in its fangs.

Down the line another leaped. Pitchfork in hand, the youth hesitated, images flooding his brain: sparkling but lifeless white glowering eyes, bristling crushing pedipalps, drooling mandibles with half-moon serrated edges slick with slime and saliva —then a fleeting glimmer of dark closing fangs. His pitchfork punched through its armor just a split-second too late, twenty-inches of death ripping into his skull —instantly dead. As it happened someone else's sword lopped through the spider's connective neck felling the posterior abdomen, causing the vermin's front half to totter forward still hanging onto its prey. A Renoloi lance speared it, then again, then again, before it finally let go of him viciously turning on her. The creature refused to give up until her fourth furious thrust went all the way through pinning its head to the ground; a writhing groan, twitching with an agonal puff, then finally it lay still.

Together Tondra and Moran fought off alternating attacks, one lunging for her but missing as she dropped and rolled ramming her lance through the tough armor of its underside. His twibil took a chunk and the giant spider recoiled as Tondra, jerking her spear free, rolled backward clear of its legs and onto her feet so swiftly it lost sight of her for just the briefest instant —but enough. Fearlessly she leaped driving her lance into the cephalothorax and out through its eyes. And with a final wretched scream it glared at the intrepid warrior with chattering, vibrating jaws, until it collapsed.

Another came at Moran, fangs wide; an overhand blow hacking into its jaws.

—From alongside, the spear,

But the Hunter's momentum and size was already plowing over him, taking him down—holding onto his ax, still in its head. He was pinned beneath it as it ruthlessly tried to envenom him, narrowly missing more than once, gouging rock and ripping loose tough clods of dirt.

—Again the spear,

Twice more Moran avoided the fangs; but when the black-hearted arachnid started gathering its legs it was clear the next strike would have him.

—*Thwack.*

From down the length of the wall Nitana's arrow ripped through an eye dropping it instantly. Nerves tangled and still on his back, squirming elbows and heels, with Tondra's extended hand Moran managed to wriggle from beneath the dead creature. Finally free and back on his feet, he yanked the ax from its jaws taking a deep breath with the rush of relief. Then he saw two inches of feathers protruding from the dull eye. Nitana had already downed another and was drawing an arrow for a third when he hoisted his weapon offering a grin and salute. Her fleeting smile was her only reply; spiders were everywhere.

Farther down the line a Pilgrim buried his spear in its cephalothorax dispatching a Hunter. Screeching wildly, legs flailing, the arachnid went over backward raking the warrior with a claw —just a sudden tug— that opened his abdomen with an intestine-dump spilling onto his thighs. Taking a step, *that hurt,* he saw his blood-soaked entrails hanging out—then shock. Twitching with involuntary shakes, he collapsed.

Ames and Lent stood fighting together —suddenly rattled and jolted. Lent yelled, "Feel that?" instantly another solid pounding vibration, *going up!*

Heaving from underfoot a shockwave surged, lifting the terrain, throwing them from their feet. Panicked again and screeching wildly the Hunters scrambled, disoriented—freaked. Back onto his feet Ames shot a glimpse over a shoulder to the escarpment crevasse —*no children*— on their way out the other side. This was their chance.

With the landscape trembling and foothills quavering fractures began appearing in the sheer rock face behind them —splintering— great cracks crawling up the cliff wall —widening— beginning to sever. Then splitting, massive chunks of stone started breaking loose from the vertical wall, falling thunderously, crashing and shattering around them. He knew at any moment their escape route may be blocked.

"Everyone through the passage!" Ames shouted over the deafening noise of rumbling ground, fracturing cliff and falling stone. Pulling Lent to his feet, they and the others ran for the chasm leaping over splintering cracks and avoiding uplifting wedges as others shifted and sank, all unstable ground that was quavering and breaking. Dodging toppling slabs shooting scatter-debris stirring whorls of dust, half went through the narrow passage. The rest, a hundred more, were left behind, valiant warriors who had fallen.

Ground still quaking as he emerged from the other side of the crevasse, stopping to catch his breath Ames took a quick look around. In front of him was a place he had been once before. It was a draw rimmed on both sides by craggy granite ledges and jutting rock spires standing among scattered boulders with a number of the nearest formations broken off.

He watched them following Kalo, climbing the draw, making their way toward the top of the hill. Some carrying the smallest children, all helping one another, when one slipped another quickly lending a hand, struggling and falling then getting back up, continuing with unrequited determination born of survival. All of them, young and old alike: children in a schoolyard, their struggle, learning and surviving, the uphill climb of life.

Tectonic thunder. The landscape shuddered violently with fracture-snaps of burrowing vibrations that shifted and wrenched, prying through a land torn with cataclysm and mystery... and bathed in a curtain of rising greylight. Now finally, he knew where they were going, because it was more than an earthquake... much More.

Looking to the summit he saw Kalo, three more steps to the top.

Behind him there was a tremendous crash as a wide section of the high wall collapsed shedding broken slabs in a colossal dump of rock and debris that raised gagging boils of outrushing dust. Huge lopsided blocks of stone tumbled with deafening clatters shattering spires and crushing the few scattered trees below under monstrous smothering settling piles.

In the dissipating dust cloud a Hunter appeared in the expansive breach in the escarpment. Again, they were coming.

Death and claws, it set upon them as three Pilgrims intervened to give those climbing the hill more time, other fighters joining them, forming a line to stop the attack. With more of the adroit killers appearing in the mammoth break, once more primitive weapons mounted a barricade, a salvo of steel against dark chitin and fangs.

Ground quaking at his feet, Ames reeled, eyes flashing again to the brink of the draw, to Kalo. The young Renoloi warrior took a final step, at the top, and looked over the rim. Confused, she spun around and found him, her expression showing doubt. She now stood precisely where he had once been, where he had looked into the throat of the dragon, the zenith of T-Rex hill…

…Where face to face, a Tyrannosaur roared.

* * *

Thirty minutes until sunrise…

…With scores of the giant arachnids pouring through the break in the cliff wall Ames fell in line to help slow their advance. He and others fought then retreated, backing up the draw, defending those behind them; white eyes, raven fangs and sleek obsidian attacking relentlessly. Arrows singing in flight, the glint of sharp flashing steel, determination and muscle driving them back. Viciously, repeatedly Hunters leaped and clawed at the intrepid warriors, each ensuing rush repelled with severed body parts abandoned in the fray. Time to do or die, warriors falling in the ranks.

Pulsating, surging more powerfully with each passing moment, the ground rumbled opening ever-widening crevasses, shifting huge boulders and shaking longstanding spires until some severed and toppled. Deeply underground incredible tectonic plates were grinding with impregnable strength, the divergent plates somewhere below separating and crumbling, forming a linear zone of weakness. Throughout the region landscape continued fracturing and splintering preempting its destiny of cataclysmic change. Because it was more than a primitive world… much More.

From the summit of the draw Kalo cried down, "Mr. Ames, there is no passageway! It is only a volcanic basin."

But he knew, *that can't be*.

Behind Kalo, on the backside of T-Rex ridge lay an expansive cone basin of what appeared to be a dormant volcano, its interior plain a bowl-shaped depression hundreds of feet deep and spanning many miles. Within the vast crater valley there was no vegetation, not one blade of grass. It lay barren and dry, a dehydrated moonscape, desiccated and sun-baked as a parched desert waterhole beneath a hot August sun.

The scimitar flashed with a spray of splatter-gray cloud that divided night-vision eyes; the Hunter went down. Thick spider blood still dripping from his blade and Kalo's words still in his head, he kept scaling the ravine, trying to think. *It has to be there.* Suddenly another Hunter —swinging, missing— and that quickly Lent's twibil sent it over backward, rolling downhill. *Keep moving. Don't stop. Think!*

Constantly climbing and fighting as they fell back, the warriors kept the children ahead of them, all gradually making their way toward the summit.

Alone at the top Kalo stood waiting for Ames' reply as Tondra, still seventy yards below, was clawing her way up the hill when an arachnid bounded toward her from behind. She would not see it coming and in less than a heartbeat Kalo's arrow was in flight, and in the time that the heart beat, it ripped through glistening exoskeleton precisely centered between glowing eyes.

Too terrified to move, a small child squatted on the ground, crying. Tondra picked her up. "Close your eyes, little one," she whispered gently as the child flung her arms around her neck.

Protectively watching and covering those on the slide Kalo called again. "Mr. Ames, there is no passageway; what shall we do?"

Scrambling up the grade, searching for the answer—*pieces... a puzzle.*

The Riddle:
> *Alpha and Omega reformation... mettled.*
> *Galactic composition replenished... begun.*
> *Time captured, an hourglass... trickled away.*
> *The amalgamate turbidity... unsettled.*
> *Legends sleep within the throat of... the dragon.*
> *Shall rise to the light, invoked... the last day.*

He muttered, "Dormant volcano," and… "pieces of a puzzle, words of a riddle," and… "they must be put together, all brought together." Reciting to himself, then more quickly, over again, faster. Again, the riddle. Still climbing, scrambling hands and knees over loose rock —and at last— "Keys to the three-lock box!" he triumphed aloud.

From the summit, "Mr. Ames…"

Excited, he yelled, "It's us!"

She cried, "…the Legends are not here. What shall we do?"

"Yes Kalo, they are! The Legends *are* there!"

* * *

Across the river, in a Forsaken Land…

…The volcano vented steam and ash of opaque plume that rose in sullen updrafts to a congealing sky born of fire and molten rock. The landform cauldron disgorged orange bubbling froth of abomination that boiled over the rim and poured down the mountain like blebby candlewax of despair. Churlish, the particulate canopy spread out once more creeping insidiously across the dim ashen sky while heat lightning played a violent frolic of now-you-see-me —flash in the dark, then again over there— another coruscating, vanishing flare. Splashing through charcoal and gray, the flickering white light trailed signature sparks of afterburn embers that faded away. It was all an omen scrawled in predawn grey.

At the base of the volcano, cloaked in shadows and menace, from within the very darkest abyss and the depths of the chasm, came the hollow, gritty, monochromatic sound of vibram sole crunching stone beneath three hundred pounds of muscle, evil, and humanity's hate.

He was the epitome of meanness; from his stubble-gray hair, pockmarked face and fat porous nose, to nicotine-stained, chipped boxer's teeth clenching a stub of cigar. With a tree-trunk-thick chest and iron-muscle arms, to the intimidating scowl spoken with deep-set eyes: penetrating, cold, hateful... and the gray of death. Wearing black spit-polished boots and a perfectly tailored military uniform… Smith stepped forward, out from the Dark.

Surveying the intended acquisition he glowered with derisive contempt. Purposefully he turned to the volcanic mountain towering behind him, eyes traveling the abrupt faces of congealed igneous rock. Considering, he stood silently a moment, and satiated, listened to the guttural rumblings and sizzle of pulsating magma within the monstrous mountain.

Brow furrowing, his eyes narrowed in a glint of evil. "It is time." Sinister, malevolent, whispered words.

From hairline fractures in the obsidian walls, basaltic slides and runs of scattered pumice; from cracks and fissure wormtrails furrowing the mountain face, emerged liquid amorphous slime of black motion. Crawling and slithering, mimicking serpentine movement his army crept forth from hiding. Oozing out, bubbling up in raven foam and gliding as slime trails; then bunching, gathering and coagulating they changed to wriggling black larval maggots. The Dark Ones squirmed and twisted blinking oscillating miniature red eyes that peered from a primordial jet-black exudate of liquefied ooze.

The Dark Forces grew acquiring the size of tarantulas. Repugnant, prodigious maggots squirming restlessly in black oily mounds, they concealed the mountain's slides with a flowing commotion of putrid waves and wretched sickness. Impatiently they rose and fell, sliding in segmented coils of undulating larval piles, until from somewhere within the multitude of smidgen scarlet eyes there came a repulsive mongering utterance. "We are waiting, my liege."

Malignantly, "Patience… very soon now," Smith revealed.

* * *

Legend Mountain…

…"Listen to that thunder," Reed said scanning the overcast.

"How quaint," P.T. observed sarcastically.

To Barnum, "Not much time left," Wilson advised. Then to Reed, "Can you move your legs yet?"

Looking at his feet and grimacing as though wrenching them loose from an invisible trap, finally flexing his ankles and wiggling his toes, "Yeah, some."

"Well keep working at it, and do it quickly," Wilson fretted. He and P.T. scurried to either side of Reed, each grabbing an arm and sitting him upright with an ungracious, swift jerk.

Ambivalent, "Aw jeez—take it easy you guys."

"No time," P.T. told him. "Gotta hurry."

"Your legs, Reed," Wilson instructed, "bend your knees." As the man began slowly to draw his legs, much like someone carefully limbering stiff joints, the dwarfs bustled to his feet, each shoving one forcefully enough so his heels bumped his butt tipping him over backward.

"Give me a break, will ya?" he groused.

Disregarding Reed, Wilson turned to Tian, "Can you make it?" She forced a nod and fragile smile, affirmation enough for the dwarf and he mindfully helped her to her feet. Carefully both little men and Tian began toward the cavern entrance.

With perhaps just a tinge of indifference P.T. called over a shoulder without looking back, "Time to go," as mounting thunderclaps slammed overhead.

"What's the big hurry?" Still grumbling but struggling to his feet in spite of himself, taking two wavering steps, following them —the ground suddenly heaving— shaking rigorously, shifting sideways, teeth-chattering hard, a powerful quake.

Teetering, "Jesus…" falling, "Christ on a…" he hit the ground, "crutch." He lay ineffective, being bounced helplessly by the pounding vibrations of seismic activity. His head rattling, "Oh…" teeth chattering, "jerk me…" body jostled, "with a frantic dither."

"Reed—" Tian cried weakly, "hurry!"

Rolling onto his side he watched them making their way toward the cavern's imposing amphitheater entrance. "Easy for you to say," his vision vibrating like a television image with flawed tracking, the rumbling now pounding above and echoing below. "I'll just wait—for the tremor to stop—before I get up—okay?"

Wilson turned succinctly sternly stomping his foot, "Reed, quit fooling around; we've gotta go—now!"

The dwarf was dead serious, so he forced himself up, staggering and stumbling, following them into the gray-black megalith of the cavern and Legend Mountain.

* * *

On T-Rex hill...

..."Mr. Ames," she cried, "the Legends are not here. What shall we do?"

"Yes Kalo, they are; the Legends *are* there!" focusing on the girl on the rim of the ridge. "There is no passageway, but the Legends are there." His mind working; the thought of his friend and the woman he loved. "You must find Tian. Reach inside, within you; use your gift. Call to her; she will hear you."

"But I am only a Renoloi warrior; how can I do such a thing?"

"You're wrong—" he yelled as an arachnid leaped from behind him the same instant —*thwack*— Lent's twibil splashed through its head splattering Ames' back with muck. Concentrating on Kalo the man barely looked back. Lent didn't understand, nor could he realize the scope of their conversation; but he remained close to Ames, covering his back, knowing this must be important.

"But Mr. Ames..."

"—Kalo, *believe!*" he cried out. "It's us! *We* are the keys to the three-lock box."

She looked at the volcanic basin, then again to him. "But it is only an empty valley."

"—No, the Legends are there!"

Uncertain but willing, "What must I do?"

"Call to Tian. Only you can find her!" Confident now, he told her, "Reach inside, search within yourself. The riddle is the catalyst. Recite the riddle!"

379

On the summit of the ridge Kalo turned, faced the volcanic basin, and whispered…

"Alpha and Omega reformation… mettled.

Galactic composition replenished… begun."

And as she recited the parable, inside, Kalo felt it. *Yes, because I believe.* Repeating again, softly, closing her eyes, drifting away, entranced—a fragment of destiny, going within, reciting…

"Time captured, an hourglass… trickled away.

The amalgamate turbidity… unsettled.

Legends sleep within the throat of… the dragon."

Raising her arms, spreading them wide, drawn by a compelling and mystical energy from out there and within, reciting… an earthquake tearing the world apart at its seams.

* * *

Inside Legend Mountain cavern…

…Exhausted, panting for breath, Tian writhed with pain. Doubled over she fell to her knees; but refusing to cry, even though she still hurt so badly inside. On either side of her 'Just Plain' Wilson and P.T. Barnum each lay a compassionate pudgy hand upon her shoulder trying to comfort as best they could.

The earthquake persisted; ground vibrating intensely, cavern walls and floor trembling, quavering, a primitive world shaking around them.

Finally catching up with them and having recovered from the effects of the Hunter's neurotoxin, Reed staggered inside the cave, his limbs functional again. He quickly knelt beside Tian gently taking the laser from her, slinging the weapon over his shoulder as she turned her face to the floor wrapping her arms around her abdomen trying to squeeze the pain away, her torment now almost unbearable.

Lovingly, caressing her cheek with his hand he reassured, "We're gonna make it, Babe."

Her brow beaded with perspiration and her body slivers of pain, she looked up at him and said, "Yes, we will… my friend."

Frustrated, irritated with his inability to comfort her, Reed turned to Barnum. "P.T.—do something. Can't you help her?"

Shaking his head the dwarf apologized, "There's nothing we can do."

That made him angry. "Why not?"

The world shuddered. Flashes of lightning.

The sky trembled. Hammering thunder.

Understanding, P.T. told him calmly, "We don't know how," as gently, lovingly, he stroked the Renoloi's head.

"Well, don't you have a magic lamp —you know— and we get three wishes or something?"

P.T. frowned, "Cute, Reed."

"Well?"

"—Reed, hush," Tian entreated lightly laying her fingers upon his lips. Eyes round with surprise he quit talking and watched as she slowly turned her face to the cavern ceiling, closing her eyes. Her lips began to move, only murmuring at first, unintelligible, then more loudly... and Reed heard Tian say:

"Alpha and Omega reformation... mettled.
Galactic composition replenished... begun.
Time captured, an hourglass... trickled away.
The amalgamate turbidity... unsettled.
Legends sleep within the throat of... the dragon.
Shall rise to the light, invoked... the last day."

Pieces of a Puzzle, words of a riddle...
They all must be put together, brought together.
Kalo, Tian, Ames. Keys to a three-lock box,
...The Secret of the Legends.

Amazed, "What—is—going—on?" Reed whispered.

Landscape vibrating...

A Mountain rumbled. Thunder-scatter splashing rattling pulse-booms.

...An entire world shuddering!

Wilson answered reverently, "More than you know."

"What?"

Barnum mildly scolded, "Reed, please." He turned, studied the dwarf, saying no more.

Entranced, Tian recited the riddle again, more clearly… then louder.

The Mountain shifted…

Everywhere, everything, an entire world quavering, the canopy roaring throughout with explosions of thunder.

A *Primitive World* Trembled,

…And Quaked!

P.T. Barnum smiled mischievously. "Reed, I strongly suggest you take this opportunity to grasp some object firmly."

"What—why?" Reed asked. The entire mountain vaulted. *"Holy shit!"*

"Because Mr. Ames and the others need your help…" P.T. beamed; then amidst the roar and confusion of a trembling, tumultuous world, P.T. Barnum yelled,

"…And we are going up!"

CHAPTER TWENTY

Twenty minutes until sunrise…

…A fragment of destiny, going within, reciting on the summit of the ridge Kalo watched venerably, with wonder as the basin and mountains quaked at her feet. The volcanic valley began cracking and giving way with spiderweb rifts unearthing sinkholes that collapsed as slabs lurched exposing monstrous wedges of shattering rock. Before her immense chunks of moving landscape snapped then splintered and crumbled, expelled with intense gutsy crushing forces of grinding shearwave compression. Shaking and quavering the surface was crackling and breaking, razing destruction heaving huge slabs with brittle hard breaks and gritty fracturing sounds.

Pushing through… the peak emerged.

Sliding aside colossal plates of the volcanic basin cascaded crashing together, pulverizing one another with the oppressive weight and unimaginable pressure of converging terrain. Uplifted and sideslipping they smashed into one another, some overriding and others subducted, being ground under with the awesome power of tectonic rift and cataclysmic movement. Grating upon one another they grumbled echoes from the depths as unbelievable sheets of earth and rock skidded and crumbled then rolled until it poured.

And incredibly… the mountain began rising.

While in the Forsaken Land—

Spewing sulfuric poisons the volcanic cloud hung as congealed sable-gray smog above the vent of toxic amber corona. Sultry with acidic steam and thickened with ash, the plume churned volcanic and dark, a billowing malignant child slowly rising from a caldera of misery forming an atmosphere of ominous satanic halo.

Weeping, the volcano's glass-like obsidian cliffs dripped sizzling rivulets of fiery orange pungent with gagging, regurgitated rotten-egg stench. Splattering, it poured onto the creeping commotion of pandemic pestilence waiting to be summoned, the flow of molten firefall pumping life and energy into the unnumbered maggot larvae of Dark Forces waiting so impatiently there.

Across the river—

In a tumultuous rattling world Legend Mountain rose, its peak pushing up from the expansive basin like a mighty Goliath of monolithic dark stone shimmering of feldspar, mica and quartz heaving huge slabs of overlay aside. Colliding, grinding and sliding, the ground moved with grating, shattering roars more thunderous than the concussion-rush of booster rockets bound for space and the unknown. With the incredible upheaval terrain shifted then crumbled, outcroppings and ledges falling as entire cliffs and ridges toppled then slid thrusting and crushing vast sheets of landscape so violently it seemed the entire world was being torn apart.

The draw—

Climbing, all of them climbing. Shaken and struggling with the unparalleled seism, warriors kept scaling the ravine bound for the rim of T-Rex hill. Many were stumbling and falling, but were somehow mysteriously spared from the pushed-up rockslides cascading over the rim of the dormant volcanic basin as Legend Mountain rose in its center.

Hunters trying to circle around the resolute army were crushed in the deluge of huge tumbling rock and onerous sliding slabs, or buried beneath suffocating volumes of sloughing dirt and debris. Being dragged under hundreds of them were squashed and milled to smears of sticky gray ooze and greasy stone-ground black powder veined with unsightly slime. Rolling boulders and sliding granite blocks pushing marauding flows of suffocating dirt and pulverized rock poured down in all directions except the narrow draw where the people climbed.

A world quaking, trembling—

With awesome splintering strength moving untold volumes of landscape, the mysterious, incredible mountain slowly rose from below; and through the gloom of predawn grey the coarse crystalline granite glittered with sparkling, shimmering might. Consummate, powerful and indomitable, staggering, center stage amid the intensity of shearwave destruction, unfailing, Legend Mountain climbed.

Inflamed, the Forsaken Land—

Volcanic explosions pounded from the landform spewing orange-melt and wrath with surging waves of querulous magma blasting flame and pulsing steam to an expanding, ever-darkening sky. Thunder peeled in the clouds and rattled with the wind as the firmament glowed amber with anger etched by crooked fingers of tainted flashing fire. The abject barren countryside was absorbed in unworldly omen and darkness as scintillating lightning illuminated the Forsaken Land beneath eerily demonic clouds, drifting for miles and miles.

While across a river—

Still rising. From the depths of this world Legend Mountain continued to ascend, incredible beyond scope, invincible beyond measure, beyond mortal comprehension...

...Invoked.

Pushing up. Landscape trembling, an entire world rumbling, until finally its peak jutted through the churning amalgam of volcanic clouds towering somewhere high above. What once had been, then was mysteriously gone...

...Legend Mountain had returned again.

On T-Rex hill, the plateau—

Kalo stood still, unable to speak, witnessing the most unbelievable event of her life. She viewed majesty beyond mystery, an enigma beyond imaginings... and More.

When at last the mountain stopped rising there was a ground-shaking shudder and incredible surge of the jolt, followed by leftover tumbling rocks clattering aside, and dilatory remnant trickles rolling into the shadows of predawn grey. Then finally the sprinkling-scatter of loose gravel and dirt dribbling from nearly vertical rock faces, forming inclines of soft piles.

Before her, a massive amphitheater-shaped opening in the sheer mountain wall…

A pause. Almost silence.

…And from within the huge cavern came the slightest moan of labored breathing, and shuffling sounds of bare feet treading upon errant loose stones, followed by small crunches of work boots—children's, size twelve.

Together, Reed helping Tian, the four emerged onto the strip of level ground, a plateau now encircling the mountain peak. She stepped laboriously, a halting walk, bent with pain, but her eyes conveying joy and relief when she saw Kalo standing on the summit of T-Rex ridge. P.T. and Wilson marched side by side, purposefully and businesslike, low-key expressions, short legs pacing and Lilliputian arms vigorously pumping their pint-sized bodies along.

Elated, marveling at their return and watching while the four quietly approached, Kalo's countenance conveyed amazement and incomprehension of the miniature twins, the identical P.T. Barnum and 'Just Plain' Wilson. Her heart welled with admiration for Reed, destined to become one of her dearest friends; and for Tian, an undying love and respect that would transcend all limits of imagination.

Eyes passing from one to the other emanating unspoken warmth, their mutual smiles said it all, more than words would ever be able. After so long, finally reunited.

Warriors running—

By now Pilgrims and Renoloi were on T-Rex ridge hurrying upon the level strip of ground circling the towering peak of Legend Mountain, anticipating another attack. Not knowing how they could be there, but pressed for time, the others only glanced and wondered as Tian, helped by Reed and Kalo, hobbled to the edge of the slide at the top of the draw. Kalo and Reed on either side, Tian between them, they looked down the hill.

In the draw—

Ames, Lent and Nitana stood together fighting on the near side of the ravine while Tere, Deet and many others held the center of the slide; and Tondra, still carrying the child, and Moran fought alone on the opposite flank. Consumed in combat, people were scaling the hill with the arachnids pursuing from below, the warriors steadfastly repelling each attack.

It was pandemonium of climbing, stumbling and danger that came as a furious rush of demonic fangs and glowering eyes. The battleline was a confusion of flashing blades and glistening exoskeleton, defiant warriors valiantly warding off the relentless horde in disarray of sight and sound where combatants were all splattered —some drenched— in gray and crimson blood.

Seeing the Hunters below and P.T. Barnum's words still lingering in his head, *because Mr. Ames and the others need your help,* anger began simmering inside him; his eyes narrowing, hand tightening upon the weapon. Without a grain of reservation the pulse laser came up, and from the hip —Reed fired!

—Shrill whines and bright flashes scattering spray of pulse laser flames, his voice rang from the top of the hill…

"…Hey Doc, we're *baaack!*"

Ames heard him and reeled —and there— standing upon the ridge was Reed, one fist clenching the weapon, the other Tian, flaming muzzle blasts sizzling into the horde. Flaxen hair listless and limp, he saw her, and felt it, the enduring love in her pain-stricken eyes. And standing with them was the one who had persevered alongside him as confidante, mentor and inspiration, Kalo, the young Renoloi warrior.

Already on the plateau with the children, Seana immediately looked with the sound of his voice, her heart welling with disbelief and happiness, eliciting tears of joy in her pained, tired eyes. Seeing him she whispered hushed words heard only by her, "My Reed, you have finally come home."

Eyes narrowed, holding a weapon of war in his hand and revenge sewn with resolute wire in his heart, from the summit of T-Rex hill Reed killed the hostiles with the justice of retribution and deliberate cold-blooded vengeance. He killed and killed —for all the pain he and others had suffered, for friends who were lost in this harsh and primitive world. He killed and killed —for all those who died by obsidian fangs merely because they were on the same world by happenstance. He killed and killed —for those wanting only to live in peace, doing no harm, simply struggling to survive…

—Shrill whines, the bright flashes—he fired and killed!

…*Payback!*

The creatures below were possessed with insatiable hostility and the proclivity for unreasoning violence —he fired and killed. The Hunters would not, could not leave them alone —he fired and killed. They had pursued the people with unrelenting savagery, and hounded, bedeviled and hunted them with incessant villainy —he fired and killed. Now it was their turn, for all the senseless, abject indecency. Repayment in kind. Now, Reed the piper would exact their due —so he fired and fired and slaughtered and killed!

—Shrill whines, bright flashes—white shattering blasts!

Linear light of ripping power seared from the precipice like tracer rounds tearing ragged holes in hateful black hulls. Ectoplasm clouds splashed gray in the air and rained windsprays of stench as chitin shards spun and twirled like broken china chips in a furious storm.

Below, a spider leaped—

The intercepting light blast shredded the Hunter's head with such horrific force it blew completely apart shooting its marble eyes out. Then again and again, whirling dismembered pieces spinning as gray vapor and broken spare parts. Tens —multiples of tens— spiders died in sync with the furious drone of the laser's pulsing white light.

Nitana, Lent, Ames and the others resumed climbing, all now approaching the summit. Pilgrims and Renoloi defending midway across the draw were also nearing the top, however, carrying the child Tondra and Moran had fallen behind, so others from the center of the ravine began moving laterally to help them. Now below the ranks of the withdrawing army and alone on the far flank, they were the most vulnerable targets —and they had been noticed.

Singling them out, Hunters appeared from everywhere, clamoring over boulders, crawling around broken spires, clattering and clawing as they closed in. Converging in a sinuous black commotion they swarmed the ravine as an eye-speckled shroud of imminent death.

Laser streaks flashing past on either side or inches over their heads, Moran and Tondra were being overrun by the horde; he swinging his twibil, she wielding her spear. Hunters kept exploding around them, as stabbing and slicing they kept moving backward, fighting as they retreated while more fighters descended to assist them. An arachnid leaped —above them— detonating in midair and spinning away. But by now black chitin was everywhere, overtaking and overpowering them.

Stepping back again Moran stumbled as three monsters pounced. The quickest swish of sound sliced air as Kalo's arrow sank in one's head. It tumbled. A flash of ripping light. Another burst. But the third was viciously upon him, its fangs boring between his ribs, the young warrior ballooning —swollen, liquefying— as a spear from above slammed home through its eyes. But Moran was already dead when the spider collapsed. Not quite in time.

Alone now, Tondra rammed her lance into one's jaws as a sudden lightflash splashed through its head, the violent impact-spray pitching her off-balance. She stumbled, went down. But even as she fell, the courageous warrior protectively tossed the child up the hill as far as she could, away from the claws coming from below. Petrified, the terror-stricken child landed and cringed on the ground too frightened to move, almost even to breathe; then she opened her eyes, recognized him —and she screamed, *"Uncle Reed!"*

Eyes to the voice, he saw her, wresting torrents of emotion and vehement dread —gigantic dark killers closing— heart stalled with the vision of Jade an instant from death, brain pounding and burning with adrenaline rush; analyzing, calculating, not a second to spare.

His soul burst with flames of anger, hate and revenge, and in that single instant a surreal image flashed through his mind. A different day, another battle, a monstrous Tyrannosaur slamming into a gnarled tree in the lowland, its roots ripping from the ground with an erupting huge wad of dirt, the tree shuddering and listing. Then the haunting, frail echo of scream as Tarin plummeted to her death beyond his reach.

Panic rush…

That forbidding chill of frigid fear and deluge-flush of nausea. That sickening feeling wrenching ice shivers from the back of the neck down the length of the spine. Helplessness, that spear of frustration and the anger that it boils in the guts. Cold electricity racing toward fingertips and toes stabbing anxiety swollen-up in the groin.

…All within that solitary millisecond of realization.

And the sudden stone cold of unequalled resolve that swept through him —*No—not again—not today. Little girl, you will not die!*

Tondra screamed, *"—Jade, run!"*

—Reed, moving!

He let go of Tian as he leaped from the plateau. Attention riveted, deciphering critical information: Jade and Tondra trying to flee, Hunters everywhere, more coming up, arrows pouring upon them. His eyes absorbing images that were smears of speed then transmitting encoded neuro-impulses in circumstantial bits of data. In the whirlwind his brain analyzed calculating threats —search, focus, target, squeeze— whines and bright flashes. As quickly as his eyes swept identifying one arachnid then another, the laser blasts spit through them with the devastating force of sound pulsed with light.

Running down the hill, furrowing tracks with his heels and kicking out stones with his feet, skidding onto his buttocks, firing, sliding, rising again, running and firing —undeviating— focused upon Tondra and Jade.

On the near flank and almost to the summit, Ames, Lent and Nitana saw him and spun. Nitana's arrow took one. From the precipice Kalo let fly felling another, more arrows whisking into the horde from the rim of the plateau.

Trying to get to her feet Tondra rolled sideways, onto her knees, but was unable to stand as a Hunter landed then rose up directly above her. Poised to strike, its chelicerae were opening, fangs dripping — flash of laser explosion— hurtling it back. Still more black chitin and claws crowding in, as quickly as the first vanished another was on top of her appearing so suddenly there was no escape. Kalo's arrow split a hole in its eyes and the ghoul collapsed upon the Renoloi knocking her down a second time. Trying to free herself, Tondra groaned wedging her legs against the coarse rocks and prying with her arms, another exploding above her —then another.

Finally, she squeezed free and made it to her knees just as — *snap*— black fangs sank into her throat and the back of her neck. Eyes frozen wide with instantaneous terror and pain, and the penetrating, constricting force choking her scream; she reached grabbing the fang —a sudden gush— and felt instant nausea with the gruesome fluid-rush of injection that flushed through her head and boiled into her chest. Frothing liquid bloat —she inflated— gagged and was dead.

On hands and knees, scampering up the hill, too terrified even to breathe, Jade saw the grisly murder of the woman who'd just sacrificed her life for the slimmest chance that she might survive. An arachnid spied her. The pounce. Jade screamed!

Reed lunged, his brain tracking the action in graphic broken-motion —just an instant of awareness— a sequence of vivid pictures flicking in his mind.

Fractions of a heartbeat slicing One Second…

In Ten Parts,

9/10th   …U

…Jade's stricken expression of horror, terrified blue eyes flashing anxious and round. Matted blonde hair stuck to her face, ends tossed in the wind as her mouth opened framing her cry.

8/10th   …N

…The gleaming blue-black sheen of obsidian as the gigantic spider came arched in a Notre Dame hunch. Bale-hook claws with serrated edges, barbed legs spread wide, dropping like a sleek parachute of glistening death.

7/10th   …C

…Sliding, the crunching sensation of his heels furrowing in gravel and cool dirt on his feet; then winds of silence in his head, sound blotted out. Sweeping whorls of confusion, surroundings a blur, absorbed within the intense focus of absolute concentration, all else lost in a smear of distance and speed.

6/10th   …L

391

…Vile, clustered, white glowering eyes peering loath from the darkness, the prismatic mosaic of his own image reflected and staring back in his face. A void without soul from the warehouse of Hell.

5/10th …E

…Finger touching the trigger, solid steel in his hand. Wrist turning, muzzle rising with that sticky-slick feeling of sweat lubricating his palm.

4/10th …R

…Lethal pedipalps open, bristling, repulsive and wide. Menacing slimy dripping jaws, glistening drool of saliva; curved hollow fangs closing.

3/10th …E

…Buttocks into the dirt —sliding— Jade's frail huddled body coming in along the left side. Reaching out for her —and touching— her thin arms and legs, so very tiny.

2/10th …E

…The Hunter's sparkling night-vision eyes, and fangs weeping —pumping— squirting yellow venom. Sweeping in, so ugly, so black and hideous, so very close.

1/10th …D

…Arm going around her, pulling her near —body contact— and momentum, still sliding —*lean back!*— going beneath it, *just above us* —the strike.

—*Snap!*

Six inches away, a lemon-cloud mist.

—*Tick!*

…One second had passed —*the son of a bitch missed!*

Confused, the Hunter wickedly peered down at the two who evaded its bite. With Jade cradled in his arm at his side, braced on an elbow, knees flexed, heels set in the dirt, the freak of nature above them… Reed glared contempt. *Revenge.*

Then deliberately and slowly the monster reared onto its hind legs. It began as a gurgle slowly rising to chatter, becoming the cackle —then that trilling white noise of savagery and ungodly animalistic scream!

Maniacally clawing and shrieking the Night Hunter towered over them glistening with black as impenetrable as its villainy; gnashing its fangs, staring down upon them, it drooled dripping venom… then it opened them wide.

Reed's eyes narrowed, drawn with vengeance —defiance— words hard as ice, dead and cold as raw winter wind… when he said, "Not this time you greasy motherfucker. *Eat this!*"

—A shrill whine, blinding flash—and again, again, and again!

The enormous spider exploded in sequences of torn craters and muck: holes shredding its head, shattering pedipalps, mandibles, chelicerae and fangs. Splattered then vanishing, its eyes disappeared like ripped buttons in clouds of gray wind. Laserfire slammed through its abdomen scattering its legs like twirling ratchet-joint sticks that whiplashed and spun; and as the ruptured hull began to collapse impact lightning bolts heaved it back up —chunks and flying pieces— just swirling black bits. Coming apart as it somersaulted, it blew up in a cloud filled with dark spinning scraps that were shredded and burned by blazing light blasts —blinding flares, tearing power, streaking sabers of white light— until nothing was left.

It stopped.

As suddenly as it began it was over, only remnant shreds twirling out of the air spiraling down. In a settling fog of torn pieces and mist the Hunter was gone.

Strangely, it seemed quiet again… momentarily.

Holding her safe in his arm as he rose to his feet, Reed squeezed her tenderly with an, *I love you*, hug. And wrapping her small arms around his neck like a miniature clinging koala, she joyfully snuggled against him letting out a heart-wrenching sigh. Her 'Uncle Reed' had finally come home.

Beaming childishly she gave him a quick peck on the cheek and a jubilant, "Uncle Reed, you kept your promise!" The tiny girl possessed with 'Thumbelina' courage bubbled, "I knew you would come back—and you did!"

The smile revealing more than his words, "Is that so?" he asked. "How could you be so sure?"

Blinking with joy she reminded, "Because you absolutely promised."

Commotion seemed to resume.

His attention again shifting between her and the arachnids, he began strafing, taking them out. "Yeah, Kiddo; and I never break a promise. But right now, we gotta go." Carrying Jade, he and the others began up the slide, slaughtering Hunters with every step.

Below in the draw there were still hundreds of them; but many seemed confused by the quake. Quavering ground was still unearthing huge chunks of stone creating onerous pours that pushed down the slopes dragging Hunters under cascades of sliding debris or squashing them beneath enormous tumbling rocks. But they were still down there, and they were still coming.

—White noise of savagery, crashing, rolling, crushing boulders, and trill animalistic screams!

From the security of his arm, guilelessly Jade studied the dead spiders strewn on the slide leaking thickening puddles, then wrinkled her nose and innocently professed, "Nasty shit."

Offhand, "Don't talk like that," Reed snapped, downing another, "I'll wash your mouth out with soap." Eyes fixed on him, Jade accepted the scolding without protest as he killed several more, heels digging in, backward up the hill. "Well," he finally relented, "under the circumstances, I guess we can let it go," glancing at her, then back to the Hunters, "—but just this once. Don't say that again."

"I will not say it again." Even though he corrected her, she didn't really mind, because finally, in his arms, she had her adored 'Uncle Reed'.

Archers along the rim of the plateau sent unending salvos of arrows into the arachnids trying to scale the hill, while fighting as they climbed, Reed and the last of the warriors continued making their way up the slide.

* * *

From the deep and unknown…

...And the darkness of space; thousands, hundreds of thousands of them, absorbed within absolute silence, too many to count. They were coming.

* * *

Twelve minutes until sunrise...

...Nitana, Lent and Ames stepped onto T-Rex ridge, Lent and Nitana immediately circling the rim to the opposite side of the draw and dropping down the slide to lend Reed a hand. With the pulse laser and additional help, he could take care of himself; Ames had someone else on his mind.

"John!" the sound of her voice sent a rush to his heart, and through the ranks defending the summit plateau he saw her. There, waiting, she was reaching out for him, weakly hobbling toward him, her face streaked with tears but defying the pain, overjoyed, laughing and crying at the same time. At long last, she and Reed had made it home.

Weaving between people defending the ridgetop, pushing through the shoulder-to-shoulder crowd and into each other's arms; they embraced. So wonderful, so warm, to touch once again, the security of two halves become whole, reunited after so long and so much hardship. Their lips touched, ever so gently at first; then more fervently with passion and the intensity of their love. Parting briefly, then again holding one another tightly enough to chase the lingering emptiness from their souls... and finally send it away. At last, they had each other again.

Just one more kiss, their faces barely inches apart; then allowing the rapture to wane as concern returned with worry etched in its place. "John," she whispered, "we must get everyone into the cavern."

Quickly evaluating their army and rampart, considering it to be an ideal position, "Why? This plateau is perfect; from here we can wipe them out once and for all."

"No John, you do not understand."

"She's right, Mr. Ames," the dwarf concurred, stepping out from behind her.

395

"P.T., what are you doing here?"

Shaking his head understandably and indicating with a thumb, "No, I'm 'Just Plain' Wilson; he's P.T. Barnum. He got the good name." Barnum also sauntered into view offering a succinct nod and impish grin.

Ames began to ask, but reconsidered, trusting Tian implicitly, suspecting her intuition was more than conjecture; and somehow, he knew. Looking around and commanding loudly, motioning the people away from the precipice, "Everyone fall back—into the cavern!" Ushering the children, they all began toward the massive amphitheater opening of Legend Mountain; and looking down the slide, "Reed, get your carcass up here; we're withdrawing."

Tossing a glance over his shoulder, "On our way, Doc." Then, "—Withdrawing, to where?" As he, Nitana and Lent headed toward the summit, in passing he remarked, "Possibly he failed to notice that not more than fifty yards behind him a kick-ass mountain just popped up out of the ground."

"That's not something a prudent individual would tend to overlook, now is it, Sir?" Lent asked, agreeing with Reed and speaking for the first time.

Quizzically Reed gave him the once-over then glanced at Nitana as she reached for an arrow offering a manufactured evanescent grin, then shot a spider. Turning back to the kid, "Sir?" Reed repeated capriciously.

"Perhaps a bit maudlin; just trying to be respectful," promptly offering his hand. "I'm Lent."

Reciprocating, "—Reed," one quick jerk comprising the handshake. Reed turned strafing the arachnids and the trio continued toward the top. Climbing, to Lent: "Where'd you learn to talk like that, kid?"

"Like what?" his innocuous habit, faking the simpleton.

"Your diction is rather articulate."

Lent, not really involved in the fight because the archers and Reed were holding the spiders at bay below them, offered pragmatically, "Comic books."

"Comic books?" Crooking an eyebrow Reed pursed his lips conceding, "Yeah well, why not; really doesn't surprise me a whole lot." Then to Nitana: "Fuckit—he talks better than I do."

"Everyone talks better than you."

Reed again, to Lent: "Ah, don't mind her; she's just teasing."

"Whatever you say," Nitana's low-key response.

"Don't bug me; I'm busy." He quit firing checking the toll; then a lateral glance, "No pun intended." Back to the youth: "You're okay, Lent; I like you."

Nitana bantered wryly, "We all suspected you would."

Reed, to Nitana: "Missed me, did you?" The smile.

Encouraged that he'd taken a liking to him Lent decided, "Reed, you and I shall become fast friends." Then to Nitana: "Wouldn't that be nice?"

"Perish the thought," she replied dryly.

Reed considered what Lent said, squeezing off a few more, "Yeah, well you never know kid; shit happens."

Nitana: "Great. Now we have two of them."

Pleased at the prospect Lent grinned until Reed added, "—But first, get a frickin' haircut; then we'll see." The kid was bruised.

Still moving, the trio was nearing the top of the draw when Jade scolded, "Uncle Reed, maybe I should get some soap."

"Oh yeah, Cutie," he told her, "if you do, make it Ivory, 'cause I like lots of bubbles." Neither Nitana nor Lent had any idea what that meant.

* * *

On the summit plateau…

…Near the cavern's immense amphitheater-shaped entrance; running confusion. People entering the mountain were moving back into the passageway making room for others whom were still coming and covering their rear flank.

"Who is that?" Kalo asked, suspicion stirring omen inside, something she sensed but was as of yet unaware.

Almost quietly Tian replied, "I do not know." The dark mood of apprehension creeping over her, perceiving malevolence and that feeling of dread, the sensation of cold air in a mist, watching eyes in the darkness that causes one to cringe —looking back, no one there— the vexing taste of treachery and baseness of evil.

The outer rim, the plateau—

Approaching, from beyond their ranks the interloper stepped solid and heavy, each footfall crunching stone beneath three hundred pounds laced in black spit-polished boots. His six-foot-five presence towered ominously in the meticulously tailored drab olive-green uniform, flawlessly pressed and adorned with brass and braids from a time that had been and was now dead and gone.

With stubble-gray hair cropped skinhead close, he had a pockmarked face and fat porous nose. Stained with nicotine and tar his chipped boxer's teeth clenched a stub of cigar. He was the persona of intimidation.

Shoulders broad enough to overturn a pickup truck, torso thick enough to uproot trees, and hands large enough to crush a basketball, he was the epitome of meanness. Edward G. Robinson eyes, sufficiently cold to congeal water, and gray as the pallor of death; he was the embodiment of Evil.

Ames turned and saw him —the outsider, the intruder— a kink of anxiety catching sick in his gut then getting stuck in his chest. "It's not possible," he murmured, his heart skipping a beat, "can't be," nerves squeezing his breath. From the dregs of all that had been, somehow, he had returned, come to haunt them again... *General Smith.*

Noticing the stranger a Pilgrim turned as he approached, and uncertain who he was or what his intentions, the youth hesitated. Allowing less than casual regard Smith's saber swept up from his side with a powerful overhand strike taking the Pilgrim, opening his head —grisly, straight down through his face— out from his chest splitting his sternum in two. With their first fallen confederate the warriors realized the outsider was an enemy and six Pilgrims turned to confront him.

They intercepted Smith near the outer rim of the crowd; but with a single swipe his sword easily cut through two of their weapons opening their abdomens and spilling their bowels on the ground. Gaping, amazed, both died before they fell.

Two more tried to take him and the towering villain shattered the first's sword with a nonchalant strike, then decapitated him. Tilted aslant, the Pilgrim blinked once as his head tottered then slid backward from his shoulders hitting the ground with a ripe-watermelon thump. Dead eyes staring up, his torso squirted blood from the severed carotids while the exposed trachea's white cartilaginous membrane rings quivered in a silent scream.

Smith didn't even flinch when he ran the fourth through; he just sneered. Then turning, he flexed his wrist slicing diagonally up through the youth's chest opening his ribs and severing his heart, blade exiting between the left shoulder and neck. Blood-gush percolated onto the hapless warrior's clothes then poured down his legs, and floundering a final step, he crumpled.

Underfoot—

The primary quakes had now subsided, but the ground still petulantly quavered as pulse-shifts of aftershocks scattered smaller stones with the secondary vibrations. Then sudden quiet and still for a moment, until another tremor rumbled.

In the sky—

Virtually concealing predawn's light the volcanic plume hung heavily with sultry ash and a stir of dark soot that wound in a strange, slow-moving, almost circular pattern. Scintillating within the clouds, heat lightning flickered like crooked claw lines of vanishing fire followed by deep rumbling thunder that grumbled begrudgingly drifting away.

Across the river—

In the Forsaken Land, a volcano waited.

The plateau—

Weaving through the oncoming crowd Kalo sprang to intercept this unfamiliar enemy. Then drawing an arrow she nocked it and stopped, taking a stance.

The fifth Pilgrim dashed forward stabbing Smith in the left shoulder with his spear, just as quickly the general's saber hacking through the shaft. Seeming uninjured Smith glared venomously at the youth as he withdrew the spearhead by the stub of wooden handle making a syrupy, sucking sound. He turned it slowly, admiring it, as though thinking, *such keen edges*, then violently rammed it into the Pilgrim's chest; and with awful, frightening power it ripped through the young warrior bursting from his back as Smith buried his entire fist in his chest. Spearhead protruding with his severed spine, and the broken shaft solidly lodged, *snug as a bug,* the General let go and withdrew a monstrous bloody hand from inside the Pilgrim's chest. Then taking a casual drag on the stub of cigar, eyes twinkling virulent wickedness, Smith grinned, *there, take that with you.*

Feet spread, body angled to one side in a fighting stance, she drew the bow. Kalo aimed, concentrating, choosing her target.

Frightened by Smith's savagery but unwavering, the sixth Pilgrim lunged at him. Avoiding the flail Smith spun with his sword and struck a whirling-full blow, across the back, cleaving through his spine and out below his ribs slicing the Pilgrim completely in two, both halves plashing onto the plateau in a heave of scarlet and warm slop.

She inhaled, expelled half the breath, held it. The target: an evil black heart below gray smiling eyes. Absorbed, focused, Kalo released the bowstring with a powerful —*snap, ssst*— arrow in flight.

Gloating, Smith surveyed the piecemeal Pilgrim at his feet; then nonchalantly shrugged his massive shoulders and straightened his blouse. Next, without even looking, and crisply, with uncanny speed —*ssst*— reached, and at arm's length snatched the arrow in mid-flight. He'd sensed it coming. And through the crowd, from a distance, Ames saw it.

A trifle, rolling it in his palm momentarily Smith toyed with it, examining the arrow, and allowed, "Crude, but effective." He looked up searching with pallid gray eyes, then spied her. He knew *this one.* The foolishness of youth, the obstinacy of faith, the threat of determination, and the design of prophetic nemesis... surreal imaginings of a time yet to come.

Smith sneered, and with a bratwurst thumb snapped the arrow's shaft in two. Consumed with malediction he cast the broken pieces aside and walked toward her, thick as a treetrunk, boot heels crunching stones, regular, hulking footfalls on a granite plateau.

Kalo stood firm, frightened but unflinching.

Beneath the miserable sunless gray of volcanic gloom Smith turned the dripping sword in his hand, its blade reflecting the shimmer of cold steel and crimson veneer of blood. Solid lumbering strides betraying three hundred pounds of swaggering malevolence and despise, he approached the silent Kalo. Intent. Determined to kill her. Closer.

Methodically, wickedly, saber held low at his side, each onerous step brought him nearer, crunching rocks with laced, spit-polished black leather boots… and an obsidian-vibram *soul*. The grey of early light companioned with the gray of his eyes concealed a mystery of predawn and harbinger of past-dawn from the realm of woebegone.

Near the great cavern entrance Tian apprehensively whispered, "John, he must not enter Legend Mountain."

The stage was set. *Pieces... the Puzzle.*

Over there—

Kalo refused to yield, or to run. Nearing her was the most fearsome adversary she would ever confront, born within the embrace of a destiny secreted within Legend Mountain long ago, and forgotten by Tian, even now. The young warrior stood her ground, her foe approaching, his heavy footfalls conveying the weight of death on his heels and the blackest curse of darkness churning blasphemously within him.

Smith glared the cold of evil in his empty gray eyes, narrow lips curled in a sneer, shoulders hunched, fists clenched, grinding a stub of cigar with stained, chipped boxer's teeth.

The silent Kalo waited.

Across the river, a Forsaken Land—

The composite landform rumbled and groaned as it moved with the undulating commotion of millions of maggots; constantly oozing, whining and squirming. Black, hideous ones peering out from a seemingly endless mire of red sand-speck eyes.

Above and around them—

Heat lightning flared silent etchings of fire and white-splash-voids that burned holes in the sky. A wrought world trembled as shifting ground rumbled shedding echoes with aftershock quakes. Distant thunder tumbled and rolled mysteriously foreboding cataclysmic change.

An enigma, a conundrum... *the Puzzle.*

Before her—

Sword in hand, towering over her, the relish of victory in his eye and derisive contempt on his lips; glowering, gloating, Smith glared down upon Kalo. Ashtray breath with the stench of dead meat, he muttered words laced with venom, "Young Renoloi warrior, it is time to die."

Silent. Kalo stood motionless, not even a breath.

Smith threw his head back and bellowed hideous, vicious laughter that climaxed in a roar; then savagely he swung at her with an overhand strike...

—*Brrring!*— mere inches from her face Smith's weapon clashed with the scimitar's steel in a supernatural, unworldly, savage collision of splashing red flame and explosive —shattering— violent blue-violet sparks!

...And P.T. Barnum yelled, *"Mark!"*

A world out of time that was frozen and still; nothing moved, no sound, absolute silence and calm... everything, everywhere ...suspended. A man, a demon, and two dwarfs were all that there was. The rest of the world watched from the realm of mystery and dreams.

And with relish, Wilson counted, "One-thousand-one..."

Stopped where they were, unable to move —amazed— Reed, Nitana and Lent, just arriving at the top of the slide and peering onto the plateau beheld a surreal vision. Running warriors were captured then frozen in mid-stride, arrows stopped-still in midair. Smoke and dust were inert, hovering debris. Overhead, lightning was halted in ragged fingers of fire. On the slide below wicked, unmoving Night Hunters were paused and suspended —dangling— in postures of momentum or outstretched in mid-leap. Rocks boiled up with the quake were hovering everywhere. A distant erupting volcano was stayed with dead quiet. Everything around them, an entire world of cinematographic motion was —frozen— a solitary, stop-frame image of action —all of it— the churning sky, landscape, fire and smoke, people, wind and arachnids —absolutely still— absolutely silent, except...

"One-thousand-two..."

Furious red flame and shattering blue-violet sparks of sword and steel! Ames lunged heaving Smith's blade aside —away from Kalo— deflecting the blow. Still bellowing, now strangely distorted vicious laughter, the general turned swinging ferociously, missing as Ames dove and somersaulted avoiding him. Tuck and roll —recall ignited— Ames was back on his feet when the neuro-flash fired in his head. *De'ja vu—the sixth sub-level—we've been here before.*

Smith reeled lashing out at his face. Ames reacted, the incredible blade sweeping up intercepting Smith's blow—searing burn of red flame and fiery blue-violet sparks! With the shimmering blade before him, Ames witnessed the scimitar's mysterious might. It began to glow, to flicker, to luminesce with blue-white tensile and remarkable light. Astonished, not understanding he stepped back deflecting blow after menacing blow thrown by the indomitable, intimidating being attacking him.

"One-thousand-three..."

His sword dripping blood that flicked away in the sparks, time and again Smith struck out as viciously—as powerfully as he could, each succeeding strike causing the scimitar to radiate more brightly. Red shattering flames and indigo blue-violent sparks splashed glimmering ribbons of sparkling bright light illuminating the dark as it peeled and resisted with resonant collisions screeching of steel.

Perspiration dripping in his eyes, hair sopping wet, his armpits and back slippery with sweat; until it came to him, and he began to understand. It was more than chance that he had taken the scimitar rather than another weapon. Smith swung; he struck back —explosive red flames scattering blue-violet sparks— this extraordinary weapon had been waiting for him. He had not picked the magnificently swept blade; the scimitar had chosen him. Smith swung; he ducked. *For everything... there is a reason.* In his hand he held a weapon endowed with more than steel; and with that realization his confidence grew.

—*Brrring,* shattering red flame and indigo blue-violent sparks flashed esoteric mystery upon an arena of granite plateau!

Satisfied—excited, P.T. Barnum grinned. He could see it in John's eyes.

And Wilson counted, "One-thousand-four..."

Countering Smith's blows, Ames spun courageously repelling each furious strike—then striking back. More agile and quicker he blocked, dodged and swung faster than the tyrannizing general could move.

Shattering light of life or death, his eyes absorbing it all in cinematography of distorted slow-motion; he was only a man yet he defied Smith in a pivotal struggle of good versus evil. Smith's sword spit hell from its hilt held in monstrous hands capable of crushing his skull, him with the mystery of hope molded then woven in scimitar blade. He stood fast and defiant —deflect and fight back— strike, duck down and roll, then again to his feet, fighting in blurred broken-motion scattering piercing red flames shedding blue-violet sparks, all of it happening in a smear of greylight and an interval of time.

Relentlessly he defended the vision of a pioneer one room schoolhouse with weathered steps, clapboard walls and twelve children playing outside at recess; a fragment of dream in a world that was frozen and still. He was only a man, just a piece of a puzzle, a conundrum, an enigma within the matrix amalgam. But he was blessed with reason and logic, emotion and more, so much more. He was one of the creatures God had granted freedom of choice, and named mankind.

"One-thousand-five..."

Right-hand swing with the sword —then left with a fist— Smith struck Ames then strong-armed cudgeling with the hilt to his forehead, hurling him backward to the ground, nearer the passageway. Ames: back onto his feet. Shoving, Smith tried to bully his way forward hitting him a second time, even harder, again knocking him down. Swinging violently and wildly, whirling the sword above his head like a gladiator using a mace, he bellowed distorted, vicious laughter biting the stub of cigar so hard he sputtered spittle onto his chin. A treetrunk with hulking shoulders and staunch solid arms set on oak-muscle legs, he lumbered closer to the man and cave entrance, his frame so thick his entire body turned when he stepped.

Lying on the ground, dazed with the incredible jolt, Ames grasped the vague recollection of concrete and rebar and Smith towering over him, bellowing abhorrent laughter. *I know you—we've been here before.*

Amused, Smith howled and drooled lurid repugnance, preparing for the decisive blow. Only one, small, insignificant man stood between him and his foremost objective, to undo what would come. He loomed awesome and graphic relishing his moment, his power at its zenith, now after having waited for so long... far, far too long.

Finally, anticipating the climactic, supreme moment of Evil, its singularly powerful and hallowed, most potent time; precisely when good was at its nadir. Throughout all of eternity, the only time and place and circumstance when Satan could corrupt an entire creation, to capture and imprison all souls, for all time, at one decisive moment, inside Legend Mountain—the juncture—when creation is vulnerable. No longer using deception to collect those gone astray, harvesting one soul at a time; but to embrace unabridged victory here and now within the realm of a mountain's mystery. More than ambitious, a nonpareil goal, now within his reach.

Towering over him, Smith was aware that this pathetic little man who called himself John Ames had also deciphered the Riddle, the parable of the matrix of creation, the moment he, Smith, had waited for—for far, far too long.

From the ground Ames looked up and beheld the monster whom had deceived an entire world with the cloak and facade of military blouse. Smith, who possessed within him the very epitome of all that is Evil, every wretched thought and vile deed ever imagined or consummated by his willing adherents, his lost followers. Lying upon his back and staring defiantly, glaring into the most venomous of all —eye to eye— Ames did indeed know.

The Riddle, a parable, a piece of... *the Puzzle:*

Alpha and Omega reformation... mettled.
—The juncture in time when creation ends and reformation begins; when creations collide.
Galactic composition replenished... begun.
—All that was before, not cast away as waste, instead gathered, cleansed, and purified; clay in a mold, used to create once more.
Time captured; an hourglass... trickled away.
—A world out of time, now frozen and still; all that may or may not be in the balance.
The amalgamate turbidity... unsettled.
—The single most critical moment of all creation, that instant in time, waiting —precisely this moment— when all creation itself vacillates most vulnerable to the forces of evil, eclipsed by its zenith.
Legends sleep within the throat of... the dragon.
—Hidden from mankind in a volcanic basin cloaked in mystery and magic... and something More.
Shall rise to the Light, invoked... the last day.
—The incredible mountain that would return... with the Secret of The Legends.

Looking up, knowing Smith's objective, Ames now understood Tian's whispered omen. *'John, he must not enter Legend Mountain.'* This, above all others, was the moment creation was vulnerable.

Smith swung—Ames evaded; a Renoloi tactic he'd gleaned from Tian. Lying on his back and bracing himself with his shoulders, he pushed and jumped recoiling his legs, springing back to his feet alongside the general.

Smith reeled. The man attacked!

Marveling at the scimitar's strength, Ames defied and checked his adversary's barbarous onslaught. The blade felt unequalled in its strength, almost divine in its texture and flawless in perseverance. Infallible, venerably pure, seeming sanctified, the weapon luminesced with a shimmering razor edge gleaming like steel of pure light!

"One-thousand-six..."

Off-balanced, Smith staggered back amazed, disbelieving the man's courage and determination. Blow for blow they battled in an incredible, cabalistic confrontation, gladiators of new design. Sparkling red flames and indigo blue-violent sparks scattered upon a world that was frozen and still.

Suspended... ...Waiting.

—Swords clashed!

Enraged, time after time Smith swung with all his might unleashing his fury upon the man; but unyielding, Ames stood fast. Blinding flames shedding bursts of radiant blue sparks showered a predawn world with vibrant explosions of fire and light.

—Steel collided!

Ringing clear —deafening— resounding fury upon a granite plateau, reflecting grenade-bursts of red flame and blue-violet power, both maneuvered locking swords with intense, violent attacks! Defend —deflect, incoming strike— then swing, counter the blow. Avoiding the pommel Ames leaped in front of Smith again refusing him entrance to the cavern.

Screaming rabid hatred the titan heaved with his herculean shoulders, but couldn't force him aside; Ames was forged with determination and wouldn't give way. The general's sword plunged down from above —Ames' blade coming up— crashing together with explosive fury and mystery and supernatural blue-violent fire! The man's unwavering glare met Smith's wicked gray eyes exuding wrath of despise, Ames' countenance drawn with a grimace, the general's a sneer, his chipped boxer's teeth biting the stub of cigar.

Amid the conflict and mystery Ames' mind flashed back in time to a place of clouded hidden memories—or were they only transcendental images of surreal and shadowy places?

—Now, and Then—

A sword through black leather sent fire into his chest with a rush of hot pain that kept crawling inside. It hurt so badly in his lungs and his hands and his feet, caught in that acute black confusion swirling waves through his brain.

Then overhead he could see massive unshod hooves splashing flames in the dark, pounding holes of bursting fire, trailing nebulae light. Thundering above him fluted fetlocks and lathered flanks of mighty horseflesh galloped through the night, a legion of white magnificent steeds with manes and tails swept liquid and wild in the wind.

—Boiling red flame and pyrotechnic blue-violent sparks!

Around him were dark shadows and brutality and bedlam, bright blood in the matrix, and the sadness of war. He remembered closing his eyes and drifting away to incredible pure colors, to the edge of eternity, a place with no pain… to where dreams and reality merge.

Then the memory of the voices and he saw them around him — and the music, that song— they were all enveloped within light. And the Smile, so radiant, so dazzling, so pure; it was wondrous, more than wondrous... it was Perfect, the Light.

Somehow he was moving, maybe floating, almost flowing, then on the floor in the sphere; and that sudden mind-bending explosion —there then fading, then gone— now far, far behind him. It all happened so very quickly… the end of the world.

—Here, and Now—

—Explosive red flame and blue-violet sparks, scatter of light that was spinning through grey!

Their swords clashed with the resonance of steel against steel, the echo lingering long in his mind. All around him was disorder in a darkness of grey ocean with flickering images of combat that was occurring in broken motion; sprays of fire and muddled silence, just the ring of crashing blades in a world that was frozen, entirely stayed, and strangely still.

Suspended... out of time ...Waiting.

"One-thousand-seven..." Wilson counted,

...And P.T. Barnum yelled, *"Time!"*

* * *

Six minutes until sunrise...

...Time, existence, reality —everything resumed— motion and noise and the running confusion. Clenching his fists in fury and raising his arms Smith screamed, *"No-ooo!"*

In the blink of an eye Ames spun with the scimitar clipping his midriff with its razor edge and unrealized power. Astounded Smith staggered back disbelieving, staring at the bleeding wound transecting his belly. His skin looked discolored or bruised—turning purple?

The draw and battleland were rumbling and trembling again as Nitana, Lent and Reed, still carrying Jade, climbed onto the plateau, everywhere a hodgepodge of pounding bedlam and shattering noise. "What happened?" Lent asked. "What was that?" No answer—no time.

—Another shockwave—*jolted!*

Hammering tremors crawled like underworld thunder through the ever-shifting terrain, while overhead lightning ripped raw static-flash clouds unleashing crackling concussions in an apocalyptic, dismal sky. Rotating, the heavens churned; below a darkened world quaked... the realization of a parable riddle was at hand.

Reed spied Ames and Smith as P.T. Barnum yelled, "Reed, hurry—get everyone into the cavern!"

Puzzled by the dwarf's urgency, Reed asked, "Who is..."

"—Reed!" Wilson shouted from alongside his twin, "there is no more time!"

Angry, "Well where the hell did he come from?"

P.T. ordered, *"—Just do it!"*

Suddenly Seana was beside him tugging on his arm, both she and Nitana half-coaxing, half-dragging him toward the cavern where Tian and Deet were urgently helping stragglers and wounded into the grand passageway.

Another flash of blade—Smith screamed!

Slicing diagonally through his blouse Ames inflicted a second wound. Still bellowing, his face reddened and appeared mottled or bruised; and enraged, seething with wrath... Smith *roared!*

Across the river—

Pushing and expanding with infernal pressure, the boiling magma cauldron surged overcoming the volcanic mountain's capacity to contain it any longer. Starting to weaken, hairline cracks began appearing as snap-runs caused by rock within its depths crumbling and melting; then breaks began leaking. Magma burgeoning from deeply below was seeking a vent, the unstable mountain's surface uplifting virtually imperceptibly from the extremes of pressurized bubbling froth and intense liquid yellow heat.

Snaking into crevices and squeezing through fissures magma abruptly forced its way up with furious swells of potent underworld power, suddenly pushing and prying then violently exploding — boiling, rushing and climbing— detonating with billowing brimstone and gargantuan flame-orange boil saturated with dense, choking, livid black smoke!

Shaking the world, the peak of the volcanic mountain shattered erupting liquefied rock and fiery debris as blast pulse and flamespray slammed the Forsaken Land with four miles of scorching, ground-flattening circular burn. The dark of death saturated with alizarin blaze, it was an explosive river of rushing fountainhead skyfire pounding boiling, gagging ash and mountainous volumes of pulsing, superheated lethal gas expelled in the black breath of a pyroclastic cloud!

On the plateau—

Smith screamed until he roared, then furiously heaving his weight he bodyslammed Ames knocking him down again. Eyes glowering abhorrence, for the briefest moment he loomed watching the man, his countenance vile and intimidating, graphic—pure evil.

Palms pushing, heels digging in, Ames moved *—get away from him—* retaliation was coming. Scooting back on his butt he caught a glimpse of Reed helping Seana into the cavern, and Kalo holding

Jade. To Smith —coming at him— he rolled onto his side then back on his feet, seeing Tian hobbling painfully toward him.

Spinning, "No—go back!" Then sensing Smith, the scimitar came up with a mighty collision of red fire and blue-violet sparks staggering him back. Tian was still coming. "No—stay away!"

—A second shattering red flame shedding indigo blue-violent sparks!

Smith was too close —*sseeooooo*— something overhead, through the sky—*no time, watch Smith*—blades ringing as they crashed!

Looking up, Tian had seen it, whatever it was, just a burst of bright light that was there then gone. Before he could stop her she was beside him—*no, Smith was too close*—and stomping toward them, now P.T. and Wilson were coming. Ground rattling, still quavering, Smith's eyes shifting from him to Tian—and an image of Kristina flashed through his mind, *hilt lodged between her breasts, the blade out through her back.*

Backing away he crowded Tian with an arm sheltering her behind him, the scimitar coming up, wrists in motion, the blade cutting figure-eights of whirling shield before them. *Watch Smith.*

Inhaling a drag of foul air as he shifted his weight Smith gargled a snarl that congealed to a groan; then turning suddenly he reeled throwing his sword at them, striking the mysterious shimmering barrier and shattering the saber in scattering red flames and twirling blue-violet sparks. The terrific impact knocked Ames into Tian, and both to the ground.

Smith screamed—almost screeching, he roared! Clenching his fists, detailing veins on the back of his hands, seething with anger… he began to change.

Growing larger, his boots split apart, and misshapen, his toes emerged. Throwing his arms back violently, still howling, his chest swelled filling his uniform, stretching it skin-tight popping the buttons of his coat and blouse, splitting it apart at the seams. Both of his wounds closed, his skin, or hide turning mottled, red to purple, as his thighs bulged, the left boot riding up toward his ankle.

Growing taller, his face contorted and looked like it drew more pointed; and his chipped teeth became ragged almost, like fangs. Turning pale-green his hair grew long and tangled, and flared wildly, as his eyes drew back sliding wider apart on his abhorrent skull, then narrowed. With a succeeding blink the pupils changed from round to vertical, corneas metamorphosed, now yellow-gray, hateful, and intensely deadly.

Still clenching his fists some kind of claws emerged from beneath his fingernails, pushing and shedding them like flaking scales, his hands becoming blotchy and discolored in places, and it looked like they might even be scaled. Lethal and depraved, from his cloak of deception magenta appeared. From within the hollow shell of man... he was changing.

Watching from the cavern entrance Reed swallowed a bubble of dry lump; but couldn't chance the pulse laser, too risky, could miss. Ames scrambled to his feet still protecting Tian.

* * *

Four minutes until sunrise...

...Pouring and crawling the canopy was an opaque ocean of rotating clouds forming an enormous whirlpool that attracted lightning's angry white-electric fire. Churning, it rolled as it flowed forming a deep-set core, becoming more defined, like a hurricane's eye. The firmament revolved... growing darker ...and rocketing through the sky bursts of ball lightning flared.

—*Sseeooooo*—

That time he saw it; from above the Forsaken Land a fireline of light streaking through the sky, ionizing air as it passed over their heads. Sudden wind in their faces—a cyclone gale pushing atmosphere away.

The earthquake persisted, the volcano erupting, resembling battling ground-rattling titans violently shaking the world—then an unbelievable, tremendous sudden-explosion tearing the entire landform apart, propelling the top half of the mountain miles high. And within the fiery blast of uprising molten flame boiled a colossal outrushing of Hell's fire and brimstone that catapulted unnumbered wriggling larval maggots with nefarious red sand-speck eyes. Soaring, swirling, tumbling and twirling within the monstrous gushing flood of ochre flame and gagging stench of dark clouds…

From Legend Mountain plateau—

"Come, my minions!" Smith's hoarse vengeful command.

In the river of flames, an erupting black cloud—

Hurtling within the fire highlighting a canopy of darkness, spurred suddenly to screeching and hatemongering and impelled by his command, millions and millions of them hatched.

…And in a festering, blistering plague, They came.

And they marched up over the broad earth and surrounded the camp of the saints… [in part] (Rev. 20:9)

A swarm of black cloud, their multitudes spread out over the barren, dead terrain of the Forsaken Land, millions of them bound for Legend Range. Like a derelict, despoiling sinuous dark wind, willingly they answered Smith's call.

On the plateau—

Fists clenched, head thrown back, Smith still roared!

Guardedly Ames eased back helping Tian as P.T. Barnum and Wilson scooted forward, and seeing the approaching black waves, "Oh sweet Jesus," he whispered, "what—is—that?"

Passing him, soberly Wilson answered, "*That*, is the visage of Hell. Those, are The Lost."

Out there—

From the Forsaken Land, born of vomited volcanic plasma choked with lethal sulfuric gas, now overshadowed by the eye of a storm, they came hostile and bleak. Belched from below in boiling mountainous clouds laced with ribbons of fire, they rushed onward over the wasteland. Hideous and dreadful, they were a miserable black scourge, the regurgitated stench of despair peering with the wicked denial of deception and lies, from red-glowing bloodshot-dead eyes.

Windblown and burned, the dryland was blotted from sight by their numbers. They were the cohesive maladies of ages long since past, dispatched with the menace of venom and misery from all that had been. Desolation and emptiness accompanied their swarm as they poured over the terrain in a nefarious cloud of railing, wicked debauchery convoyed by the rattling drone of dragonfly wings.

"Mr. Ames," Wilson implored, "you must get inside the mountain —*now!*"

Gouging clawlines in the rocks, Night Hunters were emerging from the draw scrambling onto the plateau shrieking white noise of savagery and trill animalistic screams.

Crowded together at the huge cavern's entrance, weapons braced and holding their breath, the warriors watched Ames and Tian. All eyes shifting between them, Smith and the dwarfs on the plateau, Hunters clamoring over the rim, the Forsaken Land where the volcano was erupting, to countless waves of black sin pouring over the wasteland. Coming for them.

And so it was—

On an unimaginable shimmering mountain, still climbing from the draw Night Hunters scuttled mindlessly gaining a foothold on the plateau, intent on killing them. Warriors were waiting, ready to fight.

In the Forsaken Land, ground-shaking pyroclastic explosions boiled volcanic fire and viscid smoke that stained the sky, while spreading across that wasteland of decay was a boil of black wind, something —or things— they couldn't even identify. Now nearing the river and blotting out the eyesore of dead landscape, the unearthly, depraved black fog of clamoring darkness and wings was maliciously crossing the terrain. Coming for them.

And before them… was it Smith?

Still rotating, the canopy congealed with mercurial power, a sky churning volcanic ash in dark gray, because they were people on a primitive world just struggling to survive.

Lightning flashed. Thunder pounded then rattled as it peeled across a granite plateau… on this, The Very Last Day.

* * *

Backing away from him…

…Moving carefully, easing slowly toward the cavern entrance, Ames watched Smith.

"Mr. Ames," Wilson shouted, "you must get inside the mountain!"

Over their heads —*sseeooooo*— a forerunner's burn of incredible destruction only minutes away; then many miles beyond and behind them somewhere —*ka-whooomm!* The world shook!

"He's mine," Smith gurgled, his fists clenched sledgehammer hard.

Interceding, both dwarfs stepped between them and Smith, prodding and taunting him with their walking sticks. "You were too late and the moon is not full," P.T. countered, allowing Tian and Ames a chance to escape.

"John—please—we must go now!" another harbinger searing overhead. Two steps behind him, refusing to cry, she was hunched with pain, terror etched in her eyes.

Still hesitating, the man glanced back and P.T. ordered, *"Go!"* —then he turned taking Tian's hand, and ran…

—*Sseeooooo*—

Just a glimpse, both saw it, a spear of bright light coming in low, then seconds later —*ka-whooomm!*— shatter-explosion ripping a billion cubic yards from the base of the plateau six miles away, the dim light instantly flaring bright white with a world-shaking surge. The ground vaulted —everything blurry— slammed by a head-battering shockwave of sound!

Stones flying through the air, Tian tripped and went down; he stumbled and stopped. Tears of desperation in her eyes, "John, I cannot run—leave me!"

"Not on my life. *Not ever!*" And scooping her into his arms, he ran…

—*Sseeooooo*—

From low in the sky above the Forsaken Land, slicing through the amalgam of canopy a bullet of light streaked over their heads. Then another appearing, even more, shooting stars blazing through the churning clouds and crossing the sky. The sullen canopy becoming darker and breathing more deeply, still revolving as the vortex compressed tightening toward the crux of a black angry storm.

Along the horizon of the wasteland harbingers began striking the malignant, ragged landscape like enormous stray-monster raindrops. Forerunners burning through the embroiled clouds were impacting with incredible rippling detonations as they flashed in with unbelievable speed and explosive bursts of bright light. Then even more of them, and more, scattered incoming asteroids were bombarding the horizon; until opening like a torrential cloudburst there were suddenly dozens, then hundreds plunging like rain ripping out great wedges of terrain in a spectacular hailstorm of epic destruction.

Eighty feet to the cavern entrance.

Running, four steps —*ka-whooomm!*— a fiery intergalactic bullet slammed into the bottom of the ravine three miles away, the entire plateau heaving as it quaked! Staggered and shaken he stumbled and fell, then struggled, getting back up dodging flying rock of scatter-debris.

Sixty feet.

Tian in his arms, as fast as he could run, legs and back straining, every ounce of his strength…

On the plateau—

With slingshots and walking sticks, P.T. Barnum and Wilson confronted Smith, taunting him. P.T. winged a cat's eye hitting him solidly in the chest as 'Just Plain' Wilson jabbed him with his stick then retreated looking up venerably announcing, "The Light of The Legends."

Ames darted a glimpse to the sky; but it must be directly above him. The others were all inside the cavern now; they couldn't see it.

Forty feet.

Running again, but compelled, he glanced back; a burning orb of asteroid coming in high —then a brilliant beam of bright light that by far outshined it, bursting through the core of the dark revolving sky, the whirlpool canopy just beginning to open…

"Doc, *Hurry!*"

Thirty feet.

Impact! A mile above them —*shatter-explosion!*— then the blast pulse flash that slammed them to the ground. Stunned by the blast he went down hard protecting Tian, but couldn't avoid striking his head. He hit hard; dazed, injured. Great irregular blocks of falling stone and fractured rock tumbling onto the plateau, crashing thunderously, shattering violently gouging craters when they struck…

…Reed, at the cavern entrance: "No—frickin'—way."

He leaped onto the plateau running all-out, plummeting rock still landing with tremendous collisions of splintering spray peppering deadly projectiles and boiling gray dust. Seconds later he grabbed his staggered friend by the arm jerking him to his feet, rockfall and stone clutter still coming with crashing earsplitting crunches, dust roiling around them. In one quick movement he scooped Tian from the ground, she going limp in his arm, his other fist grabbing Ames by the nape of his collar, carrying the woman, half-dragging the man. A house-sized chunk of stone shattered on the plateau nearby, rocksplatter shooting lethal bullets.

"Doc, we gotta go!"

Ames staggered a few steps being towed by his friend, blinking dust from his eyes until his vision came back. Then they ran…

Twenty feet.

In the Forsaken Land, more impacts were ripping up huge wedges of landscape, mountains and deadlands being splintered to fragments and fire. Sheetplain was hurling miles high, great soaring slabs on fire, flaming destruction and rocketing jettison-debris…

In the sky, it was coming straight for them, a horrific white boil of shooting star and death…

The revolving canopy unfolding, a piercing brilliant spear of white light beginning to burn through the core, the whirlpool vortex opening…

Ten feet.

With Tian in his arms Reed dove *"—Doc, Run!"*

Almost there, a bullet of intergalactic flame coming at them…

Jade's voice exclaiming, "Kalo, there is my angel!"

Reed carrying Tian, leaping, going into the aggregate of people breaking their fall, himself just an instant behind…

He dove! Arms reaching out, hands grabbing him…

Jade's voice: "Uncle Reed, my angel!"

Landing in the pile of strong waiting arms; Lent, Deet and others catching them…

Reed's voice, half-disappearing in the people with a jerk of his head, "—Where?"

—Then *Incredible Light!*

The cavern entrance was instantly sealed with brilliant white light, a sudden whirling veil of dazzling starburst flashing down behind them.

Reed: "—What the?"

A voice: *"It is forbidden,"* —and outside a rattling monumental explosion causing the entire mountain to shake!

Inside Legend Cavern—

To Ames, bodies seemed to be everywhere. Pumped with adrenaline and tight breath, climbing out of the pile; others were helping them sit up as Reed gently let her down. Trembling with pain and anticipation, pressing her face to his chest Tian flung her arms around his neck. He was her friend.

"What's going on?" Reed wondered whispering in her ear, helping her then his friend, get untangled from the pile. But she did not respond, all carefully managing to get to their feet. It all seemed incomprehensible, just too incredible, and as they backed farther into the cavern moving away from the entrance, Ames slipped an arm around Tian, his other taking Kalo in by her shoulder. Together now, all inside, crowded behind the great cavern's entrance, Seana nudged closer to Reed.

* * *

Two minutes until sunrise…

…Out there, intermittently, more muffled explosions.

The spear of brilliant light that burst from the whirlpool's core had sealed them within Legend Mountain. The rampart was sparkling starfire of glimmering microcosmic explosions, a veil of living texture ribboned with motion and the mystery of exquisite distant nebulae. It was incredible, ethereal, constantly flowing and changing; and at its base along the cavern floor, cool shimmering white fire sizzled emanating no heat.

The mysterious, dazzling mantle before them was intense and beautiful, wound with esoteric splendor of ebullient sparkling starbursts, minutiae quasars, and pulsars that shimmered white to color, color to clear, to color, to white... over and over with fascinating, dizzying repetition. Meteoric streaks and pinpoints of light, it was wondrous and hypnotizing; and unable to resist the impulse Lent reached out to the glimmering veil...

"Do not touch it!" Tian warned —but too late.

...As his hand penetrated the luminous mantle it disappeared within its volatile mystery. Reflex —he jerked back and gasped— his hand was gone, as breathless, those near him stared in silent wonder. Shimmering with beauty, pulsating with life, almost breathing, the light had painlessly whisked it away; and as he and the others watched, sparkling beams of pure starlight swirled from the vivid barrier and whirled around his wrist... touching him with tinglings of compassion that flowed peacefully through him ...then Warmth. And astonishingly his hand reappeared.

Bewildered Lent looked at the shimmering veil. "What is it?"

Drawing their attention Tian reverently said, "Things the Renoloi do not understand. Magic. The Light of the Legends."

The Light.

Quasars: hovering with faith and pulsing with life; then whisking away yielding shimmering, radiant sparkles trailing brilliantly colored comet tails. Pulsars: beating the quiver of a hummingbird's heart, whirling and exploding then recompressing and contracting to minutiae pinpoints of white; and erupting again, then evaporating and vanishing. Before them flowed a rushing waterfall of motion and mystery, clear to colors, to purest white. Born in the vast and distant celestial nebulae, swirling, sparkling and glittering with transparent crystalline starbursts, it was a firefall kaleidoscope bursting over and over, mesmerizing beyond magic, pure beyond the opulence of pigment, gorgeous and lush in its vividness and texture. Beyond worldly realm.

They all felt it —*a rush*— incredible beyond what they could comprehend; and outside, mellifluous, enchanting music. A beautiful song.

* * *

One minute until sunrise…

…From the deep and unknown, and the darkness of space, thousands, hundreds of thousands of them arrived. The primary cluster appeared at the rim of the planet's atmosphere with absolute silence and interstellar velocity. Some enormous, others small, they came from the unknown regions in the depths of 'out there'. Porous, pitted chunks of mineral, frigid rock and ice, they were asteroids and swarming clustered meteoroids. Without a sound they'd hurled along a circumscribed, finite path bound for a primitive world destined for cataclysmic change.

Entering the outer reaches of atmosphere they erupted with friction-burn as gargantuan fireballs in the stratosphere —then suddenly the sky ignited with plasma flame and tremendous explosions of firefall and incredibly brilliant light!

—Shooting stars,

—Fireballs from the dark and cold,

—*Starflashes blinding bright!*

Thousands —hundreds of thousands— they came. Meteoric rain trailing miles of flame yielding ribbons of fire and aerial tendrils of winding, twisted smoke. They were an incoming celestial hailstorm of screeching rock and ice and fire...

…And Change.

Encompassing comas enveloping them, surging fire before them, their extreme frictional compression created intense pulse-waves of blue-white flame and dynamic heat. They seared from space, bursting from the dark —flashing, pouring and sizzling— burning and descending with the screeching roar of jet engines in an ecliptic blur of speed. Pitted nickel-ferrite pores breathing an awesome shrieking hiss and roar, they sliced the atmosphere, ionizing it and setting afire the sky's invisible bonds of oxygen and hydrogen — broken apart— consumed, and gone.

—Incoming…

And he who sat upon the throne said,
   BEHOLD, I MAKE ALL THINGS NEW. _(Rev. 21:5 RSV)_

…Then explosions!—

Thousands of rattling sonic booms detonated with the flare of sound that was rushing out, the shockwaves far outdistanced by the meteors' velocity —starflashes— and incredible, pealing, thunderous roars. Absorbed in screaming earsplitting wails, the firmament boiled with white-burn incineration —and tailflames. Roaring, they pounded explosive surges like thunderclaps sending shockwave blasts through the grey then luminous sky. Seething, slamming into the atmosphere trailing ribbons of fire, they burst forth with superheated dry wind in their wake.

They came, a firestorm of skyfire hurling toward the planet.

An entire troposphere was pushed out of the sky, compressed toward then beyond the planet by an incredible onrushing wave of inferno projectiles as the landscape rattled with an immeasurable vibrating sensation preempting thousands of imminent simultaneous impacts…

   —Atmosphere baked, the sky rushed away,
     —An entire world shuddered, anticipating,
       —_Primary Force Impacts!_

…Screeching and screaming, the first asteroids of the main cluster struck blasting immense craters with instantaneous shockwaves of circular-rush crashing deeply down into the crust —through it— then outward!

Shatter-flash of ripping destruction and shearwave eruptions of unbelievable detonations swept over the face of the world. Speeding forth, flashing out —blowing it up— fracturing, splintering, pulverizing —tearing it apart— everything, all of it! The world quaking in upheaval as thousands of asteroid explosions shattered mountains and landscape to shards of oblivion. Thundering, rattling, pounding surging pulse-wave swells of blinding, rushing, boiling incineration and nonpareil detonation-burn of vaporous fireflash white light!

Hurtling up, monstrous tectonic plates and expansive regions of terrain propelled outward with rushing, rising, fracturing tear-waves. Seismic explosions and eruptions pealing as detonations flared burning terrain in flashwinds of apocalyptic destruction — obliterating the surface!

Instantly destroyed, the Forsaken Land and jungle were completely engulfed, absorbed and wiped away. Lost within the monumental rush ancient gnarled trees and verdant countryside vanished. An active pyroclastic volcano was swallowed, dissolved, gone. The river disappeared in a millisecond of million-degree heat, too instantly even to vaporize.

All life disappeared. Crickets, frogs and candleflies cloistered within the false security of tree bark were swept away with moss and water lily fronds in a pristine pool and an overhanging flat rock where two people swam together not so long ago. The dismal murk of a black water swamp and quarry where Trogs once stood were absorbed in holocaust flame. A misplaced ocean and an extraordinary aggregate mountain of Accumulation vanished.

Countless astonishing and unworldly hailstones blasting craters into the mantle, the asteroid thunderstorm continued to rain down with incredible explosions of rent and rising landscape, tearing the planet's surface apart. Flashing the circumference of a primitive ephemeral world, in little more than a heartbeat it was all gone; landscape slammed and torn then swallowed in fireflash of rupturing, vaulting waves of blue-yellow then white-rise destruction!

—Compressed atmosphere rattled!

Fireballs impacting again and again —crashing, exploding and erupting in scatter-bright fire! Entire regions were hurtled upward, then —still vaulting— rising with the upward thrust, gargantuan slabs of stratum being struck time and again by more incoming fiery meteors, shockwaves battering them, tearing the world's surface away. Thundering beyond measure, deafening beyond sound — pelting asteroid hail and firefall storm— it happened so quickly.

The downpour of plummeting asteroids and meteors fashioned a deluge of destruction and shooting stars smashing incredible sheets of soaring landscape and tectonic plate, until broken and crumbled, completely pulverized —obliterated— nothing remaining larger than granular millings and particle bits in a hailstorm of flaming, unparalleled proportion. So violent and intense was the destruction that the very core of the world trembled and quaked!

Shatter of fracturing, rushing shockwaves splashed fire and debris hundreds of miles high creating an infernal holocaust that swept the planet rocketing its crust upward, into and beyond its compressed atmosphere. It was an unparalleled tsunami that tore the surface from its core. Pulsing with white fire of disintegrating, dissolving crust there was an incinerating rush of all things organic —a shatter-flash of ripping destruction— and an exploding world in the wind and sky!

And amidst the destruction glimpses of an inner world, middle Earth... a 'Hobbit Land', began to appear.

* * *

Scatter-burn of confusion...

...Chaos and pieces of debris-world whirled away, spiraling up through the planet's gaseous envelope of troposphere, fanning out as it soared quickly beyond the layered stratosphere and into the mid-layers of mesosphere. Until at length its momentum diminished and slowed, where countless particles glimmered trailing into the thermosphere, purified by the extremes of temperature at that great distance. And finally, into the far-reaching margins of exosphere and merging space of interplanetary medium where the incredible clouds of dust, glittery ejecta, and shards of slivered crust, at last drained of momentum… flowed.

There it tumbled, spiraling and twirling in gentle cascading rolls, until at last it was captured and carried in streaming gravitational winds.

In the calm and dark at the edge of space limitless particles were now benignly transported along... buffeted by the pulse of solar winds. An incredible creation shimmering with reflected sunlight, beautiful with colors of rainbow hues, the dust particles circling the entire planet; spellbinding and gorgeous, magnificent beyond description.

The rings of Saturn by new design,
The Creator's promise,
Never again to destroy this world.

* * *

Persevering through the cataclysm,
And rampage of reformation,
The ReCreation.

A towering, solitary, gray-black mountain remained, lofty and indomitable, sealed and shielded within a protective rampart of Guardian Light.

The Light.

Clear as the crystal of faith, pure as the integrity of truth, dazzling and radiant as the endurance of hope… an unexplained passageway.

Breathing, Living.

Scintillating with starbursts and minutiae of luminescent quasars; hovering, glimmering. Then as though evaporating, they began whisking away, effervescent pulsars of pinpoint bright light. As they left, they sparkled then burst and disappeared, returning to the realms of mystery and dreams… and Belief.

Disappearing, going back to where they came from, they were spiraling, whirling starlight embers of pristine love and compassion shimmering with mystical texture and an elusive enigma of splendor. Winding strands of mysterious starlight they returned to somewhere near the edge of eternity.

Legend Light… the incredible celestial corridor.

And sequestered within the Light were secrets to unanswered mysteries, still not revealed, yet to unfold… beyond imaginings.

A Light and a Power from far, far away, the realm of Beyond, where reality and the dream world merge in a kaleidoscope of brilliant colors too pure to conceive... a place transcending the limitless reaches of infinity.

CONCLUSION

Legend light vanished...
   ...Those within the cavern viewed Sunrise,
      A New World.

Hesitant, reverently, they emerged from the cavern of Legend Mountain. Ames, Tian, Reed, Seana, Lent, Kalo, and all the others; moving slowly, quietly they walked to the precipice of the plateau. The draw was gone. The slides were gone. The Renoloi territory of ancient gnarled trees and jungle, the barren terrain and hostile swamp of the Forsaken Land… were gone. All that had been was no more. Legend Mountain towered magnificently and supreme, granitic and mighty, its snow-capped peaks brushing the sky.

   Miles below lay a completely new world,
     Untouched,
       Never before seen, except by two.

Reed turned to Tian. Both smiled.

Inching above the horizon the sun rose before them, the morning rays illuminating the mountainside washing the grey shadows down from the summit. Its jutting ledges and sheer faces gleamed and sparkled as they were touched by the purity of sunbeams; and doing so the gray-black glitter of quartz, feldspar and mica embedded within the granitic monolith of mountain transformed, faded... slipped away in the light. Like feathery evaporating breezes of mystery, or candleflies flickering into the sky, Legend Mountain changed taking on the color and texture of stone huts, gray-tan.

Many miles below lay a pristine region that spanned the horizon in an arc defining the convergence of morning sky and untouched terrain. Before them, with the ascending, unfolding sunlight washing over the land, their world was revealed… an enchanted forest, a 'Hobbit Land'.

Below, craggy mountains jutted from fertile ground of dark loam where remarkable severed rock columns and massive spires stood stark and stately like sentinels watching over the countryside, as far as one could see. Meandering valley basins reached out carpeted in meadows of gorgeous emerald grasses ribboned with cascading brooks of clean water rushing in riffles, then quieting, unfettered in marshes of rushes, cattail bogs, camass and pampas grass stands.

The world was new and its pigmentation was new, a plethora of violets, blues, reds and yellows, phenomenal fluorescent displays interspersed in casual array. It was a land drenched with warmth and vivid color.

Flowers grew in profusion, and free. Tulips, hyacinths, four-o'clocks, azaleas, daffodils, morning glories, asters, roses and a thousand others; like a watercolor blanket of midday bloom and undulating, wild hues. The rolling foothills were forested in mature oak, walnut, hickory, weeping willow, sycamore, maple, and aspen; fringed with stands of evergreens. A season changed, the shades of autumn were gone, now everything green and new... budding with the onset of spring.

Animals chirped and riveted in thickets and meadowlands: bugs and butterflies, reptiles and amphibians, and fish frolicking clean waters teeming with life. This world was enchanting and captivating; their world, uncharted, unexplored, restored, recreated... Reborn.

Visibly moved Deet whispered, "What happened? Where did they go, the Hunters, that big guy, whatever —and that light?" Then doubt crept in. "It was real, wasn't it? We did see them, didn't we?"

Nitana replied softly, "I do not know, but..." as she gazed upon the world now before them, "it is so beautiful." Then she looked to the sky with its corona of Saturn-like rings. Glimmering, shimmering, incredible.

"Sure is," Deet agreed absorbing the vista, unconsciously fondling corn kernels in his pocket. Seana snuggled closer to Reed.

Jade's simple appraisal, "All new," as she reached for Kalo. Reed handed her over, and with Jade's arms and legs wrapped securely around her, affectionately rubbing noses with the child, the silent Kalo smiled. Tian took Ames' hand in her own. Neither spoke.

"Shall we go down?" Nitana asked Deet and Lent. Both simply nodded.

Solemnly, deferentially Renoloi and Pilgrims began filing down the mountainside from the plateau. It was time to become acquainted with their new home, following the winding trail, a new path… one step at a time.

Tian and Ames, Seana and Reed, and Kalo with Jade, remained behind, standing together on the rim of the plateau. For a while they were all very quiet, absorbed in thought and emotion, watching as the others descended.

So much had happened.

At last, concluding their silence, Reed cast a side-glance to Ames and remarked, "Nice vest, Doc," then droll, "real trend setter. I see you've got your fingertip on the pulse of the fashion industry." He tugged at the bottom. "Need to take a bit more off right here. It's cut crooked."

Ames flicked his friend's hand away. And smiled.

Watching the people making their way toward the valley below, Kalo stepped forward. "Reed, you met Lent, and the Pilgrims?"

Without looking, "Uh huh."

Kalo wondered, "You were not surprised to learn others were on this world, besides ourselves?" She was both eagerly curious and dubious.

Deadpan, surveying the landscape and sky, "Oh—no, not really. Not much surprises me here anymore." He sighed. "Might even be a good-looking kid if he'd get his hair cut."

Puzzled, shifting Jade's weight to her hip, Kalo inquired, "Cut his hair… why?"

Reed looked at her, then again over the vast landscape below. "Bugs, Kalo." Serious, he frowned. "Cooties —shit like that."

"Do not pay any attention to him," Seana said squeezing Reed more tightly and jostling him. "He is only teasing you."

"Of course," the girl agreed, and playfully, "after all, he is —*just* Reed." Her wisecrack made him smile and Reed squared with her, eyeing her as she defiantly returned his playful glare… until finally each grinned.

Behind them, near the base of the mountain came scuffling noises from a burrow —and a walking stick popped out; next, barely audible, was the disgruntled voice of petulance from within.

"P.T. knock it off; you're kicking dirt in my face." Quickly the first dwarf emerged from the hole snickering and grinning like 'Lewis Carroll's Cheshire cat'. Scampering, he retrieved his staff, as the other appeared wiping dirt from his face, spitting it out, his mouth ringed with black smudge.

Upon hearing the pair, the small group turned.

Reed: "P.T.?"

Brushing himself off as he approached, "No, I'm 'Just Plain' Wilson. He's Phineas Taylor. He got the good name." And almost sarcastically, "Can't you even tell us apart?"

"You're identical; how are we supposed to know who's who?" Reed threw back.

Wilson offered the pretense of self-examination, then cast a disapproving look in Barnum's direction. "Really, Reed? I should imagine he's much cleaner and certainly less disheveled than myself." Still brushing dirt from his watch cap, flannel shirt and bibs, Wilson tendered his regards. "So nice to see all of you again." They reciprocated with greetings and curiosity as P.T. scurried nearer joining them.

Suspicion evident, Reed asked, "Okay, the both of you seem to have an uncanny knack for just randomly popping up —you know, for no apparent reason. But I don't buy that. How do you two midgets figure in to all of this?"

Both ignored him.

"Little people," Ames corrected.

"Yeah, whatever."

P.T. smiled appreciatively; then amiably commented on the scimitar still in Ames' hand. "Quite a magnificent blade. Yes indeed, Mr. Ames, that is an elegant weapon."

Having forgotten, reminded he was still holding the sword and flattered by Barnum's accolade, the man raised it admiringly. "Yes, it is." Turning it venerably, the razor-sharp blade shimmering, reflecting sunlight. "The edge is virtually flawless," Ames told him. "I found it in the Accumulation." His thoughts digressing, "It seemed almost as though... I was drawn to it."

"Indeed?" P.T. feigned innocently as he grinned knowingly. "What a coincidence of good fortune that was." Nearby, eyes twinkling, Wilson blinked twice; and in the recess of his mind Ames recalled, *tracks in the sand.*

Changing the subject Reed asked, "Wilson, why were you counting?"

The dwarf's extemporaneous reaction was surprise. "You remember?"

"Yes," Reed answered, "—for seven seconds."

"Was I counting?" Wilson contemplated aloud; then almost denying, "I really don't recall."

"Don't give me that. Don't *ee-even* try to tell me you don't remember."

Wilson looked at him, direct eye contact —blinked twice.

"'And on the seventh day God finished his work which he had done, and he rested...' [in part] (Genesis 2:2 RSV). Seven days, seven seconds," Reed mused, then stopped. As quickly as the words were out of his mouth, he wondered how he knew that... and why he had said it.

Reflecting, Ames said almost inaudibly, "It was all for only seven seconds." Sadly, "All we went through, the suffering, all those lost, everything... for only seven seconds of time."

"Not at all, Mr. Ames," Wilson corrected gently, "actually, it was for all of this..." gesturing with his stubby arm, presenting their new world, "all that you see."

And as he spoke... new creatures appeared.

From the meadows and marshes, from forests and mountains they rose in flight and incredible plumage. Resounding raucous caw and warbling song, flitting with butterfly motion or gliding and soaring on strong, feathered wings.

"Reed," Seana murmured, "they are so beautiful. What are they?"

"Birds," he whispered, "thousands, millions of them."

They were everywhere: birds of prey, waders, shorebirds, woodpeckers, swimmers, and perching birds. Coveys ran the grasslands and marshes, throngs skittered among thickets and shrubbery, innumerable flocks filled the skies and a new world. Untold varieties: warblers, finches, ducks, geese, hawks, falcons, quail, nuthatches, rails, cardinals, egrets, eagles, herons, condors, swifts, larks, swallows —and on and on— seemingly endless diversity and array.

The new creation was complete.

As he studied the landscape below, without looking at the dwarfs Reed persisted, although this time his voice was softer. "You still haven't answered my question, Wilson." Wilson hesitated, did not reply.

"Which question was that, Reed?" P.T. queried on his twin's behalf.

"What do the two of you have to do with all of this?"

P.T. Barnum sighed sadly, serious now, careful with his words. His reply: "Reed, let us suppose there was a race of beings —only hypothetically of course— a race of beings whose most profound achievement was their propensity for killing one another."

"Mankind," Reed proposed, not a question.

Reluctantly Barnum allowed, "Well, I suppose we could *pretend*, and use mankind, for exemplary purposes only."

Reed nodded, agreeing, "For exemplary purposes only."

P.T. continued. "Imagine that mankind's propensity for self-destruction was far greater than could have been anticipated, and as a result mankind brought his existence to an end prematurely. Therefore, the juncture of the next creation was lacking, for..."

"Seven seconds," Reed said almost involuntarily, his eyes focused upon the dwarf. Lips trembling, "How?" he stammered uneasily. Wilson immediately clasped a hand over P.T.'s mouth silencing him. Reed whispered, "How could you possibly know something like that?"

Wilson assured, "He's such a showoff sometimes." Then minimizing and dismissing his twin, "Quite a delusional braggart as well, if you know what I mean." Reed didn't say a word. Under his breath Wilson cautioned, "You'd better shut up or you really will get us in trouble," removing his hand from P.T.'s mouth.

"—Okay, okay," Barnum conceded, "you're right of course, as usual."

"Who are you guys—really?"

Ignoring Reed, Wilson abruptly turned to Ames, and offering his hand in friendship advised, "We really must be going." After the handshake both dwarfs allowed hasty, *good-byes*, to the others, then hustled away. "Till we meet again, Mr. Ames," Wilson announced over a small shoulder.

"Wilson—" Ames called back, halting the dwarf. "Till we meet again? Will we?"

"Did I say that?" Wilson feigned innocently dismissing his slip of the tongue. "It's only an expression." But Ames wasn't entirely convinced. Wilson wrinkled his nose and offered his quaint, friendly smile while inside he grinned knowingly.

"Hold on you guys," Reed objected, "we haven't finished our conversation yet."

"Sorry, we really haven't the time; we must be going," Wilson apologized. Then turning again to Barnum, "Isn't there something we should be doing right now?"

P.T. concurred, "I believe you're right. Yes indeed, we've work to do."

"—Wait just a minute you guys." Neither paid any attention and scurried toward the burrow at the base of Legend Mountain. "P.T., Wilson—" he insisted, raising his voice.

"Reed, do not yell at them," Seana snapped, snatching his attention and the others' as well, for only an instant. "They have helped us so much," she reminded.

By the time the people turned again P.T. Barnum and 'Just Plain' Wilson had vanished; two glimmering wisps of sunbeams and starlight still wafting down.

At his feet each man found a bundle of denim material, and curious, Reed knelt and unrolled the article of clothing. First wondering, then grinning, "Levi Strauss, since 1853," holding up new blue jeans for the others to see. Pleasantly surprised Ames also knelt and gathered a new pair of Levi's.

"Sure can use these babies," Reed admitted. "Mine are really old —and cut to shreds," looking at Tian. She just grinned. Then looking again to where they vanished, "P.T., Wilson—you guys..." and he smiled.

Ames' eyes traveled, where the dwarfs had been. He walked to the spot, then knelt down and touched it. P.T. Barnum and Wilson were indeed gone... but the dust remained. The dust was real.

Flash in the sky—

A shooting star streaked through the firmament —then down— toward the summit of Legend Mountain; then slowed and finally stopped hovering near a ledge high above the people on the plateau. Effervescent, it scintillated with miniature starburst explosions that sparkled with mysterious power and radiant light. From the shimmering ethereal light materialized a manifest form; the Centurion Mystic and mighty Percheron appeared.

The vision was incredible: sparkling trails of starlight glittering with pulsars and quasars of minutiae, pinpoint starbursts dappled within the shimmering translucent texture of its presence. It was beautiful, mythical, illusory, intangible... yet very real. For a moment the five standing upon the plateau gazed reverently, absorbed in wonder.

Jade smiled joyfully, and professing a child's innocent acceptance she announced, "Kalo, Uncle Reed, there is my angel." Each offered her a fleeting smile; but neither spoke.

Without words, in a coarse, garbled, disguised voice they heard the Mystic say, *"I bid you tidings, for you have done well and ReCreation is complete... a new cycle begun."*

Exchanging expressions of uncertainty with Seana, Reed whispered, "Did you hear that?" She nodded indicating she had. "No shit?" A sigh of relief. "That's good; then I didn't imagine it."

"Who are you?" Tian asked softly.

"I am the breath of tomorrow, the winds of consciousness delineating thoughts of good and evil, defining who you are and will be. I am the juncture of mortality and immortality. I am a Mystic, the soul of a dream, the heartbeat of honor, the breath of spring flowers, and a love from Beyond. From the origin and conclusion of all that has been and will be...

Alpha and Omega ...and the Light of the Legends.
I am a disciple. I follow the Light.
I am a Time Warrior."

The massive steed pawed impatiently striking sparks on the rock, then arched its neck and tossed its head, mane and fetlocks windswept, swishing waves of illusion. It was incredible; eyes of aquamarine, soul of the Lamb. Shimmering reflection and the radiance of lorica segmentata, the rider affectionately patted the mount then gently stroked its muscular neck; and the horse calmed, then stilled.

"John, this night when you hold Tian and make love, you shall know she is transformed; for the Renoloi possess a gift. Just as this world has changed, so has Tian. The Renoloi is gone. She is human."

Ames blinked with wonder. Soft-spoken words, "But how—how is that possible?"

"It was intended to be. More, need not be known." Within a shimmering veil of light and the cloak of a visored helmet, green guardian eyes smiled. Then the Mystic went on. *"Tian, you are with seed; and soon you will bear a boy child... the first in this New World. Now, the world is changed."*

"The 'Prophecy of the Strangers' is complete," Tian murmured, reciting, "They must go Beyond; then rise up like the Phoenix... and they would change our world." She turned to the man she loved and smiled. "It was in the Legends, John. I hoped; but I was not certain."

Reed grinned mischievously. "Doc, you knocked her up? That's great!" He beamed and winked at Jade. "I'm gonna be an uncle—again." Jade giggled bashfully.

"Reed," the Centurion informed calmly, *"Tian shall be the first, and Seana will soon follow."*

"She's pregnant?" He squirmed as he said it.

"Good going man of action," Seana chided. "That explains why my shoulder will not heal. Reproductive debility."

Reed: "Reproductive—what?"

"Debility. The Renoloi experiences a degenerative interval of magnified infirmity and susceptibility to injuries during the reproductive cycle."

Reed fidgeted. "You shouldn't even know words like that, girl; you know it."

Tian murmured, "It was not the mushrooms."

Reed stammered, "I—I can't have kids." Timidly, almost disconcerted he explained, "I can't afford kids. I don't even have a job. For Pete's sake, I'm as broke as a twig in a windstorm."

Seana hugged him affectionately reassuring, "We will manage."

The Mystic raised an arm, *"An abundance of life will come forth and many will be born in this flourishing new world,"* indicating the entire world that now lay before them.

Seana beamed, "That will be wonderful."

"Born nesters," Reed acquiesced; then, "—wonderful? Seana, what are you saying?" Darting a glance to those making their way down the mountain headed for the valley, "Look at 'em. They have absolutely no idea what sex is even about. For crying out loud, they don't even know what their different parts are for."

"You could teach them, Reed," Tian volunteered.

Waffling, reluctant, "Oh—no, I couldn't." Then mulling it over he conceded, "Well, I suppose—yeah—I 'spose I could." He grinned. "Imagine that—me teaching sex education class."

Ames, wryly, "Perish the thought."

The veracity of his words stung more than his ego as Reed looked at his friend, then hesitantly but honestly admitted, "No, hell Doc's right. Truth is, most of the girls I've known were pretty crusty. Shoot, they couldn't get laid by a respectable guy even if they gave S&H green stamps—or free air miles."

"You did well enough teaching Seana," Tian encouraged.

"—But, well that's different; she's decent." Tian already knew. She merely smiled. Reed had never seen the Legends; but Tian had studied them, over and over... very carefully.

Soberly, Ames again looked up to the Mystic, and asked the question that had vexed him for so long. "What are the Legends?"

"That answer is forbidden, John."

More serious now, her attention drawn with Ames' inquiry; inside, Tian sensed it, felt it... and to the Mystic, "I know you." The silent Kalo made no sound, did not stir; and at length Tian asked, "Who are you?"

The reply: *"You are safe. Love and cherish one another, for I must leave you now,"* pulling up on the reins.

"Please, tell me," she entreated, "who are you?"

The Percheron reared onto its hind legs pawing the sky, raking showers of sparks and billowing fire. Whinnying, shimmering horse and rider, sparkling whirlwinds of starfire explosions: quasars, pulsars, minutiae of glimmering starbursts and luminous white light.

"When the moon is full... where yesterday waits, and tomorrow's been; you shall know." Then spurring the magnificent steed, *"Fly!"*

The mighty Percheron neighed and bolted scattering starfire and flame with its massive unshod hooves. Luminescent mystery and light swept in a meteoric flash —streaking into the sky— and in an astonishing splash of starlight the warrior was gone, a shooting star bound for the limitless reaches of infinity.

"How, when?" Tian appealed, her words traced with yearning. "Wait," she murmured, "come back, please. Do not go."

But the Centurion Mystic and Percheron had vanished in a transitory flametrail of incredible white fire. Both were gone. Above them and before them lay empty sky and mystery...

...Something yet Unfinished.
All of them watching the sky, Ames pulled her to his side as Tian barely whispered, reticently, wondering, "Will we ever meet again?"
Still hoping, listening, there on Legend Mountain plateau, all of them, and the silent Kalo heard a garbled, disguised voice...
From out there, somewhere,
In the boundless, unending firmament,
From the farthest reaches of the territory of Heaven,
...The Mystic's reply,

"When You Believe... There Are Always Possibilities."

ENDNOTES

1   Grey and greylight: used instead of gray for mist and predawn effect
2   Renoloi… pronounced RE-NO-loy
3   Tian... pronounced TI-an
4   Seana... pronounced Shaw-na
5   Lita… pronounced LE-ta
6   Nitana… pronounced Ni-ta-na
7   Kalo… pronounced KA-lO
8   Kimo... pronounced KE-mO
9   Sargasso: olive-brown seaweed having air bladders on its stalks.
10   Tere… pronounced Terry
11   Deep scattering layer: jellyfish, squid, shrimp and myriad fishes dwelling within the protective obscurity of the ocean's depths; then rising to shallower water under the cover of darkness.
12   Dira… pronounced DE-ra
13   Nemuk… pronounced NE-mook
14   'Big Brother'…ref. George Orwell's novel 1984 written in 1949, depicts life and conditions when citizens are under constant surveillance of an intrusive, out-of-control government.
15   Gog (gog), and Magog (ma' gog): In Biblical prophecy, the nations led by Satan, that will war against the kingdom of God. Funk & Wagnall's Standard College Dictionary: Harcourt, Brace & World, Inc.
16   Combination of bloodroot and amanita is very likely lethal. This is entirely fictional (for this story).